S0-BJL-082

29.95

EVENSONG

Also by Gail Godwin
in Large Print:

Father Melancholy's Daughter

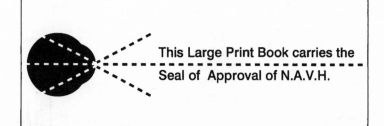

This Large Print Book carries the
Seal of Approval of N.A.V.H.

EVENSONG

Gail Godwin

Thorndike Press • Thorndike, Maine

Copyright © 1999 by Gail Godwin

Published in 1999 by arrangement with The Ballantine Publishing Group, a division of Random House, Inc.

Thorndike Large Print ® Basic Series.

The tree indicium is a trademark of Thorndike Press.

The text of this Large Print edition is unabridged.
Other aspects of the book may vary from the original edition.

Set in 16 pt. Plantin by Rick Gundberg.

Printed in the United States on permanent paper.

Library of Congress Catalog Card Number: 99-93828
ISBN 0-7862-2008-2 (lg. print : hc : alk. paper)

TO ROBERT STARER

טובים השגים מן האחד

קהלת ד:ט

EVENSONG, n. [ME.; AS. *aefensang;* see EVEN, n. & SONG] a worship service said or sung at the onset of evening to mark the close of day and to compose the mind and renew the spirit for the coming day.

I

Shield the Joyous

It all began on a Friday evening. I mean "began" in the old storytelling sense, for oftener than not what we call beginnings are fulfillments of things set in motion a long time ago.

It was the Friday evening before the first Sunday in Advent, that season of spiritual expectation in the Church calendar: a clear, frosty evening at the end of November, with a bite to it. Winter in the Great Smokies would shortly be upon us, the winter that would see us into the next century and the new millennium. Other things were on their way to us as well, things we neither anticipated nor, in some cases, could even imagine. This is the story of how we met them and were changed by them.

My husband and I had eaten an early supper together, some of his chili, perfected during his extended bachelor years, and then he was off to the school again. I was rinsing our dishes under the tap, brooding — but with a fair amount of equanimity by this time — over the fact that he had neglected to kiss me again. I heard his car start, but it didn't go

7

anywhere, and then there he was, back in the kitchen, his face already ruddy from the cold.

"Stubborn girl. You were supposed to lock the door behind me."

"What did you forget?" To kiss you, I was hoping he would say.

"Time for my wool cap. 'While the earth remaineth, summer and winter shall not cease,' and the bald head shall cry anew for its covering." Adrian liked to improvise on scripture. "Now where did I —"

"All your hats and gloves are in the box in the hall closet. Labeled 'Winter.'"

"The things you do for me, Margaret."

"I did it for myself, too. My winter things are in there along with yours."

During the minute or so that it took him to dash down the hall, locate his old Navy watch cap, and return to the kitchen in the act of pulling it snugly down to his eyebrows, I was granted a little blip of respite. Things had not been well between us since last summer, but during this momentary spot of light, I entered a different kind of time. Significant memories pressed close with the intensity felt when living them, and recalled to me how much I had wanted this life with this man and how equally much I had feared it would never come to pass. And yet here we were in it, "for better for worse." In the wedding service the four words exist as a unit, unseparated by even so much as a comma. Had I expected to

8

live only in the better side of the phrase? Into this wider perspective hope was allowed room, and something of it must have communicated to Adrian, because he now remembered what he had forgotten his first time out the door.

"Well," he said, touching his lips to mine and actually looking at me as if I was there with him, "hold the fort, as your father used to say. And please lock up this time."

"My father and I never locked the rectory back in Romulus. I don't think the vestry ever bothered to give him a key."

"Those were more trusting times, before people started blasting each other to smithereens over parking places. And your father's rectory wasn't so near the bus station that any fruitcake on foot could be at your door in five minutes."

"No, but once in Romulus I came back from church and found a woman upstairs in my bedroom closet, going through the pockets of my clothes."

"You never told me this." He looked intrigued. His hands stayed on my shoulders. "What was she doing in your closet?"

"She *said* she was looking for cigarette butts."

"Was she a parishioner?"

"No, she'd just showed up at church. But she never came back after that."

"Well, I don't wonder." His eyes rolled upward and I knew he was picturing the scene. Then he laughed, a typical Adrian-laugh. The surprised laugh of a reserved man ambushed by the gift of ludicrousness. Making me wish I had ten more such anecdotes stashed away to keep him standing there holding onto me and laughing. But then it was over and I could tell from his face he was already out at the school. "I'm not going to carry over my flannel pajamas yet," he said, releasing me. "That would be capitulating to winter too soon."

He'd taken to spending most weekends out at Fair Haven School, where he was chaplain — and now acting headmaster, since the sudden death of Dr. Sandlin late last spring. All faculty who lived off campus took turns spending nights at the school, along with the resident staff. A founding principle of Dr. Sandlin's had been the importance of consistent family routines for these seventy-five disaffected teenagers whose parents preferred to maintain them long distance via their checkbooks. Some of the students came from backgrounds so unfamilial that even meals in common were foreign to them. "You have to force them to do things with others," Adrian was always saying.

As I passed the hall closet on the way to my study, to finish my sermon for Gus and Charles's wedding tomorrow, I sniffed the lingering cedar odor from the briefly opened

10

box in which our all-cotton clerical shirts from Wippell's in England crossed the Atlantic together, and where our winter things now snuggled side by side even if we no longer did, and I was mystified anew by this whole thing we humans do when we take it into our heads to love one particular person.

It would be the first marriage for Gus (Augusta) Eubanks, a local architect, and the second for Charles Tye, the medical director of our local health clinic, whose wife had left him and their daughter three years before. We'd had the wedding rehearsal this afternoon, precocious twelve-year-old Jennifer Tye strutting about like a proud mother hen. Jennifer was convinced that her efforts had brought about this match, and to a large extent she was right. Gus and Charles were both extremely busy people who tended to neglect their personal lives, she had explained to me, and so after she determined Gus would be ideal for her father — and herself — she had plotted to make sure they got together. Like many children of alcoholics (in Charles's case, a recovering one), Jennifer felt she was responsible for everybody in the world. After the rehearsal, I discovered that she had gone around to all the pews and inserted white ribbons with the numbers 1, 2, and 3 into the appropriate pages of the hymnals so tomorrow's wedding guests would be sure to find their places

11

quickly for the chosen hymns.

Through the closed windows of my study I could hear the muted scrape-scrape of fallen leaves on the weathered bricks of the garth that connected the rectory to the church. Dry, tentative agitations similar in tone to those of my well-bred parishioners, shuffling and murmuring among themselves at coffee hour over the latest assault (usually mine) on All Saints High Balsam's time-honored customs, or deploring the fast-crumbling status of the world as they'd always known it. I scribbled a reminder to myself to get someone to clean our gutters before the snow came. Otherwise Adrian would be up there on the tall ladder, and he already had more jobs than he could handle.

What form, if any, was Gus's prenuptial nervousness taking? Was it different when you were forty-two? Six years ago I had been twenty-seven and terrified my marriage still might not come to pass because I desired it so much.

On the eve of my wedding, I sat in my seminary room, almost afraid to move, and said a certain collect for evening prayer over and over until I knew it by heart.

Keep watch, dear Lord, with those who work, or watch, or weep this night, and give your angels charge over those who sleep. Tend the sick, Lord Christ; give rest to the weary, bless the dying, soothe the suffering, pity the afflicted, shield the joyous; and all for your love's sake. Amen.

That final entreaty never fails to arrest me. *Shield the joyous.* The very arrangement of the words calls up joy's end even as you're evoking pictures of its many manifestations.

What else to do but pray for the person on the verge of realizing a cherished hope, for the couple about to consummate their love, for those children running on sure feet toward a mother's open arms? The future arches above us all like a giant question mark, looming or embracing by whims and turns. Just as in those medieval drawings, the wheel of fortune inexorably revolves, pitching today's celebrity into tomorrow's trash heap and raising yesterday's beggar to the throne. Rapture gets smothered in the rumple of dailiness; the clean, passionate pledge becomes choked with weedy extenuations. Children stumble and hurt themselves and cry, and even die. Mothers and fathers go away and never come back.

Or just imagine the elation of that first Cherokee scout when he reached the summit of High Balsam in whose shadow our community now barricades itself complacently. I see him gazing out incredulously upon the vast blue sweep and swell of peaks beneath the sky vault. He gains his breath, utters a prayer of thanksgiving to the Great Spirits, then lightfoots back down through bounties of bark and berries and flashings of game to

13

tell the others: there's no one else here! All this is ours because we found it.

Surrounded by such uncertainties, whether they play themselves out in a year, or ten, or a thousand, what else can we do but appeal for mercy and protection to a love beyond clocks and calendars and mortal frailties, a love wise and faithful beyond all imagining. Yet somehow, over eons, we *have* become able to imagine it — in part. And sometimes even to practice it — in brief spurts.

When Adrian and I were driving through Yorkshire on our honeymoon, the landscape was dotted with newborn lambs. Up and down the green slopes they raced, tottering on their wobbly legs, deviling one another, nipping at their mothers' undersides. Though we must have seen hundreds, we never tired of the sight. The lambs were of the same vintage as our own beginnings. Then one windy day we stopped for lunch at an inn up in Blanchland and Adrian innocently asked the only other person in the big drafty dining room, "What will become of all those lambs?" "Oh, we keep the females with black faces for breeding," said the man. "The rest will live out their carefree lives until September, after which you might well make the acquaintance of one on your dinner plate." He spoke in a languorous, educated, sarcastic voice. At first we'd taken him, in his tweeds and brogans, for an elderly English academic, touring the north country like ourselves. While we waited for our lunch, which was slow in coming, he'd walked us over to a huge empty fireplace and pointed out an ancient shelf built high up inside the gigantic flue. The shelf was furnished with a table, chair, and oil lamp. "Priest's hole . . . more of 'em around here than mouse holes, you know. This village began as an abbey." That's when Adrian had asked casually about the lambs, and it turned out the man himself was a sheep farmer, in town on some errands. After he'd made the remark about the dinner plate, he glanced at me, probably expecting some squeamish protest, and quickly added: "They're stunned with darts, you know; don't feel a thing. We take them over to the abattoir. However, my *wife* . . ." and here his crusty old face grew charmingly defenseless. "Every year she takes a fancy to one of the lambkins and pleads for his life. As a result, we have a bachelors' club of useless old rams braying about our place."

He's still in love with her, I thought. The sarcastic old sheep farmer was still in love with his wife. And I glanced sideways at Adrian, imagining how we, too, would grow old together and joke with strangers about each other's foibles, and I was profoundly stirred.

One spring weekend when I was a senior at the University of Virginia, I had come home to see my father and was cutting his hair in the garden behind the rectory when a man sauntered around the side of the house, carrying two books under his arm. My father introduced him as a new friend, an associate priest at the other Episcopal church in town. Then my father went inside to change his shirt after the haircut, and the man and I stood in the garden and talked. Before the sun had gone down on that afternoon I had set my heart on Adrian Bonner.

By Easter my father was dead of a stroke suffered on Good Friday during a reconsecration service for our church's vandalized outdoor crucifix. I graduated from college in May, moved out of the rectory to make way for the interim priest, and by the end of summer was living in New York with my mother's friend, Madelyn Farley, the set designer and creator of controversial theater pieces. That I had chosen to go off and make my home with this person who had destroyed my father's marriage, scandalized our parish, and robbed me of my mother when I was six, offended or baffled everyone who knew me. My oldest friend, Harriet, declared my act deranged. "Remember that nasty old witch you told me about? The one you were scared would drag you off into the closet and make you live with her when you were little? So what's the first thing you do when you grow up and get free of the closet? You look up the witch, you call her up on the telephone, and go and live with her."

There was truth in what Harriet said, but, like that other literal-minded friend, Horatio, she left a lot out.

The two years I stayed with Madelyn in Greenwich Village were, certainly from Horatio's viewpoint, the other side of the moon from the Virginia parish life in which I'd been reared. But beneath its surface irregularities, my living with this person my mother had gone away with was a natural and constructive progression. Having experienced Madelyn Farley throughout my girlhood as the enemy and the witch, I now as a woman needed to understand how my mother had experienced Madelyn as artist and agent of transformation. And in doing this I believe I came closer to discovering real glimpses of the person my mother had been, rather than tending the sputtering embers of the myth my father and I had made of her after she left us.

Those supercharged late suppers in Madelyn's loft with her artist-friends: how strange and intoxicating they must have been to my mother, Ruth Gower, who had gone straight from her Southern women's college to her older husband's rectory. Madelyn wasn't interested in food for itself, only as fuel for her artistic energies, or as an incentive to gather others around her for lively conversation. Except for her famous "energy grains," often gobbled like dry candy straight out of the jar, she existed happily on work, wine, and talk. Her young assistant, Shaun, who built exquisite and precise table models of her sets and then oversaw their life-sized construction for the stage, usually made a third at our long refectory table, where sketches and swatches of material and notes for Madelyn's latest theater piece were shoved to the far end to make room for pizzas or take-out Chinese. But frequently there were other friends: theater people or poets or painters, most of them gay men. They definitely did care about food, and would bring jumbo-sized containers of delicious things from their local delis or from their own kitchens.

I had never, at home or at college, partaken of get-togethers quite like these, where everybody was fair game for irreverent dismantlements. Anything at all, sacred or profane, was eligible to be zestfully ripped apart — and then just as enthusiastically restored to life in some unlikely new form. Of course, tearing things up and reassembling them in shocking ways was Madelyn Farley's forte, it was how she had made her fame in the theater world. The first time I ever met her, she could hardly wait to announce to my father that she was wearing a shirt a costume-designer friend had made for her out of a cut-up altar frontal.

I imagined my mother, a sheltered female of twenty-eight when she left us, suddenly transposed to Madelyn's loft and set down in the middle of these saucy rollicks. Ruth's whole life had been spent among people who spoke in low-voiced, careful codes, the very cadences and word choices of their speech calculated to talk *around things:* to smooth over, prettify, or exclude. Had she at first found Madelyn and her friends ill-mannered — even blasphemous? But perhaps, given my mother's own play of mind and her aptitude for parody and caricature, which she'd had to squash in her role as rector's wife, she had simply discovered herself to be home at last.

I remember one evening in particular, the evening of Madelyn's "new birthday." She had proclaimed that from now on she would celebrate her birthday on the date of her successful triple bypass the previous year, when she had been born again.

During dessert someone happened to remark that we were thirteen at the table that night, and Madelyn immediately leapt astride her pet hobbyhorse, turning religion to her own purposes, and began casting us for a reenactment of the Last Supper.

She chose Shaun for John the Beloved Disciple, who languished against her shoulder. The leading role she assigned to herself ("since it *is* my party"). Fernando the dancer mimed his part as a creepy, supple Judas, slinking around the table to listen in on conversations and fawn over Jesus. Harvey the acid-tongued poet got to be Peter, jealous of John. ("It beats me what He sees in that mooning wimp.") Pru, the costume designer who had cut up the altar frontal to make the shirt for Madelyn all those years ago, insisted on being the woman in the kitchen making the dinner ("I think it's time we realize that supper didn't get cooked by itself! I can come out and serve it and look decorative — and maybe wash your feet with some precious oil, Maddy"), so that meant one of the men had to play two disciples. I was cast as Thomas, Madelyn explaining that the doubting role would be good for me "after your lifetime of unquestioned belief."

As the preacher's kid, I was also called on to supply thumbnail sketches of the lesser known disciples so the others could get into their parts: Matthew the tax collector; earnest and literal-minded Philip; Peter's brother Andrew; John's brother James; skeptical Nathaniel ("Can anything good come out of Nazareth?"); Bartholomew, who was probably the same person as Nathaniel, which was just fine since one of us had to be two people; Simon Zealot, who some say was a Palestinian revolutionary; and James the Less, who may have been Jesus' brother. With so many brothers at the table there were ripe opportunities for sibling rivalry scenes

(James the Less: "Mom always gave Him the biggest piece of fish at home").

Though my judgment was no doubt affected by all the wine we'd consumed, I remember being elated by our performance that night: our inspired spur-of-the-moment dialogue, the actors fleshing out their roles with such brio. While Pru was washing Madelyn's feet in a little porcelain basin of diluted Vitabath, Shaun raised his glass to Madelyn: "Here's to you, Teacher," he said feelingly (and you felt he was Shaun saying it to Madelyn as well as John saying it to his beloved teacher), "and here's to eternal companionship."

When things had reached their peak, Madelyn, with her stage sense of knowing when to quit, held up a hand and spoke the final words of our performance: "Shhh, fellows, the photographer's coming. Everybody who wants to be in the picture come and sit on this side of the table."

Our festive party turned out to be a Last Supper in its own right. That group of friends was never to gather around Madelyn's table again. Within a few months Fernando was gone, and before Madelyn's next new birthday, four more were dead, including Madelyn herself. (Later, in seminary, when I was writing a paper on Eucharistic Celebration, I fretted for days over a worthy definition until I recalled Shaun's toast. "The Eucharist is eternal companionship," I wrote.)

As immersed as I was in Madelyn's world at that time, I kept a solid foot in my old world. I went to St. Luke's-in-the-Fields, and worked in outreach programs there. The idea of following my father's choice of work never lost its allure for me, but I was trying to heed the advice of those in his profession who urged discernment. How much of my desire to be a pastor came from a need to imitate and honor him and perhaps even to miss him less by becoming what he had been? What other life had I known? Didn't I owe it to myself to test alternative life choices outside the safe and familiar Church cycle of my girlhood before applying to seminary? I knew they had a point. I also knew that I had no choice. If I didn't accede to this trial period, they wouldn't support my candidacy for ordination.

All through this period and beyond it, Adrian Bonner remained constant in my thoughts. He was the link between the old days with my father in Romulus and my New York life. He was the one I always carried with me.

I wrote to him first, and he wrote back. Naturally, I put my best image forward in these letters, but as I grew surer that the letters were welcomed, I let more glimpses of unvarnished self slip through. I confessed insecurities, elaborated on (some of) my faults.

I knew he was a solitary man with an unhappy history, but I hoped to court and disarm him from a safe distance with my letters. I also used them to work out certain spiritual qualms (Madelyn's remark about my "lifetime of unquestioned beliefs" had been typical Madelyn-hyperbole). Given Adrian's interests and training, I couldn't have found a better sounding board if I'd ordered him out of a catalogue.

At times our letters seemed to me like a fascinating correspondence course; except that always behind them was the physical memory of the neat, solidly built man I had been drawn to in my father's garden, with his wide-spaced gray eyes and tough-boy's chipped front tooth, who spoke in terse, ruminative sentences — such a contrast to my father's agile cascades and embellishments. Our theological discussions came effortlessly, being as old as our acquaintance. That first afternoon, the word "sin" was dropped casually into the conversation, and I asked if he had a definition of it. "A falling short from your totality," he said after thinking for a good hard minute. "Choosing to live in ways that interfere with the harmony of that totality." I liked the way you could watch his whole square-jawed countenance working up a thought. He wasn't one of those wishful pietists whose assurances roll smugly off their tongues. He made it seem that my presence helped to shape his answers. In his letters he sometimes sounded as though I was guiding *him*.

"Where is God in all this?" I once typed angrily to him from seminary, after a week on the third-floor ward at St. Luke's Hospital when I was doing my Clinical Pastoral Education. "Twenty-five beds filled with rape, shooting, and dope victims, and here's this young woman of eighteen, born to be beautiful, with oozing, fresh razor scars all over her face *and* sickle cell anemia, and the nurse in charge is withholding her morphine simply because she's a sadist exercising her power. I was able to intervene about the morphine, but I never could look directly at this young woman's slashed-up beauty without fighting down the urge to run out of that ward and forsake my presumptuous dreams of improving the world."

He wrote back, by return mail that time:

Your question may be the only one that matters. Despite all the convoluted guesswork of theologians ever since Job's friends hunched beside him on the dung heap, "Where is God in this?" (just the question itself alone, I mean) may be enough to keep us busy down here. Maybe the thing we're required to do is simply keep asking the question, as Job did — asking it faithfully over and over, whatever ghastly thing is happening around us at the time — until God begins to reveal himself through the ways we are changed by the answering silence.

As for your follow-up question, after your week in that hellhole (I also did my CPE at St. Luke's, you know): how can you be sure that ministry is your vocation? I can only offer this conjecture. Something's your vocation if it keeps making more of you. Neither I nor anyone can tell you whether the ministry will ultimately do that for you. Look at my own case: at seventeen I ran away to the monks, but quickly found out their life wasn't for me; I'd already had enough submitting to the wills of others at the orphanage and then with my sadistic adoptive parents. After the Navy I did theology at Chicago until I realized I didn't want to spend the rest of my life teaching other people's theories of what God was like. Then the Jungian route to self-knowledge beckoned and off I went to Zurich. After analysis unshackled me in certain (but by no means all!) respects, I fully expected to end my days as an analyst, until I happened to attend a lecture in Zurich on "The Trinity Working in Human History" by an American theologian named Ferguson Stroup. And that, as you know, led me back home to General Seminary and ordination, and from there to my job as pastoral counselor at St. Matthias in Romulus, where I was fortunate enough to find your father across town at St. Cuthbert's. Like Stroup, Walter Gower turned out to be another prod toward transformation. Your father did so much for those in his care, even when suffering from such intense disbelief in himself. His example set me to wondering whether I, too, might risk serving others with parts of myself I had kept under wraps. Will it surprise you, Margaret, if I tell you that even as I'm writing to you now, I'm not sure I've found the right job yet?

Something else was happening in our correspondence. As Adrian was my link with the old days, I was his link to my father, who had been his spiritual director in Romulus. Judging from the revelations that accumulated with the letters, I suspected he was transferring some of his admiration of my father to me. The lonely orphan boy inside Adrian romanticized the family life my father and I had led. The orphan stood outside the window of St. Cuthbert's rectory and hungrily spied in retrospect on Daddy and me discussing esoteric spiritual subjects over wholesome suppers; he saw me growing up as

26

part of a dedicated father-daughter team serving a parish and a community. (The first afternoon I met him, he had described my father to me as someone who "lived by the grace of daily obligation.") He knew of course about Daddy's depressions, everybody in town did — my father's parishioners called him "Father Melancholy" behind his back — but despite all the allusions I made to my own dark, resentful moods as a motherless girl, I think Adrian continued to idealize my upbringing and to credit me with more wisdom and maturity than I had.

But what pursuing lover regrets an advantage? If I had fears that I might disillusion him later, I'd deal with it when the time came, I told myself. If I could just have him. And, though I had been scrupulous about admitting some of my shortcomings, to prove I was only human, I had chosen those shared shortcomings judiciously. I omitted to offer to him *one* aspect of my life as a young woman, and for this I would pay up later. But right now it was: *if I can just have him.*

Madelyn used to groan when I got his letters. "Here we have it, ladies and gentlemen: a textbook case of the daughter flinging herself into her mother's frying pan."

"What do you mean?" I'd demand eagerly. Madelyn's warnings were to me then the sweetest of predictions.

"A young woman in college who's lost both

her parents initiates a correspondence with a crusty old bachelor priest who came to her school to lead a retreat. He writes back, they discuss metaphysical poetry and high-minded topics, and the next thing you know she's Mrs. Crusty Old Priest, trapped in a Gothic Revival rectory in the Southern boondocks."

"Well, I'm not in college like Ruth was; I'm out on my own. And Adrian isn't crusty. Neither was my father, for that matter. If anything, Adrian is rather boyish —"

"Okay, a bald bachelor boy, twenty years older than you. Sixteen years wasn't enough, you had to go Ruth one better."

"He's not bald. You've never even seen him."

"You've described him enough times. Not tall, thin hair on top, chipped right front tooth — you find it 'rakish' — and pensive, 'wide-set' gray eyes. Balding people do eventually become bald, so I'm within my prophetic rights."

"He has a beautiful head and I couldn't care less about the hair. He has a strong, square, manly face that can stand by itself."

"Ha, but what about the rest of him, can it stand by *itself?* At least Walter was able to make a baby with Ruth."

"Oh, Madelyn, don't be gross."

"I'm just being practical. If Ruth were alive to talk you out of this gloomy infatuation,

28

she'd have said the same thing."

"Do you really think so?"

Madelyn always gained a point when she threw out one of her Ruth-would-have-saids. In the year they'd lived together, before Ruth was killed in the accident, Madelyn would have learned much about my mother that I wouldn't have picked up on as a child.

"She'd have said it her way, of course. 'Now, Margaret honey, have you, um, given any thought to what might transpire in your all's bedroom?' "

I had given a great deal of thought to it in my nighttime fantasies, but I certainly wasn't going to share the details with Madelyn. Her arch hints that she could see around to the backsides of the stage sets people presented as their lives had irked me ever since I was six years old and she had swaggered up our front walk bragging to my mother that she had known beforehand our house was going to look "Gothic." Yet here she had just resurrected Ruth with a single quote. I could hear my mother's voice saying it.

It was in the paradoxical nature of my relationship with Madelyn Farley that I often felt gratitude and revulsion toward her at the same time.

During those two years I lived with Madelyn, I was gainfully employed. My job description was the same as Shaun's: we were her "Personal Assistants." We had workmen's compensation, disability insurance, and W-2s, all kept up-to-date by Madelyn's accountant. She was a generous employer. (My starting salary, when I became rector of All Saints High Balsam wasn't much more than Madelyn had paid me.) Whatever her faults — and she was untidy, demanding, arrogant, rude, inconsiderate, and self-absorbed — stinginess wasn't among them. Shaun constructed her set models (and cooked and cleaned on the side), and I shopped and ran errands and did the research for her new theater piece — I'd given her the idea for it, in fact. I also provided stand-in daughter services for her cantankerous father, who lived a hundred miles upstate, with whom she squabbled constantly until old Farley painted his last moonscape, put his brushes to soak, and either had a heart attack or fell asleep and froze to death on his front porch.

I was the one who found him, having driven up to Overlook that December weekend to check on him at Madelyn's request. He was toppled stiffly sidewise on a tattered sofa on the porch, his brushes held upright by a thin crust of ice in the jar. Madelyn insisted I keep the little gouache painting, a December moon scudding between clouds in the night sky. It hangs in my study now, and whenever I look at it I am awestruck that Madelyn's selfish, foul-mouthed old parent could have produced a work of such rapturous delight.

Just as I was touched with wonderment when Madelyn was dying and asked me to read aloud her extensive sketches for the unfinished theater piece, "Abbess of Motherwit," about St. Hilda of Whitby, whose story I had told her when we were traveling in England after visiting the place where my mother was killed. How was it that the same person whose notorious *Pas de Dieux* had caused my father so much pain, based as it was on a debunking of his sacred rituals (some of which he had unwittingly coached her in himself), could so convincingly render the motions of a holy woman's mind?

Soon after Madelyn's death, I entered General Theological Seminary, sponsored in my postulancy for Holy Orders by the Committee on Ministry at St. Luke's, and with letters of recommendation from those in the profession who had urged me to disentangle my vocation from that of my father's and "test other realities" first. This second group obviously felt satisfied that my two years of living and working with a theater artist whose prize-winning works were mock burials of God and other such travesties of religious themes qualified sufficiently as an alternate lifestyle to the sheltered churched cycles of my Romulus childhood.

★ ★ ★

Now began my next task in the art of convincing people that something I wanted would not be bad for me — the object of my desire this time being not a particular job but a particular man.

Anyone who has ever been warned off the person she or he has chosen to love will recall the dedicated muleheadedness such resistance requires.

Everyone from my childhood friend, Harriet MacGruder Gaines, to Adrian's own former teacher and mentor at General Seminary, stepped forward to elaborate on why, in their (unsolicited) opinion, I would be wasting my time, running from my life, or ruining my life, if I persisted in what Madelyn had termed my "gloomy infatuation" with Adrian Bonner.

Harriet, in medical school in Atlanta, having married the (surprisingly unexceptional) person she wanted, phoned New York regularly to elicit news of my life, and then, having gathered enough evidence against me, proceeded to attack.

"I've been a student of your temperament since first grade, Margaret Gower. This crush on the Reverend Bonner is a perfect way to go on satisfying your sweet tooth for self-obliteration."

"My *what,* Harriet?"

"You heard me. You sacrificed your normal childhood to a needy, depressed clergyman father. What could be sweeter than the prospect of sacrificing your normal womanhood to a needy, depressed clergyman husband?"

"But Adrian's not depressed. He's not the ha-ha jovial type, he's a serious, scholarly man, but he has a nice understated sense of humor. And how can anybody say he's *needy*, when he spends most of every day listening to other people's needs?"

"The same way your father, who was a gifted listener and counselor, was needy. My grandfather said it operated as a kind of trade-off: in order to be the effective pastor he was, your father demanded constant reassurance from those closest to him. And then it took its toll on *them*. I saw Adrian when I was back in Romulus visiting Granny last weekend. We passed each other in our cars. He didn't see me, of course."

"Oh, how did he look?"

"The way he always looks. Inward and remote. But maybe he was having some understated humorous thought I couldn't see."

"I wonder where he was going."

"Someplace exciting, no doubt. The new car wash on Main, or over to St. Matthias to assist Jerry Hope with one of the many services on their crowded menu to please everybody, or maybe back to his counseling office on Acacia Street to meet with his next neurotic."

"How is your life, Harriet? How is Georgie?"

"Making money hand over fist in real estate, I'm afraid. He can't seem to stop himself."

"It's interesting, isn't it? All of us following family inclinations." Harriet's grandfather had been our physician. And Georgie — dubbed the "Blimp" by Harriet back when she would have killed anyone who suggested she might marry him — after dabbling in stockbroking, journalism, and half a semester at divinity school, had, as I was about to do, embraced the paternal calling. Greedy Gaines (my father's nickname for Georgie's father, who had leveled half the hills in Romulus with his condo developments) also had been unable to stop making money hand over fist in real estate.

"Some family inclinations are healthier than others," Harriet ungenerously replied. "I'm just trying to keep you from throwing away your life before you ever live it, Margaret."

"This may have to remain an eternal mystery to you, Harriet" — it was my turn now to be caustic to my old friend, whose concept of the good life had always pretty much excluded the intangibles — "but I *have* been living it as far back as I can remember."

★ ★ ★

"Now, Margaret," said Dr. Ferguson Stroup, the first time he invited me to tea at the seminary, "as you know, I haven't been an advocate of female priesthood. Doctrinally, I still can't reconcile myself to it, but in personal cases, such as your own, I'm inclined to make emotional exceptions."

What was I supposed to say to this? I was his guest, at his tea table, in his apartment filled with icons and ancient altar cloths: all sorts of ecclesiastical booty that Madelyn Farley would have loved to snatch and cut up and rearrange for her religious deconstructions. A demure "thank you" on my part, or a respectful silence and lowered head would brand me as false to my own beliefs and a traitor to my fellow female seminarians.

"My father had some of your reservations, Dr. Stroup, but I think if he were alive today, now that I've gone into the subject more thoroughly myself — well, I believe we'd be able to sit down together and work out our differences."

"Oh, you do, do you?" The handsome old man jutted his chiseled features aggressively forward. "Are you implying that your father's knowledge of the subject was in some way inferior to yours?"

"My father had so many things on his mind. Parish duties, raising me by myself, his own self-doubts. Don't you think we all

35

store much of our knowledge on back shelves, until something . . . some new urgency . . . compels us to go back and reexamine it? In this case the urgency would have been my wanting to be a parish priest, like him. That would have made it personal and immediate. Maybe that's how changes in people have to start: with something close to us. Like you said, something we can accept emotionally."

"Hmpph. You're an engaging combatant, my dear. Take more butter on that scone, you can afford it. I wish I had known your father. Adrian Bonner speaks so admiringly of him. As he does of you, by the way. But, just between us, Adrian never struck me as the marrying type. If I may venture another emotional prompting, you may not be destined for the married state, either."

My best outward defense to this last remark *was* respectful silence and a lowered head, because Dr. Stroup had thrown me into total perplexity. My father had once said he thought Adrian would remain a bachelor, so I'd heard that one before, but this was the first time I was hearing *myself* slotted for this lonely category. Had Dr. Stroup picked up on something about me that I wasn't aware of myself?

"Some of us aren't suited to partnership," Dr. Stroup said. "I'm not talking about homosexuality, either. Many a homosexual I have known is ideally suited to lifelong intimacy with another person. I'm speaking about those of us who, whether from cussedness or special grace, are given to find our complete satisfaction in serving God through what we do. In the first category I would place myself and probably Bonner. You seem more marked by grace. More *chosen* than cussed. Did a religious vocation ever cross your mind?"

I was appalled. "You mean . . . like a nun?"

"Not *just* a nun. Don't get me wrong." He lifted his teacup to me gallantly. "Old reactionary that I am, I'm not suggesting for a minute you relinquish your new canonical rights. I'm only saying it strikes me, from what I've heard of you from others — and from my personal observations — that you might be suited for priesthood *and* a religious vocation. The Church needs such attractive combinations."

I saw myself veiled *and* vested — though the chasuble would be awkard to slip over a veil — elevating the host in some convent chapel, afterward scraping the dishes in the kitchen with my sisters in Christ. Never remotely had this scenario figured among my daydreams.

What could Stroup have heard about me that made him picture me thus? Had Adrian told him something? The thought depressed me. Did *Adrian* think I was good material for a nun? Is that why he considered it safe to write to me about himself and, more recently, sign his letters "Yours"?

Or was Dr. Stroup merely trying, as older people frequently did, to fashion me into a worthy carrier of his own idealisms and proclivities? He himself was a bachelor-priest, at sixty-eight still in full swing as a popular lecturer at home and abroad on esoteric Church subjects. Students in his Eucharistic Celebration class called him "Stroup the Swoop," because he rigorously trained his apprentice-celebrants in the grand sweeping gestures of the high Anglo-Catholic mass. It was said that he had been within a hair's breadth of going over to Rome in 1976, when ordination of women had been ratified by the convention. But his well-appointed apartment at the seminary and his comfortable expertise in the rituals and ceremonies of the Anglican Communion prevailed, and he had obviously decided to stay and make the best of things. If he couldn't keep females out of the sanctuary, he could at least groom and choreograph them into its gentlemanly, circumspect rituals. He could do everything in his power to disincline them from the appurtenances that would deface their office: lipstick, earrings, perfume, nail polish, jewelry, hair that flopped forward into the face or into the chalice, anything that jiggled or jangled or distracted from what John Henry Newman

38

had called "the sacred dance of the ministers." ("Old Fergie would put breasts and pregnancies on his list of distracting 'appurtenances,' if he dared," an outspoken woman in Mass Class, as we called it, once said to me.)

He wasn't an out-and-out misogynist (earrings and wild hair came under the ban for men, too, as did slouching, slumping, clattering and clumping, tugging at vestments, and awkward or halfhearted genuflections — "If you're uncertain of your balance, for God's sake stay upright, keep your legs together, and execute a slow *respectful* Sarum bow"); but he *was* as professionally biased toward his own gender as he was toward patrician behavior. He was fond of quoting some nineteenth-century Church of England divine who said that the ideal look for a priest at the altar was "that of a Roman citizen practicing good manners before his superior." The vestments of the Church, Dr. Stroup liked to remind us, had come straight down to us from the fashions of Roman gentlemen.

However, by far the most unsettling of those who warned me off Adrian was Ben MacGruder, Harriet's younger brother. He came to New York often — there was always the excuse of his recording studio over in Hoboken, or his visits to a ninety-year-old jazz player up in Harlem who helped him work out some of his arrangements. Whenever Ben blew into town, he would rout me out. He had a tiresome knack for "intuiting" where I was likely to be (abetted by his sister Harriet, who knew my schedule and now encouraged his intentions toward me, in view of the unsavory competition). So there I'd be, browsing in the corner bookstore near Madelyn's loft, or, later on in seminary, daydreaming of Adrian outside on a bench in the close, or recollecting myself in the chapel, and guess who'd pop up like an old song? In Ben's case, it was a song trailing penitential memories.

During a lonely Romulus summer, when I was home from college and Ben was seventeen, we had been — I never could bring myself to use the word "lovers." I hadn't loved him. He, on the other hand, did have to his credit that he insisted he had loved *me* ever since an Easter egg hunt, when I was six and he was three.

One day during that regrettable summer, we were alone together on a raft in the middle of a lake and he told me of his love. He had related it in his typical prankster style, leading me on a wild goose chase first so that I was lying there shocked, thinking he'd gotten involved with a married woman in town he babysat for. Then suddenly he kissed me in a way that left no doubt who the beloved was. I was so startled I dived straight into the lake and swam away. The lake contained memories of my mother teaching me to swim in it, and stirred up all kinds of other elemental stuff. Why was I, a twenty-year-old college woman, still a virgin? Was there something wrong with me? My mother was not there to instruct me in physical matters. Finally I got tired of swimming and turned back. Little Ben, whom I had hoisted by his wet bottom into a tree, that long ago Easter, so he could claim the Golden Egg he alone had spotted — the egg my mother had made and sent from New York — that little boy had vanished from the raft. In his place was stretched out a manly stranger with curly golden hairs all down his chest and legs. Long before the end of that summer, I had repented of making him into the object of my free-floating lust. Ben was more in love than ever, but I felt cheap and false. We were deceiving his family and my father, all of whom believed me to be an older-sisterly "good influence" on young Ben. Sometimes I thought of myself as a child molester. Then followed the painful process of extricating myself from the sex part while trying to save our friendship: there was so much about Ben that I enjoyed and admired. He was a rarer bird than his conventional sister, much more original and adventurous. At first he was heartbroken and infuriated by my withdrawal, then reproachful, then resigned to biding his time.

41

He remained adamantly convinced that because I had "belonged to him" first, I would eventually belong to him again.

"It's an aberration, Margaret, this thing you're cultivating for that desiccated therapist-clergyman. You've got this rare, beautiful, shapely pot and rich, generous soil, and you're trying to grow a leafless, dry old stick in it."

"Ben, please save your picturesque language for your lyrics. You've been doing very well with them there." Ben had fulfilled his family's worst predictions for him by dropping out of college and hanging around Melody Station, a nightclub for young blacks in Romulus; then he'd gone on to flabbergast them completely by forming a vocal group, named after the club, with three other Melody Station habitués, and becoming a success.

"Oh yes, I'm doing very well with everything except *you*. What's the use of all my beauty and talent and good fortune when you spurn me?"

"Well, Ben, don't put yourself in a position to be spurned."

"Harriet said you've actually got yourself engaged to him."

"We're engaged to each other, that's the way these things usually work. We plan to marry when I finish seminary."

"Not in much of a rush, is he?"

"It was a mutual decision, Ben. But maybe

we'll get carried away and do it sooner. Would that suit you better?"

"He's the last person I can imagine being carried away. Whereas you, Margaret, are a passionate person. Yes you are. I *know*. I have my memories."

"Well, it's unchivalrous of you to throw them in my face under the circumstances."

"What I can't understand is why you love him when you can't love me. I've tried and tried — I just can't figure it *out*."

"Stop trying. I don't try to. He came around a corner and something in me went out to meet him. Some things are mysterious. They can't be figured out."

"You don't have to sound so fucking *smug* about it. Have you made love with *him?*"

"That's none of your business."

"You haven't! I can read it in your face. I've been reading your face since you were six. That day of the Easter egg hunt I saw you *renounce* finding any eggs. You turned away and walked down the slope with your sad, resolute little face. *I* was the one who spotted your mother's golden egg in that tree, I was the one who got it for you."

"Oh, how sick I am of that egg story —"

"You may be sick of it, but it's an important part of your history. Just as *I'm* in your history and you can't get me out. What's his history? He grew up in an orphanage, everyone knows that. His parents dropped him off at a Catholic orphanage and never came back."

"Well, we're fellow sufferers, then. My mother went off and left me and never came back."

"That's low, Margaret. You know I didn't mean that. I meant who knows what kind of background he comes from?"

"Oh, God! You sound like some prissy ass in the Mayflower Society. What he's made of himself is enough for me. *He's* enough for me. Why can't you just accept that, and be done with it?"

"I *cannot* accept it and I never will 'be done with it.' I'll never be done with *you*. He's some kind of delusion for you, this dry old stick old enough to be your father that you've never even seen undressed. I can't even imagine him *proposing*. I'll bet anything you had to ask him, he would never have thought of suggesting such a warm-blooded thing himself —"

"Now I've really had enough, Ben."

"— and for some 'mysterious' reason you smugly claim not to understand, you're hell-bent on climbing in the pot with him and watering the soil from below with your tears. Boy, there'll be little fountains gushing up all over the place, you wait and see, fountains of your own tears. . . ."

"Do me a favor, Ben. Save it for your songs."

Alas, he was to do just that.

Did Ben vex me more than the others because he *did* have a flair for reading people's secrets? He had spent his early childhood at diplomatic posts with his parents in Africa and the Middle East, and often boasted that he and the Nubian servant who slept outside his door in Egypt could enter each other's minds without speaking. It was like getting into a warm bath with the man's thoughts, Ben said, and he maintained he'd been able to do it with people he cared about ever since. He'd done it with his albums as well. He seemed to be able to intuit what was simmering up through the soup of the collective culture's mind, and be there to catch it at the top before it bubbled over. Before multiculturalism and sacred music had even reached the boiling point, his *Mattokki Moon Fever* release was high on the charts, his own arrangement of Nubian worship and courtship songs. He was somewhat in arrears with rap and chant, but made up for it with his catchy lyrics and unusual instrumental combinations in *The Inner-City Rap-Chapel*. And though Ben did tend to exaggerate his "extrasensory" capabilities, I'd had previous experience of them before the infuriating occasion when he had guessed correctly that I'd never seen the man I intended to marry undressed, and that

45

Adrian hadn't, exactly, proposed to me.

Though I hadn't, exactly, proposed to him, either.

After three years of letter writing, and half a dozen of Adrian's visits to New York to see his old mentor Dr. Stroup and take me out to dinner afterward, our decision to marry came about in the following manner.

One foggy November morning in my middle year at General, walking down Ninth back to the seminary from a coffee shop, I came upon an odd trio at a deserted intersection. An old man in a shabby coat was bent over double, as if from sudden sharp pain, and two young boys seemed to be trying to support him from either side. I hurried over to join the Samaritan effort and found instead that I'd interrupted a mugging. One of the boys turned his knife on me, while the other searched frantically through the old man's pockets. Throughout the whole procedure not a word was uttered. The incident had a dreamlike aspect as the four of us pantomimed our parts in the damp muffling whiteness. The boys couldn't have been more than eleven or twelve. I remember worrying as I wrestled with my young assailant for the knife that I might be hurting him. Then there was a snap, like a twig breaking. Oh God, I've broken his wrist, I thought, feeling a sympathetic pain in my own. Then they ran off. The old man, too — surprisingly

46

fast. I looked down to see my wrist drooping in an unnatural way and realized it was my own pain I had been feeling. On the sidewalk lay the knife. I picked it up with my left hand and examined it: a small un-lethal-looking penknife with PRESSAC LIMITED stamped in silver upon the electric-blue metal casing. I still have it. Then, also with my left hand, I retrieved my purse from the sidewalk, slipped in the penknife, still open, because I couldn't use my right hand to close it, and walked back to General.

The first person I met inside was the dean of the seminary, coming out of the bookstore. I was in a lot of pain by now, but I tried to be humorous as I related what had happened, because the dean looked so distraught, as if the whole thing were somehow his fault. My arm had ballooned skintight inside my raincoat sleeve. We had to borrow scissors from the bookstore to cut me out of it. Then, with the same dreamlike wooliness of the episode on the street, the dean and I were bumping conversationally uptown in a taxi to his orthopedic surgeon's office. He was carrying a paperback on Ignatian Spirituality that he had picked up in the bookstore and forgotten to pay for, and I remember we joked about this and then discussed the pros and cons of this sort of regulated mental prayer. The next thing I knew I had been installed, woozy with painkillers, my right arm encased in a cast from wrist to shoulder, in one of the bedrooms of the dean's house in the close, being fussed over by his gracious wife.

"You'll stay with us, Margaret, until you get the big cast off. Longer than that, if we can keep you. You can't be traipsing down all those stairs from your dorm room."

"But, Evangeline, I didn't break a leg."

"No, but everything'll be twice as difficult, so you might as well be in a comfortable place with your own private bathroom right next door. I remember when I broke my arm at fourteen. You'll need help dressing and doing your hair, even after you get the shorter cast next week. The simple act of taking your *panties* up and down is going to require forethought. You're a nifty girl, Margaret. I could never in my life have walked up to two muggers and wrestled away their knife and saved an old man."

"But I thought they were trying to help him and I simply went over to help *them*."

"Yes, but then when you saw what was going on, you didn't run away. Most people would have. I certainly would have."

"But maybe you wouldn't have, Evangeline. How can we know how we'll react to something until it's actually happening? And they were just little boys."

"Well, one of them was strong enough to tear your ligament and fracture your ulna. *Little children* are killing people every day in this city. But Tom's right, you're as modest as you are valiant. He said you were calming *him* down in the taxi."

At Thursday evensong, the same week I got my short cast, the dean appeared in the chapel with a man in a dark coat and hat. Immediately after, they were blocked from sight by students filing into the row ahead of me. When I was able to see again, the two men had settled into the dean's pew, and the visitor, coat and hat removed, had slipped to his knees to pray. It was Adrian.

After the service they were waiting for me on the chapel porch. "A visitor from home to check on our heroine," announced the smiling dean.

"Adrian," I said.

"Margaret, it's good to see you." He looked older than when I'd last seen him and it made me love him more. My coat, a sheepskin from a St. Luke's rummage sale, was draped about my shoulders to accommodate the cast. Steadying me lightly by the empty sleeves, he kissed me on the mouth.

"How are you feeling?"

"Oh, I feel fine. I just can't write, or dress myself very well."

"Evangeline's been doing up her hair," the dean reported proudly.

"Oh, yes?" Adrian continued to hold me gingerly by my coat sleeves and gaze at me

49

with a preoccupied air.

"Will you two join us for dinner?" asked the dean.

"That would be nice, if Margaret's free," Adrian said.

"I'm free," I said.

The three of us walked across the close to the dean's house in the damp blue evening air. "Did you see Dr. Stroup this afternoon?" I asked Adrian, assuming he was following his usual procedure of visiting his old teacher, then looking me up. Though always before, he'd written me well in advance and suggested times and meeting places.

"No, I just got here. I caught the shuttle from Washington. I phoned Fergie this morning, to see about coming up sometime before the Christmas break, but when he told me about your injury, I decided to come today."

Adrian was not an impetuous person; and he always took the train.

"What about all your appointments?" I asked.

"I rescheduled them," he said.

"You're welcome to stay here with us at the seminary," offered the dean. "Since there isn't a single bishop or Russian Orthodox prelate or Nag Hammadi scholar booked in till the New Year, I can even offer you one of our VIP suites." He laughed. "Each one comes with a tempting choice of English

50

Breakfast or herbal tea bags, a refrigerator with vintage ice trays from the 1940s, a phone you can call out on, without being stopped at the switchboard, and your own iron and ironing board."

"I don't need to be tempted," said Adrian.

He stayed over the weekend, meeting alone with Dr. Stroup several times and taking me out to dinner on Friday *and* Saturday nights. He was very protective of my immobilized arm, shielding me from swinging doors and anticipating when I needed him to cut my meat. He seemed more concerned that I might have sustained some inner damage. Was I sleeping all right? Any nightmares?

"I haven't had a single nightmare," I told him. "To tell the truth, I'm embarrassed by all this attention. People confusing my naivete with heroism. But the experience has made me sadder about some things."

"What things?"

"Well, that life can already be spoiled for people when they're so young. I can still feel how childlike that boy's wrist was when I grappled with him. And yet his future is almost certainly booked in some prison. I've touched him and been touched by him, but now I'm safely back in the close, surrounded by attentions and friends. My wrist will heal, but who'll come along and save that boy from his dreadful future?"

Adrian reached across the table and picked

51

up my left hand. After examining it thought-fully for a moment, he said, "Chances are you're right about his future. But sometimes a saving person does come along. Who knows, I might have been rotting in jail myself if one or two good people hadn't been exactly in position when I needed them. He might be lucky, like I was."

On Sunday, Dr. Stroup had the two of us for luncheon in his apartment. He'd just acquired a new piece of art, an acrylic rendering of "Cast your nets," done in the iconic style by a Staten Island painter. We remarked on the numinous quality the artist had evoked. Out of a dark blue and purple nighttime seascape, some of the disciples were returning to shore with their surprise harvest of fishes. The single area of brightness comes from the glow of the charcoal fire on shore where Jesus, returned from the dead, is cooking their breakfast. All three of us were drawn to the painting and continued to talk about it over lunch, along with the mysterious final chapter of the Fourth Gospel on which it was based.

"There's an interesting Greek word, *kalchaino*," Ferguson Stroup told us. "Literally, it means 'to search for the purple fish.' Either of you heard of it?"

"No," I said, thinking it kind of him to include me when he knew I was just starting Elementary New Testament Greek.

"No," said Adrian, "but I like the idea already."

"Well, of course you do, dear boy. It's your favorite element, those waters where the purple fish swims."

"Now I'm really curious," I said, looking at Adrian, who was smiling and who seemed, in the last two days, to have grown younger again. Stroup sent me an indulgent look. I sensed something new in his demeanor toward me: could it be he had given his tacit blessing to my interest in Adrian?

"The literal purple fish was a shellfish highly prized by the Greeks for its rich purple dye," Stroup told us. "Divers went to the bottom of the sea in search of this elusive fish. That's how 'searching for the purple fish' came to be the Greeks' expression for plumbing the depths of one's mind. I asked the artist, who's of Greek descent, if he'd known this, and he was delighted. He said, 'Then you see why my sea is predominantly purple and all the fish in the net have purple shadings, and why the ones Our Lord is cooking are the purplest of all.' "

Stroup had propped the picture on the sideboard facing our table, so we could look at it while we ate.

"The artist told me he took the whole fish theme of John Twenty-one to be an invitation to ingest Christ. The net full of fish Christ helped them catch — 'throw out your net to

53

starboard and you will make a catch' — as well as the fish he's cooking for them on shore *after his death*. The artist said he interpreted all these fish as assurances that we're ready to take in the full meaning of Christ himself."

"That makes sense," commented Adrian, "because in the language of the unconscious, when the dreamer is about to eat something, it's often a signal that there's submerged content ready to be assimilated."

"Yes, yes, it all fits, doesn't it?" said Stroup, pleased. "And those two fish on the charcoal fire look almost done, don't they? A hopeful sign, I would say. Margaret, you're pensive. What are your thoughts on the matter?"

He'll be leaving on the late afternoon shuttle, were my thoughts. He made this unexpected trip because I was hurt. He kissed me on the mouth in front of the dean. He picked up my hand in the restaurant. He looks at me on this visit as though I'm precious to him. I think he may love me, but does *he* know he loves me?

"Someone returning from the dead to give advice and sustenance to loved ones when they are most in need of it . . . that's the aspect that moves me," I said.

How welcome a few words of instruction and encouragement from either of my dead parents would have been in my present situation. Daddy had been Adrian's confidant, his spiritual director. And my mother surely would have had some ideas about how to net an abstruse bachelor.

"My dear, you provide the crucial third element of this luncheon triad. I'm the old academic, Adrian is the deep-sea diver, but you remind us what it's all about in the first place."

"And what's that?" inquired Adrian of his former teacher.

"Love, old fellow, love. He's out there cooking their breakfast because he *loved* them, and they knew it. Margaret, shall I cut your lox into more manageable strips for you?"

"Oh, I've been doing that for her," said Adrian, reaching over for my fork and fish knife.

"Then, dear boy, you'd better keep doing it, hadn't you?" said Stroup, smiling on us benignly.

"Margaret, is there anything I can do for you before I go?"

Adrian walked beside me in the close. The luncheon was over. Soon it would be time for him to collect his things and catch a cab to the airport. The weak November sun cast a sad pinkish light on the brick and brownstone buildings of the seminary. Oh Walter, oh Ruth, oh God, what do I do now?

"There is something, as a matter of fact," I said.

"Command me."

"If you wouldn't mind coming up to my dormitory room for a few minutes."

"Anything you say." But he looked perplexed.

"It won't take long and it's the best place to do it. I don't want Evangeline to know, until it's too late."

"Well, I'm intrigued," he said, following behind me up the four flights. He was slightly breathless: from nervousness, or from all the stairs?

"It's nothing very intriguing, but it will make my life a whole lot simpler."

I unlocked the door to my suite. Nobody in the common room and my suite mate's door was closed. Thank you, God. And into my own room.

"So this is where you live," he said.

I had left the door ajar, so as not to alarm him too much.

"I hope to be back up here soon. Tom and Evangeline are so kind, but I really study better here."

"I had the same oak dresser when I was at General. Same desk, too."

As I took what I needed from the dresser, I could watch him in its mirror as he leaned over my desk. "What a good snapshot of Walter. He looks so happy, serving himself pink punch from that bowl. What was the occasion?"

"A party at Elaine Major's. It was his six-tieth birthday."

"The last he ever had. You know, I often drive home the long way, just so I can go past St. Cuthbert's. I still miss him. Why are you giving me these scissors?"

"Evangeline's been setting her alarm every morning so she can put my hair up in a pony-tail."

"You can't mean you want me to cut your hair, Margaret."

"If you don't, I'll have to after you leave. With my left hand — and that will be a mess." I turned my back on him to face the mirror. "All you have to do is start cutting right here, just below the earlobe, and then cut straight around to the other earlobe."

"Shouldn't we take it out of the rubber band first?"

I laughed. "Good point. You'll have to do that, too, I'm afraid."

"All this nice hair. It seems a shame."

"It will grow back. I used to wear it shorter, anyway."

"Shouldn't I brush it out first? To make sure I get it even?"

"You should, but guess what? My brush and comb are over at the deanery."

"Maybe we can make do with my pocket comb. Not that I much need it anymore. I'll be bald as an egg soon." He was studying himself critically in the mirror as he stood behind me. His squarish chin came just above the top of my head. Before I met Adrian, I regretted not being taller. Now I was happy to be exactly as I was.

"I like your head," I said as he began combing out my hair with his comb. "It's beautifully shaped."

A silence. "Well, it's kind of you to say so." He seemed to be having difficulty with some tangles. "But I must seem decrepit to you."

"No, you seem . . . just right the way you are. Please don't worry about those tangles, you'll be cutting above them."

"Fergie has been telling me about an interesting man. He's opening a year-round therapeutic high school in the North Carolina mountains. Hiram Sandlin, a professor of psychology and neurobiology. An unusual combination. He's taking early retirement to start this small boarding school, only about seventy-five students. Fergie says he's evolved some highly effective methods for motivating young people, rescuing their imaginations from passivism . . . turning them around when everything else has failed. It's going to be privately run, but the Diocese of Western North Carolina is very enthusiastic about the venture. The retiring bishop will serve on the board of directors and hopes to be an active supporter. His granddaughter was in one of Sandlin's experimental residence schools at Chapel Hill. She'd dropped out or been kicked out of three previous boarding schools and spent a year in drug rehab, but now she's a graduate student in poetry at Johns Hopkins. Sandlin's looking for a chaplain with training in clinical therapy for his school, and Fergie told him about me and he's interested. I must say it sounds like the kind of job I've been dreaming of."

"A job that would keep making more of you."

"You say such wise things, Margaret."

"I'm just quoting your own words back to you, Adrian."

"I said that?"

"You wrote it in one of your letters. Would the job also involve those risks you spoke of?"

"What risks?"

"In the same letter you said you'd like to risk serving with parts of yourself you'd so far kept under wraps."

"Now I do remember writing that, so I'm not completely senile yet. Yes, from what I understand, this position would come fully loaded with that sort of risk. Starting a school is an enormous risk in itself. And a school for young people at risk is even more of one. But it's a risk I'd love to take."

"Then why not take it?"

He stopped combing and began pulling apart another tangle with his fingers. It was way below the "cutting line," but he appeared to be untangling something in himself and so I kept quiet.

"You make me want to take all sorts of risks today," he presently said.

"Then why not take them?"

"Well, I'm wondering if I should."

Deciding to take a risk of my own, I said, "If any of them involve me, I wish you would."

"If it were simply an old-fashioned case of your being willing to join me when you finish here . . . but, Margaret, how can I limit your prospects before you've even begun?"

"Why would you be limiting me? Why shouldn't our having each other make more of us both?"

II

The Light in the Crypt

May their having each other make more of them both.

I printed this in block letters at the bottom of the four-by-six note card for Gus and Charles's wedding homily tomorrow.

Then I underlined the words and sat looking at them. Recycling my life for use in my work. A man with two books under his arm enters a garden where a young woman is cutting his friend's hair. Later, after the friend is dead, the same woman stands before a mirror and the man cuts *her* hair, and this act becomes the means through which their love can speak. The words said by the woman to signify her willingness are taken from a previous phrase of the man's, which has significance for them both. And later again these same words will serve as a prayer for another couple's marriage.

Would Gus and Charles, as involved in their building and doctoring as Adrian and I were in our schoolmastering and pastoring, be able to live up to the words better than we were doing? I hoped so. I hoped so for their sakes. I sketched a Celtic cross in the left-hand corner of the card and began shading in the background. What had happened to Adrian and me? In my more pragmatic moods, I tried to settle for the practical explanation: our jobs were making so much of us that we had no time left to make much of each other. But by nature I wasn't a pragmatist; I was a digger, a delver into complexities.

I isolated the Celtic cross with its shaded background in a square and began decorating the square with ivy leaves. When had our shadows begun? When we had lived out at the school together, things were still very bright. When I was curate down at St. Francis-in-the-Valley, commuting back and forth every day, things were still good. Shortly after I was ordained to the priesthood, I got pregnant, and things were even better. Then, after sixteen weeks, I miscarried, and we were both desolate for a while.

Then I came out of it, but Adrian didn't. He remained stuck in his low period. For the first time, I was forced to acknowledge the melancholy likeness to my father that Harriet had plucked out of her arsenal when she was trying to dissuade me from marrying Adrian. Only, there was a chilling difference between hearing Adrian go on about how he had narrowed my professional chances and brought more sorrow into my life and remembering my father telling Ruth how he had curtailed her art and limited her life. At the bottom of

my father's Slough of Despond, I now realized, had burbled a dependable tiny well-
spring of lugubrious self-love: somehow he
had been at ease lolling in his melancholy.
Whereas at the bottom of Adrian's despon-
dence, I had discovered, lay a flinty bedrock
of self-hatred. But if my father had been
something of a loller, my husband was a
fighter: his whole history testified to this.
He'd work hard and achieve a profession,
then heed a call to a fuller use of his potential,
bravely pull himself up by the roots, and ex-
pand his skills: from Chicago to Zurich, from
Zurich to seminary, from seminary to the
church, from church to this experimental
school in the mountains of western North
Carolina. "A falling short of your totality"
was how he had defined sin on the day I met
him in my father's garden, and he was still at
work trying to fill out his own totality. But
then there'd be an emotional setback — the
death of my father, the death of our unborn
daughter, the death of Dr. Sandlin — and,
whereas anyone would be plunged into grief,
he plunged *beyond* grief, right back down to
that hard, cold floor of self-hate.

When I received the call to All Saints High
Balsam, a plum of a parish by most people's
standards — and a sort of miracle when you
consider that I was barely thirty years old and
they had never called a woman priest before
— there'd been a glorious reversal in Adrian's

63

mood: he was elated. He was obliged to concede that maybe he hadn't ruined my life by bringing me down here to these isolated hills. He moved into the rectory ("My wife's rectory," he proudly referred to it every chance he got) and we painted walls and hung our pictures and made him a study upstairs next to our bedroom, and then there followed two and a half extremely busy years for both of us. Most nights, however, we were together, and they were good nights: this was our era of connubial friendship. We were best friends who were also lovers — when we weren't too tired.

And then: Hiram Sandlin's sudden death last May. Adrian was knocked flat by grief, but then, by unanimous staff consensus, hauled to his feet while still in shock and talked into serving as interim headmaster. His reluctance to assume such a role expressed itself in an overconscientious drudgery that soon wore him out and made him increasingly irritable. Yet, almost as if to punish himself, he continued to take on responsibilities that could have been left to others. He started spending nights at the school. On the nights he slept at home, he was overconscientious about our lovemaking, with the not surprising result that he became impotent. The self-hate syndrome kicked in with a vengeance this time; he seemed to derive pleasure from making bitter jokes about

December graybeards who took to themselves May brides. But worst of all, he punished us both by withdrawing from the intimacy of our friendship as well; he took to staying up late reading in his study on the nights he was home. And when I had to go off to New York for two weeks last summer, he offered a mordant little scenario of how I might leave him one day for good — which had the effect of putting into my head, for the first time, the possibility of doing just that.

And yet all it took was a moment like the one in the kitchen this evening, when he came toward me, pulling his watch cap down to his eyebrows, remembered to kiss me, then let himself be waylaid by laughter, and I was recalled to my long-term self, the one who had prayed for this husband and got him, the one who still wanted more than anything else to see what life would make of us together.

Such were my musings, that Friday evening before Advent when more than we could ever imagine was on its way to us, as I sat in my study listening to the dry leaves in the garth below and, having over-foliated my squared Celtic cross, began sketching flowers and more leaves around the *M* of the *May* of my prayer for Gus Eubanks and Charles Tye.

The phone on my desk gave its jarring electronic bleep. It was Kevin Dowd, the interim priest down at the Chapel of St. Francis-in-the-Valley, the only other Episcopal congregation in Bruton County.

"Margaret? Am I interrupting anything?"

"Oh, hi, Kevin, I'm just putting a few finishing touches on a wedding sermon for tomorrow."

"Grace Munger just phoned me again about us joining that Millennium Birthday March for Jesus she's organizing up here."

"That woman's persistence is daunting! I told her no again this morning."

"Yes, that's what she said. But now I think she's pestering me on behalf of us both. Apparently every church but our two have committed to the march."

"The Lutherans aren't having any part of it. I saw Dick Miller at the post office this morning. He said her ad in the *Balsam Bugle* with that 'Christian Manifesto for a Wounded Town' tacked on at the bottom put his congregation off."

"Oh. Maybe she hasn't got wind of that yet."

"Or wasn't telling you if she had."

"You've got a point there. But did she ever work me over just now!"

"I can imagine. She hangs on like a tick." One of Charles Tye's colorful similes that I had appropriated for myself.

"But you know what's worrying me a little now, Margaret?"

"What?" Grace Munger had obviously

66

punctured his skin.

"Well, I'm wondering will we be sending the wrong signals by refusing to join?"

"What sort of wrong signals?"

"Well, these are such explosive times, Margaret. After that awful shooting in High Balsam last summer and all the publicity about it, people around here have gotten so *polarized* about socioeconomic differences."

" 'Class War Comes to the Peaks of Southern Hospitality.' " I quoted one of the most quoted headlines.

"Even the word 'class' has become incendiary," Kevin said, almost in a whisper. "And it's all tangled up with religion, too, you know. I mean, I'm sure you've heard, for instance, how certain of the locals refer to your parish."

"All Saints High-Horse, but that's ancient history, Kevin."

"Yes, but what concerns me, Margaret, is will people think we consider ourselves too exclusive to join this community event?"

"Some will, probably."

"But, doesn't that *worry* you?"

"Not as much as it would worry me if I marched behind a banner supporting Grace Munger's Christian Manifesto."

"Her ad didn't actually come right out and condemn any specific groups."

"It didn't have to. By now the remotest hermit in these hills, even a hermit *without* a satellite dish, knows the agendas behind her phrases."

"Maybe *we* should run an ad in the *Bugle*?"

"We who?"

"Well, us and the Lutherans."

"Saying what?"

"Oh, just a brief, diplomatically worded letter . . . about why we've chosen not to participate in the Millennium March."

"Why? When you decline someone's invitation to participate in a public function, you don't take an ad in the paper to explain why."

"But wouldn't it win us more friends than polite silence?"

The prospect of not being liked obviously worried Kevin a lot. This might have been one of the reasons why at age forty-five he was still waiting for a church to call him as its full-time leader.

"I'm not sure whether either response will win us any more friends. I'm not sure winning friends is even the point here, Kevin."

"The thing is, you know, Margaret, we *do* all worship the same God."

"I'm not so sure about that, either."

He laughed nervously. "What I mean is, we're kind of all in the same club, aren't we? I mean, if we all call ourselves Christians, how do we justify separating ourselves from this bothersome march? Where do we draw the line between us and the Grace Mungers?"

"At the point where certain club members

take it upon themselves to issue 'manifestos' in the name of the entire club."

"Hey, we could write *that* in the letter."

I counted to ten and didn't reply.

"All this damn Millennium fuss anyway. It brings out such extremes in people! I'll be glad when it's over, won't you?"

"Well, the Greenwich Observatory's been telling us for years it doesn't even begin till *next* year."

After we hung up, I sat cluttering my note card with more and more leaves and flowers until I realized I'd have to copy the notes onto a new card if I wanted to make any sense of my sermon tomorrow. As I proceeded to make the clean card, I wished I could as easily untwine myself from the tangled skeins of Kevin Dowd's not wholly unjustified unease.

In my unmarried days I would have begun a long letter to Adrian immediately, laying out the situation with all its sticky tentacles as best I could, listing pros and cons of possible actions, and laboring throughout for an expression of my quandary until it began to clarify itself through the words I chose.

I would have described Grace Munger's ferociously "knowing" voice as it had come to me over the telephone in our two exchanges: a voice stout and hard with convictions that allowed no compromise, a voice one had heard far too much of in recent politics *and* pulpits. I would of course enclose Grace's *Balsam Bugle* ad, with its provoking, yet equally savvy 'Christian Manifesto for a Wounded Town,' followed by her rallying summons to heal it all by joining her march. Then after having put in my two cents about the cannily worded document, I would have invited Adrian to apply his explicatory prowess to it. For a humorous touch, I would have quoted my parishioner Lucinda Lord on the national fad, exacerbated by the Millennium, for public religious displays: "Thank goodness Episcopalians don't *demonstrate!*" However, I would then feel obliged to qualify that, in Lucy's case, the utterance was not a gratuitous outburst of snobbery, but an expression of relief that she belonged to a denomination known as much for the independence of mind of its members as their shared love of tradition.

It was bittersweet to realize that this helpful form of communication was now denied me because my correspondent and I were married and living in the same house. At least when he was home. Of course I could always start writing letters to him again, but it had not quite come to that yet.

Kevin had been right about the polarized atmosphere since the shooting last summer. You didn't have to step very far outside your door, even in idyllic High Balsam, to realize

70

there was an "us" and a "them," and that both had suddenly awakened to their differences and were warily keeping track of each other.

Paranoia and mistrust between the haves and have-nots had sprung up in our lowlands in the mid-nineties shortly after the elections, about the same time the big cigarette paper plant and two sportswear knitting factories shut down in Clampitt, putting several thousand Bruton County people out of work, and spread like poison sumac all the way up to High Balsam, whose natural beauty and hospitality had been its twin sources of livelihood since the town's incorporation in the 1870s. (WE LOVE OUR VISITORS, announced a sign as you entered town. "A scenic community, 4,000 feet above the cares of the world, filled with cherished traditions and respect for all types of folks," the Chamber of Commerce advertised every summer on the cover of its thick giveaway tabloid.)

That congenial "live and let live" High Balsam was not immune to the fly-off-the-handle epidemic raging four thousand feet below in the world was brought home forcibly to every one of us when a year-rounder snatched a twelve-gauge from the gun rack of his pickup and blew off the head of an elderly summer home owner for refusing to move his car out of the fifteen-minute parking spot in front of the hardware store. What completed the devastation of High Balsam's cherished image of itself was that the gunman worked for the same private security company that patrolled his victim's gated estate.

In his own defense, the local man claimed he was "made crazy" by the manner in which the other man had spoken to him. "But my husband never even raised his voice," protested the victim's widow, who had emerged from the beauty shop in time to hear the argument and witness the bloody aftermath. "My husband was simply trying to reason with the man in a civilized manner." "You don't have to raise your voice to make someone feel lower than dirt," the local man had been quoted as saying.

"The poor fellow probably *was* shot because of his language," my parishioner Judge Tim Stancil, in whose court the case would have been tried if the attorneys had not moved for a change of venue, had remarked to me at the time. "A really disturbing aspect of this whole affair, Margaret, is it's the kind of language any of us might have used. We learned it at our mother's knee: it's the speech that 'nice people' use to avoid confrontation and 'keep things pleasant' — but it can also be interpreted as social arrogance and be enough to get you blown away in this day and time. When there are so many unhappy people among us, you have to use judgment about what you say to strangers —

no matter what they might be yelling or calling you."

Gus had been suggesting, half seriously, that I get myself a little companion like her "Pearl," the Lady Smith & Wesson .38 special with a pearl handle that she carried in her purse.

"Firearms have been part of everyone's normal equipage in Bruton County since tomahawks went out of fashion, Margaret. Your predecessor toted a snub-nosed little friend when he went traveling these back roads. I'm referring to saintly old Father Lindsey, not that vile intermediary who carried *his* weapon in his pants, where it self-destructed on him."

The vile intermediary, "Father Al," now unpriested and serving a prison term over in Mountain City's big new jail, had in his single year as rector seduced two parishioners and an acolyte. I sometimes wondered whether his disastrous ministry hadn't been a strong factor in motivating the shaken congregation of All Saints High Balsam to lift its tacit embargo on women priests and risk calling the ordained wife of Father Bonner over at Fair Haven Academy. Wasn't she already doing supply work in the area? And she had grown up in a church in many respects like All Saints, and she was visibly devoted to her husband — not likely to go around preying on parishioners and minors. (And, unlike

73

some candidates, she was a good sport about submitting herself to the Church Insurance Company's background check for sexual misconduct.)

"I wouldn't know what to do with a weapon," I told Gus. "I'd probably end up killing Adrian or myself."

"I'll take you out to the range and teach you. It's a thrill, the first time you actually hit what you aimed at."

"Not when it's alive, I hope."

"You know I don't go around shooting at live targets. I used to go duck hunting with Grandpop, but that was mainly for his company. I never enjoyed causing those bright creatures to plummet to earth, and I don't think he enjoyed that part, either. But I surely *did* enjoy shooting out the lightbulbs and scaring the britches off those cheap polecats when they were stealing my fixtures out of Hazel Grove Nursing Home. Some of their own grannies booked to go in there, one of the guys on my construction crew, and there they were ripping out the fixtures before we'd even finished drywalling!"

"But *everybody* in High Balsam isn't armed, Gus. I'll bet you're my only parish lady who carries a pistol in her purse."

"Oh, well, if you're talking about the privileged ladies in the summer crowd. I meant us year-round hillbillies, who don't have electric fences and rented security guards for every time we go uptown to buy a birthday card."

Gus loved to refer to herself as a hillbilly. Though in all but a few externals — her work clothes and the truck she drove, and Pearl nestling in her shoulder bag — she was every bit as much of a "privileged lady" as any of our summer parishioners who drove their Volvos and Mercedes up the mountain from Charleston and Savannah and Boca Raton after Memorial Day and closed up their summer homes before Thanksgiving.

Her great-great-grandfather had been sent up from Charleston as a young man to the newly opened High Balsam Sanitorium in 1871, to nip an incipient tuberculosis in the bud. He had taken to the mountain air and the quaint, courteous ways of the highland people and stayed on to learn construction and build summer houses for other wealthy people from the lowlands and eventually to construct a year-round lodge for his family and their visiting summer friends. Gus's great-grandfather had been the architect of All Saints, and her grandfather, August — after whom she was named — had added on our extended sanctuary and the social hall jutting eastward out of the crypt. Gus now had plans to renovate August's crypt, in the meantime updating our kitchen and correcting some serious drainage problems.

She and her cousin Smathers Eubanks were the fifth generation of Eubanks Construction Company. Sociable Smathers ran the big Mountain City side of the operation, making the contacts, and Gus occupied her late parents' house in High Balsam when she wasn't traveling around to sites. She and I had become friends when Adrian and I lived out at Fair Haven, whose main structure had been the former lodge of her great-great-grandparents. I was still unemployed, except for my supply work, and so I had the spare time to court her. As had been the case with Adrian, I recognized a kinship between us at once; only, with Gus, I had the immediate assurance that the feeling was reciprocal, and I wasn't afraid I'd scare her off. She was out at Fair Haven every day, overseeing the renovations that had transformed her ancestor's lodge into Dr. Sandlin's school. And then, at a later point, when she was building the new cottages on the grounds, we did some interior painting together and had a great deal of uninterrupted time to talk. This was after my miscarriage, when Adrian's sadness had metabolized alarmingly into morbid self-blame, and I was grateful to have someone with whom I could elaborate on my sorrow as much as I needed without damage to that person's equilibrium.

As I laid aside the new sermon note card before I cluttered *it* with doodles, my gaze was arrested by old Farley's moon painting, which hung between the two windows in my study. Every time I looked at it I of course thought of Madelyn and the changes she had wrought on our family simply by walking into our house and being Madelyn Farley and walking out again the next morning with my mother. But the painting itself remained a rich source of contemplation for me. That round white disk riding the night sky between its trail of bright clouds had been created on a dark, freezing porch by an ill-humored old man who in his last years had become fixated on the moon. Why? Because its fast-rising, elliptical variations were so hard to trap in pigment and water? Or were all his moonscapes a (conscious or unconscious) exercise in self-portraiture: obsessive studies of a cold, hard, cratered, dark thing, like himself, that nevertheless had been endowed with the capacity to reflect light and beauty? Even after Madelyn told me Farley's secret technique ("First he sticks an Alka-Seltzer tablet over the part where the moon's going to be, then he lays in a dark wash all around it and spends the rest of his time working up the surrounding clouds. When he's finished, he removes the Alka-Seltzer and that's that."), the rapturous effect of the final work was diminished not one jot for me.

All Saints rectory sat on an incline above the church, and in daylight I could look down from my study windows, without getting up from my desk, and take in the garth below and our much-prized English perennial borders, tended even during the winter season by watchful parishioners with green thumbs. At night I could see the red glow of the sanctuary lamp through a north leaded side window, and the windows of the crypt directly below, either lit up or dark, depending on what was or wasn't scheduled down there.

The trouble was, I realized at some point during my contemplation of Farley's moon painting that the windows of the crypt weren't dark this evening and they were supposed to be. No outside groups were on the calendar for this Friday: no AA or NA, no Internet Abusers Anonymous, karate class, or Parish Reading Group. So who was down there? A church person with a key on a legitimate errand? Or someone who had found a way in without a key, as had happened occasionally?

Of course I'd go over and check it out, despite Adrian's husbandly caution about bolting doors behind him. All Saints High Balsam *was* only two blocks from the bus station, making both church and rectory ideal homing places for the desperate and afflicted, as well as the seasoned charity hustlers who knocked confidently on my door with the most imaginative of hardship tales. I couldn't entirely account for it, but ever since my encounter with the boys robbing the old man in

New York, I felt only the healthy minimum of fear at the prospect of confronting desperate people. Despite my smallish gunless person, despite the weakened right wrist that still swelled sometimes and ached on damp days, that struggle had left me with an odd — perhaps foolhardy? — faith that I would never be completely overwhelmed in the course of my work.

Here the Old Guard contingent in our parish would be quick to point out that I myself had attracted these "elements," as bugs to a porchlight, by installing All Saints' first-ever churchyard bulletin board (what my father had called a Roadside Preacher), which lit up by itself at dark.

"But we never had one before," certain vestry members predictably chorused when I first brought up the idea. ("To let people know we're here and they're welcome to join us" was how I'd approached them.)

"But everybody does know we're here!" cried Lucinda Lord. "We're right off of Main Street. We're on the National Register of Historic Buildings. A lit-up sign is just not us, Pastor Margaret. We've always been low-key people, here at All Saints High Balsam."

"Why, if we suddenly went and put a lit-up sign in our front yard" — Warden Van Wyck Sluder, pacifying me with a little low-key All Saints' humor — "people might think we'd gone into business or something."

"But we are in business," I said.

Van had munched his gray moustache as if I'd made a slightly indecorous comeback but he was too polite to say so. Lucinda Lord's eyelashes batted up at me in curious inquiry. Our youngest vestry couple, the Freedgoods, who had taken over the family gem business in town and who wanted more young members so we could have a nursery and active Sunday school, perked up.

"We're in the business of hospitality," I said, tempted to indulge in a bit of low-key humor myself by reminding them that the people of Sodom and Gomorrah were destroyed not just for their sexual misconduct, but for abusing the sacred duty of hospitality to strangers. I decided, however, to save it for another suitable occasion; there was sure to be one. In those first months at All Saints High Balsam, as I searched for ways to shake up their conservative hearts without giving them heart attacks in the process, I recalled my father saying he sometimes felt his most vital mission at St. Cuthbert's wasn't to comfort the afflicted but to afflict the comfortable. "We can't all be so fortunate as to minister to lepers and thieves and prostitutes," he'd say. "Some of us are called to the much less dramatic task of stirring up the sediment in complacent souls."

As I got up from my desk to go over to the church and see who was up to what in our crypt, it struck me that the muted sounds outside this rectory could have been the same night sounds from my childhood in my father's rectory in Romulus. A convocation of scraping leaves in an enclosure, a passing car on the street, the lonely bark of a pent-up dog in a neighboring house. No different, really. Probably my father's childhood streets in Chattanooga had been exactly the same.

Yet this was the eve of the Third Millennium. We had at last reached the countdown hours, which had been heralded so exhaustively by the blare of commentary that the actual event seemed already to have happened. Here we were, almost at the end of the Psalmist's thousand-year day, about to begin a new one, and yet it already seemed threadbare from overexposure.

For the last five years, almost every day's worth of newsprint, every nightly report from our ubiquitous screens, brought us some bizarre new manifestation of apocalyptic acting-out, or egged us on toward some new extreme of "last days" behavior.

Shocking confessions, whether written, televised, or just suddenly announced at a public gathering by the unlikeliest of people, had become a choice form of entertainment. People vied with one another to reveal the most appalling aspects of themselves. (Our own "Father Al," bringing more unwanted publicity to our quiet little town, had recently permitted a national TV crew to tape a half-hour interview with him in prison, part of a series on "Penitent Priests," during which he gravely detailed the most salacious elements of his "sun-porch seductions" in All Saints High Balsam's rectory.)

In high schools around the country there had sprung up a rash of "Virgin Clubs," initially endorsed by pleased parents, church groups, and civic organizations, until a pall was cast over the trend by the stoning to death of a girl in Maryland for secretly having sex with her boyfriend. They hadn't meant to kill her, the contrite club members explained sorrowfully in a series of interviews and news specials: it was meant to be just a "chastisement ritual."

Throughout most of the decade people went around violently advocating extreme views on almost everything, only to recoil from these views in equally violent backlashes. Political reforms, unctuously signed into law one year, were denounced and repealed the next. Instant communication of anything and everything had cluttered the air to such a point that anyone intent on keeping up with the latest developments in the world risked being buried alive under a junk heap of ephemera. Old and powerful symbols, shorn from their original contexts, would be snatched out of mothballs, dusted off, and repackaged for the frenetic millennial market, soaring up the charts one day and skydiving like fallen angels the next.

Prophets arose on every street corner, offering a broad menu of salvations ranging from self-sacrificing to self-serving, harmlessly eccentric to hate-and-murder-driven. Cults staked out headquarters in posh corporate offices, took over abandoned factories or military bases, or sat in dark rooms and tapped their gospels across Internet space. Some jumped the gun on millennial rapture by committing mass suicide. Holy men and women, mad and sane, traversed the country on their missions, wearing homemade costumes or the traditional garb of established religious orders. Soul rallies catered to the chiliastic fervor. People were angry, or they felt they had missed something and didn't know what it was, or they were tired of waiting for the end, so they formed groups (men and boys who'd had enough of feminism, survivors of fatal diseases, the downsized and the dumped, the Yogic Flyers Natural Law Party, even one group calling themselves "The Disenfranchised Atheists"); they rented auditoriums and stadiums where they held national conferences, or sat in bleachers and shouted in unison their sins, their gripes, and their vows; they attempted by various means — chanting, marching, meditation, levitation — to force Apocalypse by sheer mass desire. On a Mississippi levee,

John the Baptist reincarnated himself in a seven-foot black man wearing feathers, who took his predecessor's personal diet one step further: a recent prime-time special showed close-ups of him hand-feeding live, wriggling locusts dipped in honey to his repentant followers.

Perhaps to help soothe the mania, Our Lady had generously spread her mantle around the globe, offering motherly solace not only to innocents in faraway war-torn villages but to members of our own receptive citizenry out on their farms or in busy suburban shopping malls. A year and a half ago, within twenty miles of High Balsam, two reservation children had sighted her embracing the beloved eighteenth-century Cherokee chieftain Attakullakulla atop an ancient burial mound. We were still getting traffic jams on the first Tuesday of every other month, the reappearance dates announced by her to the Cherokee children.

Poor Jesus himself had been worn ragged, crisscrossing the world on a hectic travel schedule to keep all his one-on-one channeling appointments with housewives, inmates, stockbrokers, lunatics, twelve-steppers, novelists, and multidenominational gurus, all of whom raced one another into print or onto our flickering screens with his personal voice speaking through them. There was everything from Norman Mailer to *The Corporate*

Jesus to *My Roommate at O'Hare*, a homeless woman's best-selling account of her life with Christ at the Chicago airport where they had lived together for one year. Unlike some of the wishful pieties and bold scams flooding the market, this came across as a surprisingly appealing testimony; I'd picked it up cynically in the Balsam Bookworm one Saturday last spring and skimmed it while waiting for Adrian to get our lawn mower serviced next door. (We had, in fact, parked our car in the same fifteen-minute parking spot that would bring death and notoriety to our hospitable town two months later.) The woman, neither a bag lady nor deranged — a person of young middle age with a round, plain face and granny glasses in her author's photo — had been instructed by Jesus to give up her apartment and her good job as a radiologist and put a minimum of clothes into a suitcase on wheels and go feed his lambs at the airport, and she had done it. Once there, Jesus gave her concise practical instructions. He softened the hearts of certain of his friends working in fast-food franchises, taught her to love salad bar leftovers, packets of saltines, and tinned apple juice (she lost forty-eight pounds, as a result). He advised her to walk briskly and purposefully along the concourses with her head held high, wheeling her black suitcase behind her, to sit waiting for a specific flight, and, as soon as that flight was

85

boarding, to go immediately to another gate and repeat the procedure. She was to wash her hair and sponge-bathe herself and wash her drip-dry outfits in a different ladies' room every night, and then take her rest (and hang the drip-dry items) in a certain maintenance closet — with ventilation — in a first-class passenger lounge. Throughout the day her assignment was to observe everything that went on around her, enter into conversation, or be available for it, with the "lambs" Jesus himself elected for her, pass on to them anything he thought they needed to know, writing down his comments as soon afterward as she could. His remarks and asides were pungent and memorable, often edged with a biting humor. He frequently employed the tools of paradox and reversal of expectations. He was tough on the selfish and self-righteous and had a soft spot for people who were confused or poor or in distress. He said, in fact, the kinds of things to this woman that even the picky Jesus Seminar scholars would concur had most likely been the historical Jesus' style. Whatever her education, she was a natural-born writer, a close and unsentimental reader of the gospels, as well as a woman who had intuited the needs of the marketplace.

"I envied her a little," I told Adrian as we drove home with our oiled and sharpened mower. "I mean her ministry at O'Hare. Not now, when she's on all those interview shows and staying in big hotels. What would you have to do, I wonder, to make yourself available for an experience like hers?"

"Well, for a start, I guess," he said, squinting ahead at the traffic that had sprung up overnight, "you'd have to be willing to put everything in one suitcase with wheels and leave your skepticism behind."

It was after the first of May, when our one thousand winter population had begun to multiply toward the twelve thousand summer count. I looked over at my husband in his red and white checked shirt with the cuffs rolled up and remembered how my antennae had gone on the alert that spring day in Romulus when he came swinging around the corner of my father's house carrying those two books. I still remembered the titles: *The Gnostic Scriptures*, by Bentley Layton, and *Insearch: Psychology and Religion*, by James Hillman. Yes, he's the one, I relayed back to that younger me, he's the one you're going to marry.

I was on the verge of sharing this little time-travel excursion with him, but suppressed myself because I was feeling hopeful on this fine day and didn't want to risk eliciting one of his self-put-downs I had grown to dread, such as the wisest thing I could do for that young woman would be to warn her off her misguided attraction in time.

"And it would help greatly if you weren't overly sensitive to ridicule," Adrian went on in his musing way, puzzling out the answer to my question for himself as much as me.

"That leaves *us* out, I guess," I said with a sigh.

"Probably. Look at all these people on the streets, Margaret. Did all of them just arrive *overnight?* And I would think a lack of reserves would be an important requirement."

"What kind of reserves?"

"Oh, anything you keep in reserve. Possessions. People you consider yours. Attitudes. Your high opinion of yourself. Your own preconceptions of what a visit from the divine would be like. Maybe *especially* that. A nun studying with me at the Jung Institute in Zurich once told me, 'Beware of ever finding a God totally congenial to you.' "

"Adrian, why don't we try and get away this summer? We haven't been off on our own since our honeymoon six years ago."

"Why not?" he surprised me by answering, without a single qualification. "Now that the Jeffersons have settled into their cottage at the school, we certainly have enough on-site staff. When do you think you would be free to go?"

"Oh, any time after Pentecost. Though probably the earlier the better. Before we start gearing up for Stewardship in late July, when all our summer pledges are safely settled in their cool homes and counting their blessings and feeling generous."

"Where would you like to go? The beach, or somewhere abroad? What's your idea of a good place?"

"My idea of a good place is anywhere alone with you, without parishes or schools."

"I'll speak to Hiram first thing Monday," he said, bypassing a great opportunity for a self-put-down. This *was* hopeful: he had accepted the homage and even sounded pleased. What's more, he slipped his arm around me and pulled me to him, and we drove down Main Street with our lawn mower sticking out the back end of our car, just like any couple in love.

But by Pentecost, Hiram Sandlin was dead of a massive heart attack, and Adrian was serving as headmaster, in addition to his duties as chaplain and counselor, while the search began for a person capable of taking on Sandlin's vision. Not an easy assignment. For a brilliant scientist and student of human nature to found an experimental school based on his own research and run it himself is a risky but straightforward proposition. Finding a smart, tough administrator who is flexible and secure enough in himself to carry on the work of an original and courageous mind is another story.

Sandlin hadn't been the corporate idea of a good administrator himself. He was an easy-going version of the old-fashioned authority figure, comfortable in the role of leader but not giving the position much thought. An intuitive extrovert, he operated almost wholly from enthusiasm and hunches, Adrian said. Sandlin had his brainstorms, worked them out, then passed them on to others, managing to retain his initial excitement and confidence throughout. A man less able to transmit his ideas would surely not have succeeded in populating a school at the end of the twentieth century whose charter, quoted in the prospectus, stated unequivocally: "Young people aren't being given the necessary minimum of intangibles to grow on. They suffer from psychic undernourishment. Wisdom is developed in young human brains by the curriculum of conversation, thought, imagination, empathy, and reflection. Young people need to generate language and ideas, not just listen and watch as passive consumers. At Fair Haven, we attempt to build the type of intelligence that is joyously able to contemplate a wide range of things not simply for 'career goals,' but out of *the mind's affection for its own proper objects*. We also strive to restore the endangered virtues of kindness, introspection, and disinterested love: doing things not for gain, but because they are there to be done."

Within days of his becoming acting headmaster, the toll on Adrian became evident.

Administration, with its constant round of diplomacies and consensus-seekings, its high visibility, was hostile and exhausting to his temperament. He was best, he had insisted to the others who wanted to make him headmaster, in private sessions with one student at a time, or researching and preparing his Moral Responsibility seminar for seniors, and training acolytes in the liturgy and conducting the chapel services. This was all he had desired from the job, and that much was too much for him sometimes. Even then he had needed frequent escapes for reading and praying and just being off by himself.

And yet he had acceded to their wishes and taken on the headmastership for now. Why? I asked myself this increasingly as the summer went on. He could have simply said no thanks, fellows, elect one of yourselves. Had he, then, believed himself to be the best person for the job, until they could get somebody better? Had he even perhaps secretly hoped he might grow into it permanently, shape it to his personal style? ("Something's your vocation when it keeps making more of you.") Or had his reluctant acceptance been some form of self-punishment? To punish himself for what, this time? For Hiram Sandlin's dying on him, as our baby had died?

On top of all this, he was grieving for Sandlin, whom he had loved and admired and now deeply missed. He had accompanied Hiram on his medically prescribed daily three-mile walks (the headmaster was overweight and suffered from high blood pressure and diabetes), and that's when they cooked up their best schemes to make the school more effective. Hiram confided freely in Adrian, and in me, if I was around. He was an easy confider. A widower, with no children, he had been maintaining a long-distance courtship with a lady down in Mountain City right up until the week he died — "taking those hairpin curves between us like a reckless, lovesick teenager," he told us, laughing at himself. He and Adrian had balanced each other in so many happy ways: Adrian's caution and skepticism steadied Hiram's carefree optimism. Hiram's affection and daily-voiced admiration for Adrian's gifts had the predictable effect of relaxing and inspiriting Adrian; Adrian's contemplative bent made Hiram more reflective. Having each other had made more of them both.

In the first weeks following Hiram's death, I waited — I even anticipated the development — for Adrian to share his new burdens with me. I would make time to go on the three-mile daily walks he had taken with Hiram. But he kept his problems to himself. If I asked what was happening at the school, he would wince and answer in monosyllables; if I persisted, he withdrew from me more.

With growing resentment at his selfish stoicism, I was obliged to stand by and watch him spiral down, down again, back to the cold, lonely floor of his self-hatred.

Then I got a letter from Shaun in New York, saying he had AIDS and was going home to Ireland and spend what time he had left with his brothers in Connemara. Did I want him to look for someone else to rent Madelyn's loft, which she'd left to me, or would I rather come up and interview prospective tenants myself? "It would be great to see you again, Margaret," Shaun wrote, "but if you're too busy I'll try to find someone reliable for you; though I can't promise they'll have my compulsive-obsessive neatness and my domestic skills!"

I gave Adrian the letter to read.

"Of course you should go," he said, before he'd even looked up from the page. "You'd like to see him again, wouldn't you?"

"Yes, I would. Oh, my poor Shaun. He's not even thirty, Adrian. Oh, *hell*."

"It is hell," Adrian agreed. "I only met him once, at our wedding, but I liked him. And the way he prepared the place for our wedding night: I'll never forget that, either."

"I can't imagine someone else living there: a 'tenant.' I'm tempted to sell while I'm up there and be done with it. I don't want to be a landlord."

"I don't know," said Adrian. "You might

regret not having it later."

"Why?"

"Because it would be closing a door."

"A door to what?"

"Well, to leaving me, if you ever want to."
He sounded almost smug as he said this.
Then, seeing its effect on me, he passed it off
with an apologetic laugh, adding, "Or, even if
you don't, you may be grateful to have kept
an escape hatch for the times when I'm
making life unbearable for you."

"Like right now, you mean? Or do you have
worse scenarios in mind for us, Adrian?"

This brought him around. "I shouldn't
have said that. I'm sorry. You know how I
tend to get negative when I'm under pressure."

"My father was always saying things like
that to my mother when he was in his 'negative' periods. 'You need a vacation from me'
was one of his abiding favorites. One day she
took him at his word."

"I deserved that," said Adrian. But he
laughed.

When I left for New York (I'd decided to
drive so I could bring back things if I did sell
the loft), Adrian walked me out to the car.
"We've got a promising nibble at the
headmastership," he said. "I hesitated to say
anything to you until we interview him, but
. . . just to send you away on a note of hope
that you'll come back to a simple chaplain."

"I'll come back to whatever you need to be," I said, "whether it's a chaplain or a headmaster or something else entirely. But whatever I come back to, I doubt it will ever be simple, Adrian."

We both laughed at that. Then we kissed and stood pressed together in the Smoky Mountain fog of an early summer morning.

What a strange trip that was. Across the mountain to East Tennessee, then up 81, passing very close to my old home in Romulus, then over to 95 and on to New York. During the first part of the drive I mourned for the vacation Adrian and I were not going to take. I missed him until my throat and chest ached. And as our recent difficulties receded into the mountains I was leaving behind, I replaced them with happier pictures from earlier in our marriage, and from our honeymoon six years before.

Then somewhere past Roanoke, in thickening midday traffic, I saw a sign for the exit to Staunton, where my mother and I had shopped before Romulus got its mall, and I realized that any moment now I would begin driving the portion of the road that my mother had driven with Madelyn Farley when, unaware as yet, she was leaving my father forever.

Was this the way it was going to happen to me, too? A kind of skin-prickling madness came over me as I steered straight toward the junction where my destiny would inevitably mesh with hers. Tears fell behind my sunglasses as I recalled Adrian's body pressed against mine one final time in the cool morning mist of High Balsam: ". . . just to send you away on a note of hope that you'll come back to a simple chaplain."

It was as though I had already left him.

I switched off the lamp in my study so I could spy down on the crypt from a dark window. No suspicious shadow moved behind its leaded windows. Except for the portable microwave and the slide projector and the VCR, there was nothing much down there to excite a thief. The good stuff was locked away upstairs in the sacristy vault: the antique hand-embroidered chancel sets from England; the silver candlesticks; the chalices and patens in precious metals; the Elsa Van Wyck Memorial Ciborium, with Van's grandmother's diamonds and garnets embedded in the base; the thurible made from the Georgian silver muffineer of Lucinda Lord's great-aunt. We even locked up the wine in the vault now, due to the "attractive nuisance" clause in our insurance policy.

Probably not a thief. And any homeless person successful enough to have gotten in certainly wouldn't risk losing such a comfy shelter by turning on lights.

A *sane* homeless person wouldn't.

Might as well put an end to this guessing game. Tugging Adrian's suede jacket from its hall closet hanger (the less I saw of him, the more I had taken to wearing his clothes), I went to investigate. As soon as I was outside the rectory, however, I saw Gus's shiny red truck, with EUBANKS CONSTRUCTION CO. lettered in black and gold on the door, parked in front of the church.

So much for the stranger in the crypt, bringer of who knew what new danger or grace — or uncommon call on our hospitality. I felt vaguely let down. What had I been secretly wishing for, a one-on-one millennial visit from Christ?

I imagined myself mounting to the pulpit on Sunday, taking a deep breath, gazing down at the upturned faces of my depleted winter congregation. "On this first Sunday in Advent," I'd begin, "we have a distinguished visitor. On Friday evening I was sitting in my study, working on my sermon for the wedding which many of you attended yesterday, when I happened to look out the window and saw that the light was on in the crypt. As there were no meetings scheduled, I went over to investigate. . . ."

The looks on the faces of specific people. Would the visitor go up for Communion? Would he have the foggiest notion of what Communion was? Should I have asked him beforehand to concelebrate with me? (Would

he have any problem about women priests?)
At coffee hour, who could be counted on to
overcome their reserve and make him welcome?

("Please allow me to introduce myself,
Lord. I'm Lucinda, cochair of All Saints'
Welcoming Committee. I hope you won't
think this disrespectful of me, but I'm a Lord,
too! I mean, my husband is. His branch is
from over in east Tennessee; I imagine yours
is, well, from further off. Oh, and this is our
warden, Van Wyck Sluder. Van, meet Our
Lord.

("It goes without saying, Sir, that we're all
honored by your presence. I hope you
weren't too discountenanced by Pastor
Margaret's public acknowledgment. Father
Lindsey never introduced people of consequence from the pulpit, not U.S. senators or
the governor of North Carolina, or even our
presiding bishop, who has worshiped here
with us on several occasions. But our Margaret's a gifted woman, she's brought new life
to our parish, and we are very fortunate to
have her and her husband in High Balsam."

("Lord, I'm Buddy Freedgood — Freedgood's gem shop, on Main Street. Love to
have you come in and show you around. This
card here entitles a new customer to a ten
percent discount on their first purchase, but
I've crossed out the ten and put twenty-five,
seeing it's you.")

Had Gus developed a case of bride's jitters and, being at loose ends this evening, decided to do a reconnaissance of the crypt for her proposed re-Eubanking of its kitchen and social hall? Between her efficient self and her supremely organized little daughter-to-be, everything had been arranged for tomorrow, every foreseeable glitch anticipated. (When we were putting the rings away in the safe, tied to the white heart-shaped pillow Jennifer had provided, Jennifer announced to us that she had placed her own manicure scissors in the book rack of the front pew "for the best man to use just in case he gets nervous and can't get the bow untied.")

First Sunday in Advent: "Cast away the deeds of darkness and put on the armor of light," said our lighted sign. I'd slid in the Roman letters myself, after the wedding rehearsal. Then eight and ten A.M. services listed below, and the name of the rector and VISITORS WELCOME, in all caps. A casual passerby would see an ordinary traditional church sign, but I saw a $3,053 handcrafted aluminum frame and gabled cornice, painted with automotive paint the color of dark walnut stain. After fourteen meetings our conservative vestry had finally voted to spend the extra money so that the sign would resemble custom lumber mill work of a quality fit to stand beside a building on the National Historic Register. An automatic photoelectric switch lit the sign at dusk and turned it off at dawn. The spotlight on the church building itself, a recent security measure required by our insurance company, also came on at dusk.

"With one of those awful lights up on a pole, we'll look like a ball field!" Lucinda Lord had wailed. But once again compromises had been made. A friendly Power and Light representative paid a call and showed us how we could illumine the building from below, thus preserving, as Gus put it privately to me, "our illusion of ourselves as a parish church lifted out of a seventeenth-century England and plunked down miraculously in the wilderness of a nineteenth-century North Carolina, even though the cocaine causeway from Charleston to New York runs practically next door to us now."

Other pastors in the area were always telling me how lucky I was to "have" All Saints High Balsam. I did feel an aesthetic-possessive lift as my eye traveled up its sturdy structure of pale old bricks (handmade in Charleston) to the third-story bell tower above the choir loft level, spotlit in its yellow glow of tasteful security. "All Saints is not Gothic Revival," Gus wryly remarked, "it's transplanted Gothic *Sur*vival. Because while church architects over here were busy knocking off copies of Upjohn's Gothic Revival designs, my great-grandfather went over to England and ripped off from actual *existing* Gothic churches."

After I had been short-listed for rector of All Saints High Balsam, Van had taken me on a proud tour of the building and grounds. As he pointed out its features and treasures — the English memorial flower beds in the garth, the Crucifixion rood screen, the carved lectern with its grapevine and pelican motif (commissioned in 1910 by a student of William Morris), the trussed ceiling and sanctuary paneling made of local chestnut "and when we ran out of chestnut in the narthex, we 'made do' with wormy chestnut, ha ha," said Van, checking my face to be sure I understood that wormy chestnut was valuable, too) — I had felt more like someone being vetted for the curatorship of a small, exquisite museum than the pastor of a mountain church.

I went down to the crypt by the outside stone steps and, sure enough, there was Gus in her jeans and lumberjack shirt, crouched on the black and white tiles of our social hall in that enviable long-legged squat of hers, extending her steel measuring tape in front of her like a wand.

"My father had an enduring squat like yours," I said. "He could go on like that for hours in his garden. I always had to drag along a plastic garbage bag and sit as I went."

"Oh good. I was hoping you might drop

over." Reeling in her tape with a metallic snap, Gus pocketed the cylinder in her shirt and sank back on her heels, smiling up at me broadly. She was a dashing woman, with her clean, long lines and patrician face and boy-short blond and silver hair. I had been dumbfounded when she once told me she had grown up believing herself unpardonably gauche and ugly.

"You should have come over to the rectory," I said.

"I hate to intrude on your home life."

"What home life?" I plucked at the soft suede jacket as I sat down on the floor beside her. "The nearest I get to my husband anymore is wearing his clothes."

"No headmaster in sight yet?"

"The one they wanted turned them down for another place, then they found another one who seemed too good to be true. And he was. They submitted him to one last computer check and discovered he'd falsified his graduate school credentials."

"God, how awful. How *stupid!* So it's back to square one?"

"Pretty much."

"And Adrian doesn't want the job?"

"That's what he says. He obsesses too much about the responsibility."

"Charles thinks he'd be wonderful, if he'd just let himself be the headmaster and delegate the dog work."

"Maybe Charles should tell him that. He doesn't seem to want to hear it from me."

"Oh, well, speaking of obsessing, Jennifer's banished me from my house. Charles dropped her and her friend Sue by on his way to night clinic, and now they're over there decorating my bedroom for our wedding night. Then she's spending the night at Sue's."

"Decorating it *how?*"

"That's a deep dark secret. She's given me orders that I can't go upstairs when I come home. I've been assigned the spare room off the kitchen that used to be the maid's room. She's already made up the bed for me."

"But how will you get dressed tomorrow? Are you allowed upstairs for that?"

"No. I'm to be dressed by Jennifer in the dining room. Everything's already laid out there." Gus laughed. "She even lugged Daddy's cheval glass up from the basement, so I can check myself out full-length. She's anticipated everything, down to two extra packages of panty hose, in case I tear not one but two pairs in my nervousness while getting dressed. I wouldn't put it past her to have two *more* pairs stashed away in case I keep on tearing them, and two more pairs after that."

"Are you nervous?"

"Not too much for myself, but for *them.* Jenn especially. I do want everything to come up to her expectations for tomorrow. And

103

after tomorrow, too, if I can manage it."

"That's a pretty tall order, to fulfill all someone's expectations, Gus."

"I know. But her own mother jilted her, and I've had a heavy dose of the Bad Mother myself. You know what I was doing when you walked in? I was hearing all the things Annabel would say to spoil my wedding for me tomorrow if she had lived to see the day. I told you what she said at my high school awards dinner, didn't I?"

"You told me what she said at your debut. . . ."

"Oh, yes, that. Well, the awards dinner was the same *genre* of thing, but several degrees deadlier. At the debutante ball she merely whispered in my ear while our family unit was posing for the photographer that *now* she could enjoy the rest of the evening because I hadn't tripped when I curtsied. But at the awards dinner, after I'd come back to the table with my fifth award, she got this coy look on her face and I thought, 'My mother's getting ready to say something nice at last. She *has* to; I've won more prizes than anybody else in the history of this school.' And then she tittered and said, 'Your feet sounded so *loud*, Gussie, every time you went up to get another one of those prizes.' "

"It's interesting how we go on hearing their voices."

"Isn't it! Just now I was hearing her playful

little undervoice in my ear: 'Well, Gussie, at forty-two you finally caught one.' Or, 'What a graceful, attractive little stepdaughter — I couldn't take my eyes off her when she preceded you up the aisle.' *Or* — this is the one she couldn't have resisted: 'Charlie Tye's a *good* sort . . . he's not the dreamboat Ed Gallatin was, but what's a girl to do when her Great Love comes back to town and falls in love with her male cousin?' "

"Perhaps it's just as well I showed up when I did."

"Oh, it was kind of amusing. I'm glad I'm going to spend the rest of my life with Charles. It would have been calamitous if the fates had given me Edmund when I was pining away for him. And I'm really looking forward to being Jennifer's mother. I already love her. I admire the way she set to work to make this marriage happen. I enjoy thinking of all the ways I'll be able to help her. By the way, she's finally agreed to take the master bedroom and bath for herself."

"So I gathered, when you said she was decorating your bedroom. How did you accomplish that?"

"Point-blank candor. I said, 'Look, Jenn, I agree with you that my parents' house is ideal for us. I believe we have every chance of being happy in it even if they weren't. It's not the *house's* fault they weren't happy. It's a well-planned house with some gracious accoutrements that will suit your young adult life very well. But I'd rather not begin my married life with Charles in my parents' bedroom, even though it *is* the master bedroom. There are too many old ghosts.' "

"And how did she react?"

"She shrugged and said, 'Okay, fine, I'll take it. I never met either of them and I don't believe in ghosts.' But now she's after me to knock out a linen closet and enlarge the hall bathroom for Charles and myself."

"That child thinks of everything! What do you think she and Sue are doing to your bedroom right this minute?"

"I'm not supposed to think, I'm supposed to be surprised. Not *too* surprised, I hope." Gus laughed and resettled herself cross-legged on the floor. "Not making it into a virgin's bower, I trust. She knows Charles and I have already been to bed in that room. I would think something more like balloons and little presents, maybe some romantic touches."

"Someone did that for Adrian and me. Not balloons or presents, but making a romantic setting for us."

"Really? You never told me that. Where *did* you spend your wedding night?"

"In Madelyn Farley's loft, in the Village."

"But wasn't she dead by then?"

"Yes, but she'd left me the loft."

"I never knew that either."

106

"I didn't live there very long after her death. When I moved to the seminary, I rented it to her former assistant, Shaun, he was kind of like a younger brother to me. He transformed the place — made it very sparse and beautiful — Madelyn was a horrible housekeeper and clutterbug. But when Shaun heard that Adrian and I were going to spend our wedding night uptown in a hotel — we were flying to England the day after — he insisted we stay in the loft. He said, 'This is your place, Margaret, and I'd like to send you off in style from it. I can stay with friends. Leave everything to me and I promise you won't be sorry.' "

"And was it nice?"

"A lot more than that. It was beautiful, and imaginative. He'd thought of everything. I'd had qualms beforehand. Adrian hadn't known Madelyn, he didn't know Shaun, but he was receptive to the idea. He said the loft had been my first home after Romulus and he liked that I'd be coming to him from a place that was part of my history rather than some impersonal hotel room."

"Coming to him. Oh, dear Adrian. I like that. And the home part, I like that, too."

"Yes, well, things to do with *home* are very important to Adrian, as you know. So that's what we did. We got married the Saturday before Lent in the seminary chapel, the dean and his wife gave us a reception afterward for a few of our friends, and then we got in a cab with our suitcases and rode down to the loft. Where Shaun had prepared everything in the most appealing, unintrusive style and vanished. As I mentioned, he was austere in his tastes, and he was also a meticulous housekeeper, but still. It's quite a feat to remove all traces of yourself from the place you live."

"I should think so."

"The surfaces were shining and bare, except for some vases and jugs with fresh flowers and ferns. The refrigerator was stocked with just what we might want but it wasn't overdone."

"Like those parties where there's an indecent variety because the host is afraid of not having the right things —"

"Exactly. There were two bottles of Veuve Clicquot, several bottles of Adrian's favorite lager — which really touched him — some fruit, the makings for a light supper and early breakfast. Madelyn's refectory table had been set for two, with tall candles, and he'd made up the bed in the big bedroom with these incredibly soft white linens."

"Now was this *his* bedroom?"

"I think it must have been. It was the best bedroom. It had been Madelyn's bedroom."

"And how did you feel about that? Any ghosts?"

"Well, there was this one curious aspect. . . ."

"What was that?" Gus leaned forward and

gripped the bleached-out knees of her jeans.

How much of this story was I going to tell? Gus and I had exchanged many confidences, she had told me terrible and funny stories about her hopeless passion for Edmund Gallatin, who now shared a life with her cousin Smathers in Mountain City. I had filled her in on Adrian's orphanage life and its aftereffects on him — and she had of course heard all about my mother going away with Madelyn Farley and its aftereffects on my father and me. But so far both of us had been reticent about our intimate lives with our men.

"There was this mural in Madelyn's bedroom. It covered the entire wall facing the bed."

"Something she'd done?"

"No, a friend of hers painted it. A set designer who'd developed this sideline to tide him over in his unemployed periods. He painted murals for people, based on some significant episode in their lives. You'd give him old photographs and tell him stories about your past, and then he'd paint a scene that captured what he thought was the essence of why you were you."

"*He* got to pick the scene? What if the person didn't want to live with the result?"

"I guess you paid him his fee and then painted over it. But Madelyn loved hers. She was always showing it to people and explaining what it represented."

"What was the scene?"

"It was a meadow on top of a mountain, with other lower mountains in the distance. In the foreground of the meadow there was a man sitting in front of an easel, painting the far mountains, and a young girl beside him standing in front of another easel, also painting the view, and then there was a third easel next to them with a very small painting on it. The man and the girl have their backs to you, but you see their paintings. The abandoned easel is angled so you can't see what's on it. And in the middle distance, a woman is lying curled up in a fetal position under a shade tree."

"A pastoral idyll?"

"It might seem that way at first. But the woman under the tree is Madelyn's mother. She's having severe stomach pains and wants to go home. Madelyn's father has told her to lie down, he wants to finish his painting; he says she'll feel better after a while. And he does finish his painting. The mother almost dies of a ruptured appendix."

"And the girl was Madelyn, I take it?"

"Yes, she finished her painting that day, too."

"And she didn't mind sleeping in the same room with such a memory?"

"She loved it. You'd have to have known Madelyn to understand. That mountaintop scene was like her escutcheon for the completely selfish artist, which she was always telling everybody she was. As a matter of fact, she told my mother and father that story at our dinner table, the night before my mother left with her."

"And *you* didn't mind spending your wedding night in the bed facing such memories?"

"The mural was covered. After Madelyn died, Shaun and I couldn't bring ourselves to paint over it, so Shaun made a curtain out of a beautiful old tapestry and hung it in front of it. If someone wanted to see the mural, the curtain could be pulled back on wooden rings, but otherwise you only saw a floor-to-ceiling hanging. When Adrian and I went to bed in the room that night, the curtain was closed, but later on, when we were lying there talking, he said, 'Margaret, you've told me so much about this person who altered your childhood. Why do I lack a true sense of her?' Even with all the Madelyn stories I'd told him, he said, he still couldn't discern whether she had been a person who acted from deliberate design or from defenses. So I put something on and switched on the lamp and went over and opened the curtain. And then we lay in bed looking at the mural while I told the story."

"That *was* a curious pastime for a wedding night."

"What happened afterward was part of it,

too. After Adrian had finished conjecturing about Madelyn — he thought she must have decided early that it was safer to be a selfish artist than a suffering woman, and that there was a *choice* to be made, and that her mode of living probably had been her own blend of design *and* defense — he asked me what my mural would be. I said, 'You mean if I chose it, or if I were the set designer choosing it from my old stories and pictures?' He laughed and said he guessed under the circumstances it would have to be both, wouldn't it? So I thought about it and pretty soon a mural presented itself. It was the scene of an Easter egg hunt when I was six, the first Easter after my mother left us. She had made a golden egg and sent it to us by UPS from New York; the rector's wife always made the golden egg, and I guess some mixture of guilt and pride drove her to do it, even though, under the circumstances, it had elements of a mockery. But it was a fabulous egg, my father went around bragging about how artistic it was; it had a hole in the top and a little painting inside. I later learned from Madelyn that her *father* had done the painting. But that day of the Easter egg hunt, I thought my mother had, and, you see, I wanted that egg so much that I knew if I didn't *relinquish* it, I would crack in two. My mother wasn't there anymore, so what use was the egg? That was probably the day I resigned myself to being without her forever, although I couldn't have understood it then. Anyway, it wasn't a scene I particularly wanted on my wall, but I wanted to play fair in this game with Adrian and be the set designer zeroing in on the fateful image."

"This is interesting as hell, Margaret."

"Then afterward, I said to Adrian, 'Now it's your turn.' He had much more trouble thinking up his mural. It was a boyhood scene from his orphanage, and it came out of him very slowly. Adrian's an abstract thinker more than he is an image person. But when he finally began to describe it, he got upset. And then he got *more* upset about being upset, and I wished we had never started this. After all, it was our wedding night, and nobody wants a wedding night with upsetting memories."

"Lord, no. What did you do?"

"Well, at first I didn't know what to do. So I just held him and didn't say anything. I rubbed him a little, sort of briskly and impersonally, the way you'd rub someone who had the chills. And then I started to feel — it's hard to describe — I've never talked about it before — I suddenly had confidence that however I touched him would be the right way. Whereas, well . . . earlier we had been two rather shy people trying to get through our wedding night without offending or disappointing each other. Which we managed, but with a good deal of formality and restraint. But now I knew instinctively how to touch him and didn't hesitate because I had realized, I mean realized with my body, that we had married each other and the act of marriage itself would teach us what to do with each other. So I sort of enfolded him with my confidence, and he began to relax, and then I said to him, it was a weird thing to say but it just came out of my mouth — I said, 'Just think of it, Adrian, here we are naked together in the middle of all our complicated murals.' And he started shaking. At first I thought, oh no, he's crying. But he was laughing! And then . . . well . . . to conclude this indiscreet tale indiscreetly, pretty soon after that we became truly joined for the first time under the gaze of Madelyn's mural. Except no one was looking our way but the poor mother under the tree, and she had her mind on her rupturing appendix."

"Oh, Margaret, what a great, *great* story. It's not indiscreet at all! I'm forty-two years old and, until right now, no one ever told me the story of her wedding night. *Thank* you." She threw her arms around me with such fervor that we both almost toppled sideways to the floor; then, embarrassed by her awkward display of affection, she sat upright and blushed. "Though I'm sure Annabel would have divulged some gross tidbit about Daddy and herself if she'd been here for my prenuptials. She'd have made something up if she had to, that would replay itself over and over in my head and spoil my wedding night even if Charles and I have already been to bed. But your story gives me all sorts of delectable things to chew on in my maid's room tonight. Naked together in the midst of all your murals! I love it."

"I was angry with my dead mother, too, the night before our wedding. I felt sure she could have told me crucial things if she had stayed around. Yet, now I think . . . maybe she couldn't have. Maybe her own wedding night was a disappointment, and if she *had* stayed on with my father, she would have felt bound to maintain a sporting silence."

"When did you know you wanted Adrian?"

"This is going to sound like someone bragging about her instant conversion, but the moment I saw him."

"You were physically attracted to him, you mean?"

"It was more like I saw him coming and knew he was the one. I went out of myself to meet him and then couldn't get back inside without bringing him with me. And then after we began to talk, I was aware of being physically drawn to him."

"I was attracted to Charles physically from the first, but I didn't know I was going to marry him until one night in bed — in the room Jennifer and Sue are now decorating.

We were telling each other about our respective workdays and he said in that deadpan mountain-boy singsong of his, 'Well, today at the clinic I gave an old woman a pelvic on the floor, because she said heights made her dizzy.' And this rush of delight surged through me. I knew Charles Tye was the person I wanted to lie beside and tell stories with for the rest of my life."

"Oh, Gus, that's priceless."

"I almost told it when we were having our canonically required counseling sessions with you, but I wasn't sure Charles would approve. You know, his country modesty —"

Gus's expression suddenly altered. "It seems we have a visitor," she murmured, tipping her face up to smile politely at whoever had soundlessly approached behind us.

"I saw the lights on down here," a cracked voice said. When I turned around to look, I was surprised to see a man. The voice had been more like that of a fragile old woman.

Not that he wasn't old, but his small figure was more robust than his quavery voice. His open duffel coat revealed a black belted habit whose slightly muddied hem ended just above a pair of black Nikes. He was in the act of lowering to the floor a battered green Samsonite suitcase that looked like it might contain a load of bricks. The bright, surely dyed, reddish-brown hair with its perky boyish fringe provided a freakish contrast to his tough, deeply weathered face.

"Hello," I said, getting up from the floor along with Gus.

"Are you . . . Margaret *Bonner?*" He pronounced my name with the eager relish of someone confronting a celebrity.

"Yes, I am. Have we met before?"

"No, ma'am, but I recognized you from your picture. The article about you and your husband, Adrian Bonner? In *The Living Church*, I think it was."

"I think you must mean the item about us in *Episcopal Life*. But that was quite a while ago. It was just after I was appointed rector here."

"Oh, then maybe I — it was a back issue I happened to pick up at the monastery — I guess I must've got it wrong." He seemed overly perturbed at his mistake.

"But I'm still Margaret Bonner all the same," I said, offering him my hand. "And you're . . . ?"

"Tony. I'm from the Abbey of the Transfiguration, up in Esopus, New York." His rough hand in mine shook slightly.

This scraggy old customer one of our Benedictines? Yet how many monks looked like Bellini's St. Francis? St. Francis himself, who was reported to have been quite homely, hadn't looked like Bellini's St. Francis.

"I've met Father Cecil, your prior," I said. "He was down here year before last to lead a prayer school in Mountain City." The eloquent little prior had worn a habit and scapular and black belt exactly like this one. Only he looked neater and dapper in his.

"Father Cecil died this past September. It was a big loss to all of us."

"I'm sorry to hear that. He was such a warm, impressive man."

"He was a good man. A good friend to me, too. Father Ted has been elected prior now. He's impressive, too, in his way, but not so warm."

"Are *you* on your way somewhere to lead a prayer school yourself?"

My question first seemed to astonish him; then his lips parted, showing nubby little tobacco-stained teeth and he dissolved into whispery cackles. "Oh, no, no. I'm making a little pilgrimage on my own. My community presented me with one of those Greyhound Millennium Passes. A whole year to go anywhere I want. But I have to take it in easy stages. At eighty, I'm beginning to slow down." He bowed waggishly. "I only came as far as from Knoxville today. The Reverend Jim Anderson kindly put me up for several nights. Do you know him? The rector of St. Luke's in Knoxville?"

"No, I'm afraid I don't."

"Oh." He seemed disappointed by this. "Oh, well, Jim and his wife, Sally . . . and their kids, Jamie and Brittany and little Paul

. . . the whole family couldn't have been kinder." It was as if my not knowing the rector in Knoxville had cast some doubt on Jim Anderson's existence and he felt obliged to back up their validity with all these names.

"They sound like a very nice family," I assured him.

What was supposed to happen now? Was he expecting me to put him up at the rectory for several nights, so he could then get on another bus and go on to rectories in Mountain City and Charlotte and offer as his next calling card Margaret Bonner and her husband, Adrian, who couldn't have been kinder? And if so, how could I refuse? How could I refuse hospitality to a member of an order famous for its hospitality for fifteen hundred years? And one of *our* Benedictines, and an eighty-year-old one at that? We'd of course had visiting monks at All Saints in the past, but always before they had been part of some parish mission. Correspondence had gone back and forth between us and their monasteries for months beforehand.

I stalled by introducing Gus. "This is Augusta Eubanks, a parishioner. She's an architect and is going to remodel our kitchen down here. Make it more up-to-date."

Gus, who had been observing the proceedings with her usual congenial sangfroid, stepped forward to shake hands. "How do you do. Is it *Father* Tony?"

"Oh, no, no," he protested. "Just Tony, please." He looked embarrassed. "I'm only a lay brother." Again the absurd little waggish bow. And another whispery cackle. "In a good position to appreciate an up-to-date kitchen myself."

Then I saw his shoulders sag forward with weariness. I felt I could procrastinate no longer.

"Have you a place to stay tonight, Tony? If not, we have a guest room over at the rectory."

"Oh, well. Now, that's very kind of you. If you're sure it won't be putting you and your husband to any trouble . . ."

But the way he demurely lowered his eyes made it pretty clear to me that he had been expecting nothing less.

III

Hospitality

We turned out the lights and locked the crypt. Tony tripped on his habit going up the stone steps and would have fallen if Gus hadn't been right behind. "Careful," she sang, steadying him. Neither of us made a move to relieve him of the suitcase, as he had proudly declined our offer in the crypt. I was glad Gus was along; I wasn't sure what I had gotten myself into. But what else could I have done?

We paused at the top of the steps, expecting Tony would need to rest. I was about to ask if he'd like to see the inside of the church, so he could catch his breath, but he bounced right on in his Nikes and we had to catch up with him. Momentarily in the crypt he had sagged like a weary old monk, but now he was in full stride, a man with a purpose.

A dark sedan with its engine running was parked directly in front of Gus's truck. As we approached the rectory, a large woman in a voluminous red cape came sailing down the front walk, having just stuffed a hefty manila envelope halfway into our mailbox. Her momentum was definitely that of someone who had accomplished her mission and was intent on fleeing the scene had the three of us not materialized inconveniently out of the darkness and intercepted her.

"Hello," I said, stepping forward into the light from the porch. "Were you looking for me?"

With a whuffing sound, she and the cape swirled to a full stop. She was a tall woman with a thick upsweep of dark hair and a haughty elegant face that set itself off from her massive body like a delicately carved figurehead on the prow of a bulky ship. Panting slightly, she looked me up and down.

"I didn't expect you to be so *small*, Reverend Bonner," she said almost accusingly.

I knew that voice. "Grace Munger?"

"How did you know?"

"From our telephone conversations." How would she have reacted, I wondered, if I had counterattacked by saying I hadn't expected her to be so large? "Did you want to see me?"

"Not really, though it's time we met, since we're both doing the Lord's work. I was dropping off materials about the Millennium Birthday March. Are these people in your congregation?"

"This is Augusta Eubanks, who is. And this is — Brother Tony, who's visiting."

"Oh, yes, the Eubankses," said Grace Munger, with a brusque nod to Gus. Her attention was all for Tony's long skirts beneath the duffel coat. "Are you a monk?" she demanded.

"Yes, ma'am," replied Tony. When she continued to stare at him boldly, he added with an apologetic cackle, "At least I do my best to pass for one."

Gus giggled, but Grace Munger's face registered not an iota of amusement. "So you profess Jesus Christ as Lord?" she pressed on.

"Yes, ma'am, I do." Tony hefted his suitcase to get a fresh grip on it.

"How long are you going to be in town?"

"Well, I don't —"

"Our friend is tired, he's been traveling all day," I broke in, none too soon. Why was rudeness so intimidating, I asked myself, not for the first time.

"Yes, it's been a long day for all of us," replied Grace Munger coolly. Rebuffs appeared to slide off her as easily as humor. "I've been on the road all day myself, coordinating this march. Reverend Bonner, I hope you'll peruse the materials I left in your box, and after you've prayed over it perhaps you'll join us and allow your congregation to share in lifting up His name. Brother Tony, our march is the Saturday before Christmas, the eighteenth. May I count on you to join us if you're still in town?"

"Well, if I'm still here, I'd be honored, ma'am, but —" He looked uncertainly from Gus to me.

"You'll be such an asset. Now it's time we *all* got some rest. Reverend Bonner, I'll be looking forward to hearing from you. The number where you can reach me is in the envelope."

And off she swept before I had a chance either to decline her invitation a third time, or to explain as courteously as possible that being pastor of All Saints High Balsam did not include "allowing" or disallowing my parishioners to march in parades. Though courtesy, with Grace Munger, was beginning to feel like a handicap.

"So *that's* how Joel Munger's daughter turned out," Gus mused as the three of us sat around the kitchen table. She and I were sipping cider to keep Tony company while he had bread and cider and a microwaved bowl of Adrian's chili. "How strange for her to be back in High Balsam."

"Who's Joel Munger?" I asked.

"He was the pastor of Free Will Baptist Church until — let's see, it must have been twenty years ago, because I was a senior in college. It was a huge scandal. His congregation considered him a sort of magus-saint until he was caught in some highly irregular money finaglings and sentenced to federal prison. But he and his wife burned themselves up in their house first. A gasoline and rags affair. Many people thought he took it on himself to extinguish the whole family, others thought Mrs. Munger was in on it, too. But Grace managed to escape. They found her unconscious next door in the church in what was left of her nightgown. The lower half of her was badly burned. Some relatives came and took her away to the burn center in Mountain City, and after that we heard that they'd legally adopted her and sent her away to school. But here she is back in town, still calling herself Munger and organizing a Jesus rally. I'll have to ask Smathers about it, my cousin's an archivist of all the juicy gossip between here and Mountain City over the last fifty years."

"How old was she at the time?" I asked.

"Oh, ten or eleven. Which makes her what? About thirty now."

"Very forceful lady," said Tony. "But a smasher, even with the weight," he added with a feisty grin.

Gus burst out laughing. "I haven't heard that expression since my grandfather died, Brother Tony."

"Please, just Tony. That's because I'm probably the same vintage as your grandfather. Did you make this chili, Margaret?"

"My husband did. Chili's Adrian's specialty."

"Is that so? I make a pretty fair chili myself. In fact, his reminds me of mine. It has character and an afterbite to it. Will he be home soon?"

"No, he's spending tonight out at Fair Haven. It's a year-round boarding school."

"Yes, the article said about the school. He's the chaplain, right?"

"Well, at present he's headmaster as well, which means I don't see much of him at the moment. But he's promised to be back in time for Gus's wedding. Gus is getting married tomorrow."

"My congratulations," said Tony to Gus. "Headmaster, eh?" He seemed impressed. "That's a very responsible position."

"It's only temporary. He and the board are searching for a new one. Adrian likes being chaplain better."

"Couldn't he do both?" Then, perhaps fearing he'd overstepped, he added, "Not that I know much about these things. But I'm looking forward to meeting him."

"I hope you'll come to my wedding," Gus put in cordially.

"That's very kind of you, ma'am. I like weddings." He cocked his head at me. "Did you and . . . *Adrian* have a nice wedding?"

"Why, yes, we did," I said, somewhat surprised by the question. "We were married in the chapel at General Seminary in New York. Six years ago this past spring."

"All your family there?"

"No, it was just us and some friends. Neither Adrian nor I have any family left."

"Is that so?" He was solemnly thoughtful

for a moment. "Well, I didn't mean to pry."

"Not at all," I said, rising to take away his dishes. "I'm going to go and make up your room now. You must be quite tired."

"I'll come help," said Gus, jumping up, too.

"Can I get you anything else, Tony?"

"Would anyone be offended if I sat here and had a smoke? But if you prefer, I'll go outside."

"Here's just fine." I fetched the little ceramic canapé dish I always gave Lucinda Lord to use as her ashtray.

From a deep pocket in his habit, Tony extricated a worn brown pouch, a book of cigarette papers, and an old Zippo lighter. Gus and I lingered, fascinated, while he expertly tamped out a straight line of loose tobacco and rolled his own cigarette, sealing the paper fastidiously with his pointy tongue. He seemed to relish our watching. After he lit up, he inquired of Gus, "What kind of finagling did the preacher do to get him the federal prison invitation?"

"Well, first," said Gus, "he was investing his own money using the church account numbers. So he wouldn't have to pay taxes on the investments. That's how it *began.* Then he got more ambitious, and every time he'd take out his personal monies to reinvest them, he'd siphon off a little of the church monies at the same time . . . a little here, a little there. The whole enterprise was conducted with great ingenuity. That's probably why it took them so long to catch him at it."

"Criminals can be very creative people," remarked Tony. He blew out a stream of pungent smoke and smiled shyly up at us with his little stained teeth. "Father Cecil, our late prior, had a very active prison ministry — we've got four correctional facilities within an hour's drive from our abbey. Father Cecil always said the most imaginative crimes are committed by people whose creativity has been misdirected."

"First time I ever saw a monk roll his own," Gus said under her breath as we made up Tony's bed on the glassed-in sun porch, which Adrian and I had turned into a guest room. "For that matter, it's the first time I ever saw a monk who dunked his hair. You're going to phone Adrian, aren't you?"

"What for?"

"Don't you think he ought to know you have a strange man spending the night alone in the house with you?"

"Come on. An eighty-year-old monk?"

"He was fit enough to walk from the bus station lugging that cumbersome art deco suitcase."

"Adrian has enough to worry about. If I'd been a single woman living in this rectory, I would still have offered him hospitality. I mean, what else do you do when a Benedictine shows up at your door? St. Benedict wrote it into his Rule that you should receive all guests as Christ."

"Christ in black Nikes, rolling his own. I guess you wouldn't consider letting Pearl spend tonight in your bedside drawer?"

"Having Pearl in my bedside drawer would make me far more apprehensive than having Tony in the house."

"Aha, so you admit you're apprehensive."

"Only in the sense I don't know how long he's staying!"

"What exactly is a lay brother, anyway?"

"A monk who isn't ordained."

"Oh. I thought they were the worker-bees in a monastery. The blue collars."

"That's what they used to be. Then it was made more democratic. Now lay brothers sing the choir office and have chapter rights and are considered full monks. Though in some communities it's starting to change again. Many new monks coming in *want* to spend the majority of their time doing manual labor and skip the choir and study."

"Well, worker-bee or not, he doesn't come across as someone who's spent years in cloistered tranquility."

"He may have joined up late in life and done something untranquil first. I knew a monk who was in the coast guard until he was forty-five. And at the seminary, there was a man studying to be a priest who'd been on the New York police force for twenty-five years."

"I still think you ought to let Adrian know. What happens when he walks in tomorrow morning and bumps into an old guy rolling a cigarette?"

"Good point. I will phone him. After I get Tony settled. That's a promise."

"Thank you. Now I'll be able to go home and sleep soundly in my maid's room. You've fixed up this sun porch so attractively. Ex–Father Al's ex–Seduction Porch. Weren't you tempted to exorcise it first?"

"Oh, we did. I asperged while Adrian read the benediction for a clergy-house from an 1890s priest's prayer book in his collection. There was a perfect line about unclean spirits being driven out. Then we took off our stoles and put on our jeans and started painting the walls white."

"Well, you've made it very inviting. What's the story behind that colorful icon with the three angels sitting around the outdoor table?"

"It's a wedding gift from a man who taught both Adrian and me at General. The angels represent the Holy Trinity, as they appeared to Abraham. Abraham and his wife Sarah are inside the house preparing them a meal, even though these men are complete strangers. Our guest room seemed the perfect place for it. 'Be not forgetful to entertain strangers, for thereby some have entertained angels unawares.' "

"Does Shaun still live in your New York loft?"

"No. When he found out he had AIDS, he decided to go back to Ireland. I went up to New York last summer and sold the loft."

"You mean those two weeks when Father thingy took over the services?"

"Those were the ones."

"Well well, Miss Margaret. This has truly been an evening of revelations. First you tell me you had a loft in New York, and now the same evening you're telling me you've gone and sold it." There was just a touch of a friend's reproach behind her teasing tone.

"No one knew about it but Adrian. To tell the truth, I usually forgot about it myself, until a check from Shaun would arrive, or a tax bill or something. I guess I felt funny about it. It was so incongruous with the rest of my life."

"Country parson maintains hideaway in Sin City."

"Something like that. As long as Shaun was living there, it felt right to hang onto it, but when he wrote that he was leaving, my impulse was to get rid of it as quickly as possible."

"Too much hassle?"

"Umm." I folded Tony's top sheet over his blanket. The ex–sun porch did look inviting, with its lamplight on the white walls and the bookshelves holding Adrian's and my spill-over books (and some of my father's) and the neat, fresh bed, and the icon of those majestically calm figures in their bright raiment, already in full knowledge of how they are going to reward Abraham and Sarah for their hospitality. Friendship was a form of hospitality, too, and I owed Gus a little more than that "Umm."

I did some unnecessary extra-smoothing of Tony's blanket and added, "And also, when you consider my family history, and the fact that Adrian and I weren't getting along too well last spring, I suppose I wanted to remove any chance of an easy getaway from my husband."

"Ah," breathed Gus.

I straightened up and turned to face her. "Yes, that's how it was."

"And are you still glad you sold it?"

"Once it was done I never looked back. But I did some soul-searching up in New York. That's a story for another evening."

"I'd love to hear it. Maybe one evening when Charles and I have been squabbling and I'm contemplating a bolt."

"Marriage is a great mystery," I said. "To quote St. Paul."

"Who never tried it himself."

"Now that might have been a case for bolting!"

"You mean Mrs. Paul from Mr. Paul, of course."

"Of course," I said.

"Well, my friend, this well-appointed sun porch is making me drowsy. I'm off to my maid's room. Thanks for your company on my last evening as a spinster. A memorable evening all 'round."

"Thank *you* for being my friend, Gus. If Jennifer's still over at your place decorating the bridal suite, will you remind her that I'm counting on her for the prologue to my Sunday sermon."

"As if she needed reminding! She's practically memorized that litany of unpronounceable names."

"She doesn't have to *memorize them*."

"You know my Jenn," said Gus proudly. "She always goes the extra mile."

"Can you think of anything else you need to make you comfortable?" I asked Tony, showing him to his sun porch. "I put out towels and a washcloth for you in the bathroom next door. If you want it warmer or cooler in this room, you just turn that knob on the space heater. Five is the warmest setting; it's on three now."

He hefted the green suitcase onto the bed and looked around him with hardly contained elation. "Oh, I'll be very happy here," he purred in his soft croak. "Such kindness . . ."

("Oh, they were very kind to me in High Balsam, Margaret and Adrian Bonner. I only meant to stay overnight, but a gracious lady invited me to her wedding, and a *forceful* lady asked me to stay on for a Jesus March the Saturday before Christmas, she said I'd be an asset, and then Christmas was almost upon us and my kind friends the Bonners insisted . . .")

"I'm usually up pretty early," I said, "but if you get up first, just press the On button on the coffeemaker. It's all set up to go. There's bread in the bread box and cereals in the cupboard directly above and, let's see, milk and butter in the refrigerator."

"God bless you, dear." Were his old eyes watery from exhaustion or tears? Whichever, I felt ashamed of my forebodings about an extended stay as I said good night and closed the door to the exorcised sun porch.

I started upstairs to bed, then backtracked to retrieve Grace Munger's envelope from the mailbox. I'd look into it before I went to sleep, or first thing in the morning. I was kind of curious to see what kind of materials *these* would be.

I shut the door of our bedroom and phoned Adrian's office first, on the off chance he might have lingered over more of his never-ending administrative work. Then I tried his room in the main building: no answer there, either. He must have set out on his nightly rounds already. When his recorded voice came on, I left a short message saying we had a houseguest, an eighty-year-old Benedictine monk who'd walked with his suitcase from the bus station, and not to be startled if he came in tomorrow morning and found the old man having breakfast or smoking a hand-rolled cigarette. There, that should count as honoring my promise to Gus.

Adrian as chaplain had started the custom of night prayers with individual students. Initially, N.P.'s, as everyone at Fair Haven called them, had been conceived as a bridging ritual for new students who had recently been taken off their medications and were prone to be anxious or restless at bedtime. But other students heard about it and wanted them, too. If you wished a staff member to knock on your door between eight and nine and say night prayers with you, you made a little sign and put it outside on the door. Some students just scrawled a last minute "N.P." on a piece of scrap paper and taped it up; others made careful cardboard signs, with cutouts of stars or drawings of animals in pajamas. On peak-demand nights there could be as many as thirty N.P.'s hanging outside doors in the main house and in the cottages; the staff had to hustle to squeeze them all in.

"At first it surprised me, the popularity of it," Adrian said, "but it shouldn't have. Many of their parents were never home to tuck them in at night, or review their day with them."

"It's a wonderful idea," I said.

"But I got it from you, Margaret."

"From me?"

"You told me how your father came to your room every night and reviewed the day in his prayers. He read poetry to you, too. We don't have time for the poetry. There's never enough time to give them all they need."

As I undressed for bed, I mentally followed his evening route. The Jeffersons were on duty tonight; they'd cover the dorm quarters in the main house, and he would do the seniors, who lived six boys or six girls to a cottage. When Adrian and I had lived out at the school, before I became rector at All Saints High Balsam, I had helped with the N.P.'s. I took the younger girls' wing in the main house. I enjoyed knocking softly on the doors with the N.P. signs and entering into the aura of each personality. All students had private rooms at Fair Haven, even in the cottages. And how myriad are the ways we comfort ourselves and ward off anxiety through the arrangement of our personal surroundings! One girl had covered every available surface of her small room with framed photographs of herself and her horse — no pictures of anyone else; another had papered her walls with blown-up ads from fashion magazines:

androgynous torsos twining around each other in skintight jeans . . . snarling models in black leather with spiky purple hair and matching claws. One night I found myself praying beneath a poster of Ben MacGruder and his Melody Station group.

"I've never prayed in my life," a new girl, Josie, challenged me. Yet she had painstakingly nail-polished a big N.P. and a circlet of pink flying angels on a piece of paper and taped it to her door. "But what else is there to do in this spooked wilderness at night? How do you start?"

Josie's wall were still bare. Her boxes and laptop and study lamp and new books were all piled in a corner of the room, as if she hadn't made up her mind whether she'd stay. She was distracted and spacey, having been taken off Ritalin before arriving at school. "Education, not medication" was a cornerstone of Sandlin's method. His research on the neocortex had convinced him that there was no evidence that psychotropic medicines altered attitude problems. Part of the brain's structure evolved from the way it was *used*, he said. If young people's habits and experiences changed significantly, so would their brains. Wisdom would be developed in these young human brains by Fair Haven's curriculum, which stressed the intangibles, but for this *time* was needed, and an adequate staff possessed of those habits themselves and devoted to *taking time* with each student. That's why the school had to stay small.

"You can start praying in as many ways as you can start a conversation with somebody," I told Josie. "It depends on your mood, and how close you feel to the person. Sometimes I simply say, 'Here I am,' and then wait."

"Wait for what?"

"Well, for what I need to know next."

"You mean like a *reply?*"

"In a way. For something else to get a word in edgewise. Or, other times I start with a phrase from a psalm I like. 'For you my soul in silence waits,' for instance. Or sometimes I begin by saying aloud the names of people close to me, or people that I want to pray for."

Josie cocked her curly head and gave me a strange look, then slammed her eyes shut and spieled off at least twenty first names without pausing for breath.

"Like that?" she asked, fixing me with an aggressive stare.

"That's quite a list. It's good you have so many people you feel close to or want to pray for."

She gave a high, skittish laugh. "What's next?"

Though her parents had written "Christian" in the "religious affiliation or preference" blank on her application form, she said she was unfamiliar with the Lord's Prayer. I read both versions to her from the prayer book.

"What else have you got?" The practiced young consumer being introduced to a new kind of merchandise.

I tried the Twenty-third Psalm.

"Could you run through that again? I've got an attention problem since I went off my meds."

I ran through it again.

"Well, I like it better than Our Father."

"Really? Why?"

"You're not begging for anything and you've got company. Someone's going with you."

In her gradually unpacked room on subsequent nights, we'd begin with her rattled-off list (always the same names, though never in quite the same order: Laurel, Trevor, Tad, Dixie, Margo, Caleb, Kirk, Bo, Billie, etc.) and then we'd shop for psalms. I had left a Bible with her. At first she triumphantly showed me her "turn-off" psalms.

"God, what a whiner this person is! He thinks everyone is picking on him and only he's perfect and God ought to make him the teacher's pet."

"Haven't you ever felt like that?"

"Well, sure, but it's pretty childish, isn't it? And just look at this one: how can it be a *prayer*, when you're asking God to dash your enemies' children against the rocks? It's not the *children's* fault! How can cruel whiny stuff like this be in the Bible?"

"Because the psalms were written by humans and humans are a messy, contradictory lot. They grow up very slowly. The reason these psalms still speak to us is because the writers showed us ourselves as we are and yet put it in a larger container. They're reporting to God what's going on inside them at the moment. They rage and lament and give thanks and praise for their good fortunes and curse their enemies some more and blame God for abandoning them, but they also write down God's voice telling them things they need to know, telling them that they are loved and special. It's a mixed bag, but the point is it's all *in* a bag, bigger than they are, called God."

"I thought the Bible was supposed to be a book that told you how to be good."

"No, it's a record of a people keeping track of their relationship with God over a very long period of time. The amazing thing is, this constant accounting of yourself to an unseen other does make you change and grow. Sooner or later you become more conscious of what you're doing. People go through some pretty awful stages as they fumble toward what they're meant to be. As you put it, cruel and whiny. It takes a long while to complete the transformation from 'eye-for-an-eye' sandbox whiner into a loving person — a lot of us never make it."

"Haven't *you* made it?"

"In spurts, I have. Sort of like little grasshopper leaps. I'm hoping that as I go on, the spurts will get longer."

Josie gave her high-pitched skittish laugh. "Like maybe a helicopter-spurt?"

"Oh, Josie, that's wonderful. What a great image! Yes, I certainly aspire to a helicopter-spurt one of these days. There's another fascinating angle about all this, too."

"Like what?"

"Well, that my growing up and your growing up retraces the growing-up pains of the entire species. All of human experience is stored in each of us. So it's understandable that an omnibus like the Bible, produced by many human beings down through the ages, should contain every variety of mood and behavior from the bloodthirsty whiner to the divinely compassionate."

"Now I *liked* that psalm that goes, 'you put my tears in your bottle.' You know the one?"

" '. . . and recorded them in your book.' That's one of my favorites, too."

"You're kidding. What are some of your other favorites?"

"Oh, I like, 'Lord, You have searched me out and known me.' And I'm especially fond of, 'You rescued me because you delighted in me.' The actual psalm says, 'He rescued me because he delighted in me,' but at some point I changed over to the more personal form of address and never wanted to change it back."

"You also took out the 'he.'"

"True, I did. That's very perceptive of you, Josie."

"We both like the ones where there's someone to go with you," Josie said.

One night, after I'd been away doing supply work for a vacationing priest in Mountain City, Josie named only four names, all new. Gone were Bo, Billie, Trevor, Tad, etc. When she finished she eyed me shrewdly.

"Short list tonight," I said, puzzled.

"But they're real."

"Real?"

"They're real people. Sarah, she's a friend I've made here, and Nora was my grandmother, she's dead but I still feel close to her, and Dick and Felicia are my mother and father. I wouldn't say I exactly feel *close* to them, but they probably deserve my prayers if I'm ever going to get out of the sandbox-whiner stage and apply for my helicopter license. I wanted to add your name, but I was afraid you might think I was sucking up or something."

"Well, I thank you for the intention. But who were all those others, then? Bo and Billie and Trevor and Dixie and so on."

"You really don't know, do you? They're characters in the soaps I used to watch at all the boarding schools I got kicked out of before I came here. It was sort of a joke, the first night you came by, because I couldn't think of a single person I felt close to, and also I wanted to see if I could put one over on you."

"Well, you certainly did."

"It wasn't totally a joke. I mean, I kept up with them on a day-to-day basis more than I ever did with my parents. I knew more of what they were doing than I ever did with my parents. Dick and Felicia are both corporation lawyers, but they fight all the time. The only way they can stay married is to work for different firms and live in separate towns. I looked forward to my soap people and worried about what would happen to them next. They were like my family, I'd kept up with some of them ever since I was a little girl watching them with the housekeeper. So I *did* feel close to them, if that makes any sense."

"It certainly does, Josie. I'm very glad you had them to practice on."

"Practice what on?"

"The art of feeling close to people and caring what happens to them."

Josie's adoption of the soap people as her family was a typical manifestation of the kind of displacement going on all around us. Many people now found their solace in controlled simulations of reality rather than the

143

actual thing itself. (Radford Zorn, the father of another student at Fair Haven, had made a fortune creating his "Zorn Town, U.S.A." theme parks, "The Home Town We All Wish We'd Grown Up In," yet had been unable or unwilling to provide his son, Chase, with even a poor excuse for a home.) People tapped keyboards and squinted into their screens and instantly visited the Louvre, or cruised down the Nile aboard virtual reality. At least one didn't step in a wad of chewing gum in front of the Mona Lisa, or lose one's passport, or brush against a threatening stranger on board a real boat. This avoidance of the human medium was one of the malaises that Hiram Sandlin had been waging war on with his curriculum to coax young minds out of the psychic poverty of the passive mode and teach them to risk encounter.

I was glad for my time spent out at Fair Haven, because it had given me an insider's understanding of why Adrian was so possessed by his work. It was an immensely satisfying thing to be able to create a kind of compost out of the gifts and lacks from your own childhood and sprinkle it as fertilizer on a new crop of spindly young souls struggling toward the light. When I had been just Josie's age, a woman in her late thirties named Katharine Thrale started coming to my father's church and she befriended me. She told me stories of her spiritual odyssey, taught me some rudimentary Greek, and showed me how to make incense from rosemary and sage. Together we built a dry wall of bluestone to save Daddy's iris beds from erosion caused by Greedy Gaines's excavations. I plotted to make a match between her and my father, but she'd already committed herself elsewhere. Yet during the short period she was in Romulus, she gave me something I very much needed: time spent in the company of an older woman I looked up to.

Adrian's earliest mentors gave him things he needed, too. But unlike the unalloyed benefits of Katharine Thrale's friendship, the patronage of Mr. Dumas and Father Mountjoy — especially Father Mountjoy — came packaged with pathology.

Alcoholic and nerve-damaged from World War II, Mr. Dumas was unemployable, but he was a simple-hearted, faithful Catholic from a respected family in the area, and the priests at the orphanage gave him room and meals in return for maintenance and repair jobs. When Adrian, starting out on a solitary walk soon after his arrival at the orphanage, passed Mr. Dumas's basement workshop, the man called out a friendly greeting and asked him about himself. Adrian carefully explained to Mr. Dumas that he was not an orphan like the others, that his parents were only *boarding* him here so he could be in school until they found work. Every day, during those first months, Adrian would walk down to the fence at the end of the orphanage grounds and stand peering through the slats of the high fence, watching for his father's car. For quite a while he kept up the belief that his parents would return as promised, as soon as they could provide a home for him. He clung tightly to his difference from the other children. "Any sign of 'em yet?" Mr. Dumas asked every day. "No, not yet," Adrian would reply, not minding the question because Mr. Dumas also seemed to take their return for granted.

One afternoon, Mr. Dumas asked Adrian to stick a few empty bottles inside his jacket and take them to the woods. Soon Adrian was performing this service routinely. "The fathers knew he drank, but they didn't know how *much* he drank, and Mr. Dumas had the wits left to know it could lose him his home. On my average trip to the woods, I'd have fifteen or twenty pint bottles crammed inside my jacket. Mind you, I was only about four-foot-two when these trips began. I had to walk very slowly so I wouldn't clink. Afterward, my shirt always carried the sweetish stench of Four Roses."

One day Mr. Dumas's hands were shaking so violently he hammered his finger while replacing a rotten panel in a screen door. He asked Adrian to finish the job for him, showing him where to put the nails. "That was the beginning of my carpentry apprenticeship, which lasted as long as *he* lasted at the orphanage. Four years later, Father Mountjoy arrived and packed him off to the county infirmary. He was pretty much of a mess by then, though I think the other fathers would have been willing to close their eyes to it a while longer. I like to believe my assistance with the bottles *and* the repair work helped keep him there as long as he was. Later, after I was adopted by the Schmidts, there was a woodworking teacher at the high school and I mastered some finer points of the craft before I ran away. But I saw Mr. Dumas's face and heard his voice long after I had stopped trying to force memories of my parents. He may have been an addled drunk, but he *liked* me, and I responded to that. And he showed me how to occupy myself with something useful and practical while I waited in vain. Redemptive people can come to us in the unlikeliest of shapes."

Soon after Father Mountjoy became director of Adrian's orphanage, he summoned each boy for a private conference. Starting with the oldest and working down, he skillfully converted the earlier interviewees into star witnesses against the rest. When Adrian's turn came, Father Mountjoy made it clear that he knew everything about him he needed to know, plus things Adrian hadn't known about himself.

"I am an alumnus of this orphanage," Father Mountjoy crisply began. "I was dropped off here at age four — in circumstances similar to yours, I might add — and I remained here until age sixteen, when I entered the seminary, so I know my way around the place. I know where boys hide, where they go to smoke and do their other forbidden things, what contraband they keep under their mattresses, and where their hands are under the blankets. I know that *you*, Bonner, over a period of four years, singlehandedly despoiled these woods — which are church property — with unsightly mounds of cheap brown bottles. Yes, yes, take that look of outraged innocence off your face. I know *you* didn't drink the stuff, not a drop, ever — that shows good judgment on your part — but you abetted, you accelerated, the ruin of a poor simpleminded sot. Don't you imagine there's a special place in hell reserved for accomplices and abettors? I myself have always pictured it as a narrow ledge above a pit. Those who helped others to sin must slink back and forth along their precarious ledge for all eternity, flattening themselves against a jagged rock wall to keep from falling into the pit, gazing down forever on those they have ruined. Sometimes they long to lose their balance and fall into the pit with the others and have it over with. Not a pleasant prospect, is it?"

"No, Father."

"Fortunate for you you're not in hell yet, isn't it?"

"Yes, Father."

"You're still on this earth, imperfect as it is, where redemption remains possible until the last minute. You will be provided with a wheelbarrow and sturdy trash bags, and starting tomorrow you will spend your recreation hour each day hauling every last one of those loathsome bottles from the woods. You will be given a chance to make reparation."

"For him, too?"

"I beg your pardon?"

"For Mr. Dumas, too?"

Father Mountjoy gave him a sharp look. "I don't quite follow you, Bonner."

"Well, if I can abet someone's ruin, why can't I abet them back to redemption?"

"Because you're not Jesus Christ," snapped the director.

"But you said *I* would have a chance to —"

"I said you would have a chance to make reparation. You're confusing reparation with redemption. Take care with words, Bonner. By cleaning up the mess you made in the woods, you will merely be making reparation. As for redemption, yours or anyone else's, that's up to God. All you can do is pray for it."

"Then can't I pray for Mr. Dumas's redemption, too?"

"You may certainly pray for his soul. But

removing the empty bottles isn't going to remove the damage and dissolution from his body. You're not a miracle worker, Bonner. I've been told you're a very smart boy, but take care not to be presumptuous."

It took nine weeks for Adrian to clear the woods. With every load he trundled out in the wheelbarrow with the wobbly wheel, he prayed for Mr. Dumas's soul and for as much restoration as it would not be presumptuous to ask for Mr. Dumas's damaged and dissolute body.

Father Mountjoy sent for him. "I took a walk in the woods today, Bonner. Impressive job. You raked and cleared some brush, too, I noticed."

"There's still more to do," Adrian told him.

"More?" Father Mountjoy regarded him strangely. "What more?"

"Well, I'd like to take Mr. Dumas's bow saw and cut off all those low dead branches in there."

"Removing the bottles was your mortification, Bonner. I don't require you to turn the place into the Vienna Woods."

"No, Father, but I'd like —"

"Consider your project at an end and go back to the playground with the other children. Our woods are much changed for the better. What about you, are you changed for the better?"

"I don't know, Father."

"Disappointing answer. Enlightenment is a by-product of mortification — with intelligent people. You had no thoughts, no epiphanies, while engaged in your hard labors?"

"I had thoughts. I'm not sure I know what epiphanies are, Father."

"An epiphany is a revelation. Something new shows itself to you. Was anything new revealed to you in the woods?"

"Well, not revealed, exactly, but —"

Expertly, Father Mountjoy built Adrian's "disappointing" answers into a table model of the boy's secret thought processes and laid them out in clear sight for him to examine. He soon extracted from Adrian that he had performed his woods penance not for Mr. Dumas's restoration alone. At some early stage of his bottle trundling, a notion had come to Adrian that *if he restored the woods to the way they had looked when his parents had left him, then they would come back as well.* As his project neared completion, the "notion" became an "assurance." *On the day when the woods looked just as they had before he'd begun cluttering them with Mr. Dumas's bottles, a certain gray car would slowly turn into the drive and . . .*

When all the bottles had been disposed of and no gray car came, a new proviso floated up in Adrian's mind: he must make amends to the *woods themselves* for having forced them

151

to bear the shame of so much ugliness for four years. He must rake and clear brush and make them *better* than they were before he arrived at the orphanage. And when no car came after that, another new proviso floated up: he must dispose of all the ugly dead branches, and *then* the car would come. . . .

"That is magical thinking, Bonner. A foolish and dangerous activity. It's taking God's gift of natural reason to you and flinging it back in his face and then setting yourself up as a play god, who has only to 'will' things for them to happen. An utterly futile — and presumptuous, I might add — undertaking. *You* can't 'will' the flimsiest pine needle to drop from its tree. And you most certainly can't 'will' the return of an automobile with people in it who most likely never intended to come back for you in the first place."

"That's not true!"

"Let's look at your folder here, and see what conclusions you draw. Using God's gift of natural reason to you and not magicking around with what you'd 'like' to happen. You're an excellent reader, I'm told. Let's see if you can make out my predecessor's notations on your record, even though his handwriting is deplorable."

" 'May twelve, 1952 . . .' " Heart skittering oddly in his chest, Adrian began to decipher aloud Father Connor's cluttered script while

Father Mountjoy watched him. " 'Adrian Bonner, Catholic boy age six, admitted by parents Joseph and Evette Bonner to board with us for two to maximum of three months. The boy appears to be in good health, though slightly undersized for his age. He will have to have his inoculations again, as parents did not bring along any records. Mrs. Bonner recently suffered miscarriage and is too weak to care for the boy at this time. Father very likable man — shows respect and seems trustworthy. He left five dollars on account toward first month's fee with balance to follow as soon as he finds work in the area. Describes himself as a skilled mechanic so prospects seem good. Meanwhile in case of emergency, we are to write to Adrian's maternal grandmother, Mrs. Ida Rameau, Route One, Manistee, Michigan. (Mrs. Rameau is deaf so does not have a telephone).' "

Adrian looked up. "A grandmother! I wonder why she's never written to me."

"Read on," Father Mountjoy enjoined dryly.

There was only one further clump of difficult handwriting. As his eyes raced ahead of his voice, Adrian wished in vain that it would become *more* difficult. A few illegible words might have left him with a sliver of hope. " 'December ten, 1952. As we have had no word from Adrian's father, I wrote to Mrs. Rameau in Manistee on first November. The letter was returned yesterday stamped 'Addressee Unknown.' This morning I made some telephone inquiries. Employment bureau had no record of any Joseph Bonner asking for work. Called the automobile repair shops in the area. Nobody named Bonner has been by. Looks like another case of abandonment.' " Adrian sounded out the last word bravely, but his lips were not working right and he childishly mispronounced it "abandomment."

"Look up at me, Bonner."

Adrian reluctantly obeyed.

"You are hating me at this moment," said Father Mountjoy. "How do I know it? Because I've stood in your spot. The director who dashed *my* illusions was new to his job, just as I am. He was sweeping the place with a clean broom, only he had only one arm to sweep with. He'd lost the other in combat in the First War. He informed me I was old enough to know that all evidence pointed to my mother's willful desertion of me and that I could either feel sorry for myself the rest of my life and blame all my future failures on this early bad luck, or I could make myself into a competent, self-respecting member of the human community. The choice was mine but he strongly advised the latter. I hated his cold-blooded voice and was disturbed by the empty black sleeve pinned back on itself. 'I'll run away,' I thought. Why didn't I? Why do you think I didn't run away, Bonner?"

Adrian looked at the director with his pressed black clothes and austere bearing and saw no trace of any boy who needed to run away. "I don't know, Father."

"Because, like you, I was too intelligent to fool myself that I'd get very far. And where, pray tell, was I going to run *to?* I next fantasized doing away with myself. In recent history a bed wetter at the orphanage had tried to hang himself after being made to come down to breakfast wearing his wet sheet. This just preceded the arrival of the new director, who had forbidden such punishments. I saw my own little corpse dangling successfully from its better-constructed gallows, bringing censure and disgrace on the new director. And my mother, wherever she was, would read about it in the newspaper and be sorry forever. This fantasy sustained me until I realized its impractical aspects. A dead boy can't watch others feel sorry, he can't experience revenge. The revenge would be to keep living and become so self-sufficient that if I ever met my parents again, I wouldn't need them. And here I am, Bonner, living proof that this child did better without them."

"But you might have done even better if you'd had them," Adrian dared to say.

"I assure you not. That became abundantly clear when I met my mother again. As for my father, I seriously doubt she had the slightest idea who he was."

"But you found her?"

"She found me. She'd known where I was all along, she just didn't want the bother of raising me. Now I didn't need her anymore, my boyhood 'revenge' wish had come true. She needed *me*. She was pitiful and cunning. Not an attractive combination. I helped her as I would have helped any degraded, destitute creature it was in my power to help. I used my influence to get her into a comfortable place where she could live and be cared for, and I visited her regularly until she mercifully died. But I assure you, I'd rather have carried the unsolved mystery of her to my grave. And despite whatever you're imagining now about your parents, you may one day feel the same. Take God as your parent and be your own disciplinarian. That's been *my* winning combination. That's what I'd counsel a scrupulous, intelligent boy like yourself to do. I like you, Adrian. In some ways, I see my history repeating itself in you. Perhaps I can give you the advantage of a few shortcuts."

"But how can I be my own disciplinarian?" Adrian asked, puzzled. He felt the heat rising into his face from the unexpected praise. It was the first time Father Mountjoy had ever called him by his first name, and the soft sound of it on the director's lips made him feel specially anointed by this imposing man.

156

"By doing everything assigned to you the way you did the job in the woods: with staying power and thoroughness. *Minus* the magical thinking. Keep busy. Keep making things, repairing things, improving things. Keep repairing and improving yourself. Be tougher on yourself than anyone else is. Mortify yourself as often as required."

"Mortify myself how?"

Father Mountjoy grimly smiled. "I'm going to show you." He opened a drawer in his desk and removed a black cloth bag. "Go and lock that door, please."

While Adrian did this, Father Mountjoy drew the blinds over the windows. Then, opening the drawstring of the black bag, he took out a small whip with leather cords knotted at the ends. He passed it across the desk to Adrian. "Have you ever seen one of these before?"

"No, Father."

"It's a flagellum. An ancient instrument of discipline for the religious. I am going to demonstrate its proper usage."

Father Mountjoy stood up. Reaching behind his neck, he unsnapped something, then worked his clerical collar out of the front opening of his black shirt. He laid it, a stiff white curl, on the desk next to the flagellum. He unbuckled his belt, whisked it from his trouser loops, and dropped it with a neat thunk next to the other items. He did not look at Adrian at all as he took off the long-sleeved black shirt and draped it carefully around the back of his desk chair: he might have been alone in his office. Then he pulled his white undershirt over his neatly barbered head and stood naked from the waist up. In the dim light of the drawn blinds, his well-developed chest was a bluish white, boyishly smooth except for a sprinkling of black hairs across the nipples and a few moles. Without his official garb, he seemed like a different being.

He picked up the whip and, still not looking at Adrian, addressed a point near the room's high ceiling. "When the desert fathers practiced corporal mortification, they drew blood, we are told. We don't do that anymore. The object is to inflict as much pain as you can stand, but not to break the skin. Though that cannot always be avoided. I use a two-phrase prayer to accompany the discipline: 'I scourge my body/to make it my slave.' One phrase per stroke."

When the priest turned his back, Adrian was shocked to see the pink scars already disfiguring it. Father Mountjoy bent forward from the waist, raised the whip backward over his shoulder, and began to thrash himself. "I scourge my body . . ." *whap* ". . . to make it my slave . . ." *whap*.

As angry red whelks crisscrossed on top of the scars on Father Mountjoy's back, and his repeated prayer became muffled and more breathless, Adrian grew worried. If this was supposed to be a *demonstration,* hadn't it gone on long enough? Faster and harder the whip lashed until it and Father Mountjoy's hand seemed like parts of the same machine bent on the destruction of Father Mountjoy's poor back. The chant grew more gasping and slurred until suddenly the priest broke off with a strange, high cry and doubled forward.

Adrian started toward him.

"Stay back," ordered Father Mountjoy, still doubled over and breathing raggedly and clutching the whip to his groin in an odd way. "I'll recover myself in a minute."

"And he did," Adrian told me on our wedding night, as we lay in Madelyn's old bed, facing her mural and painting our own for each other. "Father Mountjoy recovered himself admirably and promptly. The black shirt went on, then the belt and the collar, and he sat down behind his desk and the whip disappeared into the bag and the bag vanished into the drawer. But when he dismissed me, his voice was so unfriendly and remote that I felt I had disappointed him and he regretted showing me the discipline. Weeks went by without a summons from him. When I'd try to catch his eye in the dining room, he'd give a cold nod and sometimes say, 'Bonner,' and that was it. There was no sign

159

of the man who'd praised me and called me by my first name and said he liked me. I felt *dropped* in some awful way — worse than my parents dropping me at the orphanage and not coming back. This was so deliberate and cold. There was something metaphysical about it — like being sent to hell and not being told why. More inexplicable than my parents abandoning me, which now seemed to me — after I'd read Father Connor's comments in my file — more like a last resort for two people down on their luck and not because of anything I'd done. Even my few memories of them were of unreliable human beings, sometimes affectionate and playful, especially my father. Shortly before I went to the orphanage we were playing hide-and-seek behind some machine parts in the place where he worked and I fell against a radiator and knocked off a piece of new tooth coming in — that's why I have this chip. I remember my mother crying and screaming at him when we got home and she saw my mouth. She was sick then and stayed in bed most of the time. After that he lost his job and they argued a lot and one night we packed up the car and just drove away from our house in the middle of the night. When I got older, it occurred to me that we must have gone away like that because they couldn't pay their rent. After I read the file, I saw their failure to come back for me as an error that could still be reversed when their luck improved and they realized how much they missed me.

"But Father Mountjoy's sudden negation of me seemed to cancel me out as the worthwhile person I had just begun to believe I could be. The person he himself had assured me I could be."

Adrian cut himself a sapling in his cleaned-up woods and fashioned the middle part of it into a supple whip handle, to which he attached strips of rubber from a piece of inner tube. He knotted small rocks into the ends of the strips. He took to slipping off to the woods, removing his shirt, and disciplining himself the way Father Mountjoy had demonstrated. As he lashed himself he repeated the priest's two-phrase prayer, "I scourge my body/to make it my slave," one phrase per stroke.

"It hurt, but it made me feel strangely better," Adrian told me. " 'Keep making things, repairing things, improving things,' he'd said. 'Keep repairing and improving yourself.' Well, I'd made my own flagellum. And I was repairing myself, improving myself, by using it as often as required. That's what he'd advised. 'As often as required' soon turned into 'every day' for me. It was my secret thing I looked forward to whenever I could get away from the teachers and the other kids. I started to crave it, it became bound up with something else. I went deeper into the woods and found myself a hidden spot where I couldn't see if anyone crept up on me. This made it easier to fantasize that one day he would come walking in the woods and find me doing it. I daydreamed this over and over, embellishing and perfecting it a little more each time I flogged myself. . . . Margaret, I'm not sure we want to go on with this."

"Why not?"

"It's disturbing stuff."

"You mean for me, or for you to remember?"

"Oh, I don't forget it, ever; I accept it as part of who I am. I went through all its ramifications during my Zurich analysis: how I had internalized Father Mountjoy and carried him around inside me all those years. I also understood by then that he had been a product of his time, when Jansenism was having its last gasp in parochial schools and orphanages in this country. Mortify the body. Beat sex out of yourself — often, paradoxically, accompanied by erotic release. Later, your father reconciled me to . . . this part of my life . . . in deeper and, for me, more interesting ways. But it's another thing to tell it to the woman you just married."

"If it's part of who you are, then it's just one more part for me to love."

"You don't know what you're saying. I'm

162

sorry, Margaret. I think I'm a little out of control."

He had turned away from me in the bed. Was he shivering or weeping? I couldn't tell. I was afraid to say anything or move. An ill-considered word or gesture of mine might jinx our marriage. I'd already learned from the hour or so we'd been in bed that I had married a man who had difficulty letting himself go. I had restrained myself, in fact, so I wouldn't come across as a woman who wanted more than he could give. We had conducted ourselves adequately, with mutual respect and tenderness. And then, relieved that we had been able to do what was required of us, we settled back to talk and he asked what was behind the curtain, and I had opened it and told about Madelyn and her mural. He relaxed and curled against me like a child lost in a good story. Then the analyst in him got roused and he asked me what my mural would be. And for a while, our talking in bed had been more intimate and satisfying than our lovemaking. Until we got to Adrian whipping himself in the woods, fantasizing that Father Mountjoy was looking on.

The human mind, as we know from personal experience, is a chronic time traveler, but we are repeatedly amazed by its ability to hitch up the body, the body that resides the only place it can — in present time — and pull it along like a wagon, with its entire load of sensory equipment, backward or forward into other time zones. Telling it all — well, not *all* — to Gus in the crypt earlier this evening had brought our wedding night back to me with such physical vividness that I now felt absurdly misplaced: a married woman lying alone in bed longing for the body of her husband who is lying in his bed across town. Lovers separated by their vocations. Though we had not been lovers for some time, I ached to have him beside me now. I felt certain that if he were here right now in this bed, I could rub the warmth back into him and make him laugh with the blessed assurance that had come to me that other time: I could reconnect us at the deepmost point of that other night. All that was lacking was his present-time body next to mine.

The mind of ten-year-old Adrian, flogging himself in the woods, could lift itself off into a desired future time that never came, when a severe, unsmiling man in black steps forth from behind a tree and opens his arms to the boy and intones in a Godlike voice that he is well-pleased with his Adrian. Until one day the Adrian in present time discovers that the self-inflicted blows, accompanied by his carefully constructed phantasm of the approaching figure, can produce thrilling sensations that dependably lead to an almost unbearable rapture — until he comes to himself alone in the woods with a stinging back and his homemade whip. Thus the image of a stern but loving divine parent, and sex, and self-punishment, and Father Mountjoy, melted together into an irresistible Golden Calf that Adrian lugged with him well into his third decade — his only lover and his obsessive private religion.

"Even after I had rationally separated all the strands and finally abandoned my whip to a lake in Zurich — by then I had acquired an elegant leather whip like Father Mountjoy's — I've still reverted at times to that boyish wish: that I *could* have all of it together, somehow — minus the whip, I mean." He turned his head on the pillow and faced me again. "Does that disturb you, Margaret? It did me, until I had those good talks with your father. He said it was perfectly natural to yearn for a place large enough to contain all your unsightly edges and unsolved mysteries. We all yearned for that, your father said. He said the unsightly edges were where we'd tried to stretch beyond our capacities, and the unsolved mysteries were oftentimes the mysteries *we* had chosen because we intuited that they were the very ones that would help us grow beyond where we can see. I chose Father Mountjoy, he caught my imagination, and I like to think I caught his. Maybe he praised other boys the same way, maybe that was his method, making each boy think he was the chosen one. Maybe he got off on undressing and flogging himself in front of little boys — that's entirely possible. I'm thankful for it to remain a mystery, and I've long accepted him as *my* mystery. Soon after our last interview, he left the orphanage. The other fathers told us he was a perfectionist and had made himself ill from overwork; he'd been sent to some priests' convalescent home up in Canada. God only knows what the rest of the story was . . . or the true story.

"Shortly after my eleventh birthday the fathers decided to close the orphanage. We'd entered the era of foster parents and social workers and paperwork. I was adopted by the Schmidts. Ironically, they chose me over the bigger, stronger boys because word had gone 'round about the phenomenal job I'd done on the woods and they wanted a slave on their farm. After that came my seven years of hell on earth until I ran away. Ironically *again,* what got me through those seven years was my little whip and its transcendent pleasures and the voice of Father Mountjoy enjoining me to be tougher on myself than anyone else. The Schmidts could withhold my food, torture or kill any animal I unwisely showed affection for, beat me in front of my schoolfriends, work me till I dropped, yet legally own me as their son, but as long as I could whip myself into oblivion in the privacy of the woods, they couldn't touch the sacred and best part of me. That's how I experienced it.

As Father Mountjoy advised, I took God as my parent — even though for a while he got pretty confused with Father Mountjoy — and I became my own sternest disciplinarian. Before I enlisted in the Navy, I had my name legally changed from Adrian Schmidt back to Adrian Bonner, but the only birth certificate I possess still bears the name of Gerhard and Hansie Schmidt as my parents.

"I still pray for him. I don't know if he's still 'Father Mountjoy,' I don't know if he's still alive, I don't know if he's on that ledge in hell reserved for accomplices and abettors, looking down on all the boys he influenced. At a low time in my life, just before I abandoned my studies and went to Zurich, when I was still very caught up with Gnostic theories and fascinated by their concept of this world as the creation of a demiurge, while God bides his time on a higher level, waiting for us to look up and recognize him, I often found it comforting to speculate that hell was right now and Father Mountjoy and I were slinking along our ledge together bemoaning our ruined selves, while all the time our real Father waited for us to get sick of our sad little ledge so we would look up and He could stretch down his arms and lovingly welcome us home."

IV

Prayers

I could hear Tony coughing downstairs, a rattly smoker's cough like a defective car engine turning over and over but not quite firing. I lay listening in the dark, waiting for the present bout to subside, then the next round to start up. Did the monks who slept near him at the Abbey of the Transfiguration welcome the silence coming from his empty room? Or did they miss the customary hackings of their old brother? Tomorrow night, if he was still here, and I had a strong feeling he would be, I must remember to leave a pitcher of water and a glass next to his bed.

On another night, practically a lifetime ago, I had lain in the dark of my father's rectory and listened for the sounds of another stranger floating up from below. Madelyn Farley had been spending her one fateful overnight at our house, and my mother had stayed up late to talk to her old friend. The guest room in my father's rectory had been directly beneath my bedroom, and the duo of their voices, as much as the intervening silences, troubled me. I couldn't make out a word they were saying, but even as a child I must have recognized the tones and the rhythms of two people who hadn't had enough of each other. My mother's delighted peals of laughter exasperated me: what was that blunt, charmless person *saying* down below to make Ruth laugh? Why didn't my mother come upstairs to join my father, who had long ago gone to bed?

Now, lying in the dark of my own rectory, I tried to pray, but echoes and images from the day crowded upon the blank screen of my intentions: Kevin Dowd's nervous plaint, "How do we justify separating ourselves from this bothersome march?"; the departing red swirl of Grace Munger's cape, cutting off any further refusal from me; Tony's sharp little tongue sealing the handmade cigarette; Gus throwing her arms around me in the crypt, then being embarrassed by her display of emotion; the old monk's watery eyes as he surveyed his cozy room.

I had given up trying to fight these reruns from days when more things happened than I could absorb, or when too many enigmas taxed my limited powers of discernment. I allowed the leftovers to play themselves out, mutating into whatever they wanted to be next. Meanwhile I tried to stay connected to a quieter part of me who waited in the background for the cessation of all this outer business. After the cessation sometimes came lucidity, in which a different kind of communication could take place. More often it didn't come: the day's noises and pictures rolled on and on, I got sucked into the show, then would suddenly snap out of it with a jolt, caught red-handed in the midst of some self-serving (or equally extravagant self-defeating) reverie. Oftentimes I simply gave up, just signed myself off for the time being ("Yours truly, still stuck in my outer noise — but still yours").

When the desired communication did come, it frequently arrived from an unexpected direction or in a surprising form, which is why I had become more lenient with my shadow shows: breakthroughs had been known to mutate out of incidents in them.

Here, for instance — why? — came my father's rolling voice reciting snatches of Vaughan's poem "The Night,"

There is in God (some say)
A deep, but dazzling darkness . . .

. . . His knocking time; the soul's dumb
   watch,
When Spirits their fair kindred catch.

and with it the physical recall of his large, warm hand crowning my head as he knelt beside my bed each night and rendered to God an account of our day. His form of address was chatty, digressive, more often than not delivered in his self-deprecating mode, but he had a way of reckoning up events so that they were more than just the sum of their mundane happenings. It was as though he were refocusing them to meet God's wider-angled, longer-term perspective.

"Well, Lord," he might begin if he were doing the prayers with me tonight, "here we are on the eve of another Advent, and lots of things are on their way to us, some of them good, some of them bad, and in some cases we're not yet able to say which. Give us discernment wherever possible, and where *not* possible let us remember that we're in any event under your wing, and we're certainly reassured by *that*. Gus and Charles and young Jennifer rehearsed for tomorrow's wedding that will sacramentally combine their considerable forces and render each of them less alone. My Margaret has the wedding homily ready *and* her sermon for Sunday — she's not an old procrastinator like I was — and she was made happy this evening when Adrian remembered to kiss her. Though they've been through closer times together, he's still the one she wants, and she prays for the grace to take him as he is given to her.

"Now, this Millennium Birthday March for Jesus — well, the idea is inoffensive in itself, I guess, but why is the lady being so adamant to get everybody roped in behind her banner? That's usually symptomatic of someone on the power trail, and, oh me, what a can of worms *that* can turn into — I'll bet you've seen some dillies in your time, every variety of march from glorious to goriest — frequently an equal mixture of both — under someone's banner bearing your name.

"Of course, this is a relatively harmless local march — or is it? What's the point of it? What's the *real* point of it? And who is this Jesus they'll be marching for? The one who sat down at the table with sinners and social outcasts? Or a Jesus fashioned closer to their own desires, one who *would* see fit to cast the first stone? Can there be a successful march for conflicting Jesuses? One bunch saying, this is our boy and you'd better see him our way or you'll go to hell, another bunch saying, well, our fella's a lot different from yours, but for the sake of goodwill and liberality in this shaken community we'll stroll along with you and lift our voices in a few hymns and pretend he's the same man. Which side is in worse error? A toss-up, would be my guess. What would I have advised my parish? But in my time, there weren't all these marches for Jesus, though people took to the streets for other things. You could hardly get people to come to church or talk about God back in the secular sixties. Oh, we always had our evangelical harassers, I remember Nan MacGruder telling me how some Born Agains had tried to cut her off on the sidewalk downtown, demanding to know whether she'd found Jesus. 'I hadn't realized he was lost,' she said politely, and stepped around them. But, you see, Nan could have been shot in the face for that today.

"Tonight Margaret shelters a stranger under her roof. We're not yet apprised of the nature of this old monk's pilgrimage, but strangers and sojourners can bring us unexpected gifts. They have also been known to *remove* gifts from us — I lost my wife to an overnight houseguest, as you well know — but help us try and remember we are all, with our mixed and conflicting motives, members of your household and in your own good time you will sort us out and assign us to our rightful rooms. Until then, dear Lord, keep us generous and faithful and teach us to fear nothing but the loss of you."

Outside on the quiet street, a car slowed, idled for about fifteen seconds, then rumbled off. Had the driver stopped to read the Advent text and the "Visitors Welcome" on our $3,053 sign? Would this person show up at church on Sunday and, with who knew what expectations or former associations, slide cautiously into a pew not too far front?

Or was it the organizer of the Millennium Birthday March for Jesus, cruising back by the rectory to see whether I'd taken her "materials" out of the box yet?

This provoking image successfully routed

173

any further progress in prayer, and I switched on the lamp with an unclerical epithet, and unlatched her hefty envelope. Included were duplicates or updates of stuff I'd already had in previous mailings or seen on bulletin boards around town. There was the "Christian Manifesto for a Wounded Town" full-page ad, photocopied on eye-catching magenta paper this time, for those of us who might only have skimmed it in the *Balsam Bugle*'s black-on-white.

CHRISTIAN MANIFESTO FOR A WOUNDED TOWN

BY THE WATERS OF BABYLON WE SAT DOWN AND WEPT, WHEN WE REMEMBERED YOU, O ZION.
AS FOR OUR HARPS, WE HUNG THEM UP . . . (Ps. 137)

But, Brothers and Sisters of High Balsam, we are NOT exiled to Babylon.
We still LIVE HERE in Zion.
Babylonian elements may have leeched into Zion and contaminated our waters,
But we are NOT in captivity. Though many of us feel oppressed. With good reason.

Are you happy with your life?
Are you happy with your job? (Those of

you who still have jobs.)

Are you happy with the way your children are being educated in the local schools?

Can you remember a time when things were better here on top of God's beautiful mountain?

Then FOR THE LOVE OF CHRIST, take down your "harps that you have hung up," and come out on Saturday morning, December 18, 1999, two weeks before the NEW MILLENNIUM, and raise your banners and voices in song and declare your PERSONAL, FAMILIAL, and COMMUNAL rededication for OUR LORD AND SAVIOR.

Welcome Him into His new Millennium.

Invite Him back as King of your heart.

For He is on his way. Have no doubt about it.

"SURELY I COME QUICKLY." (Rev. 22:20)

Let us MARCH IN HIS HONOR and RESTORE HIM AS KING on our beautiful mountain. Let us raise our voices AS A COMMUNITY to proclaim renewed faith in ourselves AS HIS LOYAL SUBJECTS, who commit ourselves to live fully by the Word of the

Bible, and by the traditional morals and family values that have made us His people.

He will do the rest. *It is promised.* "I am come to send fire on the earth." (Lk. 12:49) "Be ye therefore ready . . . for the Son of man cometh at an hour when ye think not." (Lk. 12:40)

"Even so, come Lord Jesus." (Rev. 22:20)

COME AND LIFT UP YOUR VOICE IN PRAISE on Saturday, December 18! Reclaim what you have lost! Remake your community! Take charge of your life in His name!

Underneath this rousing document that had turned Dick Miller's Lutherans off was a five-page letter from Grace Munger to me, handwritten in a bold, loopy script on stationery from the High Balsam Inn. ("Traditional Southern Hospitality since 1923. National Register of Historic Places. 'Nineteen Rooms for Ladies and Gentlemen.' ")

Dear Reverend Bonner,
    After you had refused again this morning to allow your congregation to join us

in lifting up the Lord's name, I hung up the phone and straightaway took my pen and crossed off your church. Yes, I crossed All Saints High Balsam off my list.

I could clearly picture her striking her bold black line through our congregation.

"From such withdraw thyself," I said, quoting Paul's advice to Timothy concerning those puffed up with pride and destitute of the truth. I went on with my work. Organizing an entire Christian community into a successful act of public worship on the eve of the Third Millennium is no small job. There are the different church choirs to be staggered, they can't all sing the same hymns, they can't all be singing different hymns at the same time, either! Then there are the theme banners, they have to be planned and the designs effectively coordinated with one another. And there's the schedule of dancers and prayer leaders and the music at the rally and all the sound equipment. Parade routes have to be submitted in minute detail to the police department so they can control traffic.

When I was first asked by some folks who admired my father (the late Reverend Joel Munger of Free Will Baptist) to come back to High Balsam and organize this March, I flat out said no. As you must surely have heard by now, High Balsam does not contain happy memories for me. "But Grace, we need your organizing abilities," they told me. "There's been bad blood between too many factions up here, and a local person would have a hard time not being identified with one faction or another. Whereas you know the place but have been gone long enough to not be *of* it, and you have a reputation among the brothers and sisters throughout the state as a powerful witness for the Lord."

I said, "Let me pray about it," and that's exactly what I did. I was on my knees on the hard floor for one long night. At dawn the next morning I called the friends back and said, "Well, I guess I'll be coming to High Balsam." "So you prayed about it," they said. I said, "it was a *wrestling match,* I'm black and blue and slain in the Spirit. He won. And now if you'll excuse me, I have to go to bed and get some sleep."

He didn't wrestle with me this evening, but He softened my heart toward you, Reverend Bonner. Here is what happened. While I was speaking to Reverend Dowd on the phone, trying to get *him* to reconsider, I asked him what your

178

background was. I was trying to understand why you were being so inflexible about the March. He told me you were married to the chaplain of that alternative school that bought the old Eubanks house and that your late father had also been a minister up in Virginia! "Then we are both daughters of ministers of the Word," I said. Rev. Dowd promised me he would speak to you again about joining the March, and I hung up and then suddenly I found myself *writing back in* the name of your church over where I had crossed it out on my list. Now why in heaven's name did I do that? I asked. At that precise moment, the Lord's voice came out of the open grate — they gave me one of the larger rooms with a fireplace here at the Inn, though I don't light fires in it. The Voice from the grate said, and I quote verbatim: SHE AND YOU ARE SISTERS IN ME, AND I HOLD YOU ACCOUNTABLE FOR HER AND HER FLOCK.

Those were His exact words to me, Reverend Bonner. How can I, as your sister in Christ, do less than pass them on to you? How can I do less than exhort you and the members of All Saints High Balsam to join us and the rest of this wounded community in lifting up His name and preparing for the time to

179

come, when "we shall all be changed."

Grace be with you,
Grace Munger

P.S. As I will most likely be out when you call, Mrs. Fletcher at the Inn will take the message or tell you where I can be reached.

I read through this amazing composition several times. Aspects of it repelled me. My indignation was of course roused — but from someone "puffed up with pride" what else could you expect? — by all those rude red flags at the beginning. Starting off by calling someone "destitute of the truth," even when hiding behind Paul, who, some would feel, never quite shed his Pharisaic self-righteousness, was hardly a way to win someone over to your cause. (Also, I found her borrowing of Paul's characteristic sign-off, especially given her name, a little too much Grace to swallow.)

A touch more infuriating, but not without its comic side, was this business of "my refusing to allow" my congregation to join the march. For that, Grace Munger deserved to be a fly stuck on the wall when Lucinda Lord and several others got going on the subject of all the public swayings and slayings of the Spirit that had become so prevalent in the last decade. If I *were* to stand up in the pulpit and announce my disposition to join the march, inviting others to join me, I knew my independent-minded parishioners would have "allowed" *me* to do it (with a few raised eyebrows and a susurration of murmurings at coffee hour about their gifted young pastor trying out new ideas on behalf of the parish) and simply abstained, except possibly for the Freedgoods, from signing their names on the march sheet.

And then we came to the interesting matter (Dammit, Adrian, why aren't you ever around anymore at night when I need to talk these things out?) of Grace's relationship with the Lord.

Here I myself heard a voice, but it was only the all-too-familiar voice of my inner-critic, who didn't need a grate for an amplifier: "He speaks in whole sentences to her," my sardonic inner-critic said; "they *wrestle* together on the floor; whereas poor you couldn't even get in to see Him tonight. Perhaps you'd do better to spend a little more time on the floor yourself."

The crux of the aggravation was somewhere in here, and Adrian would have given it some conceptual focus. I'd never been much of a concept person, that's why I'd been mediocre in my philosophy courses. I needed all the anecdotes and parables and stories I could get to help me envision that middle ground where divine and human meet. Why is it, I would have asked Adrian, if he'd been beside me now, that I can read about Teresa of Avila falling off her mule into the mud and yelling at God, "If this is the way you treat your friends, no wonder you have so few!" and wholeheartedly believe they had an intimate connection going? And likewise have no trouble believing she did hear a voice say "Do not grieve, I will be your Living Book" after the Inquisition took away all her books? Yet when Grace Munger quotes the Lord's exact words to *her,* holding her accountable for me as her sister in Him, my flesh crawls. What makes me accept Teresa's God-voice as an authentic example of mystic intuition and causes me to reject Grace's voice as self-created emotional ventriloquism? Am I just being a snob? Why is it easier for people like me to accept the testimony of a sixteenth-century Spanish nun, softened and worn attractively smooth by time's distancings and translations, than the "witnessing" of this ferociously persistent fellow preacher's daughter and "sister in Christ" met on my own doorstep as recently as this evening?

But what intrigued me about Grace's package of "materials" was its odd mixture of fundamentalism and sophisticated manipulation techniques. She knew how to wield scriptural story to address local woes, she knew how to get under her audience's skin.

She was neither ignorant nor incoherent. The rallying call of her manifesto was squarely within the ancient tradition of the Prophet's call to repentance. And yet . . . and yet . . . and yet. Wasn't there something suspiciously swollen here, too, what Adrian's Jungians would call an inflation? Well, perhaps Jeremiah or John the Baptist would have been diagnosed as inflated by an archetype if they'd gone into analysis.

Did she really hear a voice coming out of the grate at the inn? If so, whose voice was it?

During Gus and Charles's canonically required sessions with me, Charles had told the story of his conversion at age fourteen. It was after he had gone to his first Jesus movie. Lying in bed that night, he became aware of a new sound inside his ears. *Crunch-crunch . . . crunch-crunch.* He knew it was Jesus walking on the gravel toward his crucifixion. Even after he learned that what he had heard that night was the sound of blood pumping through your ears when you lie deep in your pillow, he continued to hear Christ's footsteps in the gravel. The conversion, he said, had already taken, like a vaccination, however skeptical and scientific he was later to become.

What was the difference between Charles's *crunch-crunch* and Grace's Voice? Adrian would probably say that Charles had been able to integrate his unconscious God image and draw nourishment from it, whereas Grace was still projecting hers on an empty grate.

But by myself, through the medium of my own inner voice or the internalized voices of those I loved, I could get no further with these puzzles tonight. I was more than willing to accept the sound of the toilet flushing in Tony's downstairs bathroom as God's final word to me for the day.

V

The Night

All was dark and clear. Something unusual was abroad in this night. Another car patrolled our quiet street. If not Grace, then who? Someone else interested in us, someone who wanted to look in on us and change our lives in some way. The car slowed and turned into our driveway, idled with a murmuring of engine, as when people are extending their farewell, then switched off.

Now I knew something was going to change. This car was bringing back someone long wanted. I was partly myself and partly my father, but that seemed perfectly normal. I *was* partly my father, every child is. I knew that I was dreaming, and that he as part of me was dreaming in me, but for both our sakes I had to finish this dream. Because I knew whose car had pulled into our driveway and what two people were inside talking, and I knew that only one person was going to get out of that car, which was Madelyn Farley's silver Mustang, in which Ruth had driven away from us forever in 1972. I knew that the real Mustang was long gone and that I myself had watched Madelyn's coffin being lowered into the ground in Overlook, New York, but I also knew with an equal certainty that on this one special night it was going to be possible for Madelyn to return Ruth to us in the phantom car and for us to welcome her home for good.

She had entered the house now; I heard the faint jingle of her keys as the kitchen door opened, then closed softly behind her. How best to greet her so as not to stir her remorse and drive her away again? How best to compose ourselves so that she would stay unfrightened of the changes she had wrought on our lives by her long absence?

I lay rigid in the dark, afraid to move, my eyes fast shut, my heart thumping. I must keep perfectly still and breathe deeply; I must act convincingly asleep, so that she can enjoy full luxury of *repentance without recrimination.*

Her step was on the stair. Oh, keep me still in this dream until our faces are touching once more, under the cover of the forgiving darkness.

The steps are in the hallway, a floorboard squeaks, the knob of the bedroom door is slowly turning. Keep breathing the even breaths of the peaceful sleeper as she enters then shuts herself in. And now there are two sets of breathing in the darkness, my counterfeit peaceful ones and the other person's truer uneven ones, fast and slightly ragged from climbing stairs.

Then I go prickly all over because I'm not dreaming now. There *is* someone in the room with me. Why hadn't I listened to Gus and borrowed Pearl?

"Margaret, are you awake?"

"GOD!"

"No, only Adrian, I'm afraid."

I was so relieved to hear his voice and at the same time so vexed to have lost the dream that I let out a strange sound halfway between a groan and a sob.

"I didn't mean to frighten you."

"I was dreaming you were my mother coming back."

"Ah, poor girl. Sorry to disappoint you again." He sat down on my side of the bed and laid the back of his hand against my cheek. "You're so warm," he said admiringly.

"You're so *cold*. Your hand is freezing." Then I quickly grabbed his hand before he could interpret my remark as a complaint and pull it away.

"I've been running through swamps and woods, chasing a boy."

"Which one?"

"Chase Zorn."

"Chasing Chase," I murmured sleepily, rubbing his hand between my two.

"The stinker." He sighed dispiritedly.

"He hasn't done something too bad, I hope." Chase was Adrian's pet black sheep.

187

"He broke into the chapel and got at the wine again."

"Oh, no."

"Oh, yes. Only this time it wasn't just the evidence of his breath and the compassionate chaplain the only sniffer. Baxter Jefferson caught him red-handed. Having himself a solo cocktail party. He might have gotten away with it, if he hadn't lit the votive candle for 'atmosphere.' That's how Baxter caught him; he looked out of his bedroom window and saw the flickering red light in the sacristy and went over to check it out. And there was Chase, drunk as a sailor and using matching language."

"Oh, Adrian, I'm so sorry."

"So am I. Even though I know it was a rather pointed piece of acting out, a second offense is a second offense. The first time I warned him and he promised he'd never do it again. But now, if I don't ship him the same as I would anyone else, everyone loses."

I had never seen Chase, but felt closely connected to him through Adrian's interest and his many stories about the adopted child of Radford Zorn, the happy hometown theme-park mogul. Chase had begun his career of getting shipped from schools at the tender age of eight, and by age fourteen had six expulsions under his belt — one for each year. The charges ranged from "harmful influence on peers" to "insubordination and disruptive behavior" and, most recently, alcoholism. At fifteen, he'd been arrested and, thanks to a devoted psychiatrist's intervention, merely put on probation for vandalizing the house of his father's ex-girlfriend, stealing her car and driving it to Daytona Beach without a license, and totaling it on the return trip (she refused to press charges). The same week he was released from the hospital, he was arrested again for helping himself to a case of wine off an open delivery truck and kicking the driver, who ran after him (and did press charges). This time he was sentenced to a stint on a juvenile "work farm," with his father's enthusiastic approval, but rescued once again by the efforts of the devoted psychiatrist and remitted instead to the Menninger Clinic for three months of intensive treatment for alcoholism. The Menninger therapist knew about Sandlin's school and suggested to the father they try to get Chase into Fair Haven. "*You* can try, if you want to," Zorn had told the psychiatrist, who reported it to Adrian, "and I'll pay. I'll pay *you*, as I've been doing for far too long with no results, and I'll pay the school if they're stupid enough to take him, but that's all I'll do anymore for his sorry butt. This is the end of the line for me with that ill-tempered little Peruvian bastard. My wife at the time wanted to send him back the moment she saw him, and I wish we had.

Only I felt sorry for the little spic; he had fight in him, I liked that. Well, it was one of the few times I should have listened to her. And if he screws up at this last-ditch school, tell them just to send him on to the nearest prison. He's old enough to be in with the big losers now. And if you have any trouble getting the *prison* to take him, say I'll be glad to pay his room and board."

"Oh, Adrian, I'm really sorry," I repeated, rubbing his cold hands between mine.

"Well," he said with another sigh, "it's his pattern and I of all people should have been on the alert. And I bear some of the blame for it, as well."

"How can you say that? You've devoted more time and attention to that boy than anyone else."

"I did at first, when he came to us, but then I got overloaded with so much other stuff — schedules and spread sheets and faculty personalities and the search for a new headmaster — and it all changed. When I finally caught up with Chase tonight — or I should say when he finally let me catch up with him down in the swamp behind the ball field — he treated me to a brand-new repertoire of maledictions and would have hit me if I hadn't grabbed him first. When I was force-marching him back to the school, I tried to calm him down with a humorous comment about the sound of our wet shoes squish-

squishing along together, and he said, 'I hope you catch pneumonia from this and die.' Then he added, 'I hope we both die.' "

"You didn't deserve that."

"No, but I can see it from his side. I gave myself, then I withdrew myself. After all, I've had it done to me."

"If you're thinking of Father Mountjoy, it's hardly the same thing. You've given Chase hours and hours of your best. You went for all those walks with him, you taught him how to tolerate an environment of peace and safety, you taught him to have *conversations*, you let him know you liked him. You got him interested in the liturgy —"

"Ah, yes. Here I was, training him to be my sacristan, and guess what he was drinking out of when Baxter found him tonight?"

"I hope not a chalice?"

"Not just any chalice. The Sandlin chalice that the bishop consecrated when he was here and that we were planning to use for Christmas."

The Sandlin memorial chalice, hand-crafted by a local silversmith, set with local gems, had been Adrian's own gift to the school.

"He really wanted to hit you where it hurt, didn't he?"

"Well, that's his trademark, isn't it? He finds your soft spots and then uses them against you. The father's girlfriend who let

191

him stay at her house and drive her car gets her house trashed and her car smashed. And you remember that composition of his, don't you? The one I brought home to show you."

"Oh, God, yes." I was still rubbing his hands, though they were warm now.

How proud Adrian had been of that composition. "Look, Margaret, the boy has used his intelligence and creativity to smoke out his *own* weakness, for a change." The assignment had been, "Write about a memorable person in your life, either using the character sketch or story form." Chase, choosing the latter, had written about an elderly black woman who, because of her reputation for handling bad children, had been hired by a rich man to take care of his "bad little boy." She first turned the rich man down, saying her babysitting days were over, but he "kept shoving money at her" until he forced her out of retirement. By her intimidating presence, she has successfully hidden the fact that she has gone blind, and when she comes to the rich man's house, she takes the boy's hand and makes him give her a slow and thorough tour of the house, room by room, corner by corner, describing every object and piece of furniture, complete with the history of it.

This gets them through many days. The days turn into years, and when the boy becomes old enough to realize her secret, he colludes with her in order to keep her with him. Until, one inevitable day, she crosses him, they have a battle of wills, and he betrays her and gets her fired. "She loved him with blind love," the story concludes, "and in her case it really was blind. After she left, the awful boy was sent off to school, where he continued to excel in his awful ways. Sometimes he missed her."

"You're right," I told Adrian. "It's the same pattern all over again. Pulling the rug out from under someone who cares about him. But hasn't he run out of schools? If you ship him —"

"There's no if about it," Adrian said bitterly. He reclaimed his warmed-up hands and rubbed them slowly up and down his face. I could hear the sandpaper scratch of stubble. "All that remains to decide is when. I ought to get him out of the school by tomorrow. Meanwhile, he's under house arrest over at Coach's place till I can get in touch with his father. After the great chase, I went back to the room to change shoes and that's when I found your message on my machine. That's all this day needs, I thought; I lose a promising boy because I'm never around anymore, and now what if this houseguest is a lunatic or a felon disguised as a monk and I come home tomorrow morning and find Margaret murdered in our bed because I'm never at home anymore? So I phoned Baxter and told him we had an unexpected visitor and I was needed at home."

"You are needed, and I'm glad you're here. But I hope you took time to change your socks as well as your shoes."

"Thank you, I did. I can't afford to catch pneumonia and die, even if it would satisfy Chase. There's too much to do if we're going to keep the school going without Sandlin."

"Plus a few people would miss you. And our houseguest isn't a lunatic or a felon. He's one of those Transfiguration Benedictines from Father Cecil's monastery in upstate New York. Father Cecil just recently died, Tony said."

"Tony?"

"He's a rough-cut old lay brother who wants you to just call him Tony. He rolls his own cigarettes, and Gus and I are sure he dyes his hair, but he's funny and kind of sweet. I'm not certain what the purpose of his trip is, other than seeing the country without spending anything on motels, but I'm sure it doesn't include murdering anyone. But I'm glad you came home. Why don't you come to bed?"

"I think I will. Chase has done me in properly. I'll go get my pajamas."

"No, don't get them."

"Well . . . then I won't."

Now, this kind of banter goes on between married folk all the time, but it was a first for

194

us. During six years of marriage I had never asked my husband to forget about his pajamas, and he had never forgotten them. Each couple develops its own style of intimacy, which is nobody else's business. I wouldn't be telling this much now if it weren't a vital part of this tale, and even this much may be too much for the one I am remembering it for.

Anyway, for the first time in our marriage, my husband came to bed naked because I had asked him to. If I had been thoroughly awake, I would never have suggested it. The forward approach just wasn't part of my bedroom persona. And certainly in view of our recent difficulties, it would have been the last thing I'd have thought of doing: he might interpret it as a demand for something he couldn't give. But thinking had little part in this. It just came out of my mouth, like the thing about being naked in the middle of our murals on our wedding night. On both occasions I may well have spoken directly from the desire to have not just his body naked but himself stripped to his essentials, smoothed of all those scratchy barnacles of self-doubt and self-defense.

And now, because a boy had blighted his chances and run off into the night, and an old man with a suitcase had shown up out of nowhere and I had invited him to stay at our house, here I was holding a naked Adrian, wrapping my warm feet around his cold ones, telling him about the sudden manifestation of the old monk in the crypt and Grace Munger's larger-than-life presence and her red cape and daunting persistence. It was as though we had lain casually entwined like this every night since the night of the murals in Madelyn's loft, telling stories and in the meantime absentmindedly taking incrementally larger liberties with each other as we conversed. During all my worrying about how and when and whether we'd ever get together again, I had neglected to imagine we might slip back together as naturally as a dislocated joint slipping back into place, followed by an ardor more straightforward than either of us had been capable of before. I had neglected to imagine what it might be like between two people who, whether from relief on the part of one that the other has not been murdered in her bed, or from a drowsiness on the part of the other that frees her from fear of his rejection, are able to let go of their respective reserves and complexities and simply express their appreciation of each other through their bodies.

Anyway. Enough.

Then we slept so profoundly that when the noise drilled into us, it took me some time to identify it as coming from an object called a telephone, on my side of the bed, and then it

196

took a while longer to recollect just where and what nature of thing I was and how it had come to be that Adrian was not out at the school but pressed warmly up against me without either of us wearing nightclothes.

"It's Grace Munger wanting to see if you've capitulated about the march," Adrian mumbled into my hair.

But it was a nurse calling from the ICU at Bruton Memorial Hospital, trying to reach Reverend Bonner.

Still thick with sleep, I passed the receiver across to Adrian.

"Hello? I see —"

Please don't let Chase Zorn have committed suicide, I was now awake enough to think.

"— oh, that's my wife you want. Yes, I'm one, too, but she's the rector of All Saints High Balsam. I know, it can be confusing." He handed the receiver back to me. "I'm afraid it's you they're after."

A retired couple from Ohio taking the leisurely scenic route across the mountain down to their winter home in Florida. They stop for dinner at the Treadwell Lodge, are about to set off again for Mountain City, where they have reservations for the night, when he collapses in the parking lot. Rescue Squad arrives promptly, shocks his heart into action again, gets him to Balsam Memorial, where signs look hopeful then less hopeful on the

197

monitor. They're Episcopalians and the wife wants a priest. Father Dowd at St. Francis-in-the-Valley is the nearest to the hospital, but the nurse can only get his machine. So she tries the only other Episcopal church, fifteen miles up the mountain.

I got out my clericals and went into the bathroom to dress. When I came back, the light was on and a groggy Adrian, in trousers and sweater, was sitting in a chair lacing his shoes.

"What are you doing?"

"I thought I'd drive you," he said.

An offer I would have jumped at ordinarily. But when he raised his head after tying his shoe, I saw how drained and exhausted he looked.

"I'd much rather think of you here in bed, keeping it warm for when I get back."

"But you know how these things can drag on into the morning."

"All the more reason for you to stay here. Somebody has to be here for Tony."

"Ah, Tony. I forgot about him. Poor Margaret, you look so sleepy. And you've got the wedding tomorrow. Well, I'll walk over with you to the sacristy to get the oil stock."

"I'll take the pyx, too, in case he can swallow the host."

"What about your chewing gum?"

"New pack in the car." For some reason, chewing gum gave me added confidence when driving mountain curves at night.

"How about quarters for the coffee machine?"

"Now those I could use."

He plucked out coins from his stash on top of the dresser. "Take all my quarters," he said with a meaningful look, capsizing a handful of them into my jacket pocket with sweet jingling clinks.

It was a road I knew very well, the two-lane highway from High Balsam to Bruton Memorial, having driven it in summer's Smoky Mountain downpours, October's soupy fogs, winter's snows and ice storms, and spring's mudslides. I knew where the hairpin curves came, where the "surprise" fogs were most likely to spring up suddenly from a gorge below, where the steepest grades and compensatory escape pits for runaway vehicles were, and where the little blue phone boxes waited faithfully to convey your helplessness. The first seven or eight miles down were the problem, if there was going to be one — but tonight's drop in temperature made for one of those clear nights of such radiance that trees cast moon shadows along the road.

Nevertheless I was loyal to my chewing gum. For the first few miles out of High Balsam the reception was so good that the radio picked up a classical music station in

Chicago. A two-piano concerto filled the car with rhapsodic sounds that prompted replays of Adrian's and my reunion. I was hoping the station would stay strong until I could learn the name of the work, but it was probably just as well on these curves that it didn't. As soon as static began to scrabble at the edges of the music, I punched on to the next station, where the gruesome voice of Clampitt's own Whispering Dan effectively jolted me out of any more hazardous reveries.

A former tobacco auctioneer who had been Saved and called to prophesy after his radical laryngectomy, Dan broadcast his nightly warnings of the Coming End via an implanted valve between his esophagus and trachea and a microphone pressed against his throat. His amplified new voice had the incantatory spookiness of robotic engineering. Whenever he had to stop and force air through the valve, which was frequently, he filled in the pauses with eerie browsings on his electric organ: snatches from familiar hymns strung together with his own menacing tremolos and chords. He had a loyal following among the disgruntled and the insomniac, as well as late night drivers like myself who were drawn in by the sheer creepiness of his sound effects.

". . . it's all going according to plan, good buddies . . . fulfilled prophecies kicking up all around us like flying gravel . . . the night air is swollen and foul with the devil's done deals . . .

". . . Why, no, Dan, you say . . . it's a beautiful moonlit night up here in the Smokies . . .

". . . Yes, my friends, but it's slap dark and stinking in the spirit world . . . *filthy* invisible things are abroad in this western Carolina night . . .

". . . Satan's infected . . . looking for an opening into your weak and sinful heart . . . like the plagues that have already carried off so many of our unclean . . .

". . . Your own Dan here, he played host in his heart to Satan . . . and lived to repent and testify . . . God gave him a second wind and a second voice . . . God speaks to you now through Dan's shriven voice when I say to you: repent, good buddies, the end is at hand.

". . . Regain *your* immunity NOW . . . and stay awake with Whispering Dan and watch for the beautiful end . . . when Satan's infected will be zapped like bugs in God's all consuming flame . . . and the rest of us will be taken up and clothed in glory . . ."

Flying gravel, "the infected," and the "immune"; Jesus as Grace Munger's personal trainer, night-wrestling her to his purposes on the floor, God as Bug-Lite, zapping his foes: regardless of what crackpot ideas fueled these self-appointed ministers, anyone in the preaching business had to concede them their striking images.

Safely down the worst curves, I prowled the airwaves for more music and intercepted a late-night interview program in which an affable-sounding man was explaining why he had called something *An Evening Gone*. Curious to learn who this assured, intimate voice belonged to, I stayed tuned.

"Well, what first appealed to me about it was its evocative sound — *An Evening Gone* — because this is an evocative work. It's a form of memoir . . . my first try at a memoir, if you really want to know the truth."

A writer.

The interviewer commented on the "memoir epidemic" of the past few years. "And do you tell all?" he asked sardonically.

"Well, I do and I don't," hedged the man with a soft laugh. "But before we go on to that, let me finish answering your question about the title, *An Evening Gone*." A person used to being interviewed, who knew how to take control. "I borrowed the phrase from the well-known hymn, 'O God, Our Help in Ages Past . . .'"

" 'O God, our help in *a*-ges past . . .' " the interviewer intoned in a facetious off-key. "I know it well. My dad was an elder in the Presbyterian Church. My kid brother and I were dragged out of bed every Sunday morning, rain or shine. . . ."

The man laughed obligingly, but continued right on: "The fourth verse of the hymn, as you probably remember, begins:

> *'A thousand ages in thy sight*
> *Are like an evening gone . . .'* "

His own voice lifted into song, true and clear, flirting at the edges of countertenor. A trademark, evolved from his teenage adoration of Aaron Neville and adapted with great advantage to his own better-trained voice. I had heard him sing this hymn many times; we had sung it together in his car. Ben MacGruder was the man being interviewed on the late-night program. He was a bit on the young side to have written a memoir, but then, he was a popular singer and probably had stories to tell about other popular figures he had met.

"That's on the new video album, too, what you just sang," the interviewer said. He paused to remind his listeners that his guest was Ben MacGruder.

A new album, then. Good for you, Ben, I thought magnanimously. Seven years had gone by since our last encounter, when he had told me I would be burying myself by marrying Adrian, and I could feel happy in his good fortune. How confident he sounded. I even found it in myself to wonder what his life was like now.

"Yes, I begin with the unaccompanied hymn against a background of sky and cirrus clouds. You know, the kind of sky that's been doing the same thing for thousands of years. The long-term view. The instrumentals don't come in until we focus in on the personal scene, an Easter egg hunt in the early 1970s."

"Where the boy falls hopelessly in love with the preacher's daughter." The interviewer chuckled allusively. "And it goes on from there, doesn't it?"

"Yes, their love story is a kind of Dante-Beatrice thing. He falls in love with a child — he's also a child in this case. Only, unlike Dante and Beatrice, their love is later consummated. But ultimately she spurns him. But . . ." Now it was Ben's turn to chuckle allusively. ". . . hopefully, he has turned it into art. At one point she tells him to save all his images for his songs, and he does just that. Only I've tried to put the experience into a millennial setting. *An Evening Gone* is my personal story, my 'love-memoir' if you like, but it's just as much about how art can give you back what you've lost if you're willing to play around with time and look at the long-term view. For instance, the final song on the album is a replay of their love story, but this time I've set it in ancient Egypt. And this time the boy gets the girl. I spent my formative years in Egypt, my parents were in the diplomatic corps, and I had this Nubian babysitter, about eight feet tall, who used to sleep outside my door at night. The last song on the album is a combination of two Mahasi wedding songs I learned from him. The first one celebrates the beauty of the bride and the generosity and bravery of her tribe, and the second describes the groom's courageous personality and character. So, in a larger sense the album has a happy ending."

"If you're willing to go back to ancient Egypt to get her," said the interviewer.

"Well . . ." Ben laughed ruefully. "What other choice did I have?"

"*Was* there a preacher's daughter in your life, am I allowed to ask?"

"You're allowed, but for discretion's sake I'll just say I had my Beatrice all right, and it all started at a children's Easter egg hunt."

"And did she later spurn you?"

"Oh, definitely. Yes."

"And, tell me, do you feel vindicated now that you've transformed the experience into art?"

"Well, I'm not sure vindicated is really the point here. But why don't we go ahead and listen to the title song and let it convey its own mood?"

"Okay, Ben MacGruder. Here we go. The title song from your new 'memoir' album, *An Evening Gone*."

"Easter shadows on a lawn,
Children of an evening gone
We ran and plundered

205

Filled our baskets — All but you:
The preacher's daughter.
You turned and walked away
You — the only one I wanted
Ever since that evening gone . . ."

It went on. Ben's recorded voice accompanied the preacher's daughter, now a middle-aged preacher herself, down the moonlit curves to the mountain hospital where a man lay dying, or not dying. I heard the words of the song, though not all of them. My thoughts and feelings were all over the place. Mostly — except for some lines that made me cringe ("You took me as your lover, you embraced all of me, but you don't like to be reminded of *that* evening gone") and some others that made me bristle ("You always went looking for the absent and unseen, but when you planned to wed a shadow, I asked, 'What can this mean?' ") — it flowed along, a better than average song with a nostalgic melody and a story line like country music always had. It was rendered with more purity and range than the average pop vocalist.

But by the end of the song, which was also the end of the interview, I was feeling a lot less magnanimous. Every time Ben told the story about his Egyptian babysitter, the poor Nubian shot up another six inches in height. However else he had might have improved, Ben was still a wanton exaggerator.

And was his evasion of the preacher's daughter question really a sign of gentlemanly discretion, or was he just saving juicier revelations for a prime-time interview? I'd have to get the album and subject myself to the rest of it in private. If there was worse to come, I wanted to know about it before Adrian's students and the teenagers of my parishioners did.

If Harriet MacGruder and I had still been in close touch, I could have found out more from her. But in a phone conversation just before my marriage, we had fallen out over the silliest thing.

She had been baiting me, in her usual Harriet-way, this time about my choosing to take Adrian's name. Having "kept" hers when she married Georgie Gaines, she was going on about this being yet another symptom of my self-obliterating intentions, meanwhile preening over her own "gesture of independence" until finally I had enough and pointed out that it was no more independent to keep your father's name than to take your husband's, and, if she really believed independence was a matter of what you called yourself, then the truly independent gesture on her part would be to give herself an entire new name, devoid of all parental input. Harriet hated to lose an argument. But that wasn't what we were fighting about and we both knew it. I had been maid of honor in her wedding and I wasn't inviting her to mine. Though she had been archly "understanding" when I explained Adrian and I were having a private chapel wedding at the seminary, I knew she harbored a grudge. But if I had invited her, what excuse could I have given for not inviting her brother? It had been, as my father used to say about messy implications, a can of worms, and one I wanted left unopened.

We continued to communicate, but in a frostier sort of way. Her medical residencies, my ordinations as deacon and priest, the death of her grandmother, my new rectory address in High Balsam, her pathology appointment to the Disease Center in Atlanta: such milestones were exchanged in casual Christmas notes. A proud sister's references to baby brother's burgeoning career were periodically dropped, but never any personal news of Ben, which I considered tactful of her.

Will I never be allowed to put my Ben-mistake behind me? I was thinking irritably, still under the miasma of the interview, as I drove through the gates into the parking lot of Bruton Memorial Hospital.

Then the disquiet was compounded by a painful parallel that was just surfacing. Here we go again! *Another* person from the past using my life and my family's life as raw material for art.

It flared up like the stab of an old forgotten toothache: the hurt and indignation my father and I had suffered when Professor LaFarge, fresh from a cultural jaunt to Manhattan, walked into Daddy's rectory with news of Madelyn Farley's religious travesty based on liturgical details innocently provided by my father some years before. And then Professor LaFarge had handed over the program of the performance itself, with its poisonous program note in which Daddy was portrayed by Madelyn as a nameless obtuse muse of a clergyman who tells a trivial story about goose feathers as he drives with her to the morgue to claim his wife's body. When Daddy had gone to England to bring my mother's remains home, he *did* drive Madelyn to the morgue and he *had* told a story about an old lady who had once given him goose feathers for a pillow when he was serving as a curate in England, but there had been more to it than that: he had been trying to spare Madelyn pain as they drove along the route where my mother was so recently killed.

But Madelyn had left that whole side of it out of her program note, either because it didn't serve her purposes or because she could be very obtuse herself when it came to recognizing genuine acts of kindness in other people. Nevertheless, my self-punishing father had kept that odious program in his desk drawer till he died.

And now what unwelcome goose feathers awaited *me* in the rest of Ben's "memoir" album?

VI

Widow

A lanky, drooping silhouette in jeans and anorak dipped and lurched erratically across the parking lot of Bruton Memorial Hospital. I was on the alert to do some self-protective zigzagging myself when he suddenly lifted his head and the amber glow from the sodium vapor floodlight revealed not a menacing drunk but the gaunt, bushy-bearded countenance of Gus's bridegroom. Crumpled papers and empty containers dangled from his spidery long fingers.

"Dr. Charles! You're out late."

"So are you, Preacher Margaret. What's going on? I just saw Father Dowd scurrying down the hall with *his* little black holy kit."

"Oh, great. Which means I've driven down the mountain purely for the drive."

"Is it someone we know?"

"No, a retired couple from Ohio passing through. He had a C.A. at the Treadwells' lodge. The ICU nurse could only get Kevin's machine so she called me as a backup."

He saw me eyeing his stash and laughed. "I know. I try and restrain myself. I tell myself, Tye, this is not your bailiwick, this is not your clinic — you can't go around tidying up the whole damn world. But then I just can't resist that one nasty fast-food wrapper, and that squashed soda can over yonder with the dangerous edge — and next thing I know I've got my hands full of debris."

He pronounced it "*day*-bree."

"What else besides trash collecting brings you out in the early hours of your wedding morning?" I asked him.

"I just hospitalized a patient with Rocky Mountain spotted fever. It generally responds to tetracycline or sometimes goes away all by itself, but Uncle Cratis is going on ninety-eight and I didn't want to chance it turning into pneumonia or heart failure. So when night clinic was over, I brought him on down myself — to simplify matters."

I knew from Gus that Charles often shepherded his more reluctant insuranceless patients through the humiliating labyrinths of signing in at the emergency desk, a benevolence that he modestly downplayed as "simplifying matters." Shortly before his ex-wife decamped, she told Charles she had thought she was marrying a *physician,* not a backwoods do-gooder.

"Isn't it pretty late in the year for Rocky Mountain spotted fever?"

"Not when you've been leading hunting parties through the underbrush over Thanksgiving."

"When you're going on ninety-*eight?*"

"My daddy could still unload a refrigerator from a truck all by himself when he was way up in his seventies and wearing a truss. Some of these old string beans are tough as nails."

"Speaking of that, we've got a tough-looking eighty-year-old monk spending the night at the rectory. He walked from the bus station carrying a heavy suitcase."

"No kidding?"

"Gus and I were down in the crypt this evening when he suddenly just appeared."

"Is that so? I've never met a monk."

"You might, at your wedding. Gus invited him, if he's still here, and I'm pretty sure he will be. Well, I'd better go on up to the ICU, though Father Dowd's no doubt rendered me superfluous by now."

"Shame to be dragged out of your warm bed for nothing."

"I told Adrian to keep it warm for me. He wanted to drive me himself but I wouldn't let him. He'd been out chasing an angry boy through the swamp and was wiped out." I ducked my face out of the light, embarrassed. It had sounded like an announcement that I'd been to bed with my husband. Then I had to remind myself that Charles didn't know I'd revealed anything out of the ordinary.

"Are they still looking for a new headmaster?"

"Yes, but nobody can replace him, Adrian says."

"What I don't understand is why Adrian doesn't just go ahead and run the school himself. Delegate the gruntwork to others."

"He thinks he has to do everything himself or it won't get done."

"Well, I've been there, too. I was the same way myself until I took that leave of absence from the clinic. Nobody could do it but me. Trouble was, I did it right all day and saw that everyone else did; then, come nighttime, I'd get fall-down drunk at home. And when I came back from being dried out, all kinds of things *had* gone to hell in my absence. I was looking at a patient's folder, and I said, 'Your last cholesterol test was fantastic, Minnie. Your HDL is up and your LDL is way down.' I read her the numbers. 'You must really have stuck to the diet we worked out before I left,' I said, 'congratulations!' 'Doc,' she says, shaking her head, 'That report's someone else's.' Well, I looked again and sure enough it *was* someone else's. Stapled into her file. 'Min, you're right,' I said. Then I started to go into orbit like the old days. 'Dammit to hell, did they do *anything* properly while I was gone?' And she looks at me, real pleased with herself, and says, 'Well, Doc, I knew it had to be wrong, because I didn't do a single one of those things you told me to.' That's when it finally and truly hit me, Margaret, that I could only do so much and I better be content with that."

He started laughing, standing there in the parking lot with both hands full of other people's trash, and so did I. "I wish you'd tell Adrian that story," I said.

Going up in the hospital elevator, I tried to rid myself of my annoyance with Kevin Dowd for being out when he was wanted and then beating me to the scene. The Episcopalian tourist from Ohio would either be still alive or not. By now Kevin would have taken care of the anointing or the appropriate prayers of commendation. Unless he had been at the hospital on some other mission of his own and was unaware of the message waiting at home on his machine. But given the smallness of this hospital — twenty-four beds for acute care, seventy for long-term — this seemed unlikely. Word would travel quickly between units, between floors. ("Lord, I wish that reverend lady from High Balsam would get on down here . . . my patient's sinking fast." "But Rita was on her break just now and she saw Father Dowd getting coffee out of the machine downstairs." "You mean he's here in the hospital? Phone down to dispensary and tell them to step across the hall and grab him.")

In either case, there was still the wife. Spouses were often in dire need of care themselves. During my CPE at St. Luke's, another

215

seminarian and I once held an old man steady for twenty minutes so he could stand and howl after his wife was pronounced dead. Another time at St. Luke's — I wasn't present for this one, but heard about it when I came on duty — a woman, after being told that her husband hadn't made it through surgery, put her head down in her lap and sat very still; it took the doctors a while before they realized she had suffered cardiac arrest and died.

When I reached the ICU, I was met by the nurse who had phoned. "I'm sorry to have brought you all this way for nothing, Reverend Bonner. We just didn't know what else to do. Father Dowd arrived a few minutes ago and he went on and did the last rites. Mr. Britt didn't make it."

"I'm sorry to hear that."

"He's been gone close to an hour now. The nurses had left the wrappings open for you, but then, like I say, Father Dowd showed up and took care of everything. Someone from Grover's will be over shortly to take the body back to the funeral home for cremation. Such a nice lady, it's a shame. They traveled with copies of their living wills and burial instructions. She had all the papers in her pocketbook. I wish more of our elderly tourists would be as practical."

"Where is Mrs. Britt now?"

"She went down with Father Dowd to that little waiting room next to the morgue. She wanted to stay with the body until Grover's came."

"I'll go join them."

"He was hoping you would, but said not to feel you had to, if you wanted to get back up the mountain. He felt bad about going ahead when you were already on your way, but Mrs. Britt wanted to go on and get it done. Like I say, she seems a real nice lady, but she's one of the cool, efficient ones. Of course, they're the ones that sometimes fall apart later, but at least we don't have to pick up the pieces while they're here."

Kevin Dowd, clerical collar peeking above a fuzzy brown crew neck that made him look like a friendly teddy bear, was leaning forward in his chair, gesturing to a poised little woman in a stylish gray pantsuit and white turtleneck who sat straight as a queen under a cloud of white hair, attending from the adjacent sofa. He was in profile, but she was facing the open door of the little waiting room next to the morgue, and as I approached down the hall I saw her take me in with a practiced sweep. When Kevin saw me, he leapt up and fell all over himself with apologies. After he'd spoken to me on the phone earlier in the evening, he'd suddenly felt a crying need to escape from his pastoral burdens and had burned rubber down to Clampitt Tech, where he still counseled part-time in their vocational program, in time to catch the second half of the Lady Riveters' basketball game against the Mountain City Valkyries.

"I'm a devout fan of the Riveters. Those girls are just fiendishly good, they blasted the Valkyries 95–65. Then I got home and found the message from the ICU. Oh, and by the way, a bulletin from our friend, Grace Munger. She left a message that you were sending some monk friend of yours to march in her parade."

"Inaccurate bulletin all 'round. The monk is only passing through town, and I've only just met him."

"Oh, really. And here I was thinking, how clever of Margaret, I wish I had a monk friend to send out to the front lines and keep both sides happy! And then when I got to the ICU, I'm sorry to say Mr. Britt was gone, and though they were expecting you any minute, *Helen* here" — he indicated the queenly lady on the sofa — "said I should go ahead —" He broke off with an agitated wave of his hands.

"That's fine," I said. "A priest is a priest." My ire was flashing red at Grace Munger's blatant misrepresentation of our sidewalk exchange, but right now was hardly the time to pursue it.

I offered my hand to the widow. "I'm Margaret Bonner, from All Saints High Balsam. I'm very sorry your husband didn't make it."

"Well, I am, too," she replied with a strange upbeat little lilt. Her hand was soft and well-cared-for. "And I'm sorry you came all this way on our behalf for nothing."

"Oh, I wonder if anything is ever for nothing. Don't you think it all gets used up eventually? But since I am here, isn't there something I can do for you?"

"The Treadwells have a room waiting for her back at their lodge," Kevin said. "And Helen's stepson will be coming in by 'copter from Charlotte airport tomorrow, about midday. That's all been taken care of. Of course I've already told Helen I'm more than happy to drive her back up to Treadwells' and get her settled in, but since you've come all this way, Margaret, and it's on your route home, maybe you'd like to do the honors." He made it sound like he was relinquishing a treat. "That is, unless you need to get home." He peeled back a furry sleeve and consulted his watch. "Grover's ought to be here any minute now."

"I don't mind waiting." I sat down in the other chair. "I'll be happy to take you back to the lodge," I told Helen Britt, and realized I meant it. There was something about her that piqued my interest.

"Thank you." A formal dip of the feathery-cut white head. "I accept."

While we waited, Kevin tirelessly defended us against any threat of silence.

219

". . . they're more like *warriors,* those girls . . . the looks on their *faces* when they're charging in for the kill. Most of the Riveters came to Tech on basketball scholarships, so it's more than just a varsity sport for them . . . it's their livelihood . . . their ticket out of their mountain poverty . . ."

Helen Britt, smiling vaguely in the direction of his chatter, appeared content to sit in the windowless basement lounge with its little artificial Christmas tree decorated with tinsel and ornaments but no lights, waiting for the undertaker. The ICU nurse was right, she was a cool number. My father, distinguishing between types of grieving, used to quote Emily Dickinson: "Safe despair it is that raves — Agony is frugal." Could Helen Britt's reserve be a sign of frugal agony?

Grover's came soon after — Bob Grover himself: faultlessly attired in black overcoat, suit and tie, shoes gleaming like mirrors, every silver hair in place. He brought his air of authority with him, and also his own brand of pastoral skills. I'd become an admirer of his while serving my six-month curacy under Father Satterwhite at St. Francis-in-the-Valley, after Adrian and I had first arrived here and I was still to be ordained. Bob Grover was held in great esteem by the local clergy. As soon as Bob's overcoat whisked around the open door of the lounge, Kevin shut down in mid-sentence about the Lady

Riveters and stood up to shake his hand. Bob's dignity wore off on people.

The undertaker exchanged personal greetings with Kevin and me, introduced himself to the widow, informing her that he'd already spoken to her son Bill who had phoned from Cincinnati, sat down beside her on the Naugahyde sofa, asking her permission first, and turned himself over to her completely. It was something to watch how smoothly they swept off together into the business at hand.

"We were prepared, of course," Helen Britt told Bob Grover in her dry little lilt. "Some might even say we were overprepared. Paul had had two major heart attacks, and I've had some health setbacks of my own, but we decided just to go on the way we'd been going and not sit home waiting for the other shoe to drop."

"Much better," agreed Bob Grover, "to die living than to live dying."

"I'm glad you understand. Now here . . ." She slid some folded papers out of her black envelope purse and separated them on her lap. ". . . here is his living will, which we won't need anymore — though I'll certainly hang onto mine . . ." A brief ironic smile. ". . . and here are his burial instructions, which you may want to have on file, even though you and Billy have arranged all about the cremation and shipping of the ashes."

"If only more people," said Bob Grover,

sweeping his glance over the document approvingly, "would follow your example and get their wishes down on paper ahead of time! Your son says you two thought of everything. All that's left for him to do, he says, is fly down here and escort you home."

"Billy helped us think of lots of those things; he's a fine attorney. He's my stepson, actually, but he's been very good to me. You won't mind, will you, Mr. Grover, if I step next door with you when you take the body away? There was a little ritual of mine I observed all through our marriage: I always watched Paul out of sight whenever he went away."

"But, you know, Mrs. Britt, you could ride with us back to the funeral home, and I could run you on up to Treadwells' in my own car afterward. It would be my pleasure."

"That's very kind of you, but I've already accepted a ride with the Reverend Bonner. She's waited here on my account."

"Please don't mind about that," I said. "Whatever feels best for you."

"That's right, Helen," said Kevin, "we want *you* to be comfortable."

"I'm quite comfortable with our present arrangements," Helen Britt assured us. "I'd just like to say good-bye to Paul here at the hospital, since it's the last place we went together. So, Mr. Grover, if I could go with you to that room next door and watch you take

222

Paul's body away — if you'll indulge me in this whim."

"It's a very *understandable* request," replied Bob Grover, after the slightest hesitation. "Let's go and see what we can do." The undertaker seemed suddenly a little sad, either from having his offer of the ride rejected or because, as a recent veteran of a very acrimonious divorce, he found himself touched by Helen Britt's precise last ritual and whim.

"Mr. Grover was so accommodating. I put him to some trouble, I'm afraid," said Helen Britt, walking beside me to the car. A large red plastic bag with the High Balsam Memorial Hospital logo bumped against her leg as she walked, and I could hear the shiftings and jinglings of her late husband's belongings moving around inside. I remembered the sweet clink of Adrian's coins falling into my pocket and the way he had said, "Take all my quarters," like an added wedding vow, and this led to the unwelcome image of myself carrying away a plastic bag like this some night.

"Paul would have liked Mr. Grover," continued Helen Britt. "The reason we were away so long — what should I call you? What do they call you at your church?"

"Most of them call me Pastor Margaret. It's a form just coming into use in our church that we all feel comfortable with. Though one

223

old lady who didn't like me at first made a point of calling me 'Mother' for a while. One time a little boy who was visiting called me Father — because of the vestments, I guess. But I wish you'd call me Margaret."

"Well, Margaret, the reason Mr. Grover and I were away so long was because I asked if I could see Paul's face one more time. Up in Intensive Care, things got so hectic just after he died. The nurses were trying to take things away and tidy up the room for the next patient without seeming to, you know, rush me out of there while we waited for the priest. And then Father Dowd came and there was some discussion about whether we should wait for you, and I said let's go ahead, since Paul hadn't known either one of you. And then I was kept busy trying to follow along in the prayer book Father Dowd gave me, and say the responses with him, and before I knew it the nurse had covered Paul's face. But there was something that had troubled me. I told Mr. Grover about it and he was very understanding, but first he had to go and get someone on the hospital staff — something to do with insurance, staff has to be present if unauthorized people like me are poking around in the morgue — may I hang onto you, Margaret? I don't see at all well in the dark."

"Please do." She felt much less substantial leaning into my body than she had appeared sitting upright in her queenly calm on the sofa. Arms linked, we crossed through the amber of the floodlight under which Charles and I had stopped to talk — an hour? two hours? ago. My eyes were scratchy and the stomach grumblings of early morning hunger had set up a plaintive counterpoint to the stolid bump-bumpings of Helen's bag, but I felt extraordinarily alert. I felt contented to be exactly where I was, walking beside Helen Britt through this ordained moment.

"Anyway, we got this extra person we needed, and in his presence Mr. Grover unzipped the bag on the gurney and undid the wrappings around Paul's face and explained the cause of what had troubled me: you see, up in the ICU, when I came back from the rest room, Paul looked different — I mean, he had already died *before* I went to the rest room, but it looked like someone had injected blue dye into his ears while I'd been gone, and it puzzled me. I'd intended to ask about it and then Father Dowd bustled in and we were so busy praying. But Mr. Grover explained the blue was what they call cardiac blue. He said it would also be on Paul's shoulders and fingertips and ribs and heels if I had looked at those. If Paul had chosen to have his body embalmed, he said, the embalming fluid would clear away the blue in minutes, but that this was the perfectly normal color that went with Paul's form of death. I know it's a small thing, but I felt better. Mr. Grover asked me if there was anything else I wanted to know about the body, and I said no. I ran my finger around one of Paul's blue ears — it was cold because the body had been in storage — and I said, 'It's been fun, Paul,' and then they covered the face and zipped up the bag and it was finished. I hadn't felt it was finished the first time. Does that make sense?"

"It makes complete sense. I'm glad it was Bob Grover who came, he's especially sensitive to that kind of thing."

We drove in silence down the hospital exit road. When I suggested she fasten her seat belt before we entered the highway, she uttered a derisive little snort, then obediently buckled up. I would probably have made a similar noise myself if some stranger had reminded me to strap myself in for safety's sake, when I had just lost my life's companion.

"Why didn't the old lady like you?" she asked when we were out on the highway. "The one who called you 'Mother' at first."

"The whole idea of women priests offended her sense of propriety and aesthetics. But she was a loyal Episcopalian and stood by the decision of the convention. 'Mother,' was her way of being a stickler for form, high church people do often call their women priests Mother, but I'm sure part of her intention was to remind me every chance she got that *she* hadn't forgotten I was a female."

"Paul never minded about women priests," said Helen Britt. "He said women took better care of people and that was such a large part of the job anyway. But aren't you awfully young to be a rector of a church?"

"I was thirty-three last June. That *is* considered fairly young, but circumstances were in my favor. My husband was already a chaplain at a school here. And a priest even younger than myself — a young woman right out of seminary — had made history in this diocese a few years back by forming the first Episcopal congregation in Marble County, which is a Baptist and Pentecostal stronghold. Also, the unmarried rector who preceded me at All Saints High Balsam had just gone to prison for sex offenses, and here I was safely married and in love with my husband. And I guess there was just the right degree of mutual respect between the search committee and the vestry and myself. I threatened them sufficiently with the new ideas they knew they needed, but I did it in a familiar Southern tradition that made it easier for them to swallow. And from my side, their love for their church and its traditions attracted me more than their old-line conservatism annoyed me."

"I think you're being modest," said Helen Britt. "But I'm glad you have a husband you love. Do you have children?"

"At the end of our first year in High Balsam, I miscarried a sixteen-week-old girl." I was surprised at myself. Ordinarily I responded to this question with a simple no.

"That must have been very painful for you."

"It was. Though many people tend to regard a miscarriage as a kind of disappointed goal that can be reached later. A person is likely to say to you, 'Don't worry, you'll try again,' or even, 'A miscarriage is nature's kind way of getting rid of a faulty product.' But for us, it felt like what it was, losing a child. Even if she hadn't been born yet."

"Paul and I had no children. I was too old when we got married."

"Had you been married before?"

"No, just busy, running the family newspaper. Then Paul came to my office one day — he owned a string of weeklies and he wanted to acquire ours, *Jane's Exchange*. My mother, whose name was Jane, started it during the Second World War after she was widowed. It began as a little two-page sheet of personal ads; people had things they wanted to get rid of, she said, or wanted things they didn't know where to look for, and they needed a container to share the information. No one was more surprised than she was when it took off. By the time I got into the business, *Jane's Exchange* had become a real community voice. Then it started winning awards and even making money! Though Mother had died by then, I wasn't ready to sell. But Paul kept coming back and pestering me. And then he stopped coming and I realized I missed him. I was forty-five, but it was the first time in my life I'd ever missed anybody in that way. So I called him up."

"And did you sell?"

"Absolutely not." She laughed. "I married him and I kept *Jane's Exchange*. We ran it together after he got rid of all *his* newspapers. They were going to unionize on him, and after his first major heart attack he got sick of all the aggravation and sold the whole kit and caboodle to a national chain. Now what is that beautiful little country church up ahead of us?"

"That's the Chapel of St. Francis-in-the-Valley. That's where Father Dowd's serving at the moment." I was puzzling why the little frame church looked so garishly lit up, then realized its new insurance-required area light was of the "ball field" variety Lucinda Lord's tantrum had saved us from. "They're in the process of calling a new rector."

"What happens to Father Dowd then?"

"I expect he'll probably go back full-time to his vocational counseling at Clampitt Tech. He's just serving as interim priest now."

"Back to his Lady Riveters," she remarked blandly, but with the subtlest seasoning of wickedness, and I was suddenly reminded of my mother. She had possessed this same skill of conveying her devastating parodies and judgments via harmless-seeming understatements.

I pulled over to the side of the highway so we could look at the Chapel. "I served my curacy and was ordained here," I told Helen Britt. "The bishop arranged it so I'd be able to come to North Carolina with my husband directly out of seminary. I'd drive down the mountain to the Chapel every day and back in the evening to Adrian's school, where we were living then. Of course, it was during summer and fall, when the roads are easy, but, in summer-resident enclaves like this, the head count can more than double in a mountain parish. The rector was recuperating after a stroke, and I got to do everything except consecrate the Eucharist. I mowed the lawn, answered the mail, visited parishioners, preached the sermons, and weeded the graveyard in back. In the 1888 diphtheria epidemic here, a mother lost all four of her small daughters in four days. Her husband was away on business and there was no regular priest at the Chapel then, so she dug all four graves, made the headstones, and read the services from the prayerbook herself. The girls' names were Elspeth, Edwina, Eleanor, and Eva. The last one to die was Eva, the baby. I'd sit in front of each grave while I weeded it and think of the mother chiseling their names into the stones. What were her thoughts? Or did she just drive one letter after another into the stone and feel it vibrate in the marrow of her bones and try *not* to think? And when she got to Eva, did she wish her last baby's name had more letters so she could postpone the desolation a little longer?"

"But this was before you lost your child?"

"Yes, I didn't get pregnant until after my ordination. But it's interesting you should ask that, because after I lost the baby it seemed as if all my meditations on that mother while I weeded around those little gravestones had been a kind of training for my own loss."

"That's an intriguing thought," said Helen Britt. She turned to look back at the Chapel as we drove off again. "Of course, with Paul's health as uncertain as it was, I had ample opportunity to think about what it would be like without him . . . to *train,* as you put it. But you never do get things quite right when you're preparing for them ahead of time."

"No, there's always a part you hadn't expected."

"Always a part you hadn't expected," Helen Britt echoed in her dry little lilt.

We drove past historic High Valley Inn

231

with its rustic chestnut bark buildings and par seventy-one golf course "designed to provide a different mountain view from every hole." The inn was closed until April, but, like everything else around here where a few had so much to protect and the rest had nothing to lose, it was thoroughly bathed in the glow of security area lights.

Then on past several look-alike retirement enclaves that had risen out of the wilderness since Adrian and I moved here, each with its own man-made lake and private course — and twenty-four-hour guarded checkpoint. ("But who will guard the guards?" Judge Tim Stancil went around bitterly quoting his favorite satirist, Juvenal, after the second "security guard outrage" down in Jasper, where the ousted guards had firebombed the dormitory being built for their out-of-state replacements.)

"No, Paul thought women priests were fine," Helen Britt reiterated, as if continuing aloud a thought. "But he couldn't *stand* the exchange of the peace. He felt it diverted from worship. You know what he would do?" She laughed. "He would step across the street and buy the Sunday paper while it was going on. It was his form of protest."

"Did you go with him?"

"Oh, no, I stayed behind and shook hands and said 'peace of the Lord be with you.' I didn't mind the intermission. Paul was the religious one. Some people have religious natures; others don't. I didn't. But I enjoyed going to church with Paul. I liked spying on him when he was praying. He did seem to be in touch with something, and I felt I was included, too. I was covered under his God-umbrella, so to speak. But up in Intensive Care when Father Dowd and I started in on our little duet, I realized the umbrella was gone. I hadn't been prepared for that. I suppose I had assumed it would go on without him, like an insurance policy. It was an unpleasant feeling."

"How so?"

"There was just a sarcastic, brittle emptiness. While we were reading those beautiful words I've always found so moving at funerals, I thought, this is absurd, I don't believe a word of it, and Paul's no longer around to shield me from the absurdity. I went on with my part of the show because the nurses were watching and Father Dowd expected it, but I felt absolutely nothing. Not a single human feeling."

"You were worried about Paul's blue ears, though."

"That's true," she conceded. "Maybe there's hope for me yet."

We began the circuitous ascent of High Balsam Road: literally a shelf cut into the granite mountain. In 1930, Charles Tye's grandfather was one of the half-dozen intrepid (and out-of-work) volunteers lowered from the tops of cliffs on rope swings to plant dynamite in the mountain. Then they were hauled back up and charges set, ten-foot widths at a time, until this road was carved into the rock.

"What will you do when you get back to Ohio?" I asked.

"Since I don't have any gravestones to chisel, you mean?"

"Something like that." Beyond the dry intelligence had I heard a discreet cry for help? But Helen Britt was not a person to be consoled by wishful reassurances; neither was I.

"Well, let's see. Billy and I will unload the car. I'll unpack the box of Christmas decorations Paul and I were taking to our condo in Jupiter. We always had a tree in Florida. Then we'll plan Paul's funeral. Though if I know Billy, he's already done everything. I'll ask him to get a nice tree. A Christmas tree will make our friends feel better when they stop by."

"What about you? Will it make you feel better?"

"Our living room at Christmas without any tree would be an insult to Paul. If I can't have his faith, I can at least let myself be carried along by the forms. There's a degree of comfort in forms, wouldn't you say?"

"Absolutely. On some days the forms completely carry me."

"Now that surprises me, Margaret."

"On the other days, enough glimpses of meaning break through to keep me from feeling like a fraud."

"But you're a very smart young woman. You could easily have chosen another profession." She humorously added, "You could have started your own newspaper."

"But I wanted to do this more than anything else."

"May I ask why?"

"Probably because it will always be too big for me and I can count on it to keep surprising me. Something in me craves the mystery of the adventure, I suppose."

"And where is God for you, if you don't mind my asking?"

"No, I don't mind. Right now? Definitely in the car with us as we talk and exchange things, and change each other in the process. It's like your mother said about *Jane's Exchange*. People have things they want to give away, or they want things they don't know where to look for, and they need containers to pool their information. This night is far too large for us to rattle around in on our own. It's a perfect fit for God, but we need our containers. We need one another for God to work through us: that's something I experience every day. The concept of God is way too big for me to get my mind around, but, despite that, maybe even because of it, the relationship keeps growing and changing. Sometimes it grows so slowly it seems it's stopped. Or gone into reverse. Then when I least expect it, it takes a big leap forward. In fact, it's done that since I've been with you, Helen."

She made a funny sound and turned away to the window. I couldn't tell whether my answer had offended or disappointed her, or if she was mulling things over. Perhaps she'd simply dismissed me in order to pull her widowhood around her like a shawl and test the emptiness by herself.

But then she cleared her throat. "How has it grown?" she asked.

"I think it started the minute I saw you. Something about you, the way you observe people and take them in, the way you communicate, felt familiar to me, though I couldn't think why at first. Then when we started talking in the car, I realized that you brought my mother to mind — or how I remembered her."

"And did you like your mother?"

"I didn't have her for very long. She went away with a woman friend when I was six. It began as a short trip to New York — my father encouraged her to go — and then it turned into a sort of leave of absence from us, and then she was killed in an automobile accident in England. My father and I never knew whether she'd meant to come back or not. Yes, I liked her; I loved her. I was dazzled by her. I remember being afraid of not pleasing her, but most of all what I remember about her was how she could *not* say things and convey them very effectively. When we were together, each of us knew what the other meant. The same thing I feel with you. Maybe that's why I was finally able to understand something about my mother — when you said that about Paul and his God-umbrella."

"Oh, that just came to me as we talked. I'd never thought of it like that before."

"But it's such a wonderful image. Someone who doesn't consider herself religious, kneeling next to her husband and sheltering under his God-umbrella. Then suddenly he's gone, and the umbrella's gone with him, and she's at the mercy of the brittle absurdities. What then?"

"What then, indeed," she said, a touch forlornly. "But how does this relate to your mother?"

"Before I entered seminary, I lived with my mother's friend in New York for a while."

"This is the woman she'd gone away with?"

"Yes. Her name was Madelyn. She was always quoting things Ruth, my mother, had said to her when they had lived together for that year. Well, when Madelyn was dying, she told me something that truly upset me. Madelyn had just found out she had inoperable cancer, and she'd asked her doctor to pump her full of steroids so she could finish a theater piece she was working on. She said, 'It won't ever be produced without me, but I want to see how it turns out. I want to find out what I can make happen when I have so little time left.' Madelyn was fascinated by her own artistic processes, right to the end. She didn't finish the piece, as it turned out, but for a while she worked every day and then we'd take a walk. Sometimes we'd get only partway to the end of the block before she'd slump against me in exhaustion. On one of these walks Madelyn told me my mother had told her that she'd never taken God seriously until she met my father. 'Falling in love with Walter was like falling in love with God,' my mother had apparently told Madelyn, and it sounded just like the sort of thing my mother would say. There would have been a touch of mischief, but she'd mean it. I should explain that my father was a priest, a bit older than my mother."

"Another priest in your family."

"Yes. They'd met when he directed a retreat at her college, and then she started a correspondence with him. Well, on our walk that day Madelyn told me *her* theory was that when my father toppled from his pedestal, so did poor God, and Ruth had felt trapped in a false life as a result."

"I can certainly see how it would have been

upsetting to hear that. Do you think your father did topple from his pedestal?"

"For my mother, he undoubtedly did. My father was a good man, a lovable man, but he wasn't easy to live with when he was in one of his depressions. Then he'd undermine himself: he'd tell my mother she had spoiled her life by marrying him. But that part wasn't what got to me, it was that part about the false life. When Madelyn said that, all I could think of was, 'Then I must have been part of the false life, too.' "

"How tactless of your mother's friend to say that! Of course she was ill. She was probably not herself."

"Oh, she was herself, all right. Madelyn talked this way: she'd tell a story about someone in order to pursue some theory about her own workings. And when she got going on one of these self-analyses, she was oblivious to the sensitivity of her listener. I'm sure what she was doing that day was patting herself on the back for having been an artist — because she then went on to conclude that she herself had always had all the living God she could handle in her work, whereas my mother never found anything powerful enough to replace the emptiness Walter — and Walter's God — had left. That was the point of the story. But I was shocked. Not that my mother hadn't taken God seriously before meeting my father. What shocked and hurt was the idea that my mother might have seen me as a part — even a by-product — of her 'false life.' "

"But it wasn't your *mother's* thought! The false life idea was her friend's theory. You said so yourself."

"Yes, just *now* I did, but that day it was such a blow in the chest, the idea alone, that it was as if Madelyn *had* been quoting my mother about the false life as well as the other part about falling in love with God through Walter — or Walter through God, whichever was meant. But, see, that's where you come in. When you were telling me about Paul's God-umbrella being suddenly gone for you, it brought back the memory of that day. Then I realized that the blow-in-the-chest feeling I always get with that memory hadn't kicked in. Something had shifted."

"And how do you account for that?"

"I don't exactly know. I just, for the first time, saw it all from a different place. I wasn't me anymore, broadsided by hurt and anger on the sidewalk next to Madelyn. And I wasn't the little girl who got on the school-bus one morning in Virginia and never saw her mother again. Another perspective had come into play. Now I was some third party, watching you and my mother as counter-parts. Both of you without the umbrella you'd shielded under. My father didn't make Ruth a widow, but he chipped away at him-

240

self until he killed her belief in him and what he represented. But before her own life got cut off so prematurely — she was driving on the wrong side of the road in England one evening and smashed into a truck — I can see her in the same place you are now, asking the questions we're bound to ask once our umbrellas get taken away. And I'd rather be with her — and with you — in those larger questions. What am I supposed to do with myself now? Or, what are you doing with me now, God? I'd rather be there than back with the hurt girl on the sidewalk demanding why. My exchange with you has somehow relocated me, Helen, so I can live closer to those questions. So, thank you."

There was the snap of her purse opening. The extraction of something, then a closing snap.

"You're quite welcome." Even with her congested voice, she kept it light. A handkerchief was unfolded. "And thanks to whatever's working *through* me, of course," she added wryly, after blowing her nose.

"Definitely thanks to whatever," I agreed, laughing.

We rode on in an intimate and timeless silence, Helen Britt weeping companionably into her handkerchief. I was acquainted with Mr. and Mrs. Treadwell from the times Adrian and I had dined at the lodge. They were solid, undemonstrative people of the widow's own generation, and I knew they could be counted on to shelter Helen Britt for the remainder of her stay with the perfect blend of unintrusive sympathy and mountain hospitality.

VII

An Abundance of Grace

The innkeepers must have been watching out for us. When our headlights swung into the entrance of the lodge, both Treadwells were standing side by side at the bottom of the front steps.

"We were real sorry to hear." Mrs. Treadwell spoke first. Her voice held simple compassion. "When you all left in the ambulance, we were still hoping —" She broke off awkwardly.

"So was I," replied Helen Britt. "But it wasn't to be, was it?" Her weeping had left no trace; she was her dry reserved self again.

"If you tell us what luggage you need, Buck'll fetch it from your car."

"Expect I'll need a key, though," said Mr. Treadwell good-naturedly.

Helen dug into her envelope purse and brought out a single key. Then she gave an exasperated laugh and dropped it back in. "How silly of me. You need the *trunk* key for the trunk and it's on Paul's ring." While she rifled through the contents of the hospital carrier bag, I was pretty sure all four of us were thinking the same thought: only hours ago she and Paul were leaving here after a good dinner, walking toward their car to continue their journey, and now here she was back at the lodge alone, carrying her husband's valuables in a plastic bag. How quickly anyone's life could turn inside out.

"Buck's lit a fire in your room," Mrs. Treadwell said. "Not that the room's cold, but lots of folks appreciate the comfort of a nice fire." In her mountain dialect, it came out "farr."

"Well, I am definitely one of those folks," Helen Britt assured her, extracting her late husband's keys from the bag with a tinkling flourish. "Mr. Treadwell, my black carryall's right at the front of the trunk. It will have all I need." Singling out a key, she handed over the ring to him. "I doubt if I'll get any sleep, so I'm doubly grateful for the company of that fire."

"Shall I go inside with you?" I asked her, rather hoping she'd say yes.

"Absolutely not, Margaret. You've been out far too long on my account as it is. Go home to your husband. These good people will take care of me now."

I must have looked dismissed, as Bob Grover had when she turned him down to go with me, because she linked her arm through mine and walked us off by ourselves under the bright lights of the parking area; she took neat little marching steps beside mine, the

244

plastic bag bumping softly against her body. "You're an extraordinary young woman, Margaret," she said. "I think you were hand-picked for me on this occasion. By — what-ever." She squeezed my arm with hers. "I'm not saying it well, but I hope you hear all I'm conveying."

"I feel the same about you," I said, squeezing hers back. "God bless you, Helen."

A bereftness rode with me as I drove alone up the final portion of mountain into High Balsam. I'd been sorry to leave my warm bed with Adrian in it and go off down the mountain to comfort strangers, yet now that I was heading home under fading starlight, my spirit remained behind at the lodge with Helen Britt, unpacking my carryall by the light of the Treadwells' fire, not wanting any more light for now, not anticipating the dawn and its sharper outlines of all the day would bring.

Here an outraged stomach rumble returned me to my own body. There was that heel of ham left over from the parish dinner. And some cheddar cheese. I'd cut them both up in little squares, chop an onion and a green pepper and anything else I could find, and make a colossal omelet. Adrian would wake to the enticing smell and we'd have a rare breakfast together. Then I remembered Tony. Monks got up early, and being so close to the kitchen, he'd naturally assume he was being summoned by the smells. Then poor Adrian would have to make chitchat with a stranger while half asleep.

So I stopped instead at the Horseshoe Diner. SUPPORT RED MEAT, RUN OVER A CHICKEN, said the bumper sticker on the pickup I pulled in next to. Already at a quarter to six, the Horseshoe's brightly lit interior percolated with unapologetic tobacco smoke and working men's voices and all the bacon and coffee smells one could desire. It would have been more considerate for me to perch on a counter stool among the other single customers, but I took the last empty booth. I intended to order enough breakfast to qualify for it.

A waitress with coffeepot instantly hovered. "Transfusion?"

"Please."

"Cream's in that lil' pitcher. You know what you want, or you need a menu?" *Sandi* was stitched in white on the pocket of her pink uniform.

"I know what I want," I said.

"You been up all night?" she inquired sociably as she scribbled my order on her pad.

"How did you know?"

"Oh, I observe folks. You look wore-out, your lipstick's chewed clean off, and you're wearin' your work clothes. You're the preacher at Gus Eubanks's church, aren't you?"

"You know Gus?"

"She and Dr. Charles eat here lots of mornings. Always order the same thing. Soft scrambled with a side order of sliced tomato, and brown toast without butter."

"Not like me, huh?"

"Those two order fried eggs? And hash browns *and* bacon? Triple felony. But they're older. You still have time to repent and mend your ways."

"That's good to know."

"I'm hoping to get to the wedding this afternoon, if I can get outta here and make myself decent by two o'clock. They both invited me. Dr. Charles was my mama's physician till she passed away last July. When she got too poorly to come to him, he came to her. Mama thought he hung the moon. Don't you want any orange juice?"

"Oh yes, I just forgot to order it."

"Large or small?"

"Oh . . ."

"Might as well go whole-hog."

"Okay," I said, laughing, "large."

She hustled off with my order, sidestepping a handsome young man in a bomber jacket who looked half asleep. "For cryin' out loud, Creighton, what are you doing in here on a Saturday?"

"I got a makeup job down in Mountain

City. Supposed to go yesterday, only I put diesel fuel in my flatbed by mistake."

A delighted roar of male guffaws from the booth ahead of me. "Did the same damnfool thing myself, once," a white-haired man in suspenders called out to him. "Cost me fifteen dollars to fill the tank, and fifty to empty it."

"That must of been back in the dark ages," replied handsome Creighton, swaggering toward them with his sleepy grin. "It cost me twic't that. Not including the towing, either." He flopped down in their booth, rubbing his eyes with both fists.

I was hit by a surprise voltage of well-being. It came from no specific source I could identify — I hadn't taken even the first sip of my "transfusion" yet. I just felt overwhelmed to find myself exactly here, with these early morning people, to have been identified by my "work clothes" as one of them, and assured of a hearty breakfast someone else had cooked.

The reconciliation with Adrian came back to me with a relief powerful enough to make me close my eyes. It was only now that I could admit to myself that I had feared we might be heading straight into one of those companionable, kindly, nonphysical marriages.

When I opened my eyes, there was Grace Munger looming above me in her red cape.

248

"You were praying," she accused exultantly, as though she'd tracked me to my lair at last.

"I was, in a way," I said. "You're out early, Grace."

I waited for her to reply: you're out pretty early yourself, but she crisply rapped out, "It's never too early to begin the Lord's work."

"Will you join me?" I tried to sound more welcoming than I felt. "I just ordered a huge breakfast. I've been up most of the night."

"Well, I guess I can sit for a minute." It was as though she were doing me the favor.

Sandi materialized with her coffeepot and her smile. "The usual, Grace?" So she was known here.

"Just coffee today, Sandi." She pushed her cup forward to catch the steaming liquid. She had large creamy white hands with tapered fingers, the nails beautifully manicured and polished with red enamel the shade of her cape. "I'm speaking at a breakfast in Clampitt, but Reverend Bonner asked me to join her here for a few minutes." She made it sound as if we'd made a date.

"We've got those maple sticky buns you like so well."

"Not today, thank you." My last evening's impression of her haughty good looks held up under the diner's fluorescent light. Tony was right: a smasher, even with the weight.

249

Having dismissed Sandi with a frown, she slid the red cape grandly from her shoulders, like a goddess getting down to business. Her tentlike dress was of a beautiful soft wool whose tweed picked up the yellow, green, and orangey-brown flecks in her hazel eyes. A large Byzantine gold cross on an open-worked chain rested prominently upon her bosom. Her hair was braided and twisted into a plump dark coil, and the long white face was carefully and recently made-up.

"I've been at Bruton Memorial Hospital most of the night," I offered, largely to deflect the naked *intention* I felt being directed at me. "It was an older couple, on their way to Florida. They were leaving the Treadwell Lodge after dinner when he collapsed."

Grace Munger regarded me implacably over the rim of her coffee cup. Not a flicker of curiosity or sympathy for the couple.

"The ICU nurse phoned me when she couldn't get hold of Father Dowd —" I continued obstinately on.

"Father Dowd has indicated to me he'll march if you will." She steamrollered my story to grab her opening. "And when you've had a chance to look at the materials I left in your box, I'm still praying you'll see your way clear to joining us. If all of us gather at the top of this mountain in the name of Christ for the march, don't you agree, Reverend Bonner, our coming together in unity will begin the

250

healing of this broken community."

Here she attempted a disarming smile, but her small childlike teeth in the broad pink gums were so incongruous in the long, haughty face that the effect was rather unnerving.

"As a matter of fact, I *have* looked at all your materials, Grace." I decided to dispense with diplomacies that would probably be lost on her anyway. "I've read your letter, more than once, and I've read through all of your materials, and I don't agree with you that this march will set anything right. It may even make things worse. Some of the things you put in that Christian Manifesto for a Wounded Town could exacerbate the rifts that exist."

She drew herself up. "Can you be more specific?"

"Yes I can. 'Are you happy with your life? Are you happy with your job, if you still have a job? If not, join the march, commit yourself to live fully by the word of the Bible and the traditional morals and family values it espouses, and Jesus will come and do the rest.' Your message is provocative and it's equivocal. It's a dangerous mix."

"I have no idea what you're talking about, Reverend Bonner."

"You play on discontent and unrest; you promise things in the name of Jesus that you can't deliver. Not to mention the undercurrent of incitement that runs all through the manifesto. I mean, your choice of 'I am come to send fire to the earth' is an extremely ill-chosen passage of scripture, don't you think, Grace, when that big arson the security guards perpetrated down in Jasper last month is still all over the news? And just what *are* these 'traditional morals and family values' the Bible espouses?"

"I should think you'd know," she countered sharply, "having been to seminary yourself."

"No, I do not know. Which part of the Bible, Grace? Which traditions, which family values? Jacob brought home two wives, but we can't do that anymore in this country. People did all sorts of things in the Bible that are against the law today. But you know as well as I do that 'family values' has become a catchword for pointing fingers at people and enforcing boundaries. And your march is in the name of the person whose ministry was to break down those boundaries."

"Are you implying *he* was against morality?"

"Certain kinds, yes. He preached compassion over and against the purity code of his own religion, for example. He made a point of sitting down at the table with the wrong kind of people. He praised a prostitute who washed his feet. He said the Sabbath was made for human beings, not the other way 'round. . . ."

Her face closed down. I was talking to myself. "Look, Grace," I said, abandoning this futile method of discourse, "I must tell you emphatically: All Saints won't be joining your march. And, by the way, I did run into Father Dowd at the hospital last night and he didn't say anything to me about being willing to march. But he *did* report you'd left a message on his machine saying that Brother Tony would march on our behalf. I told him that this was mistaken information."

"It is not mistaken information," she flared. "The monk told me so himself."

"I was there, too," I reminded her. "He said, 'If I'm still here.' But he won't be. He's only staying one night, maybe two at the most, and the march is the Saturday before Christmas. And even if he were going to be here longer and decided to join you, it wouldn't be a question of his marching 'on behalf' of our church. If we wanted to march, we're perfectly capable of doing so on our own behalf."

"Then why didn't he just come right out and say so?" she demanded righteously. But a flitting blush along her haughty cheeks gave her away; she knew she'd been caught fabricating between the lines.

"Well, I expect because he was trying to be polite," I said, exasperated. "He was very tired. He's eighty years old and he'd walked all the way from the bus station carrying his suitcase. We were all standing outside in the cold."

She set down her coffee cup and glared at me with pure hostility. "You people always hide behind your politeness, when it comes down to the crunch."

It was as unexpected as being hauled off and slapped by a salesperson who the minute before had been wheedling you to try her product.

"I'm not sure what you mean by 'you people,'" I said. "Now it's my turn to ask *you* to be more specific. And hide from *what*, exactly, Grace?"

"From revealed truth when it's right in front of your face. It's too *obvious* for you lukewarm elites. Too *demanding*. To think you might have to get out there in the street with the rest of us and *witness* for your beliefs. How common! Well, you know what the Bible says about people like you."

"If you want me to quote the lukewarm passage, I can, Grace, but I don't consider myself lukewarm."

" '. . . because thou art lukewarm, neither cold nor hot, I will spew thee out of my mouth!'" she quoted, as if I hadn't spoken in the interim.

"Revelation Three-sixteen. In the King James. The New RSV translates it as 'spit,' and the Jehovah's Witness Bible translates it as vomit. I plump for spew or vomit, myself.

Spit loses something; it's a lukewarm word itself."

Her eyes were flashing multicolored sparks at me. "You know, it's so sad. You people sit inside and study your Bibles, you compare the different *translations,* but you won't —"

Sandi arrived with my steaming breakfast platter.

"Here at least comes something hot," I said.

"Here you go, Reverend . . . straight up to cholesterol heaven," Sandi announced, plunking down the platter. "I'll bring y'all more coffee. Grace, honey, sure you won't change your mind about that sticky bun? Gotta keep up your sugar level for the big parade."

Interestingly enough, the organizer of the Jesus March deftly pocketed her animosity and assumed the polite facade of the lukewarms she'd just been sending to hell. "Maybe I will, Sandi. Just a small one, though."

As soon as Sandi turned to go, Grace announced her intention of " 'visiting the ladies' " and maneuvered herself out of our booth. I watched the men's heads swivel as she sailed up the aisle between the booths. The ankle-length skirt of her dress undulated like waves around her high-heeled black boots. One of them called out, "How's it goin', Gracie?" and she inclined her noble profile his way and answered something I couldn't hear.

As I set about transferring each wobbly egg onto a triangular island of toast, a habit I had picked up from my father, I wondered — and not for the first time, either — how Bishop Athanasius would have reacted if an angel had dropped down into fourth-century Alexandria and buzzed in his ear how much mischief the Book of Revelation was capable of seeding in future generations. If he had known his canon, originally meant only for the churches under his own guidance, would become *the* canon of Christianity at a later date, would he have had second thoughts and hidden John of Patmos's vision in a drawer, to be taken out only when he, the bishop, could be there in person to teach it and explain about levels of meaning? Handing the Book of Revelation to a literal-minded person without any guidance was like presenting a child with a box of matches and telling him to go out and play. The ravings and mean-spirited agendas this Apocalyptic poem with its dramatic visions and complex symbolisms had fueled in my lifetime alone were enough to make me sympathize in my bad moments with D. H. Lawrence, who said it was the most un-Christian book in the Bible, "A gospel of hate in a gospel of love . . ."

"Everything okay?" Sandi asked, back with Grace's sticky bun and the coffeepot.

I nodded enthusiastically with a full mouth.

"Heard you two quoting scripture." She

refilled my cup. "You gonna march in her parade?"

I shook my head.

"I'm not, either. If I take off early for the wedding today, I can't take off so soon again. I explained about it to Grace, but still I felt badly, turning her down. She's got her heart set on a big turnout. She's been working like a dog. I asked her what she's gonna do if it rains or snows that day — December's just not a great time to schedule a parade even if it is the Lord's birthday, but she said to me, 'Sandi, if the Lord could part the Red Sea and drop manna down on His disobedient people, why should it be a problem for Him to provide appropriate weather for a birthday march in His son's honor?' I admire folks like her who go out among strangers and witness for their beliefs. It's not that I don't love the Lord, even if I don't get to church much anymore, but I'm up at four A.M. six days a week, and when I wake up and it's finally Sunday morning, I *do* pray. I thank Him that I can roll over and go back to sleep. I probably shouldn't be saying this to you, Reverend, but I don't think He minds one bit."

"I don't think He does, either," I said.

When Grace came back from the ladies', she appeared to have mellowed, but I strongly suspected this was merely a revision of strategy.

"You did say you'd read my letter?" she

began, almost humbly. "I believe you said more than once."

"Yes," I said, "I did."

"And did you . . ." She scowled at the sticky bun, then, picking up her fork, daintily pried off a piece. "You know, Paul says . . ." She raised the piece of sticky bun on the tines of her fork and scrutinized it, as if seeking her text in its brown-sugary whorl. "In Romans Twelve Paul says, 'Be of the same mind, one toward another.'"

"Yes," I said, wondering what I was getting myself into.

"Well, were there any parts of my letter, Reverend Bonner, where you felt we were of the same mind?"

This was said with such diffidence that I began to feel maybe I had been too hard on her.

"Look, please call me Margaret," I told her. "After all, we are contemporaries."

She frowned skeptically. "Well, I don't know. I have great respect for the cloth. For *whoever* wears it." She took the forkful of pastry into her mouth and masticated it with prim fastidiousness, the way the actresses in old movies used to chew.

"Your father was a clergyman," I said. "And so was mine. You pointed out that similarity between us in your letter."

I tried to recall what else she'd written in the letter after God had spoken to her from the empty grate. But much had happened after I'd read it and turned out the light, thinking my day had ended. Unfortunately, the parts that now sprang vividly to mind were examples of our *un*likemindedness.

She had, however, referred in her letter to her unhappy memories of High Balsam, which she correctly surmised I would have heard about, though only as recently as last night.

To have survived the fire that your father — or your father and mother together — had set to destroy the three of you must surely have left a big imprint on your view of things. (No wonder you didn't build fires in your room at the High Balsam Inn!) Perhaps the best way to locate some common ground between us was to get off the subject of the march and find out more about its organizer.

"You mentioned in your letter that you lived in-state," I said. "But you didn't say where."

"I live and work in Mountain City. My adoptive parents were from there."

"What kind of work do you do?"

"Well, right now I've taken a leave of absence to work full-time for the Lord. But I created ad campaigns and promotion materials for my clients at Brent and Bolling."

"Oh," I said, somewhat surprised, "Brent and Bolling."

"Do you think people who organize Jesus

marches are too simpleminded to work for a prestigious mainstream ad agency like Brent and Bolling?"

"I hope I didn't convey that." But she had read me accurately. This woman was far from simpleminded; but, like her "manifesto," she seemed to be a perplexing mixture of things.

"I wish you would tell me more about your life after you left High Balsam," I said.

"I take it that Miss Eubanks filled you in on what happened before I left."

"She did tell me about your father's difficulties. And about the fire. And that some relatives took you to the burn center in Mountain City and later adopted you."

"They expected me to die, otherwise they wouldn't have been so charitable. Aunt Irma was my father's cousin, she felt it was her duty. They also got a nice tax break out of it. Have you ever seen skin with third-degree burns?"

"Yes, I did hospital work when I was in seminary."

"Well, it was like that from my waist to my ankles."

I recalled some ghastly close-ups from my CPE at St. Luke's and transferred them to the skin beneath Grace's flowing skirt and handsome boots.

"Even after all the grafts, it will never be like normal skin. Yet I lived to rejoice. It's the way the Lord chose to mark me for His own.

Though it took me a while before I acted on it."

"And what were you doing before you acted on it?"

From the way she puffed up, I was afraid I'd sprung too many personal questions on her and she was about to tell me it was none of my business and get us back on the subject of the march. But presently she began to speak with a cold, accusing vigor.

"What was I doing? I was attending this snooty boarding school. I was seeing the school psychologist who stuck his tongue in my mouth and did some other things two evenings a week in his office and knew I wouldn't tell. I was loathing the other girls one minute and praying to God to make me like them in the very next breath. I wasn't their sort and they knew it. Aunt Irma knew it, too, but I think she was hoping if they kept me there long enough, a transformation would take place. Well, a transformation did take place, but not the one they were counting on." Her tawny eyes flashed at me. "It was a Church-affiliated school, by the way. Three guesses which church."

"I don't think I need three," I said. This information went a long way, I thought, toward explaining both her animosity toward me and her determination to make the Episcopalians join her march. "But how did the . . . transformation come about?"

261

"How did it come about?" she repeated mockingly. She laughed, showing the incongruous childish teeth. "The oldest way in the world, Reverend Bonner, the oldest way in the world." Her gaze swept over me dismissively. "I daresay it's not something you have personally experienced."

Then she pushed back the sleeve of her dress and consulted a gold bracelet watch. "I've really got to run," she said, as if I'd been detaining her. "I need to get in some time alone with the Lord before I address the breakfast group."

"A church group?"

"Not specifically, but they're believers. It's a bikers' organization. They contacted me after my ad for the march ran in the *Clampitt Clarion* and asked if I would come and speak to them. It's a good forty minutes' drive from here, so I'd better get on the road." She drew on the red cape, fastened its clasp with a brisk snap, and stood up.

"Tell me honestly, Reverend Bonner," she asked, looming above me once more, "do you really welcome visitors to your church?"

"Well, of course we do," I snapped crossly. "Our sign out front says so in three-inch-high letters, and I put every one of them in myself."

"Then I take it," she was rooting in her purse, "that it would be acceptable to you and your congregation — even though you refuse to march with us — if I joined you for worship one of these Sundays?"

"You are welcome to worship with us anytime, Grace."

Could she actually be letting me off, or was it the beginning of a fresh assault?

"This ought to be enough to cover my part," she said, pushing a dollar and some change across the table with her impeccable red nails. "And now, I *really* must fly."

VIII

Home Remedies

The first thing I saw when I pulled in behind the rectory was a black habit swinging on a wire hanger from the dogwood tree. I cut across the damp grass in the pale frosty light of sunrise and entered the kitchen, where more surprises greeted me.

Tony, springy and fit in Levi's and a khaki twill shirt, looking a good ten years younger than last night, was at the stove, tending pancakes on a griddle that I never knew we had. An unshaven Adrian in bathrobe and pajamas, looking anything but fit, sat hunched over a steaming cup of pinkish brew. Lined up in front of him on the table, like toy soldiers, was a phalanx of little colored bottles.

"Ah, there you are," he croaked from several octaves lower than his normal voice. "I was beginning to worry."

"Oh no," I said, knowing what that deep croak heralded.

"Don't worry, our Benedictine infirmarian here took one look at me and started to work." He waved a hand toward the little bottles. Adrian's chest colds always descended on him like a cloudburst — yet the rheumy eyes that gazed up at me were, I was happy to see, the eyes of a lover pleased with what he sees, and he seemed cheerfully taken with the old man in bow-legged jeans flipping pancakes at our stove.

"Good morning, Tony," I said. "Did you sleep all right?"

"Like a little baby who's been baptized and gone straight to heaven, Margaret. I hope you weren't offended when you saw my habit hanging outside, but it needed an airing if it's going to a wedding. And if I could borrow your iron later, to give it a good pressing."

"You're very welcome to it," I said. "It's in the pantry and the board's in the hall closet." If he was planning to stay for the wedding, I was thinking, that surely meant another night with us.

"How did things go at the hospital?" Adrian asked.

"He died before I got there. And Kevin Dowd was already at the hospital; he came home from a basketball game and got his message and beat me to the commendations."

"But you were away such a long time."

"Well, I sat with Kevin and Helen Britt, the widow, while they waited for Bob Grover. And then I drove her back to the Treadwell Lodge. We had a wonderful talk on the way. She was one of those gift people you occasionally meet. Then I stopped for breakfast at the Horseshoe Diner and was vouchsafed the company of none other than Grace Munger herself."

"What was she doing out so early?"

"The Lord's work, what else? Actually, she was on her way to address a motorcyclists' breakfast in Clampitt, but she dropped into the Horseshoe for a shot of caffeine and the Lord led her straight to my booth."

"Are the motorcyclists going to be in the birthday march?"

"She didn't say, but I'm sure she has designs on them for something. She has designs on everybody for something, is my impression."

"My wife leads an adventurous life," Adrian remarked to Tony, who was setting down a plate of golden brown pancakes in front of him. As the monk's forearm shot out of his partly rolled-up sleeve, I glimpsed a tattoo of a flying bird. One more incongruous item to report to Gus.

"I've met the lady myself," said Tony. "She's a force of nature, all right. But a smasher, even with the weight." He cut his eyes at me for approval as he repeated his vintage epithet from last night. "Now eat these while they're piping hot," he told Adrian. "The flu powder works better that way. Opens up your passages all the way down."

"Yes, Father," said Adrian.

"Please just call me Tony. I'm not or-

266

dained. Besides, I'm only a lay brother."

"But lay brothers have had the status of full monks for some time now, haven't they?"

"Well, that's true." But he looked distraught, as he had last night when he'd gotten mixed up about which publication he'd seen our picture in, and also when I'd said I didn't know the Reverend Jim Anderson over in Knoxville. Then, recovering himself, he explained, "I guess I continue to think of myself in the old way. Lucky to be there on the bottom rung."

"Is Tony your given name or did you take a new name with your vows?" Adrian dribbled maple syrup onto his pancakes from an old Stuckey's earthenware cruet. In what overlooked corner of the pantry had Tony unearthed *that*? Was it from the late Father Lindsey's solo breakfasts, or had it sweetened the morning-after pancakes of the Sun Porch Seducer's victims — or both?

"Well, it's — I chose it. St. Anthony, you know."

"The tempted hermit from Egypt, or the finder of lost property from Padua?"

"Well, the . . . second," said Tony, after a minuscule hesitation during which he seemed to be deciding which saint would please us best. "I was kind of lost property myself before I entered. I found stability later than most."

"And what did you do in your former life?"

Adrian set to work on his pancakes.

The monk gave his whispery cackle. "You name it, I've probably had a crack at it. I've fixed things, sold things, built things, dug things up. I even managed to get my seaman's papers for the Merchant Marine once, but something else transpired before I was able to use them. Did a lot of tree and roof work when I was younger. I have good balance, never minded heights. And I've done a fair amount of construction work in my time: a contractor I worked for once told me I could make a bulldozer move like a ballet dancer. One summer I actually *did* teach dancing in a Catskill resort. Saw the ad, got myself a book with those footstep diagrams and taught myself. I bought a used tuxedo and off I went to the Catskills. I was more personable in those days and the manager gave me the job on sight. But partway into my second week . . ." His shoulders began to shake with mirth. ". . . I was teaching this large lady the samba and she trampled my right foot and broke three toes. There went my job, but the manager liked me and put me to work chopping onions for the short-order cook at the pool snack bar. That's where I began developing my culinary skills, such as they are. With me, one thing has sort of led into the next. But, aside from some sewing and gardening, cooking's my main job at the Transfiguration now."

"That figures," said Adrian. "These pancakes melt like hosts in your mouth. The other monks must think you dropped straight from heaven."

"Well, some of them maybe do," Tony modestly allowed.

"What's in the flu powder?" I asked.

"Oh, just my own concoction of things from our herb garden at the abbey. Plus a shake or two of cayenne powder. Not enough to irritate his throat, but it stimulates the blood and the pods are packed with vitamin C and magnesium. If what works on me works on Adrian, the pancakes along with the hyssop tea and those echinacea and gold seal caplets will fix him up. I'm subject to respiratory ailments myself. That's why I always travel with my little family of home remedies."

After passing his hand over the colored bottles, Tony paused to rub the edge of the walnut table. "This is a handsome piece. Reminds me of some of our older library tables, when people knew how to make things. Is it old?"

"Only about ten years old," Adrian told him. "I made it myself, when I was serving in Romulus. Where I met Margaret."

"You did, really? Where'd you learn to do work like this?"

"I was taught carpentry as a boy."

"At school?"

269

"Well, it was an orphanage actually."

"You were an orphan?"

"For all practical purposes, yes. My parents dropped me off there when I was six. It was supposed to be a temporary thing, until my father found work. But they never came back for me."

"Never came back?" Tony shook his head. "Now that's hard. Do you remember them at all?" He was still rubbing his hand along the edge of the table thoughtfully.

"Not really."

"But if you were six, you must have some memory of them."

"Only the vaguest. I remember more about the man who taught me carpentry than I remember about them. I recall my mother being sick and my father being a fast-moving, impetuous sort. But it's more like the memory of a shadow, rushing in and out. Except he could play like a child. One time he was chasing me and I fell and chipped a front tooth that was just coming in. But if I met either of them on the street today — even as they were then — I wouldn't recognize them. Margaret says I'm not a visual person."

"You've still got the chipped tooth," remarked Tony.

"I could have had it capped free when I was in the Navy. But I never did."

"Why was that?" Tony asked.

"I don't know. Maybe I wanted to keep it

because it was all I had left of my true origins. Though Margaret tells me it's sexy."

"Margaret, plenty of batter left. How about letting me make you a stack?"

"Adrian's do look good. And I'm curious about the flu powder."

"You won't be able to taste it."

"But what about yourself? I've already had one breakfast."

"You two have work to do. My most pressing job this morning is to iron my habit, excuse the pun. If you're sure it won't inconvenience you if I stay for that nice lady's wedding."

"We hope you'll stay another night with us, as well." What else could I reply?

Adrian made concurring noises that sounded sincere.

"Well, that's very kind of you," said Tony, at the stove again. He scraped down the griddle, and soon three dollops of batter were widening into sizzling circles, pocked with little air bubbles.

I poured a cup of coffee, set two more place mats at the table for me and Tony and sank down, relinquishing myself to this odd turn of events, much as Adrian must have done when he stumbled downstairs to turn on the coffee machine and found a bow-legged little medicine man and short-order cook waiting to be of service.

"Speaking of work, I wonder if it's too early

to call Coach's house and check on my delinquent," said Adrian. "On the other hand, the
fact that nobody's called *me* yet is a good
sign."

"Let sleeping delinquents lie," I agreed.

Tony served my pancakes. Once again the
bird tattoo flew out from his sleeve. This time
I saw Adrian notice it.

"I don't look forward to calling Zorn,"
Adrian said. "Radford Zorn is the father of
the boy I was telling you about, Tony. The
adoptive father, that is."

"The lost sheep you were saving and now
you have to ship," said Tony.

"The lost sheep who brought on your
cold," I said. The pancakes were light and
good, with a tingly afterglow, which must
have been the cayenne powder.

"I think I was already starting the cold before my trek through the swamp —"

The phone rang. "Who wants to bet that's
my troubles for the day beginning?" said
Adrian, reaching for it. "Oh, good morning,
Coach, I was just asking Margaret was it too
early to call you. He what? Do you have any
idea where? I see. Let's hold off on that, Dan.
That's true, but once you invite the police in
— can we give it a little longer? He might re-
think and come back. *Naturally* I'll take full
responsibility, that's what I'm there for. Yes,
Dan, I'm sure you did. I'll be out there as
soon as I can shave and dress."

"I can fill in the blanks on that one," I said when Adrian hung up. "Chase has run away."

"No, Chase has *driven* away in Coach's brand-new Jeep. Just brazenly entered their bedroom sometime during the night and stole the keys out of Dan's trousers. Dan and Mary didn't hear a thing. When they got up this morning, both Chase and the Jeep were gone."

"He'd make a good cat burglar," said Tony.

"And he may soon find himself living where many a cat burglar and car thief have ended up." Adrian rose from the table. "Many thanks for the good breakfast and the home remedies, Tony. I feel slightly more equal to what awaits me than I might have otherwise."

"But if Chase is gone," I said, "what can you do out at the school that couldn't be accomplished right here at home over the telephone?"

"I can walk around in my headmaster persona and look responsible and encourage everybody to think the situation is under control because I'm there," said Adrian. His palm rested briefly on the top of my head. "Don't want to give you my cold," he said, and went upstairs to dress.

"Oh me," said Tony, suddenly slumping. "Think I'll step outside and have myself a quick puff." As he fumbled in his shirt pocket and brought out his Zippo and an already rolled cigarette, I noticed his hands were trembling slightly. "Don't want to pollute the air in here, with his chest cold. Please leave those dishes, Margaret. I've got the rest of the morning to clean up." After he'd gone out, I began to feel the aftereffects of the eventful night. My adrenaline drained out, as if someone had pulled a plug, leaving me in a kind of aware stupor. Observations continued to register, but it was like being partly anesthetized; I was able to reflect on what was in progress around me but felt powerless to influence the course of events. Adrian was upstairs preparing to plunge into a stressful Saturday when he should be home coddling his bronchi; his pet delinquent was careening down some mountain road in a stolen new Jeep; Helen Britt was embarking on her first day of widowhood; Grace Munger was addressing the bikers in Clampitt, no doubt dropping my name in some disingenuous way to advance her cause: "Earlier this morning, the Reverend Margaret Bonner of All Saints High Balsam and I shared our beliefs over a cup of coffee and found ourselves, as Paul urges us to do in Romans Twelve, of the same mind on a number of points. . . ."

And outside, Tony was puffing away, hatching God knew what plan, even if it consisted simply in making himself welcome under as many free roofs as possible on his millennial pilgrimage.

I got up to pour myself another cup of coffee and in so doing glanced out the back door and saw the empty wire hanger swaying madly from the dogwood branch. Then I saw Tony hurriedly scrambling into his habit. When he spotted me peering out at him, he made stay-inside motions and put a finger to his lips. Then, tugging his skirts down over his jeans, he scuttled out of sight.

I was still waiting, transfixed, to see what spectacle would next present itself through the glass, when Adrian returned.

"Where's St. Anthony?"

"He went out for a smoke, then I looked out and saw him hustling into his habit. He waved me to stay inside and disappeared around that corner."

"I'll go see what's up."

But Adrian had no sooner opened the door when Tony swung into sight, moving fast, pursued by an angry, dark, round-faced boy. Following both of them, like a willowy blond frowning angel, was Jennifer Tye.

"I'll be damned," said Adrian. "Well, Chase," he called, stepping outside, "I'm extremely relieved to see you, but this is a sorry performance on your part."

"Not as sorry as *his*," the boy shot back furiously. "This old sneak comes hobbling over in his holy clothes and says you're *sick* and catches me off guard when I'm talking to *her*, then steals my keys out of the ignition and *runs!*"

"I may be an old sneak," said Tony, "but your headmaster is sick. He should be in bed, but he got dressed to go looking for you." His lowered eyes as he modestly advanced in his black skirts and handed over the Jeep keys to Adrian failed to conceal his elation over this latest service to us.

"He doesn't look very sick to me," said the boy. He glared at us all and accusingly added, "You can't trust anybody!"

Adrian had once described Radford Zorn's adoptive Peruvian child (whom the then-Mrs. Zorn had wanted to return, like merchandise to a foreign store, because he was "too brown") as "a ticking bomb of justified grievances dating all the way back to the Spanish Conquest." It was the first time I had seen him up close, and the description certainly fit. The ticking bomb was small for his age, with flashing dark eyes and long, lustrous inky-black hair parted dead-center like a Rudolph Valentino impersonator in a high school play. The hair had occasioned much teasing by the other kids when he first arrived at the school, but Adrian said this had only incited Chase to grow it longer and accentuate the look with brilliantine. His exotic pre-Columbian face glowered out at us from his green anorak with the Fair Haven crest. He appeared much younger than his sixteen years: standing shoulder-high to sedate Jennifer in her leggy black jeans and over-sized pea coat, which I recognized as belonging to Gus, he would easily have been taken as the younger one.

"You can't trust *anybody*," he reiterated self-pityingly in the Dixie boy accent of his adoptive father's region.

"Coach is probably saying the same thing right now," Adrian caustically replied. " 'You take a boy into your home for the night and wake up to find your new Jeep stolen. Can't trust anybody.' "

"He didn't steal it, Father Bonner," Jennifer said, speaking up in her precise, reasonable voice. "He only borrowed it because he needed to get over here to see you right away."

"Perhaps he should have made that clearer to Coach Dan," said Adrian. "Well, here I am, Chase: what do we do now? And what brings you out so early in the morning, Jennifer?"

"Sue's dad dropped me on the way to his office. I was worried about the flower delivery for our wedding. They're sure to put them up on the *altar* or some stupid thing, and also I wanted to check them out while there's still time to send them back if they're wrong."

"But Jennifer, love," I said, joining the others on the frosty lawn, "the florist won't even be open for another hour or so."

"Well, but Sue's dad was leaving right then and I needed the ride. And you yourself, Pastor Margaret, told me worry was my middle name."

As we both laughed, she gracefully pushed away an unruly wisp of gossamer hair that the breeze had blown across her eyes and gave me a droll look. It was one of those moments when everyone suddenly realizes he is in the presence of beauty; I felt it myself and I saw it register on the faces of the others, including young Chase's.

"Is it your wedding today?" he asked Jennifer.

She gave a derisive snort of laughter. "Are you crazy? I'm twelve years old."

"I thought you seemed —"

Seeing that she had mortified him, she quickly amended, "But in a *way* it's my wedding, because I got my father together with this person who's ideal for both of us. I'm the maid of honor and the only bridesmaid, because Gus says her friends are too old to be bridesmaids anymore. Why don't you come? I want the church to be packed. You, too, sir," she added graciously to Tony.

"Thank you, I'm planning to," said Tony. "Your ideal person kindly invited me last evening." He unbuttoned his habit, tugged it over his head, shook it out, and carefully hung it back on the dogwood branch. "To continue its airing for the wedding," he announced to his young onlookers, the complacent magician after a trick.

"What are you, anyway?" demanded Chase irritably.

"I've been any number of things in my time," said Tony, "but right now I'm just an old monk on a journey. Perhaps you young folks would allow me to make you some pancakes after all the excitement."

"Chase and I have some business to attend to first," said Adrian. "May we use the telephone in your study, Margaret?"

"Help yourselves," I said. "I'm going upstairs to change out of my holy clothes."

"I'll set the table," announced responsible Jennifer to Tony.

I kicked off my shoes, dropped my collar on the dresser, and got as far as hanging up my jacket (Adrian's unused quarters still jingling in the pocket) when I realized my day was already racing away from me before I'd had the chance to commit it to God's time. I lay down in my shirttails on top of the bedcovers, which Adrian had hastily made up, propped up some pillows, and took my office book out of the bedside drawer. This was the final day for Year One. Tomorrow would begin Advent of Year Two in the companion volume, awaiting its biennial turn in the same drawer.

Lord, open our lips (although my mouth had

been running practically nonstop since the earliest hours of the morning), *And our mouth shall proclaim your praise.*

Then on to the first psalm, which today, by rather sinister coincidence, was none other than 137, Grace's clarion call to the Millennium Birthday March: *By the waters of Babylon we sat down and wept . . .*

(Dammit, why hadn't I thought to nail her on that allusion to "Babylonian elements" in her manifesto, the ones that had "leeched into Zion and contaminated our waters.")

In the newer office books, the nasty parts of Psalms were always put in parentheses in the daily assignments, indicating that it was okay to skip over them if you wanted, but I always read them faithfully, as a reminder to myself that, for all our progress, the sandbox mentality still lurked in our depths and it was better to be aware of it than not. Besides, the nasty parts of 137 ("Happy shall he be who takes your little ones, and dashes them against the rock!") never failed to evoke fond memories of my Night Prayers with Josie, who was now studying law and who still wrote to me occasionally.

If you went in for reading the office like a horoscope, the upbeat first Lesson from the Book of Micah ("A day for the building of your walls! In that day the boundary shall be far extended . . .") was promptly shot down by the next Lesson from First Peter: "The end of all things is at hand; therefore keep sane and sober for your prayers . . . Beloved, do not be surprised at the fiery ordeal which comes upon you to prove you, as though something strange were happening to you.")

Was I destined, from now on, to think of Grace Munger every time I came across a passage about fire? ("It's the way the Lord chose to mark me for his own.")

I fought the urge to lie back on the pillows smelling faintly of Adrian's sweat (I forgot to ask him did he think he had a fever) and close my eyes and float away on the reassuring music of life going on without me from below.

The next thing I knew, Adrian was sitting beside me on the bed.

"Have I been asleep long?"

"Not long enough. I didn't want to wake you, but I needed to speak to you before I go."

"You're going out to school?"

"Chase and I are returning the Jeep; Coach Dan's expecting us. Then we'll go over to the dorm and pack up Chase's things. I haven't reached Radford Zorn yet, he's between home and a work site. The housekeeper gave me his mobile phone, but I want him as stationary and static-free as possible when I break the bad news."

"What if he washes his hands of the whole thing?"

"Oh, he'll make noises to that effect; we've already had a foretaste of his 'junk Chase' rhetoric. However, he knows as well as I do that he's legally responsible for his son. But I hate to think of Chase being packed off to some maximum security military school or psychiatric facility where they'll undo the small bit of good work he's done on himself at Fair Haven. Margaret, how would you feel about having him here for a while, at least until we can decide what to do?"

"Well, I'm willing to try it, if you think that's best for now."

"It's certainly not *ideal*, by any means, but I can't think what else to do on such short notice. The ideal situation would be — hell, the ideal situation would be for him to have behaved himself and stayed at Fair Haven. He feels the same way himself — he just told me in your study that he knows he wrecked his best chance. If only he could stay away from the drinking; it makes him sorry for himself, and then his self-pity turns into aggression toward the people who are trying to help him. If I could get him into some kind of program and continue working with him the way I did as chaplain while he finishes out his sophomore year at the public high school. If we could take him that far. Beyond that, I don't dare project."

"Best not to," I agreed, my imagination neverless embarking on scenarios. What were the chances of Chase staying in a public high school when he'd been kicked out of every school paid to take him? And where was Adrian going to find those extra hours to spend with Chase "the way I did as chaplain" when he himself admitted he hadn't had sufficient time for Chase since he had become acting headmaster? Ask now or forever hold your peace, the voice of reason prompted, but I knew how much my husband had invested in the redemption of Chase, and heard myself saying instead, "We can put him on the sun porch after Tony leaves, but what about tonight?"

"Well, there's my study. I could clear off all the books on the bed. Maybe sleeping in your father's old bed will have a salutary effect on him."

"As long as *we* sleep with our respective car keys under our pillows in here. And lock ourselves in."

"Good idea," said Adrian, laughing. "Tony asked if he could ride out to school with us. He wants to see the place."

"And then do come home and rest up a little before the wedding."

"And you try to do the same, if you can." He laid his hand on mine and then, discovering it was resting in turn on the office book, which lay facedown on my stomach, gently commented, "My poor love, you fell asleep reading Morning Prayer."

"Actually, I feel anything but poor," I said, topping his hand with mine. And there we were, on the final morning of Year One, growing larger by the minute with all the commitments we knowingly and unknowingly had taken on.

IX

Wedding

Jennifer, worrying aloud as fast as she could walk, hurried ahead of me to the church. It was like trying to keep up with a chattering high-tension wire.

"I should have made a quick phone call to those florist people. Just to make sure they have our order right. I wish we weren't having the champagne punch at our house, but my father says it's not fair to the nonalcoholics and he never liked champagne anyway. You've got the license, haven't you, Pastor Margaret?"

"No, but I will have, when I unlock the safe and get it out."

"Shouldn't Mrs. Lord be here doing the altar by now?"

"If it were a morning wedding, she would be. But we've still got five hours to go."

"But the ceremony *starts* in five hours!"

"You can be sure that Mrs. Lord knows her job, Jennifer," I said testily. The girl's tension was infectious. "Lucinda has been president of the Altar Guild as long as you've been on this earth. Her mother wrote the *Altar Guild Manual*."

We had reached the church door. Jennifer kept up a perpetual jiggle beside me as I dug into my pocket for the key. "You brought your key, didn't you, Pastor Margaret?"

That did it. I spun away from the church door, key in hand, and crossed over to the stone bench. "Come over here and sit down," I said. "I think we need to recollect ourselves before we go any further."

She contritely joined me on the bench. "I guess I am pretty nervous this morning, aren't I?"

"You're a walking menace to tranquility. Everyone, including me, is going to be afflicted with the jiggle-jangles if you don't calm down." A piece of her soft hair blew my way. "But your hair smells wonderful."

"It's too fly-ey, though! I had to use Sue's shampoo this morning because I forgot mine and it's all wrong for my hair. My shampoo has the extra-body formula. Oh, I hope this breeze dies down before the wedding, or *everybody's* hair will be all over the place."

"Jennifer." I put the flat of my hand across both her knees to stop their compulsive jiggling. "Did you listen to the weather report this morning?"

"Of course." She seemed surprised I even asked. "I had the Weather Channel on before it was even light. They said clear and sunny, high about forty-eight in the sun."

"That's what they said on my car radio,

too. Ideal forecast for an afternoon wedding at the end of November, wouldn't you say?"

"Well, yes —"

"And everything is as humanly perfect as we can make it. The programs got printed without a single misspelling of anybody's name; your numbered ribbons are in the Hymnals so everyone can find their places quickly; and you saw how I marked up a Book of Common Prayer yesterday for Smathers Eubanks's organist friend from Mountain City, so he'll know exactly where the hymns go in the service. Now how about giving ourselves over to the part of the day we can't control? Let the breeze play softly through everybody's hair, or everybody who still has hair, if it wants to, and allow the winds of the spirit to find their way through the spaces we leave. Okay?"

"Okay. But . . ."

"But what?"

"Well, it's just that . . ." Already you could see where the worry slashes would soon be marking the lovely high forehead. "It's the parts I can't control that bother me the most."

"Would you want a world that you were totally in control of?"

"Good grief, no! I have enough to do as it is!"

Then, having the good fortune to possess a sense of humor which almost counterbalanced her ponderous sense of duty, she burst out laughing at herself, and so did I.

"Leave some room for the Divine margin, then," I said, hugging her in her oversized pea jacket. "You can be sure God will have a few surprises to contribute to this day."

"Well, I just hope they're —"

A car door slammed, nipping her next impertinent misgiving in the bud.

"Morning, all," trilled Lucinda Lord, tripping toward us in her killer heels, carrying a plastic-protected freshly laundered fair linen on a special "roller-hanger," contrived by Lucinda herself to prevent creases. "Here comes your ecclesiastical charwoman." Her "char" clothes this morning were a natty hunter-green suit, with spotless fichu and diamond circle pin, and a matching green trilby with a saucily tilted pheasant feather. "Your precious new mother, I want you to know, Jennifer, is one of the few people in this world for whom I don't mind changing the church from Festival white to Advent purple all in a single day. But why are you two sitting out here? Are you locked out?"

"No, ma'am," said Jennifer Tye. "Pastor Margaret and I were just recollecting ourselves for the busy day ahead."

The florist's truck arrived almost immediately after and two fast-moving young men unloaded the exact number of red cyclamen and pot-grown white heath, with appreciative side glances to spare for the young lady with flying hair who counted each plant as it was carried into church to be placed, as she instructed, "at the base of the altar, please, *not* on top." After the wedding the plants were to be delivered to the Hazel Grove Nursing Home, which Gus had built, a cyclamen to go in each inhabitant's room for Advent and the heath to be planted right away, before the ground froze, in the residents' hillside garden, visible from their dayroom.

Jennifer at once took charge of arranging the blooms in their gray-green earthenware pots, while I lurked on the sidelines admiring Lucinda's tactful guidance.

"What you'd *started* to do there, hon, was nice."

"Oh, really? I thought it was too clunky."

"It was very natural looking. Almost like they were growing together. Not so lined-up-y. Yes, that's the idea. And maybe move the white heath a little more to the right, what do you think? That way it'll have the gold orphrey behind it and won't get lost against the white frontal."

"If only my hair would stop flying around!" cried Jennifer, swatting agitatedly at her face. "And there's not time to wash it again with my own shampoo because I told Gus I'd be over to her house to help the caterers set up."

"Come to the rectory now," I said, "and I'll give you a squirt bottle of my magic calming spritz. Then I'll drive you over to Gus's and you'll have plenty of time to experiment with it."

"That sounds like an inspired idea," said Lucinda Lord, covertly shifting a cyclamen pot with the pointy toe of her shoe while Jennifer's back was turned.

"What kind of spritz is it?" asked Jennifer.

"Just one of the brand name extra-holds. I dilute it because the original dries like cement on my hair. I call it Dr. Stroup's Altar Fix."

"Who is Dr. Stroup?"

"A professor at General Seminary who taught us how to look and behave at the altar. Let's go and get the spritz and I'll tell you about Dr. Stroup."

"Yes, hon, you go along with the rector, and leave the rest of the beautifications to me," Lucinda urged, sending me a straight, sharp look of approval. It was the first time in my presence she had referred to me as rector. During our three years of coexistence, Lucinda and I had slowly been progressing out of our initial faceoff stance of Old Guard conservatrix versus young-woman-pastor-with-too-many-new-ideas into mutual appreciation. Behind her old-fashioned-female airs and euphemistic mode of operation, I had discovered endurance and loyalty and far more intelligence than she wished to own up to. On this first occasion of her calling me the rector, it was pleasing to think I had met her image of a person sufficiently worthy to lead the church she had devoted so much time and talent to serving.

As I drove Jennifer and her spritz bottle of Stroup's Altar Fix across town to Gus's house, she was unusually pensive. This lasted for a few blocks, then she burst into giggles. "That crazy boy! Asking if it was my wedding. But his father can't really pay the state to keep him in jail, can he?"

"Of course he can't," I said.

"That's what I told him. Our justice system doesn't work that way, no matter how rich or important your father is, or how many contracts he has with the state. Chase is terribly naive for someone sixteen. Still, sixteen is pretty young to be an alcoholic. He's been to the Menninger Clinic, you know."

"You two must have had quite a talk."

"Well, he was ballistic. Somebody had to calm him down, and I was the only one around to do it. He slammed out of that Jeep and was on his way to wake you all up if I hadn't taken him in hand."

"We were already awake, but that was thoughtful of you."

"And then, it was so funny, this old monk suddenly comes creeping out of the bushes like he can hardly walk, and asks Chase if by any chance his name is Chase, and he says

291

Father Bonner is at home sick, and then he sort of circles around and peers inside the Jeep and says what nice upholstery and asks to have a look inside, and the next thing you know he grabs the keys out of the ignition, picks up his skirts and streaks off! I thought it was hilarious, like a Charlie Chaplin movie or something, but Chase went into a rage. He seems to be a person who goes into rages a lot. What's going to happen to him, Pastor Margaret? He said he's been expelled by Father Bonner, but I don't think he'll do too well on his own."

"Adrian's going to suggest to Chase's father that he stay with us at the rectory and finish the school year at High Balsam High."

"That's pretty generous of you."

"Generous or foolhardy, I'm not sure which. Adrian thinks Chase has made some progress and hates to see it thrown away. Let's hope it will work out. You'll have to help us, if he comes. It looks as though you've already won his confidence."

"Oh, sure, I'll help." There was a busy silence during which I could all but hear her making a list of the ways she was going to take Chase over. "For a start," she said, "he could make himself useful by driving me to school. It's on the way to the high school, and it would free up my father for more important things. I think people feel better about themselves if they're being useful, don't you?"

"Let's see what Chase's father says first. And he can't very well drive you to school without a car." No use to add at this point that I wasn't sure Chase's license was valid, or if he'd ever had a license, not to mention whether Charles Tye would want his daughter riding to school with a teenage alcoholic with two stolen cars under his belt. "Let's wait and see," I amended cautiously.

The Joyous Kitchen caterer's van was parked in front of Gus's "Florida Tudor," as she humorously described the style of her late parents' house. ("My father, who had no natural taste of his own, was getting ready to copy some pretentious Colonial Shingle he and Annabel had admired up in Newport, when Grandpop stepped in and persuaded them to buy this nice Richard Sharpe Smith–inspired stuccoed Tudor on a sixteen-acre wooded site that had just come on the market. Grandpop figured it was too solid to ruin, but by the time Annabel finished knocking out walls and windows and paving the timbered entrance hall with Mediterranean tile and turning the oak-paneled library into a sort of Olde English sun porch, he said for the poor *house's* sake he wished he'd kept his mouth shut and let them go ahead and build their Newport jumble.")

I pulled into the circular driveway ahead of the caterer's van, intending to drop Jennifer and head out again, but Gus, in jeans and old bomber jacket, burst out of the house like a rocket.

"Morning, sweet." She hugged Jennifer as soon as the girl stepped out. Linked together, both tall and rangy and blond, they presented an adventitious mother-daughter sameness, but I was unprepared for Gus's ragged, abashed appearance this morning; she'd been so serenely at ease last night in the crypt, down on her haunches, pointing her steel tape like an extension of her confident powers. "The tablecloths are already on, and they've found enough outlets in the library for all their food warmers." She released Jennifer and gave her a playful push on her behind. "Run and take a look at those serving dishes you like and check them over for any tarnish spots. I'll be in presently."

She came around to my side of the car and stuck her head in. "The angels must have sent you," she said. "Do you have some time to talk?"

"Sure." I cut the engine and got out. "You look a little tense."

"Let's —" she hesitated, glanced nervously at the library wing where you could see the caterers setting up through the wraparound windows and French doors Annabel Eubanks had installed on all three sides, and then veered off toward the woods on the opposite side of the house. I followed.

"I went through some brand new kind of

hell in the maid's room last night," she began before we'd even reached the woodland path where we had occasionally walked before. "I need you to tell me if this is normal bride's nerves, or if I'm making a terrible mistake, and if it *is* a mistake, what on earth can be done about it at this late hour without breaking everybody's heart."

For the second time that morning, I had to take extra steps to keep pace with a distraught long-legged member of the wedding party. The path, carpeted with new-fallen pine needles, was golden in the morning light, the woods had that lugubriously satisfying autumnal smell of crumbling summer being mulched into purposeful winter rest, but my mind was already racing ahead to meet an alternative day in which a wedding must be dismantled rather than celebrated. What were the requirements, humane and sacramental, for such an undertaking? So far the worst thing I'd had happen on a wedding day was the mother of the bride getting lost on the way to High Balsam (she arrived forty minutes late, with police escort and sirens, and everybody made a huge fuss over her, which, considering the lady in question, might have been the point).

I'd as yet had no experiences of no-show brides or grooms, or last-minute changes of heart at countdown time. The only dismantled weddings I knew about came via novels or the tales of fellow clergy. Everyone shuddered at the prospect of a stranger showing up, as in *Jane Eyre*, and revealing some awful impediment from the back of the church. And my father once had a groom *and* the groom's father, who was best man, faint together at the beginning of the exchange of vows. The father was helped to a pew, the shaky groom dragged himself up to stand beside the bride. "Do you want to go on with this?" my father discreetly asked the groom, who insisted he did. But the marriage hadn't lasted, my father said.

"What happened in the maid's room?" I asked Gus.

"This is mortifying. What's that demon thing that has intercourse with people while they're asleep?"

"An incubus if it's male; a succubus if it's female."

"Well, this was a male. A specific male. Oh, this is so *unwelcome*, Margaret! But it certainly wasn't unwelcome while it was going on. And then I slowly woke out of it and realized it had been a dream and started to cry, of all things, because it *had* only been a dream! That was the part that made it unforgivable: that I was *awake* when I was crying. On the morning of my wedding to Charles, I woke up crying because I had only made love with Edmund Gallatin in a dream."

She snapped a dead branch off a pine tree,

flung it violently into the woods, and wheeled around to face me. "Margaret, as my friend and my priest, you have to help me. I have to know whether it's honorable for me to go ahead with today as planned."

Her handsome face was strained with anguish, her light eyes clouded with confusion. Totally absent from her tone was the playful disparagement that had always accompanied her stories of her long and hopeless passion for the boy from Charleston, who spent summers with his family in High Balsam, and who then returned alone years later, middle-aged and elusive about his past, ostensibly to court her but never coming around to the point — and then the absurd anticlimax of his going to live with her gay cousin Smathers in Mountain City. I had been looking forward with frank curiosity to my first sight of the legendary Edmund today, seated beside his partner on the bride's side of the church, relegated securely to his proper role in Gus's story: the extinguished *ignis fatuus* who had served his purpose by keeping her love muscles from atrophying while she was so busily pursuing her profession.

"I suppose the first thing to ask," I said, after a pause during which I myself asked for help, "is, do you want to go ahead with this day as planned?"

"Up until this morning, I never doubted we'd all three be better off for having one another. I looked forward to our new life. No, I was already in it. I already thought in terms of us and ours."

"Then, what has changed?"

"It's as though the dream, and more particularly the way I felt when I woke out of it, has separated me from Charles."

"Then tell me a little more about how you felt when you woke up." The aftermath, from her account, seemed to be where she thought her betrayal lay. This was no longer the Middle Ages, where the existence of incubi was recognized by ecclesiastical and civil law and you could feel guilty for having been ravished by one in a dream.

She suddenly sank down cross-legged in the middle of the path and put her hands up to the sides of her head as if steadying her thoughts. "It was like . . . the emptiness you feel in bereavement. Only worse, because it was for something unsubstantial. After Grandpop August died, I went around for months with this aching hole in my heart. I felt emptied out of the person who had understood and loved me most. But I knew, even as I went around hurting, that I'd *had* his love. It had been real and I would always carry it, and him, with me. Whereas, this morning I seemed to be grieving for some illusory thing I'd never had. This love I wanted so much and never had. It was frustrating and sad and, I must say, utterly degrading."

I dropped down beside her on the pine needles. "Why degrading?"

"Well, because I still felt the shape of this phantom lover. When I woke up, I could still feel the presence inside me of someone who'd never been there, or wanted to be there. But also, there was — oh, I wish I could explain this better — there was an ebbing rightness about it that I wanted desperately to hold onto. That rightness part is the killer."

"Try to hold onto it now. What was the rightness like?"

"Well, I felt him — *delighting* in me exactly as much as I delighted in him. It wasn't just sexual. I've never felt this . . . this perfect mutuality . . . with anybody, not even Charles. I doubt if I'll ever experience it in my waking life. It may not even be possible to *have* such a thing in your waking life." Her eyes welled with tears. "And yet I wanted it."

"Do you think," I picked my words slowly, "that if inclinations had been different on his side, and you and Edmund had become lovers, or gotten married, there might have been this perfect mutuality?"

"Are you kidding?" She laughed incredulously. "I may have carried a torch for him for twenty years, but even while I was busy making a fool of myself after he came back to High Balsam, I was perfectly aware that he hadn't the least concept of what I was really about. You and I have been over all this before. No, the dream lover was a much fuller being, but he wore Edmund's face and body." She paused and reflected. "Shoot, I'm not even sure about the body. There are large areas of Edmund's body that I never became acquainted with. For all I know, Edmund might have a strawberry down there." She snickered, and then cut her eyes over at me and dissolved into helpless laughter. I thought this was a good sign.

"If I'm following you so far, it's the waking up part, where you mourned the loss of that perfect mutuality you've never had with anybody. That was the part that made you feel separated from Charles?"

"Yes."

"Why? Can you say why it made you feel separated?"

"Because I would be going into the marriage knowing about something I don't have with Charles, something I wish I did have, and keeping it from him. That doesn't seem honorable. Does it? And yet the last thing I would ever want to do is call him up and tell him about it. That would be stupid and unkind. And cowardly: making him take on the consequences of my romp with the incubus. 'Oh, Charles, it's me, with a last-minute qualm. Will you listen to this dream I had, and the way it affected me, and then be honest and tell me whether you still want to marry me?' "

"Let's imagine you did make such a call. How do you think Charles would respond?"

"It would surprise him. I don't operate like that. He'd think it was a bad joke. No, he wouldn't; he knows I don't make jokes like that. Charles knows *me*."

She closed her eyes, concentrating hard. "He would listen, in that laid-back mountain-man way he listens to his patients going down what he calls their laundry list of ailments, then he'd stroke his beard until out would come something Charles-ish, like, 'What all did you eat and drink before you went to bed?' Getting it back on a practical level. But he's a gentleman and he'd go on to ask whether *I* felt any different this morning about getting married. He knows all about the ambiguous Edmund, just as I know all about his troubles with that bitch, Jennifer's mother. And I'd say, 'No, not if *you* don't. It was just a wonderful dream of perfect union, but I thought I ought to check with you because it was Edmund, not you, who showed up in the dream.' And we'd go ahead and have the marriage. But it would cast a cloud over his wedding day."

"What about yours? Would it cast a cloud over yours?" I was careful to stay in the subjunctive.

She picked up a red maple leaf from the ground and slowly smoothed it out on her palm. "Well, it already has, hasn't it? But . . ."

She was stroking the leaf meditatively, rather like her description of Charles stroking words out of his beard. ". . . it's not a poison cloud, I'm pretty positive. I don't think it's even a mildly radioactive cloud. Before I dropped off to sleep last night, I was mulling over our talk in the crypt. That was such a wonderful story you told, about you and Adrian and that mural, and I may have carried it over into some fantasy of what it would be like to finally be joined with the first passionate love of your life on your wedding night. But you were twenty-seven and your first passionate love wanted you as well. I'm forty-two, and Charles and I have been sleeping together for almost a year, so the wedding night consummation has been preempted. And my first love was simply a fantasy man I never had."

"Perhaps you had the best of him last night," I ventured.

"Hmm." She scrutinized the leaf in the palm of her hand. "Now, that's a thought. Ha. Dear old resurrected Edmund, in his never-to-be straight incarnation. But does it, or doesn't it, count as some sort of infidelity?"

"Not unless you subscribe to some awfully out-of-date laws." I told her about the civil and ecclesiastical courts of the Middle Ages. "Saint Augustine never thought it counted, though it grieved him that even after he'd sworn off sex he kept being pursued by images that gave him carnal emissions in his sleep. But he acknowledged in his autobiography that that's *all* they were and he was sure God would eventually rid him of them. The 'glue of lust,' he called them."

"The glue of lust, I love that."

"Yes, well, the whole concept of the incubus is supposed to have originated with Augustine, according to my Patristics professor at General. Before the *Confessions*, *incubo* was just a harmless little intransitive verb, meaning 'to lie upon.'"

"You're full of such wonderful lore, Margaret. Are you saying that you think it's okay if I keep my dream to myself and go ahead and marry Charles?"

"If that's what you still want to do."

"I do. Yes, I definitely do still want to marry Charles." As soon as she spoke the words, the cloudiness and tension visibly ebbed from her face.

"As far as I'm concerned, nothing you've told me has violated the papers I signed and sent to the bishop, saying that in my best judgment you and Charles intend a Christian marriage as it is described in the Canons. Do you still hold with the Declaration of Intention you and Charles signed?"

" 'A lifelong union for the purpose of mutual fellowship, encouragement, and understanding,' " she quoted from memory, ". . . and then there's the part about children, if they come along, which, as you know, we've ruled out at my age, though I certainly intend to follow the physical and spiritual nurturing part to the hilt in regards to Jenn, and then the part about being beneficial to society . . . well, Charles and I are both trying to do that already, I think. And then there's a bit more which I'm afraid has slipped my mind."

"It concludes with your engaging yourselves, with God's help, to make the utmost effort to establish this relationship."

"Oh, right, God's help. People are always forgetting that. Just like in Charles's twelve steps. You've got to ask a greater power for help."

We stood up and brushed pine needles off our backsides. "I'm afraid you've got a wet seat," she said.

"No wetter than yours. Friends are supposed to share." As we retraced our path back to the wedding, I said, "This may sound strange, but I think you should honor and treasure that dream."

"I *should?*"

"The perfect mutuality part, you should. I believe it was an intimation of a state that's absolutely worthy of your yearning. Think of it as a gift that goes beyond the Edmunds. And beyond the Charleses and the Adrians, too. I believe such a state exists and we are all groping for it, in our bumbling fashions. If it didn't exist, we couldn't have dreamed it so well."

"Do you mean exist in the sense of —"

But the rest of that conversation would have to wait for a later walk. Jennifer was hurrying toward us on the path.

"Hey, you guys? It's getting pretty late, you know."

She was trying to appear nonchalant, but her anxious face told its own story. Her sharp little radar system, always on the alert for disappointment, had picked up distress signals, and in our absence she had been tormenting herself with possible scenarios of a last-minute destruction of her hopes: some unforeseen reversal — another woman walking out on her. And in slightly different circumstances, I somberly reminded myself, such a scenario might be in its painful opening throes this very moment.

It tugged at my own mother-starved heart to see how everything about her reached for Gus, yet refrained from grabbing. "So what were you all *up* to?" she asked, dancing her long legs ahead of us on the path, but keeping her sights trained relentlessly on Gus.

"Oh, just taking my last walk as an old maid," said Gus. She gave the red maple leaf a festive twirl between her thumb and forefinger, then ceremoniously handed it over to Jennifer. "Here, daughter, a little souvenir."

★ ★ ★

Lucinda Lord's car was gone when I got back to the church, but it would have been an insult to my impeccable sacristan to go in and check things over. I knew everything would be in its proper place: parish register on the sacristy desk (with fountain pen handy for signatures), cope on its stand, Eucharistic vestments laid out properly on the table. The altar and credence would be faultlessly prepared, wedding kneelers ready on chancel steps. Her work would in every aspect live up to the bronze plaque given in her mother's memory, which hung in the Altar Guild's little annex off the sacristy:

> *Duty makes us do things well.*
> *Love makes us do things beautifully.*
> Phillips Brooks

Back at the rectory I listened to the messages on my machine. First came a call from a priest in Mountain City who wanted to make an appointment for a pre-Christmas confession if I had an hour to spare during the two-day Commission on Ministry meeting there.

Next came a rambling and annoying communiqué from Kevin Dowd: "Hi, Margaret! Hope you at least are managing to get some shut-eye after our long night in the trenches. Our mutual friend Grace Munger woke *me* up before eight this morning to say you two had ironed out major differences at the Horseshoe and you've invited her to come to your church, so I'm deducing our little tempest in a teapot is hopefully over. Now you and I can get on with more important business!"

Which meant exactly what? He was as soft and circuitous as Grace Munger was persistent and duplicitous: they made a scary duo. It was hard work trying to keep straight lines with either of them. She must have phoned him even before she got to the bikers' breakfast in Clampitt. As for "our little tempest in a teapot," I would have liked to pour it over his head.

The last message, from Adrian, was so typically spare I had to play it over again twice to get everything, which meant suffering through Kevin a total of three times.

Radford Zorn had agreed quickly (too quickly?) to Adrian's proposal and offered to pay all Chase's expenses and a monthly allowance, to be doled out or withheld as we saw fit, for as long as he stayed with us. Adrian, Tony, and Chase were going to stop somewhere for lunch after packing up Chase's things. The three of them would be back for the wedding.

I went upstairs to see what could be done in a short time to transform Adrian's study into a temporary bedroom for Chase. When Tony left, we could settle Chase downstairs in the sunroom with his own bathroom, but for to-night and probably tomorrow he would have to sleep down the hall from us. I stood in the doorway of Adrian's study: my husband's province, with its shelves of psychology and theology and medieval history, and the stacks of newer books and journals on educational theories and adolescent disorders over-flowing onto the bed which had been my fa-ther's, and my father's and mother's before she left us, and before that had belonged to my father's late mentor, Father Traherne, and his wife.

But how would Chase see the room? As a dreary, alien space? An oppressive enclosure crowded with another person's thoughts and interests, leaving no room for his own?

I raised the blinds and opened the windows and soon found myself washing the sills and cobwebby screens, sneezing into paper towels as I proceeded. The books and jour-nals I removed from the bed, and found places for them on the shelves or in our room.

As I was making up the bed that I most likely had been conceived in, it occurred to me to wonder whether Adrian had purposely kept it covered with reading matter during our strained time after Sandlin's death in order to prevent himself from sleeping in it and thus making an overt break from our marriage bed. After everything was done, I lay down on the freshly made bed and imagined how it would feel for Chase to lie here. Taking deep gulps of the fresh air flowing in through the screens, I stretched out my legs and, in doing so, recalled how high and wide and safe this bed belonging to my parents had seemed to me as a small child, and how I had reveled in leaping up onto it and spread-eagling myself exactly in the middle, so that an extremity pointed toward each of the four posters. In that position I felt that I was completely in charge of my world.

Of course, those heady illusions had come to an end very soon after, and, as my limbs lengthened, the bed's boundaries had proportionately shrunk; but the old standard-sized bed was still higher off the floor than most beds of today, and perhaps when Chase first lay back on it tonight he would be surprised by an unexpected elevation of confidence and a sense of old-fashioned containment. That was my hope, anyway.

By the time I had showered and dressed, it was just before noon. Though I wasn't at all hungry after my Horseshoe Diner binge followed by Tony's pancakes, I knew I had to fortify myself for the afternoon ahead. I was sipping a power pickup smoothie from the blender, staring meditatively through the glass at Tony's habit swaying gently from its branch in the sun, when I suddenly decided I would go ahead and press it for him.

I set up the board and filled the iron with water for steam pressing, then went out to fetch the habit. As I lifted it down from the branch, I picked up the olfactory blend of sun, cold air, pouch tobacco, and what must have been a lingering trace of Tony himself. I found myself actually *sniffing* at this trace, as if it might offer further information about him.

The habit was well-made. The wool was fine to the touch and had a nice heft to it. I sponged off the spatters of dried mud from the hem, then turned the garment inside out. All the seams were finished. I tried to picture Tony's monastic life: how he would softly enter the abbey chapel in his Nikes, what stories about his past he would tell the others, how he would look when he prayed alone.

As I began to iron one of the two deep side pockets, there was a crackle of paper. Oops. I reached inside and felt what I first took to be his cigarette papers, but it was a piece of newspaper, folded into well-worn sections. I opened it and looked down at the three-year-old photo of Adrian and myself that had appeared in the "Diocesan News" column of *Episcopal Life.* ("Clergy Couple Enhance Western North Carolina Highland Town. The Rev. Margaret Bonner, recently called as rector to historic All Saints High Balsam and the Rev. Adrian Bonner, chaplain at the Fair

Haven School.") Our names had been under-lined in pencil.

I refolded the fragile creases and slipped the paper back into the pocket. Should I go on ironing? I was no longer sure whether it would be such a welcome surprise to Tony. Unless he'd assume I had ironed his habit without looking in the pocket. What if I hadn't? Was I better off or worse off for having looked? I went on ironing and, when I was done, hung it on the hook on the kitchen door where he couldn't miss it. I didn't risk taking it to his room for fear that I might to-tally abandon the rules of hospitality and go ransacking through the rest of his things. Of course, he had told me the very first evening he recognized me from this photo in a church periodical. But that he actually had been car-rying us in his pocket when he said it — that seemed deeper.

Shortly before one, I went over to the church to gather myself before the organist came. Van, my server, would be here at half-past. Then the groom and best man and ushers would arrive and the early birds begin to trickle in.

I got the license and the rings out of the safe and put on my alb, which Lucinda Lord had pressed for me on the ironing board she kept in the sacristy closet. Maybe, I thought, knotting the cincture around my waist, if

311

each of us ironed one garment belonging to another person once a week, the world would become a kinder place. But what to do about the troubling things you came across in the pockets?

Before turning up the lights over the sanctuary and chancel, I sat down behind the rood screen and focused on the occasion ahead, trying to leave all the rest outside. But, given all that had sprung up since yesterday evening, this was no easy thing.

I hadn't made much progress when the organist from Mountain City bustled in with his briefcase and trotted upstairs to the loft at the rear of the church. I heard the twin clump of his street shoes as they dropped to the bare wood floor. The organ was switched on. A silence, in which he presumably laced up his suede-soled pedaling shoes and fiddled with knobs.

Then the startling full-volume burst of a trumpet voluntary. Which just as abruptly ceased. A rustling of pages. Then the exuberant Prelude and Fugue in D Major reverberated through the nave and filled the obscurest crannies of our trussed ceiling. He made our two-manual sound like a five-manual. Our regular organist was on indefinite leave of absence, caring for a mother in the advanced stages of Alzheimer's, and the substitutes I had so far been able to procure had made Sunday hymn singing more of an exercise in endurance than an aid to worship.

The Bach abruptly sheared off. The organist, who must have spotted me sitting in the shadows, called down in his engaging mountain drawl, "I'm not disturbing you, am I, Reverend?"

"No, please go right on."

"I like to come a little early, get into the mood of the place. This is such a beautiful little church. What's up there in the tower?"

"Just the bell."

"I thought maybe you kept old parish ghosts up there."

"No, they're still down here with us."

He laughed, then presently began to play again. This time a sustained piece that fell on my ears like the prayer I had been too distracted to say. Soft and hesitant at first, expanding into strength and certainty, then fading back into a more mysterious hush.

"What was that?" I called up to him.

"Elgar's 'Nimrod.' From the *Enigma Variations*. Strictly speaking it's not a religious piece, but I often play it as background while people are going up for the Eucharist. It works equally well at weddings and funerals."

"Are you going to use it today?"

"Unless you'd prefer something else."

"I like it very much."

Back in the sacristy, I found Charles and

his best man Haywood, a young cousin he was helping to send to medical school, leafing through the parish register.

"You two are nice and early," I said.

"Haywood kept deviling me," said Charles. "Even though there aren't any train tracks to cross in this town."

"A freight train caused me to be late for my wedding," explained Haywood Tye, "and not a day has gone by since that my lovely bride doesn't find a way to remind me of it."

The cousins had the same gaunt faces and lean, droopy builds, but the cosmopolitan Haywood hadn't a trace of Charles's mountain speech and appeared thoroughly at home in his dark suit and tie, whereas Charles looked trapped in his.

Soon after came Van, who exchanged his usual pleasantries with everybody while he vested. "Interesting book you're leafing through, our parish register there. It pays looking through. Father Lindsey was going through it once, and a marriage license from 1917 fell out. Signed and everything. The priest that day must have slipped it into the register and forgot to mail it off to the county. Father Lindsey tried to locate the couple, but nobody around here had heard of them. Wonder if they ever had any problems over it?"

He took down the candlelighter with the brass handle that we used for festive occasions. "Time to light up, I guess. There's a good number of folks already gathered."

I gave Haywood the rings and he slipped them into his coat pocket and patted the flap. "Countdown time, old son," he said to Charles. We could hear the church filling up. I recognized a few voices. Gus and Jennifer and Smathers would be waiting in the church office by now. Gus had asked Smathers to escort her down the aisle but he wouldn't be presenting her. ("I'm old enough to present myself.") When Adrian and I were married by the dean in the Chapel of the Good Shepherd at General, the dean's wife escorted and presented me, because I wanted a final parental grace note. Dr. Stroup had been Adrian's best man and carried our rings in his pocket. "All your family there?" Tony had asked last night. "Our two orphans," Evangeline had called Adrian and me at our reception. "But happy orphans," Adrian answered, his arm around me.

At five minutes before two, the Bach Prelude and Fugue soared forth, though less resonant than when the church was empty. Interesting how much sound the bodies of seventy or more people absorbed.

Van adjusted the cope around my shoulders and fastened it with the morse. He stationed himself at the sacristy door, awaiting the signal from the ushers.

"Ready to roll," he presently said.

315

The groom and best man went first, then Van. As the organist struck up Gounod's "March Nuptiale," I picked up my prayer book and followed them out to meet Gus at the chancel gate.

Smathers I had met only once, when Gus was building the cottages out at Adrian's school. There had been a question about some old right-of-access road, long since overgrown, between the school and the adjoining property, all of which had formerly belonged to their great-grandfather Eubanks, and so she had summoned her cousin ("Smathers never forgets a line he's seen in a family survey map") from Mountain City to "walk the vanished stobs" with her before she broke ground. From her descriptions, I had been expecting to meet a dry, prissy old bachelor, but he turned out to be as attractive in his quicksilvery, patrician way as Gus was, and also very funny. They teased each other a lot on the walk, and he was so vividly descriptive in his outrageous family anecdotes that I felt I knew the people. He also wooed me with tidbits of local church history and gossip, taking my arm like a courtier as we traversed the difficult spots along the route.

In his wedding clothes, he completely personified the gallant protector; as he escorted his cousin up the aisle, one couldn't help recalling the ancient reason the bride had to be on the man's right — so she wouldn't bump against his sheathed sword.

Jennifer preceded them like a solemn medieval princess in her tunic and long skirt of dark green velour, her nosegay of white heather and ferns held close to her body. The waves of her blond hair were as becalmed as those in an etching: how much of Stroup's Altar Fix had she used?

Gus was the only one in the procession who looked completely of her own time: a self-sufficient woman in her forties, an architect with a construction business who was just getting around to matrimony. Even at the tail end of this century, she and Helen Britt were still comparative rarities. Gus looked handsome and elegant in her light gray wedding suit, white high-necked blouse and garnet cross, but she also looked handsome and elegant in her lumberjack shirt and jeans.

Jennifer and Smathers and Haywood moved to the appropriate sides. Gus and Charles stood before me.

"Dearly beloved: We have come together in the presence of God to witness and bless the joining together of this man and this woman in Holy Matrimony . . ."

My eyes did a quick sweep of the standing congregation as I continued on through the Exhortation, but I couldn't spot Adrian or Tony or Chase.

". . . Therefore marriage is not to be en-

317

tered into unadvisedly or lightly, but reverently, deliberately, and in accordance with the purposes for which it was instituted by God. Into this holy union Augusta Eubanks and Charles Tye now come to be joined. If any of you can show just cause why they may not lawfully be married, speak now; or else for ever hold your peace."

No one stepped forth from the shadows of the nave to declare an impediment. I knew exactly where Edmund Gallatin, who had driven up from Mountain City with Smathers, was seated — in the first pew on the bride's side — but I postponed my closer inspection of him until the reading of the Lessons, when I would be sitting in the shadows of the chancel.

"I require and charge you both, here in the presence of God, that if either of you know any reason why you may not be united in marriage lawfully, and in accordance with God's word, you do now confess it."

Everything is absolutely all right now, Gus's warm and candid glance to me conveyed.

Then their Declaration of Consent, followed by "Come Down, O Love Divine," to Ralph Vaughan Williams's stirring tune, "Down Ampney." This had been my contribution; Gus had wanted to include a favorite hymn from Adrian's and my wedding. During the singing I saw an usher escorting in a pretty woman complete with hat and veil. It was Sandi, the waitress from the Horseshoe Diner.

Everyone sat down, the wedding party in the front pew. Smathers rose, bowed toward the altar, mounted to the lectern, and began reading from I Corinthians 13. I gave the congregation another once-over: no Adrian, Tony, or Chase. Where were they? Edmund Gallatin was now directly in my line of sight and I proceeded to study him. He was good-looking in a conventional way, but *blander* than I had pictured him from Gus's stories. His even-featured face registered no expression during Smathers's reading; he seemed oblivious to his present surroundings. It was difficult to imagine him focusing on anyone intently enough to ravish them, in a dream or in real life.

". . . For now we see through a glass, darkly, but then face to face: now I know in part . . ."

Three violent sneezes, coming in rapid succession from the narthex, obliterated the rest of the pivotal sentence with its promise of one day knowing wholly and being known. Smathers, whose face was as mobile as his lover's was shuttered, could not suppress a little scrunch of vexation, but went on to finish as eloquently as he could.

As Smathers was returning to his seat, the usher led in an old monk, a man in clericals, and a boy holding a handkerchief to his nose.

There was a pause, during which the late-comers were seated and a few of the curious could not resist looking around. The boy then blew his nose, a little trumpet voluntary all by itself. Adrian's apologetic eyes met mine: yes, as is all too evident, we have finally arrived.

When it was completely quiet, Jennifer rose, beautifully executed her Sarum bow as we had rehearsed, and, gathering up her long green skirts as if she wore them every day of her life, ascended to the lectern. "A Reading from the First Epistle of John," her clear young voice rang out. "Beloved, let us love one another: for love is of God; and every one that loves is born of God, and knows God . . ."

Then it was my turn to read the Gospel and deliver the sermon. As I was concluding with my sentence on the bottom of the note card, I looked at Adrian, flanked by the old man who carried our picture around in his pocket, and the boy who would sleep in my father's bed tonight.

"May having each other make more of them both." I said the words slowly, hoping that Adrian would pick up on our old phrase. He did; he winked, and I was glad.

Then the exchange of vows, the blessing and giving of rings, the blessing of the marriage, the Peace, right on through the Great Thanksgiving, Communion, and Recessional — everything rolled right along without hitch or glitch, as though checking themselves obediently off Jennifer Tye's wish list of the Precise Way Things Had Better Go at This Wedding. Chase's three loud entrance sneezes and seated trumpet voluntary, though I doubted that Jennifer would permit them to qualify as God's spirit playfully blowing through the planned formalities, had so far provided the only touch of the unpredictable. Of course, there was still the reception to come.

X

Dark-Thirty

As the four of us set out for the reception at Gus's house, the early winter sunset turned the mountains a glowing magenta, and Tony surprised us all by bursting forth into quavery off-key plainsong: "Now sunset comes, but light shines forth/The lamps are lit to pierce the night."

"Is that some of your monastery chant?" Chase, beside him in the backseat, wanted to know.

"It is," said Tony. "The monks sing it at evening prayer."

"But you're one of them. Don't you sing, too?"

"Oh, well, I . . . usually I just move my lips. You heard me. My voice would ruin the effect."

"But you're singing now."

"That's because I don't have any competition."

"You know when you went to visit all those guys in the prisons with that head monk of yours?"

"Father Cecil, my superior," said Tony.

"Yeah, him. The one who's dead now."

322

"What about him?"

"No, not about him. I was going to ask —"
Here Chase paused for another round of
sneezing.

Adrian, who was driving, joined him in a
coughing bout.

"Oh, man," said Tony, "our little party
here is going to be about as welcome at that
reception as Typhoid Mary. When we get
back to the house, I'll give you two another
dose of Gold Seal."

Briefly, after the wedding, Adrian and I
had had a chance to talk in our room. "He's
really very likable — and smart," Adrian
commented about Tony. "You should have
seen how quick he was to pick up on things
and people at the school — everybody he met
warmed to him, as soon as they got over the
initial shock of his absurd appearance — why
an old monk would dye his hair that prepos-
terous color is beyond me. And his presence
certainly lightened the tension when we were
packing up Chase: he made it into something
of an adventure rather than a disgrace.
Frankly, I found myself almost jealous of how
quickly he established rapport with Chase.
But I can say it now, Margaret: I didn't know
what you'd got yourself into when I came
downstairs this morning and saw him sitting
at the table."

"Well," I confessed, "now I'm the one to

323

have misgivings." And I had told Adrian what I found in Tony's habit.

"But you said he'd mentioned that picture last night when he showed up in the crypt."

"Yes, but it's one thing to mention you've seen someone's picture, and another to carry it around in the depths of your pocket. That seems more premeditated."

"Ah, well, we'll see the last of him tomorrow," Adrian said.

"So, what were you going to ask?" Tony was saying to Chase.

"Who is Typhoid Mary?"

"She was a cook named Mary Mallon who spread typhoid around during an epidemic, without getting it herself. Her name's become a kind of — help me out, Adrian, my boy."

"Her name's become synonymous for a transmitter of anything harmful or undesirable," Adrian explained from the front seat.

"You mean like me," Chase challenged him with a bleak laugh.

"I did not," Adrian assured him firmly.

"So, Chase," said Tony after a brief silence, "what were you going to ask me before we got sidetracked by Typhoid Mary?"

"About those prisoners you go to visit. What's the worst thing any of them ever told you they did?"

"By worst, do you mean grisly, or something more in the imaginative line?"

Adrian shot me a wry glance: see how well they get on?

"Oh, just something you thought was pretty amazing."

"Well, let's see now. Their stories aren't always reliable, you know. Lots of inmates embroider their crimes; others, they deny committing the tiniest misdemeanor: it was all a setup, a case of mistaken identity, somebody had it in for them — usually the judge. And they really believe their own stories. Some of them wouldn't recognize the truth if it walked in wearing a red dress. But until I can think of something more spectacular, this will give you a little taste of prison social life. Once I was playing Monopoly with some fellows in a maximum security facility. My other playmates were . . . let's see . . . going around the board that day we had an armed robber, an extortionist, a kidnapper, and a drug dealer who'd murdered his partner."

"Huh," said Chase, impressed.

"Yes, well, I can tell you, everybody kept a sharp lookout on the others. They took the game very seriously. It took us forever to play because there was so much trash talk between each roll of the dice and people kept stopping the game to accuse someone else of cheating. 'So what are you gonna do about it,' the armed robber asks the drug dealer who'd had his partner blown up, 'blow me away, too?'

The armed robber was this sweet, baby-faced nineteen-year-old who'd robbed a small-town bank, wounded a teller, got away with ninety thousand dollars, then turned around the next month and paid sixty thousand in cash for a new Mercedes in the same town." Tony cackled. "The other inmates wouldn't let him be the banker because they said he didn't know how to manage money."

"How spectacularly stupid. I would have known better than that when I was *five*."

"To pay in cash, you mean, or to buy in the same town, or to spend two-thirds of your stash on a car?"

"All of the above," Chase said scornfully, sneezing into his handkerchief.

Though we could see through the multiple windows of Annabel's renovated library that the reception was in full swing, the bride and groom remained stationed near the front door, greeting a slowly moving knot of well-wishers. I couldn't help comparing this morning's demoralized Gus, who had burst out of this house pursued by demons and doubts, with the vibrant, assured person welcoming us back into it to share her happiness.

Jennifer, like a junior radiance acting in tandem with her new mother, swooped down on us, hugging me and Adrian, who warned her away from his cold, and then put an arm each around Tony and Chase and led them off to the buffet.

"Wonderful girl," said Adrian as we stood in the archway looking after them. "You must have been something like that when you were her age."

"I worried about people like she does, but I was much less sure of myself."

"You seemed supremely sure of yourself the afternoon we met."

"Ah, but I was twenty-one by then. I'd learned to conceal my deficiencies."

He gave me a dazed look. His face was flushed and his eyes shining. Was he running a fever? "What deficiencies?" he asked, and drew me to him, right there in front of everybody.

Charles Tye came over. "Hey, you two, *we're* supposed to be the lovebirds here."

"One of the nice things about marrying the right woman," Adrian told him, still grasping me, "is that you keep falling in love all over again at the most unexpected times."

"Then I've got more good things to look forward to," replied Charles cheerfully. But I saw him giving Adrian a shrewd professional once-over. The remark was not the kind that Adrian went around making. "How long have you had that congestion?" Charles asked him.

"It's been creeping up," Adrian told him. "But it usually makes its annual appearance around this time of year."

"Last night didn't help," I said, "when you were chasing Chase around the swamp."

"There's our lost sheep over there," said Adrian. "The one your daughter is shepherding around the buffet. But he's penitent now, and he's caught a cold himself. Brother Tony's been dosing us with Gold Seal and some other remedies from his monastery's herbarium."

"Snakeroot and liverwort? Those were two of my grandmother's old standbys. The Cherokees around here were great advocates of Gold Seal. But how about letting me augment Brother Tony's pharmacology with a prescription from my witch-doctor pad before you leave here this evening?"

"Who is that boy who sneezed at the wedding, the one over there who looks like a darling little Eskimo?" Cass Morrissey asked me.

"That's Chase Zorn."

"Not related to the Zorn who's building those awful 'hometown' theme parks all over the place?"

"That's his father."

"Is the boy at your husband's school?"

"He has been, but he's coming to live with us for a while."

"Really? As a sort of experiment, or what?" Cass's avid curiosity about other people's lives had made her an intrepid jumper of the fences of conventional restraint. Which was why I secretly looked forward to being around her; only now, for my sins, it was going to be my turn to get cross-examined.

"Well, you could say that."

"But he'll still be attending Fair Haven?"

"No, he'll be going to the local high school, and Adrian will continue to work with him at home. He hasn't had a very stable home life, and Adrian feels —"

"Well, all I can say is you'd better prepare yourselves. Life won't be the same with a teenager in the house. I know, I've been through it. I had my niece staying with me last year while her parents in California were getting their awful divorce. So nasty! It made me thankful I never married. You remember when I had Sara Jane with me."

"Yes." A sullen girl I had failed to make conversation with when I went to pick up Cass for a churchwomen's luncheon.

"She turned out to be a cool one, all right. But I didn't find it out till after she left and I had gotten this lovely thank-you note from her that I'm sure my sister had written and made her copy over. I wouldn't let young Zorn have a telephone in his room; not that *that* will stop them, either. Would you believe that quiet girl you couldn't get a peep out of at mealtimes was capable of running up a five-hundred-dollar phone bill? And there was worse. Your friends never tell you these things directly, but I later found out through the grapevine that Sara Jane and Van Wyck Sluder's nephew got themselves kicked off some chat room on the Internet for obscenity! It was Van's nephew's idea to test the limits, it was Van's computer they did it on — thank God — poor Van can be such a dear naive old bachelor when it comes to trusting children — but she was the one who thought up the dirty thing that got them kicked off. I was never able to find out what it was, but I'm sure Van knows. I never got my five hundred dollars back, either. How could I even *tell* my poor sister, with all her other problems?"

I was eating a ham biscuit and sipping champagne and enjoying myself with the organist from Mountain City.

"Tell me more about that 'Nimrod' piece," I said.

"Well, Sir Edward composed surprisingly little music for the organ, considering he himself was a church organist as a young man. But the whole story behind the *Enigma Variations* is quite interesting — there's supposed to be a mysterious 'second tune' in it that nobody's managed to find yet. The piece you liked was dedicated to Elgar's great friend August Jaeger. See, Jaeger is the German for 'hunter,' and Nimrod, of course, was one of Noah's descendants in Genesis, the one who became a great hunter. Every one of the *Enigma Variations* is a musical portrait of someone close to Elgar, but they all had to have code names, otherwise it wouldn't have been an enigma, would it? 'Nimrod' came out of a long summer night when the two men were talking and Jaeger spoke very eloquently about Beethoven's slow movements. Next time you hear it, listen real closely to the opening bars, and you'll recognize a hint of the slow movement of Beethoven's 'Pathétique' sonata."

"I will. I hope I hear it again soon."

Smathers Eubanks and Edmund Gallatin came over to join us then.

"My cousin tells me that Grace Munger has transferred her colorful presence to your scenic heights," said Smathers.

"Do you know her?" I asked hopefully.

"Only what I hear from my sources over at Brent and Bolling."

"Yes, she said she was with them. But now she's taken a leave of absence to pursue her evangelical work."

Smathers laughed. "Is that what she told you? Well, I heard a slightly different version. My friend Tad Bolling presented her with a permanent leave of absence after he learned about the 'weekend witnessing' she'd been doing."

"What kind of weekend witnessing?"

"She was traveling around to abortion clinics all over the South and performing her

331

one-woman show. She'd been at it for several years, evidently, ever since it became a federal crime to picket clinics. What she'd do, she'd make a weekend appointment for a consultation, then quietly show up in the waiting room, like she was a candidate for the procedure herself, then as soon as she had a small audience, she'd go into her number. She'd suddenly see the error of her ways and get down on her knees and ask the Lord's forgiveness, and then implore the other women to leave with her before it was too late."

"Was this ever in the papers?"

"Nope. She was careful never to lay a hand on anybody, she never hit the same clinic twice, and she left as soon as she was asked; people felt sorry for her, I reckon. And it's not the sort of unpleasantness that people who run clinics *want* to call the papers about: she had made an appointment, after all, and then had a change of heart, right there in the waiting room; it might put off potential customers.

"What finally did her in was, paradoxically, she made a convert. A woman in Greenville *did* follow her out of the clinic, and they went and had breakfast together, and the woman repented and Grace let down her guard and told her a little bit about herself. Later, the woman's sister tracked Grace down at Brent and Bolling. This was after the convert had changed her mind back again and suffered bad effects from a late-term abortion. The sister first tried to get money out of Grace, and that's where Tad Bolling came in. Grace went to her boss for help. She was obliged to tell him the whole story, and he made a deal with her that he would help her — the sister had stupidly demanded money via the U.S. mail, which is another federal offense — if Grace would leave Brent and Bolling quietly."

"And here she is, back in High Balsam with us," I said, "organizing a Millennium Birthday March for Jesus."

"So Gus tells me. Well, that sounds relatively mild, after the histrionics at the abortion clinics. One marches if one is so inclined, or one politely *de*-clines."

"She doesn't seem to respond to polite declines," I said.

"I remember my mother writing to me about the Munger thing," Edmund Gallatin said, speaking up in a dreamy voice. "I'd stopped spending summers in High Balsam with my parents by then. I think that was the summer I stayed in Charleston and worked as a busboy at Perdita's. Or, no, it was the summer after that, when I was acting in dinner theater. But I do remember getting that letter from Mama about the embezzling scandal at the Baptist church and how Munger had tried to burn up his family in their house, only the girl escaped but with awful burns. I remember thinking while I was reading Mama's letter, 'How could something this sensational ever have occurred in High Balsam?' " As he rambled on in his oblivious, self-absorbed manner, Smathers rolled his eyes a couple of times, and I couldn't help wondering how many hours of these dreamy monologues Gus had endured during her era of devotion.

"I wonder what sort of music she's planning for her march," mused the organist from Mountain City.

Tim Stancil and his wife entered in an apologetic flurry of lateness. "I made the mistake of saying to Louise, 'Let's stop by home on the way to the reception and check our messages.' "

"And I said to Tim, 'You'll be sorry,' and was he ever sorry," said the judge's wife.

"Is there some new trouble?" inquired Buddy Freedgood hopefully.

"No, just the same old troubles, but with a new venue closer to home. As you may have read in this morning's paper, they've petitioned to transfer the Jasper barracks burning trial to my court, and I said yes. How could I refuse? This wasn't in the papers, but Judge Molton said to me, 'Tim, old son, we took the trigger-happy security guard off your hands after he obliterated the old gentleman in High Balsam with his twelve-gauge. Now

I'm in the hot seat myself. I'm told we can expect riots down here if we try the barracks burners in their hometown.' "

"Great," said Cal Lord caustically, "so now we get the riots up here."

"Not if I can help it. It's my prerogative to keep things moving calmly, and that's what I intend to do. No cameras and no TV. Just the young lady who draws so well and the court recorders. But the first assaults from the Fourth Estate have begun. Eight messages on my machine from reporters all over the state, some of them right aggressive. I think I'll get myself a stiff drink. Hon, what can I get you?"

"Oh, some sparkling water with a swish of ginger ale," said Louise Stancil, "since I just got elected designated driver."

"These security guards!" wailed Lucinda Lord. "Blowing off the faces of the very people who pay their salaries, firebombing barracks being built for their own coworkers. Whatever are we going to do with them?"

"You might better ask what are we going to do without them?" countered her husband nastily. He was already drunk, but everyone was pretending not to notice.

"Maybe the time has come to start trying?" It was the upbeat voice of Haywood Tye's pretty wife, who had just joined the circle. "I mean, back in the old days, people of property didn't hire security guards. They just had burglar alarms and good insurance coverage and took their chances on a robbery along with everybody else."

"And do you really think, Lucinda," her husband pursued, completely ignoring young Mrs. Tye, "that the firebombers regard those 'rotating squadrons' from out-of-state as their *coworkers?* They're their mortal enemies, my dear: they're threats to the best damn livelihood going around these parts, after cigarette paper went belly-up, and the garment and textile people abandoned us to go and exploit Asian children."

Lucinda stood up to him bravely, as if by doing so she could divert some of the focus away from his condition. "Well, Cal, it's their own fault. If they hadn't gotten greedy, there would never have been the necessity to import strangers from outside to *compete* with their wonderful livelihoods."

Cal was just about to let loose his next volley when a gentle, cracked voice intervened. "How did they get greedy?"

"I'll tell you how, Brother Tony," said Lucinda, laying her hand affectionately on the sleeve of his habit. "Some of the guards started telling their local buddies where all the valuables were. They watched the comings and goings of their clients, they learned their habits and the layouts of their houses, they spied on where they put their silver and jewelry, and then they told their thieving, out-of-work local friends. And the local friends came and robbed the houses when they were off duty. Have you ever heard of such a thing?"

"Inside jobs? Oh, yes, ma'am, in the course of my prison work, I've heard some lulus."

"What sort of prison work are you involved in?" asked Judge Stancil, who had returned with the drinks.

"Well, sir, we have four correctional facilities within an hour's drive of our abbey. I mostly listen to the inmates' stories — which is how I know so many — and I take down their requests. You know, little things they can't buy at the commissary." He cackled softly. "That is, if it isn't contraband. And I help some of them with their correspondence. My superior did the Eucharists and the spiritual direction. I'm just a lay brother, you see. But now, speaking of inside jobs, this one fellow linked up with a jewelry store owner who gave him the names and addresses of his best customers. He'd do the legwork and split the take with the owner. Then after the insurance companies had settled the claims, these same customers would come back to the store to have their stuff replaced and the owner would sell them their own jewels back in new settings."

"Ingenious, you have to admit," somebody in the monk's growing audience said, laughing.

Tony folded his arms, nodding sagely. He

appeared to relish being the center of attention. "Yes, Father Cecil used to say the most ingenious crimes were often the work of creative people whose creativity was misdirected."

"Well, if it was so *ingenious,* how come the thief was in jail?"

Everyone turned toward the source of the challenge, a boy in a suit with overlarge shoulder pads and too-long cuffs, his acorn-shaped face partly curtained by dramatic swags of black, brilliantined hair.

"Good question," said the old monk, without missing a beat. He extended his hand toward the boy, presenting him to the rest of the gathering. "This fellow keeps you on your toes. Nothing gets by *him*. It was like this, Chase. The burglar wasn't the one in jail. It was the jewelry store owner I heard the story from. The burglar was the one they caught, but he turned state's evidence and walked."

"He squealed on his partner and the partner took the rap," Lucinda Lord spoke up, looking quite pleased with her translation.

"Squealers are lower than s—" Chase Zorn paused just long enough on the sibilant to let people squirm. "— shoes," he innocently finished with a smirk.

"I'm inclined to agree with you, young man," Tim Stancil said. "We boys called it peaching when I was at school. I'll let you in on something else, too. I've never been an admirer of state's evidence. Plea-bargaining, either. Why, back when I passed the bar, there was no such thing as plea-bargaining. The whole notion of saving your own skin at the expense of someone else's appeals to people's lower instincts and invites abuse. It's just one more nail in the coffin of our higher ideals. You know: 'Bear one another's burdens,' that kind of thing."

"Not to mention the Golden Rule," Tony modestly contributed.

"Have you and the Bonners known one another long?" Cass Morrissey asked Tony.

"Only since yesterday evening, but I feel almost like part of the family, they've been so kind. I walked to the church from the bus station, and Margaret offered me hospitality."

"And are you en route to somewhere special?" Cass pressed right on.

"I find it pretty special here," he disarmingly replied. "But I wouldn't want to outstay my welcome. My brothers in Christ up at the abbey made me a present of one of those millennium passes Greyhound is offering so I could ride around and see how the country has changed; I haven't been out in the world for quite some time now. But I've got to take it in easy stages. On account of my age."

"I have half a mind to go with you!" Cass giggled. "I'd adore riding around on the bus and staying with strangers and witnessing all the kooky behavior breaking out at the turn of the millennium."

"I'd be honored to have your company," replied Tony with a little bow.

"Seriously, though, I know people who'd be glad to have you stay with them. My sister in California would just love to put up a monk —"

"The millennium doesn't even begin until 2001," Chase said. "The calendar goes straight from one B.C. to one A.D. There never was any such thing as the year zero, so we've got another whole year to wait."

"Somebody should tell the kooks that," Lucinda Lord gaily suggested.

"Hell, Lucinda, they've been in full dress rehearsal ever since the sixties," snarled her husband, looking around murderously, as if he expected to see some stragglers from that decade crashing the reception.

"Is that what they teach you at your school?" Cass Morrissey asked Chase. "That the millennium doesn't start until 2001?"

"You don't have to be very intelligent to figure something like that out for yourself," Chase told her. "Also, it's not my school anymore. I was expelled by Father Bonner this morning."

"Oh, well my goodness," said Cass. "Well, I'm sure you —" Pulling up just short of her next fence, she looked around at the others, then prudently renounced the leap.

"The Disease Control Center in Atlanta is saying this year's flu strain is going to be even more virulent than the Type A-Wuhan whammy we had back in 'ninety-six," Van Wyck Sluder diplomatically interposed. "I hope everyone has had their shots?"

"Speaking of all this fin de siècle fuss," Tim Stancil said genially, "I'm reminded of a family story. When my grandfather took his year abroad in 1927, he came across this intriguing set of cigarette cards in an antique shop in Paris. The proprietor told him these had been the artist's originals. A toy company had commissioned them in 1899 as a sort of fun thing to usher in the twentieth century. The topic of the cards was: what will life on the planet be like in the year 2000? One card had a painting of cops and robbers flying through the sky, another had aero-cab stations. Then there was a schoolroom with all the students wearing headphones —"

"What else is new?" cried Buddy Freedgood gleefully.

"There were also underwater croquet tournaments, and — get this — plush Victorian parlors with *radium* fireplaces . . ."

"My cozy, conta-min-a-ted home," crooned Smathers Eubanks in a romantic baritone, getting a round of laughter.

"And one card was an elaborate dinner party with everybody feasting on pills and little packages of concentrates."

"Lemme at the ham biscuits!" cried Buddy Freedgood, who then decided he'd better honor his own exit line.

"Did your grandfather buy the cards?" Tony asked Tim Stancil.

"No, the fellow was asking way too much. He told Grandfather they were the only set in existence, because the toy company had gone bankrupt shortly after they'd commissioned the artist."

"So what else is new?" someone laconically quipped.

"Well, I for one," said Smathers Eubanks, "will be glad when this wearisome millennium pageant is over, whether it's a month from now or a month and a year from now, and we can all get back to our humdrum little contaminations."

Charles Tye had been clinking his spoon against a plate to get everyone's attention, but not until a dozen or more guests had joined him in a backup orchestra of clanks and tinkles did a true hush fall on the gathering. Then it became apparent that someone had gone around and lit tall candles in all of the windows as well as the candelabras on both sides of the tiered wedding cake that had appeared, as if by magic, on the table.

"We're fixing to have the wedding cake directly," announced Charles, "but first I'd like to say a few words." Pulling thoughtfully at his dark bushy beard, the groom paused and gazed slowly around him. "I see so many good friends here, some of you my patients as well, and what kinfolk I've got left in the world. I'm so proud to have you all here with me to celebrate what is surely the most fortunate day of my life. I say day, though it's already pitch-dark outside. When I was a boy, I recall how folks referred to this time of day as 'dark-thirty,' which meant about thirty minutes after it got dark. It's not a phrase you hear anymore, but I always liked it. I don't know why, but it seemed to hold back the long winter evening just that little bit longer.

"I want to tell you this one story. I promise to make it short. I've rehearsed it about a hundred times so as to get it pared down to telling size — and then we'll cut the cake and continue to make merry.

"There was a man whose life suddenly went sour. Now people respond to adversity in different ways, but I have to tell you this man did not behave nobly or wisely. To the contrary, he went around slam full of self-pity and did just about everything he could to disserve himself until he wasn't worth a milk bucket under a bull.

"But fortunately this man had one good thing between him and the dissolute end he was headed for. This man had a young daughter who was as noble as he was sorry, and as sensible as he was foolish.

"One morning, his daughter insisted upon dragging him to church. It was a church in town she'd been attending with a friend. It was not the church of his childhood, far from it. In fact there's a story that when the first clergyman of this strange denomination rode into our hills for the first time and asked a woman at a cabin door, 'Do you have any Episcopalians up here?' she replied, 'I don't rightly know, sir, but my husband's got the skins of lots of varmints up in the loft. Maybe we can find you one up there.'

"But to please his daughter," Charles continued, when the laughter had died down, "the man put on a jacket and even found a crumpled-up tie on the floor in the back of his closet and accompanied her to this church. Where everyone was very nice to him, including a lovely woman the daughter seemed particularly to have taken to. He asked the lady if she'd be free to join them for lunch, and during lunch this lady, who was a builder, asked the man, who was a doctor, if he thought he might sometime find time to go with her to the site of a nursing home she'd just put in a bid to build. She wanted to design it right, she said, she wanted to feel the space and the windows and layout from the point of view of the people who were going to be living and working there. 'Why don't we all go right now?' the daughter said, while he was still hemming and hawing, thinking about times he might be free later in the week or month or year. And the lady laughed and said, 'Well, indeed, why not? *Carpe Diem.*'

"And so off the three of them went, right then, and presently they found themselves lying in different positions all around a meadow, trying to determine where the light would be at different times of day and what you'd be looking out at if you happened to be lying there in a bed with a roof over you, or sitting in a dayroom, or working your shift at the nurses' station.

"Well, I promised to make this story short, so I'll just say that the lady got the bid to build the nursing home and it later won a state architectural prize, and the man fell in love with the lady that same Sunday afternoon, though he didn't dare to speak of his love until a good while afterward, after he had taken steps to put his life in order.

"But the man never did tell her at what exact moment of that Sunday afternoon he fell in love with her. When he was courting her, it seemed kind of inappropriate, and then later when he knew her well enough to know she'd appreciate it, he decided to save it as something special for their wedding day, being as how they'd found so many things to laugh at already.

"What happened was, when they all three got up off the ground and were walking back to the car, the man saw that the lady had lain down right on top of a meadow muffin. It was all over the back of her skirt. It must have been a rather old one because it didn't smell, but there it was, all the same."

He waited, poker-faced, eyes cast down, stroking his beard while the mirth of his listeners surged all around him, the bride herself being the one who bent double and laughed longest and hardest.

"Of course, I told her what she had on the back of her. I had to tell her. And Jennifer and I helped her clean it off and then we found a newspaper for her to sit on for the trip home, and all of us had a good laugh over it. But, here's the thing: I can't truly explain it even now, but it was in the moment just *before* she knew, when she was walking along so lovely and upright and proud, even with that thing smeared all over the back of her, when my whole heart went out to her and I became a man saved by love.

"And that, my friends, is the end of my story. Now, please replenish your glasses and toast my wife and daughter and share our wedding cake."

XI

Wrestling

My hand gripped another hand. A struggle was in progress. The clasp was wrenching and hot, with a sweaty grime redolent of childhood playgrounds. Was I a child or an adult? Did the other hand belong to a child or an adult, or something not quite either? Who was the puller and who was being pulled? Who had started this, and why were we struggling?

It suddenly dawned on me that I could simply let go and end the contest, whatever it was about. But when I relaxed my fingers the other hand clung more desperately. It was then that I realized with a sickening lurch that I was not an adversary but a lifeline to this other being.

I woke up shaken, because the hand had been slipping out of mine as the dream ended. Oh, God, whose was it?

Then I felt the old gnawing in my right wrist from the struggle with the boy and his knife on Ninth Avenue in my seminary days, and I knew from the ache that the weather must have changed during the night, even before I heard the soft sizz of rain on the rectory roof. A sleeping Adrian, dosed with an antibiotic prescribed by Charles at the wedding reception last night, added his own congested rasps and sizzes. I lay beside him in the dark, gradually reconstituting my present whereabouts, while the phosphorescent digital minutes shape-shifted from 3:46 to 3:47. I stared hard at the straight-backed seven. It seemed important to "catch" it in the act of breaking in two and becoming the right-hand side of the figure eight. But when it did, I was staring so intently at it that I missed the experience. So I made myself wait for the broken lines of the eight to rejoin and form the spine of the nine. But this transformation I lost during a blink, so I had to start again: I must catch the nine as it squared off into the zero of the ten.

But just before this metamorphosis was due, I closed my eyes and forced myself to return to that desperate slipping-away hand in the dream. Whose was it? That was more important than pouncing on shifting green minutes in the dark.

Chase was down the hall from us, asleep I hoped, having ingested his own over-the-counter recommendation from the bridegroom. "It dries up the sniffles, but makes you drowsy," Charles told the boy, "so don't go operating any dangerous machinery."

"The only dangerous machinery anyone's likely to let *me* operate is my electric toothbrush," Chase had ruefully boasted.

★ ★ ★

"My wrist will heal," I had told Adrian in New York when my arm was in the cast from the Ninth Avenue struggle, "but who'll come along and save that boy from his dreary future?"

And the man I hoped to marry had picked up my left hand. "Sometimes a saving person does come along," he said. "Who knows, I might have been rotting in jail myself if one or two good people hadn't been exactly in position when I needed them. Maybe he'll be lucky, like I was."

Had the hand in my dream belonged to Chase?

Not Chase, floated up the voice of an inner commentator, try again.

A belabored phlegmy sound erupted from Adrian, like a cough being choked off at its source. He shifted his legs and groaned. Against my back I could feel the heat of his curved back inside the wrinkly damp of his pajamas. I was back in Romulus, in my father's rectory, lovestruck with my father's friend, daring to create fantasies of our being married, sharing meals, lying in the same bed, back-to-back, just as we were now, and taking each other's living heat for granted. Could such a thing ever come to pass? Though I wanted it fiercely, it did not really seem so for a long time. Which made me desire it all the more obstinately.

And here we were, here I was, despite last summer's digression out of these mountains, when I had begun to cry, driving north on 81 to New York, as I auditioned for the part of myself as my mother, leaving my husband behind in increments so as to protect myself and him from the impact of a straight-out desertion.

Yes, here you still are, the voice floated up out of its nether regions. Here you still are, holding on.

Had the hand in the dream belonged to *Adrian?* To some desperate part that needed a lifeline?

"One of the nice things about marrying the right woman," Adrian had uncharacteristically blurted to Charles last evening, "is that you keep falling in love all over again at the most unexpected times."

Falling in love with you, just as you are falling out. Just as you are letting go.

Who said that? Why do such things float up, when they're the last things we want to hear? Is it the voice of truth, or the voice of some nasty thing that finds cynical paradoxes amusing?

And I'm not letting go. We made love last night, for the first time since Hiram Sandlin's death. I wanted it as much as he did. It was a sweet reunion, as unexpected as everything else that came out of that evening. We slipped back into place.

But what is that place? Is it the place you wanted to be when you first saw this man walk toward you across your father's garden? What is left of the man you visualized on that afternoon? What is a sweet reunion, and what are you leaving out?

Am I still in love with my husband, is that what you're after?

Yes, no need to try again.

I still need and desire what I saw in him that day and on many occasions after, and in his letters. And though he spends a great deal of his time and energy undermining what communicated itself from him to me that day, I still need and desire it just as much, and can't imagine finding it in anyone else.

The prosecution rests. For now.

The manifest purpose of my trip to New York last summer, disposing of Madelyn's loft, was easily accomplished. The seminary bought it for a good price; I didn't even trouble to put it on the market. I liked the irony and the balance of it: Madelyn's lair, where she had concocted her anticlerical theater pieces, becoming a piece of General Theological Seminary. The money, a shocking windfall for a poor country parson, I asked Van Wyck Sluder to invest for me using the same prudent principles that guided his management of our church funds: he suggested diversified holdings that earned five percent tax-free and eight percent taxable dividends. On my return home with the news of our wealth, Adrian said he'd rather I keep the accounts in my name only. (Against some further day when I would get fed up and abandon him?) I had been angered by his wish; by refusing to share my good fortune, wasn't he refusing to accept a part of me? But he was intractable, and I finally agreed, probably rolling my eyes much in the same spirit as Smathers had rolled his during his lover's self-absorbed monologue at the reception last night. You loved the one you loved, rolling your eyes at the infuriating parts you didn't know what to do about, until the day came when you did know.

That day had yet to come. Even though our six months of celibacy had mercifully ended the night before, I knew there was more that had to be resolved. The man who had written that wonderful definition of vocation to me in a letter, who had confided that he wanted to risk serving with parts of himself heretofore kept under wraps, seemed, on the contrary, to be wrapping himself into a shroud woven of his own self-doubts.

Besides the assignment of disburdening myself of some real estate, the two weeks last summer had turned out to be an exercise in soul-searching. Driving past the Virginia exit of my mother's one-way trip to New York, I had "tried out," as I said, for her role as absconding wife. Yes, I had imagined it before I could stop myself, but my situation was not hers. My mother was leaving the rector. But I *was* the rector: I had a parish to return to. I had already decided that much before I got out of Virginia.

She was also leaving her child, that's true. As if I could ever forget it! But if I left Adrian, I would be leaving the child I still hoped to have with him. I would also be leaving the abandoned child in Adrian that I had taken on — even if it was a bit more than I had bargained for, in my "if I can just have him" period.

When I got to New York, there was Shaun. That took precedence over everything at first. I had thoughtlessly presumed from the upbeat tone of his letter, even though he said he was sick, that we would be going out to dinner, as we frequently did in the old days; that we would take long walks as we used to do, and Shaun, that most visual of creatures, would continue to point out amazing sights I never would have noticed on my own.

Instead I found myself helping a dying man who weighed ninety-five pounds pack up his things for Ireland. All he could keep in his stomach were his medicines and the Chinese noodles or fried rice he ordered in, and those didn't always stay down. He was horribly self-conscious about the thrush that had recently erupted inside his mouth, and kept running off to the bathroom to rinse with an antiseptic so he wouldn't "disgust me." It exhausted him to walk across a room, and he couldn't even do that without a cane.

He was touchingly happy to see me, and we spent almost every evening together. He came alive "like a vampire in training," he joked, at the hour of dusk, and we would prop up pillows and stretch out together on Madelyn's bed, because he was most comfortable lying down and it was the one room in the loft that caught the magic blue evening light he loved. We discussed anything we pleased on the scale between heaven and hell. (By tacit consent, we always kept Madelyn's mural curtain closed; there must have been enough presences in this room without her.) He wanted to know what marriage was like — "It's something I hoped for, eventually, with someone, but at least I had some awfully good fantasies" — and I found myself telling him all sorts of stories about my six, going-on-seven, years with Adrian. Those first happy months living at the school and commuting to my curacy at the little chapel down the mountain. The incredible sensual surge, almost like a swoon, that came over me at unexpected moments when I realized I was actually married to this person. The joy of early pregnancy. The lost baby. Adrian's plunge into self-blame and depression. Alarm bells going off: were we headed for some version of my parents' story? Then getting Adrian back again during the first busy years at the rectory, when both of us were often so tired from our respective jobs that on the nights we spent together we took turns falling asleep in mid-sentence. But there was that feeling of being carried along on our parallel waves of usefulness. Then: the death of Dr. Sandlin, and Adrian's sulking retreat and enervating self-doubts.

Confiding in this ethereal wraith, with his still-beautiful though almost inhumanly gaunt face, was not unlike telling secrets to a recumbent angel lying beside you at the hour of dusk. I even mentioned the impotence period Adrian and I were going through at the time, wondering as I did so whether telling a secret to a dying man counted as a betrayal, and, if it did, did it mean that subconsciously I had already decided to leave Adrian? I even wondered if my mother had lain beside Madelyn in this same bed and told more and more stories about her marriage to my father until she realized she had betrayed him and that this must mean she was never going back.

Shaun told me about his lovers, how he'd been the beloved of older, accomplished men who had wanted him more than he had wanted them. "I was the Ariel, the Puck-figure, the will-o'-the-wisp. Sometimes I'd look at myself in the mirror in the morning and pucker my lips at myself and say, 'You heartless, flighty little tease!' But I felt so powerful, I felt immortal. Then other times, I'd think, 'Shaun, lad, this has to come to an end sometime.' And I was right."

Madelyn had once made love to him when they were sharing a hotel suite during an out-of-town theater run. "I was perfectly willing if it made her happy. I adored Madelyn, as you know. But she ended up having to do all the work, and she was so furious when it was over that she slapped my face and wouldn't speak to me all the next day." He had gone after only one man himself, a red-haired construction worker he'd picked up in an Irish tavern on the upper East Side. "He was married and had kids, and said I was his first. He was second-generation Irish and my Connemara brogue made him weep. We were only together a few times, then he broke it off. Disgusted with himself, he said, and never wanted to see me again. But after I found out I was sick, I went back to the tavern to find him. He wasn't happy to see me, but I told him to go have himself tested and please to let me know because I'd worry till he did. He promised he would, on condition that I would never come looking for him again. But I never heard from him."

I took an old seminary classmate out to

lunch, the same woman in Mass Class who had made the joke about Fergie outlawing breasts and pregnancies at the altar if he could have. She was now a teacher and spiritual director at General's Center for Christian Spirituality, which emphasized the practice of ministry. She quizzed me closely about my life as a parish priest, and while regaling her with stories about All Saints High Balsam and its particular problems and colorful cast of characters, I became aware that I was presenting myself as a sort of modern female counterpart to the hero of Bernanos's novel, *The Diary of a Country Priest*. Was there some devious romanticizing lurking in my presentation of life in a quaint mountain parish? Was I dwelling so insistently on the arcane pleasures and intensities of serving in the backwoods in order to escape any criticism from her for having left the front lines? As I walked back to the loft afterward, I wondered what she had *really* meant when she said at the end of the lunch: "Listen, Margaret, anytime you can spare us the time, I can find a pastoral course for you to teach at the center." Did she mean that I might have practical knowledge to bring them from the backwoods, or was she tactfully implying that I myself would benefit from a fresh immersion in the theater of operations?

I walked more in those two weeks in the

city than I had walked in my six years in High Balsam. From Madelyn's, as I never stopped thinking of it, I walked down to the Battery and back: more like a slow swim, really, through a bouillabaisse of late twentieth-century disparity: fish, flowers, curry, diamonds, garbage, raucous flea markets, firehouses and courts, the lacy Gothic towers of a church, a storybook cobblestone mews with trailing wisteria (and, inside the trellised gate, a parked car with one of those wheel-locking devices to prevent theft). The whole brew bobbed with equal chunks of splendor and desolation. Some neighborhoods seemed more desolate; others miraculously renewed. Tompkins Square looked like an English park: what had they done with all the homeless people? I tried to notice everything with Shaun's eyes as well as my own, so I could report to him when I returned.

Usually I returned overloaded. I just hadn't been able to take it all in: the changes, the contrasts, the circus of humanity in a metropolis with all its sideshows. My senses were assaulted from too many directions at once. Yet formerly I had walked these blocks the way one absently walks a familiar neighborhood, thinking of God or Adrian, or intent on some research errand for Madelyn or what questions were likely to be on my Old Testament exam.

Had I become too acclimated to High Balsam's rarefied air, "four thousand feet above the cares of the world"? But High Balsam had its share of worldly problems, I reminded myself — and more were on the way, that summer. It was just that there weren't so many people, or varieties of people, in High Balsam.

I had lunch with the dean and his wife. I took them to Madelyn's loft several times, and the process of transferring ownership began.

I had lunch with Dr. Stroup. Fergie surprised me by asking me point-blank if I was happy, and I told him yes. This seemed to please him enormously, as if my happiness had been a personal gift from him. It was only afterward that I thought how interesting it was that this would have been the last question in the world he would have asked when I was here at General. How many people asked a single woman, or single man, for that matter, if they were happy? Yet here was the same person who had once suggested that I might not be suited for the married state — and hinted that Adrian might not be, either — looking sweetly indulgent and sentimental because I had answered his question yes. When Fergie the old bachelor imagined our married happiness, what kind of pictures did he see?

★ ★ ★

The readings in the Daily Office during those weeks seemed put there specifically to perplex and goad me. The Son of man acted so damn sure of his mission. Go borrow that man's colt, I'm going to need it. Go follow that man with the water jar and tell his landlord we'll want his upper room for our passover meal. Making his luminously cocksure plans to get himself betrayed and killed so he could fulfill his mission. How could he be so sure that it was his mission? How much, if any of it, had really happened, and how much had been imposed on the story afterward?

What had he known about himself that I didn't know — or was too small or cowardly to find out — about myself? What had been the source of his internal certainty, and how had he learned to recognize and trust it?

I walked the city blocks and got overloaded, stopped off in parks or churches — the ones that remained unlocked — or lay on Madelyn's bed after Shaun had gone off to bed. My leg bones thrumming from the unaccustomed contact with miles of pavement, I reassessed fulfilled desires and courted their opposites.

How sure I had been that I had wanted Adrian and no one else. Why had I been so sure? I had told myself and others that I had recognized Adrian as my fate the moment he came around the corner of my father's house, but what had that really meant? Had I sensed in him on first sight a person capable of knowing me as I wanted to be known? Or had something about him flashed a prefiguration of an old pattern, an alluring shape precut for me by the lives of others that I felt compelled to lie down in?

Or I would summon phantasmal Margarets of ten or twenty years hence and conduct fanciful interviews with them, trying to force a vision of my own future. ("Well, so you married him and went off to the mountains and lost a baby and got ordained and became rector of that little church. And then, following that, what happened? Oh, you did? Tell me truly, are you glad you . . . ? Do you ever have any regrets? As an older and wiser self, would you be willing to look me straight in the eye and assure me God has a plan for you? And while we're on the subject, would you be willing to tell me the closest you've ever come to this thing we call God?")

"Margaret, I don't want to put you on the spot, but I'd like to ask you something."

Shaun, lying on top of the covers beside me in the blue dusk in Madelyn's room.

"I thought I'd already told you everything."

"No, not this."

"Well?"

361

"It's not something I'd dare ask you if I were well. But I think I'm too far gone to benefit from the new drugs, and it's something I'd really like to know."

"Go ahead," I said. Whatever secret he asked, I'd already made up my mind I was going to answer. Maybe this was the way I would find out what I was going to do next.

But it was another kind of secret he was after. "What about God?"

"What do you mean?"

"Do you believe there's someone up there waiting for me? Oh, I don't mean up there, but you know. First he'll give me the devil for squandering my life, but then he'll say, 'Well, Shaun, but I see your family took you straight from the plane to old Father Gallaher and you confessed and swallowed the blessed sacrament, so I guess that sets us to rights again, and now what can I have the angels bring you for your dinner?' "

"I like that vision, Shaun."

"But is it a vision or is it a pathetic little dying fantasy?"

"It's a picture that came out of you about everything being set to rights. I don't call that pathetic, I call it farsighted."

"But do you believe there is really anybody there?"

"I'm not sure I believe as much as *recognize*. Belief seems to me something that is willed. But there are times when I definitely recognize the presence of something eternally beyond me working through me. And the more of these times I experience, the more I want."

"*How* do you recognize it?"

"Well, given the kind of person I am, it's sometimes through the tremendous creativity of a dream, when something guides me through the most amazing images and stories to knowledge I couldn't have squeezed out of my intellect alone. Or sometimes there's a flash of recognition when I'm talking to somebody or reading something. Or sometimes it comes when I'm just . . . lapsing, with my guard down. And the moments build on each other, they have a cumulative effect, like when you're learning an art or training your body for something. They leave me with a kind of euphoric rightness — like suddenly being sent an extra dose of fresh air and then realizing you hadn't been breathing too well before. You find yourself wanting more of them."

Shaun sighed and folded his hands on his concave chest. He'd punched so many holes in his belt that it went twice around him now. "Well," he said with a sad laugh, "every day I do think about God more and more; but every day there's a little less of me to think about him with. What will the outcome be? I wish I could send you back a message when I get there. And I don't mean Ireland now."

"I know you don't," I said, reaching over and laying my hand on top of his folded ones. "And I wish you could, too."

I walked from Madelyn's all the way up to East Ninety-third and back, stopping off at the Central Park Zoo to catch the afternoon feeding of the sea lions, then over to observe the leaf-cutting ants obsessively building their kingdom inside a glass case, oblivious to our huge faces spying on them from above. The arctic foxes looked hot and shabby and disoriented by the noisy human surf; a polar bear morosely paced on his giant haunches in much too small a space. To get cool, I plunged into a luxury emporium on Fifth, the artful and the artificial assailing my senses. Sleekly packaged products of the hour cried out for immediate acquisition. A shopping virus floated all but visibly on the multi-perfumed air. An unstylish woman was perched grimly on a high stool, allowing a man in a lavender smock to stroke her face and murmur coquettishly, "I'd really like to see you go a shade darker with your foundation." I sniffed in the virus and merged with the driven shopper-seekers, craving a costly silk scarf that would coil gorgeously upon my parson's black topcoat. I seriously reevaluated the shade of my own foundation. I bought a lipstick that cost way too much, and felt absurdly pleased, as if I had bought my way into some stylish club. I thought of the leaf-cutting ants and strained for the perspective of some higher consciousness peering down on us now. Had the Son of man caught a glimpse of how the world looked from God's point of view, was that it? Was that what his behavior had been all about?

A tourist of the surreal contemporary, I browsed the streets, gaping and pondering at the passing strange everywhere on parade. I grew accustomed to seeing extremes of have and have-not within touching distance of each other. One day I saw some boys peeing on a sleeping man in rags, the whole scene being witnessed dispassionately by a liveried driver waiting inside a smoky-windowed limousine. I walked on, realizing that I had been an onlooker, too.

Twelve years before, when I had first come to this city with Madelyn, my most startling encounter on Fifth Avenue's prime blocks of wretched excess had been with a well-spoken older woman wearing a hat and dirty gloves, who did a brisk business in collecting "carfare" dollars from people who believed her tale about the stolen purse. I had contributed a dollar myself on our first meeting, then later discovered her working the crowds in the narthex of St. Patrick's. Now an altogether spookier wraith prowled her beat. Somewhere between seventy and ninety years of age, with a rouged collapsed face, she minced painfully along on stiletto heels, ancient legs like bones exposed to mid-thigh in a mini-skirted black dress. She carried a worn shopping bag from Bendel's, and embedded in the scalp of her shaved head was a jeweled butterfly. I encountered her on three occasions. Unlike her counterpart of the earlier era, she stopped nobody, told no story, asked for nothing, initiated no contact at all with her surroundings. Perhaps that was the most chilling difference: there was no contact. Like a ghost come back to haunt bygone shopping trails, she merely stalked the fashionable blocks in the terrible high heels, her ghastly visage expressionless and unseeing.

I bought presents for Shaun's brothers and their wives and numerous children. He had given me a list of their names, and brief character descriptions and an extravagant amount of cash. He wanted to carry these gifts in his luggage and ship everything else. I pressed him to take whatever he wanted of Madelyn's, including the furniture. We could ship that, too.

I went to services in the Chapel of the Good Shepherd, or sat alone in the chapel trying to recall the things that had been uppermost in my prayers when I had been a student here. The Lavers & Westlake stained-glass window of Jacob wrestling with the angel had often been my focus while I prayed, and I looked to it now as an old friend, in its various afternoon and early evening lights, and meditated on what it meant to wrestle with an angel. Was that what I was doing now?

One afternoon when I was in the seminary bookstore, I bought two postcards of this window, and as I did so I realized my heart was pounding strangely. Do I want to think what I am going to do with these postcards? I asked myself. I felt a great reluctance, but also a dreadful excitement about going on with this thought.

Back at Madelyn's, I took one of the cards and propped it in front of a salt shaker on the table and lit a candle on either side of it. Then I sat down and contemplated the figures of Jacob and the angel. All right, I thought, let these two tell me what I am afraid to think for myself.

You can send one of the cards to Adrian, my own voice immediately suggested to me, and keep the other card for yourself. Why would I do that? I asked. Because the two of you would be going your separate ways, replied the voice. You would write a message to him on the back of one card, and send it, and you would keep the other card for yourself, as a memorial to your difficult decision. I then had a vision of myself years hence, in a life without Adrian, suddenly coming upon my "memorial" card in a desk drawer. I saw my hand go to my throat as I relived the emotions of our parting, which the stamped and posted duplicate of this card had announced.

At that point Shaun returned from a taxi visit to the doctor. He came closer and looked over my shoulder. "It's beautiful. Where's it from?"

"It's a window in the seminary chapel. Jacob wrestling with the angel."

"I like the expression on that angel's face. Sort of tender and far-seeing at the same time. Maybe I'll get one as pretty as that bringing my dinner. I wonder if they have Chinese food in heaven. But look at the way his hands are — they're more, like, holding Jacob upright rather than wrestling with him. Though Jacob looks slightly suspicious of the whole thing."

"Jacob was slightly suspicious of everybody. Probably because he was so devious himself."

"Didn't Jacob get a blessing out of the angel?"

"Jacob managed to get something out of everybody. But this was probably his finest moment, when he embraced his best and truest self. After that, he lapsed back into his old ways and wasn't much of a blessing to anybody. But he was the first of the patriarchs to return home. After him, it became an important part of Israel's faith: you had to make peace with the past, the way Jacob was reconciled with his brother Esau, before you could move forward into the future."

Adrian and I talked on the phone twice every day. He called me from the school in the morning, and I called him in the evening, after Shaun had retired. As we talked, various un-High Balsamic noises from my end provided background distraction: frenzied Latino music and thumpings outside the open window, a car alarm going off, then a second one in descant; excited voices arguing in a foreign language, the aggrieved "pop-pop" of an ambulance or police car stuck in traffic; an occasional scream.

"That new headmaster I dangled in front of you the day you left," Adrian began, the evening before Shaun was due to fly home.

"He's finally said yes?"

"To another school."

"Oh dear, what now?"

"We start over again." He sounded tired. "How's Gotham?"

"It's pretty fin de siècle. Except for certain enclaves."

"I hope you're frequenting some of them, too."

"Oh, yes. I had lunch with the dean and the new director of development today at the seminary; later in the week they're going to come and look at the loft. And Evangeline's invited me for dinner in the close after even-

369

song on Wednesday."

"I miss evensongs," he remarked wistfully. A silence. "We're putting in a new sprinkler system at the school."

"Are you?" I said, to fill up the space.

"What a mess." He seemed low.

"Do you ever think about going somewhere else, Adrian?"

"No." I could hear his surprise. "Do you have something in mind?"

"Not really. I guess I've just been thinking a lot."

"About . . . ?"

"About us, among other things."

"Yes?" I could tell from his tone that he was expecting the worst.

"Oh, I don't know. You seem to be in a bad place since Sandlin died, and it has crossed my mind since I've been up here that there are plenty of other things we could be doing besides undoing the damage rich people have done to their children or ministering to historic parishes."

"That's one way of looking at it." He sounded as skeptical as I felt about where this dialogue was headed. Did he also sound *disappointed* that I hadn't given him what he had been anticipating? A perverse gorge rose in me. It would serve him right if I were to give him what he expected.

But I wasn't ready to strike yet, even in playacting. "The two of us," I said, "could always come back here. I could keep this loft, we could live here in yuppie splendor and start a triage mission in some dead-end neighborhood nearby. You'd do the carpentry and counseling and detox work, I'd conduct the services and run the soup kitchen. We could get our hands really dirty for a change, use ourselves up that way."

"Would you like that?"

"Not really. I'm just feeling dangerous and confrontational."

"Yes, I can hear that. I feel used up enough where I am."

"But it's sapping you! It was supposed to make more of you, remember?" Now we were talking truth. "But the works got gummed up, somehow. You're becoming congested, restricted." I was about to add, you're becoming less of yourself, not more, but decided that was too brutal. "What is stopping you, Adrian?"

A silence. A silence where I had been hoping he'd fight back! I was expecting at the very least to hear him plead overwork, or his temperamental unsuitability to fill Sandlin's role: the chronic excuses.

"I'd be willing to go somewhere else," he replied in a calm, reasonable voice, as if everything I'd just uttered had not been said or even thought, "if that was what you most wanted."

"But what if, say" — we were off the track

now, and I was going to playact out of sheer frustration, simply to get a rise out of him — "what if I wanted to go one way and you felt you had to go some other way?"

Another pause. "I'm having a hard time imagining such a situation," he said. "Can you?"

"Imagine it from my side or from yours?"

A testy laugh. "Why not start with yours?"

"I can't, right off. But I *have* been thinking a lot about what people call their 'missions.' Do we invent them from a need to exalt ourselves — or punish ourselves — and then claim 'God wants me to do so-and-so.' Or is there a right life for each of us to be in and we forfeit it at our peril?"

"I don't think you can narrow it down to one 'right life.' Life is a series of transformations, isn't it?"

"Of course. You're right." I felt relieved to be losing the argument; it meant he still had things to teach me. "I guess then the question becomes, how can you know when you're in the right series of transformations?"

"You can't, always," he replied with maddening equanimity. "And sometimes the wrong one can lead into a right one later on."

"So you just wait, is that it?" I said irritably.

"Wait and be useful. I wish I were a little more adept at the usefulness part. I know I'm not being of much use to you now, Margaret. Either at home, or in this conversation. But that's what I'm trying to do down here, in my limited way, just give myself fully to a few people in a small place. There's really only so much personal time left to do it in."

"Live by the good old grace of daily obligation, you mean." I was appalled by the sarcasm in my voice as I quoted his own words back to him. His highest praise about my dear father. On the afternoon of the day we met.

"Something like that," he responded quietly. "How is Shaun?"

"About the same. Poor thing, this morning he was worrying that his passport picture doesn't look like him anymore and they won't let him on the plane to Ireland tomorrow. I had to get a mirror and convince him the bone structure and the eyes are exactly the same."

"That was a useful thing to do," said Adrian.

I was chastened.

Then later, after we'd said good night, I found the flaw in his argument. I considered calling him back and accusing, "But you're *not* giving yourself fully!" However I didn't. He'd just slip away from me again and make me feel more furious.

That night I dreamed I was living in this loft. I was by myself and seemed to be resolute and full of plans. I had stripped the room of furniture, laid down paint cloths, and was very professionally and effortlessly rolling white paint over the walls and ceilings of Madelyn's bedroom, including the mural. There went father, mother, meadow, tree, mountain, all the easels and the paint boxes, and last of all, little Madelyn, the selfish young artist. All gone. The room was white and new and empty again and I could put into it whatever I wanted.

At that point, I laid down the roller and went into the big room. Everything was suddenly darker. A man sat in the shadows at the long refectory table. His head was bowed and he had his face buried in his hands. At first I thought someone had broken in, then I understood this person was dead. Perhaps one of Madelyn's artist-friends who had died of AIDS. But no, it was an older man, in a black suit. I went closer, and then my heart felt like it was stopping and breaking in the same beat.

"Daddy! You've come to see me." I rushed over to take him in my arms, but he made a horrified face and motioned me back. He looked very old and shrunken and frail, not at all as he had looked in life, but I loved him just as much.

"I'm just stopping for breath before I go on," he said.

"But can't you stay with me a little while? Oh, God, how I've missed you!"

"Nope, got to catch a train. Adrian's expecting me. I'm going to keep house for him a while."

"But — why can't I keep house for you both?"

"Not possible," he answered sternly.

In the dream I had never married Adrian, though I had desperately wanted to. And now here was my father, come back from the dead for Adrian, when he had never come back for me, and he wouldn't let me go and be part of their household.

"But — *why*, Daddy?" I was weeping, holding onto the edge of the table. Tears ran down my face and soaked my hair and neck.

"Because we're going to be living in a tent, honey," he replied with sweet reasonableness, as though that explained everything. And dwindled away into a black spot right before my eyes.

I was awakened by my own moaning. I felt utterly bereft, until I regathered my life about me and realized I had married Adrian and could return to him anytime I liked. I stumbled to the bathroom, shaking my head, and splashed my face with cold water. On the way back I stopped at the refectory table, where Shaun's carry-on items were neatly stacked. I ran my fingers along the part of the table edge I had touched in the dream.

In Madelyn's bedroom I shoved back the tapestry curtain on its wooden rings. There was the mural, with all its difficult people and their thrashings and turnings that had led to more thrashings and turnings in the lives of others. An inextricable knot of messes and blessings. Adrian and I had formally consummated our marriage in front of its closed curtain. Nobody had failed and nobody lost face — or control. Later, having opened it and opened ourselves to each other a bit more through the exchanging of precarious stories, we ventured into riskier physical terrain. We trusted ourselves enough to lose ourselves in each other — well, briefly.

Someone would surely paint over this mural, and probably soon; but it wouldn't be me.

At Kennedy Airport nobody looked at Shaun's passport picture and then frowned at him and forbade him to go any farther. To the contrary, everyone was so tender and respectful and *perceptive* that I had to hold back tears. Human beings were behaving the way they were supposed to for a change. The young woman from Aer Lingus had strawberry-blond hair that matched his; they could have been sister and brother. She managed to reassure me and joke and flirt with Shaun at the same time as she settled him into his complimentary wheelchair. We hugged, and when I smelled all the mouthwash and cologne he'd overdosed himself with during his most recent bathroom stop, I almost broke down. Back at the loft he had asked me to anoint him and bless him before we left, and I had done this. Afterward I had given him one of the two postcards of Jacob wrestling with the pretty angel. He had made me sign it on the back.

Now away he went, propelled by the Aer Lingus angel. I watched him out of sight in his cream-colored trousers and seersucker jacket and perky green and blue ascot, his carry-on bag and magazines balanced neatly atop his skeletal knees, his cane cocked upright like a scepter.

When I got back to the loft, I phoned Adrian. He hadn't checked in at his usual time this morning. Was he peeved with me?

"Well, Shaun's over the Atlantic now," I said. I described high notes of his jaunty departure. Adrian seemed interested and kept asking for more details.

"You sound better this evening," I told him. "What were you doing right before I called you?"

"Sitting here at my desk, looking through résumés of some people."

"Oh," I said. "Anyone hopeful?"

"A couple of them look as if they could do the job. There's a woman in this pile. Before she got her doctorate in clinical psychology, she ran a Montessori school, and before that she worked as a psychiatric nurse."

"Does she look promising?" Was that why he sounded more animated tonight?

"No, her autobiography's rather bloodless. Not much creativity. To tell the truth, none of this batch excites me — at least on paper. In fact, I'm inclined to think I'm doing a better job myself — until they carry me out screaming."

"Maybe they won't."

He didn't respond to this.

"But you sound much better than you did last night," I reiterated.

"Do I? Well, I'm glad you think so. I know there's lots of room for improvement."

I refused to be drawn into this.

"A new boy arrived today. He was due at eleven, but his shrink dropped him off at nine because of a professional commitment later today. That's why I didn't have a chance to call you this morning. I was taking the boy on a get-acquainted tour of the place."

"How did it go?"

He laughed. "It didn't. We went out through the back door of the main building and had just started down toward the athletic field when he flung himself facedown on the grass and started rolling around."

"My God. How old is he?"

"Sixteen."

"But what was wrong with him?"

"That's what I asked him. He screamed,

'It's killing me! It's killing me!' and kept rolling around. I ran down my worst-case list. Food poisoning? Appendicitis? Alcohol withdrawal? — he was delivered here more or less straight from Menninger's. Some bad reaction from medication withdrawal? His adoptive father is in China at the moment to purchase rails for a theme park he's building, so I couldn't call him. And the psychiatrist was on the road back to South Carolina."

"What did you do?"

"I sat down on the grass and asked him what was killing him. He continued to lie there, with his arm over his head like a two-year-old. I kept on asking, until finally he screamed, 'Boredom!' I told him I sometimes had that effect on people, but it didn't get a laugh, so then I asked him, 'What would you *like* to be doing now?' "

"That was a good question. What did he say?"

"Well, this is the interesting part. He suddenly sat up and looked at me as if I'd just become visible, and said with perfect clarity, 'Man, if I knew that, I could maybe live.' I wish you could have seen the transformation in him, Margaret. It was astonishing. From a two-year-old in a temper tantrum to a young man in a matter of seconds."

"What is his name?"

"Chase Zorn. If there was ever a name that didn't fit a boy! He's adopted. They got him from an orphanage in Peru, one of those lawyer-arranged child purchases. Zorn's wife wanted to send him back — I got this from the shrink — because he was too dark in color. But Zorn kept him, probably to spite his wife, who didn't stay around much longer anyway — that's what the shrink said. Poor little bugger, he's had one hell of a rough time, but I have to say" — and suddenly Adrian burst into hearty laughter — "he certainly hasn't taken any of it lying down. His abominable records show he's given every bit as good as he got!"

"Sounds like you've got yourself a challenge." It was wonderful to hear Adrian laugh in that robust way.

"Oh, indeed. But when he sat up out of his temper-tantrum and looked across at me man-to-man and articulated himself like that! If Sandlin had been here, he would have said, 'You've just seen the neocortex win a decisive round against the old subcortical id.' The boy's a challenge, all right — there's something deeply touching about him, too. You know, Margaret, I'll probably live to regret saying it, but I believe I might succeed with this boy where all the others have failed."

There it was, in a single sentence: my husband setting the charge for his failure even as he laid the foundation for a possible success.

"Why shouldn't you?" I encouraged, ignoring the demolition clause. "You've got to keep taking those risks."

"Well," he said, after a moment, "I'm hoping you'll keep taking them with me."

And so. I went back.

XII

First Sunday in Advent

"What's the day like?" croaked Adrian from bed.

I squinted through the blinds at the first platinum patches of light struggling to prevail against the low-lying fog. "It rained at night; now it's still making up its mind."

"Any sounds from our friend down the hall?"

"I heard the toilet flushing and the shower going, and a sad little whistling that sounded sort of like a mistral of the soul. But that was a while back. He's still in there."

"Perfect description. Chase could whistle 'Jingle Bells' and make it sound like keening."

"How are you feeling?"

"Not so great."

"Why don't you stay in bed today?"

"Maybe I will."

The toilet flushed again. More water running and splashing, but nobody came out. Six forty-five, with the eight and ten services ahead of me.

Adrian picked up on my itchiness. "Tap on the bathroom door," he said irritably. "Tell him we live here, too."

"I'll give him another minute. After all, it's the first Sunday in Advent. The great season of spiritual hygiene. Time to wake up and clean up and resolve issues."

"That's great. Is it your sermon?"

"No, I just made it up right now, inspired by all those sounds of running water. Could I bring you something? Juice? A cup of tea?"

"No, thank you." A fusillade of coughing. "Just the thought that I don't have to get up is sustenance enough."

The bathroom door opened at last. Quick bare thuddings down the hall. Chase's door closing.

"Run," said Adrian.

The bathroom was full of splashings and permeated by the odor of upset intestines, but I went ahead with my shower anyway, since I wanted to wear my new tropical wool cassock from Almy's over clean skin for the first day of the liturgical year. How jealously we clung to our precious demarcations and rituals, and how easily put off we were by the slightest intrusions and leavings of others. And this boy, with his turbulent guts and all his other turbulences, had now become part of our intimate routines and also our responsibility. Had we really done this to ourselves?

Back in the bedroom, I shook down the thermometer. "I meant to do this last night."

"You went out like a light. There I was,

talking away, and I looked over and you were sound asleep."

"Well, don't talk now, it lets the air in. I don't know what's stopping us from buying one of those instant jobs that beeps in your ear after a second or two."

"Either apathy or perverse loyalty to old ways, I suppose."

"Shush."

I took the new cassock from the closet and couldn't resist rubbing my face against the soft fabric before putting it on. It was a beauty, Roman style, with round black buttons down the front, and it fit me, not some tall or roly-poly predecessor who had left it behind with all his personal smells in the sacristy cupboard. As I buttoned the buttons, I vividly recalled a dress with amber buttons shaped like little cat's heads, the last dress my mother ever bought me, and how she'd said in the store when I insisted on this dress, "Those are real buttons, Margaret. Every time you put it on, you'll have to button them all the way down the front, and every time you take it off you'll have to unbutton them." "I don't care, I want it," I'd said; "I don't mind buttoning buttons." "Well just remember, I'm not doing it for you," she replied, "I've got enough buttons of my own to worry about."

And so she must have had.

And now Adrian watches me button up in

the mirror, his face mid-center in the cross-hairs of this focal moment of past and present which, when I look back on it in future years, will contain almost too much emotional resonance to bear. The old-fashioned temperature-taking stick angles upward from the corner of his mouth as he shares my unconcealed pleasure in this perfectly fitting garment.

"Black brings out your youthfulness," he said when I removed the thermometer.

"That's good to know, since I wear it so much of the time." I held the mercury line up to the light.

"The suspense is killing me."

"Not good. A hundred and one plus a notch."

"That's nothing. My first Smoky Mountain bronchitis was a hundred and three. And in Romulus, when I had that acute bout right after your father died, Mindy Hope swore I made it to a hundred and six. But the Hopes were hyperbolic people, as you remember. Anyway, a hundred and one makes me feel less guilty about staying in bed."

"Dr. Tye made you promise to call him today."

"But not before eight on the morning after his wedding. What a superb wedding speech he gave." He succumbed to another bout of coughing. "Feel yourself kissed," he croaked, waving me off.

Hoping to avoid Tony in the kitchen, I sneaked out the front door of the rectory and all but collided with him on the sidewalk as he materialized out of the mist in his duffel coat and habit.

"Good morning, Margaret, happy Advent."

"Happy Advent to you, too, Tony. I'm off to set up for the eight o'clock."

" 'Keep awake — for you do not know when the master of the house will come, in the evening, or at cockcrow or at dawn, lest he come suddenly and find you asleep.' " Wagging his head like a child rattling off a prized recitation.

"Well, nobody will find us asleep, will they? And what brings you out so early?" I had to admit I was reassured by his ready recall of the seasonal exhortation. What if he was just exactly what he'd said he was: an old man come late to vows after an up and down life — even if he didn't sing along with the other monks?

"I mislaid my bus schedule. The station wasn't open yet, but there was one stuck up on a little card in the window. There's a bus leaving at five for Mountain City."

"Do you mean today?" Was it going to be this easy, after all?

"Every day at five, but today's the day for me. You've all been so kind, but you know what they say about houseguests and fish after the third day." His shoulders rode up and down with his dry cackle. "How's Adrian feeling?"

"Not great. He has a nasty cough and a fever of a hundred and one and some."

"Folks with susceptible chests have to be extra careful, I was cautioning him about that yesterday. Lungs are like hothouses: all kinds of rank things can sneak in and bloom over-night."

"Charles Tye gave him an antibiotic. And made him promise to call him today."

"I liked your doctor's wedding speech. Which reminds me, Margaret, can I ask a favor before I leave? Do you think you could spare me an hour for a little confession?"

"Do you mean the sacrament, or —"

"Well, now, I'm not sure about that. I'd just like to get something off my chest before I leave."

So it wasn't to be such a simple hail and farewell, after all. But what was it going to be?

"How about two o'clock? We can either go to the church office or into the sacristy."

"Why don't you decide?" Now he did look a little pale around the gills.

"Let's meet over in the sacristy, then. That way, if you decide you want an old-style con-fession, there's a door with a grille that I can go and sit behind while you're at the kneeling desk. Or, if you just want to talk, we can sit in two chairs face-to-face."

"May I think about it?"

"Of course you may."

"Do you think Adrian would mind if I took him up some hyssop tea?"

"He'd probably welcome it. Chase might need some attention, too. I think he may have acquired an intestinal bug along with his cold."

"Oh, I've got some colocynthis tincture with me. Just the thing for stomach flu." The shrewd old eyes sought mine in collaboration. "It's also supposed to be good for pent-up anger."

"Sounds right on target," I said, laughing. "I've got to run now."

Unlock church door, switch on lights. Turn thermostat up to eighty (for Addie Rogers, ninety-six, who feels the cold in her joints) and remember to turn it down immediately after the early service so Van won't fuss about our wasting heat.

Hanging from the chancel arch is the fresh-cut wreath of local juniper, pine, and balsam, thoroughly sprayed by Lucinda, one could depend on it, with the requisite fireproof coating. The Advent candles stand ready to be lit, one per Sunday until Christmas. ("We've always used *white* candles in the Advent wreath at All Saints," Lucinda had sounded me out a mite contentiously when I first came, "but if you'd rather have purple and rose ones like so many places do now, Pastor Margaret, I suppose there's still time to order one of those *kit*-things from Sikora's." "No, white by all means," I confounded her by agreeing. "And pure beeswax, of course. They burn so much better.")

I loved the winter eight o'clocks at All Saints High Balsam best. No golfers and gardeners getting their obligation out of the way before hitting the greens or plunging their fingers into the mulched soil of their perennial beds. Just a few determined souls setting forth in the first light to go and sit on wooden pews in an old brick building with a timber-trussed ceiling and a few special objects that focused their attention on something timeless they were drawn to, whether they understood it or not. No music or hymns or bells at this service, just the two altar candles lit and the readings for the day, a psalm said in unison, some scriptural musings — not a sermon — from the rector standing in the aisle among them. Followed by Communion at the rail, exchanged greetings at the door (the only social contact of the day for some of them) and then home once more through the cold.

Take vested chalice out of safe and carry to altar. Open Altar Book to Rite One for the early service. Place cruets of wine and water on credence table with box of breads, lavabo basin, and towel. Light the altar candles and the first candle on the Advent wreath. Then sit down in the shadows of the chancel and hope to gather oneself and all one's loose ends into some focused offering.

Professor Mallory comes in early, the visiting geographer from Princeton. He's always the first to arrive, the weekends he's not camping out in the Smokies, tracking the movements of a nineteenth-century Swiss explorer who mapped this entire Appalachian chain. Muted clump of lug-soled boots on a solid six-foot-four body trying to make itself invisible and soundless. Swish and pop of goose-down parka being unfastened.

He always chooses the last row, pulpit side, which is darkest because of the organ loft overhang. Doesn't unhook a leather hassock from the back of the pew in front. Just sits quietly and takes in the surroundings, stands during the service when others do, reads with them from the prayer book in his articulate reedy monotone, but never kneels.

("I'm not a churchman, but I like being here if I'm not intruding. Something about it brings me closer to the enigma of Professor Guyot. He originally went to the University of Berlin to study for the ministry. But he ended up falling under the spell of Karl Ritter, the eminent geographer, and decided to look for divine purpose in nature instead. What fascinates me about Guyot is how his lifelong obsession with God drove him to be the passionate and meticulous scientist he was, yet at the same time handicapped him so embarrassingly at the end. The same man who dated glaciers and charted every one of these hills and originated our Weather Bureau was also the man who couldn't accept the theory of evolution because only God could make a new species! Let me ask you this, since you're a pastor: could an obsession with God ever become a downright hindrance to what in fact is one's God-given vocation?" "That is a deep question," I said. "Give me some time to think about it.")

I was still thinking about it.

If Mallory from his nave shadows is observing me up here in my chancel ones, it doesn't feel like an intrusion because there's a sort of kinship between us. We're both here early, geographer and churchwoman, courting something beyond our ken in the company of these candle flames. Yet when I rise and bow before the altar before returning to vest in the sacristy, I never look out or acknowledge him for fear of intruding on his ultimate concern, whatever it may be. We always talk after the service, anyway. He is one of those, I suspect, who gets his recommended daily — or in his case, perhaps even weekly — allowance of human contact from the eight o'clock. Like many solitaries, he's loquacious on some days, and rushes off shyly on others. Once he hung around talking until I had to excuse myself for the next service. He was explaining to me that the part of the American continent to the south of the fall line was once a part of Africa, and speculating on whether it would have made any difference to the African slaves if they had known that — would it have made them feel closer to home? he wondered.

On one of his shy mornings recently, he pressed the following scrap of local lore into my hand at the door, and fled before I could read it.

Chief Drowning Bear (c. 1759–1839), who held his people firm to the old Cherokee religion in these mountains, once allowed a Christian missionary to read several chapters of the Bible to him. After the missionary had finished, Drowning Bear remarked thoughtfully, "It seems to be a good book — strange that the white people are not better, after having had it so long."

Knot cincture over alb; kiss and put on stole; secure the ends through the cincture loops. Lucinda has laid out the violet chasuble on top of the press. As its silky tent passes over my head, I pray that I may carry it on my shoulders in such a manner as to purvey your gracious presence.

Only the Faithful Four in the pews this

morning. Addie Rogers and her pet home care help Estelle, and Marie Baird, and Mallory. But we launch into Rite One like the seasoned quintet we are: Addie's haughty quaver, Estelle's Trinidadian lilt, Marie's ardent treble, Mallory's careful, enunciated monotone, as if he's reading to his students from some abstruse text he's just discovered: each of them secure that if they need to cough or yawn or turn a page, the underpinning of my voice will keep things moving along.

Addie Rogers did not always like me. She was the one who had huffed and puffed and pointedly addressed me as "Mother," when I became the first woman rector of All Saints High Balsam. She would punctiliously invite me to tea once a month, and I would punctiliously go. We would talk, but only about "social" things. If I veered into the subject of prayer or the spiritual life, or, God forbid, God, she would wince and withdraw, as though I had committed a serious faux pas.

This went on for a year. Then one day I went to tea at her house, and, limping from her painful arthritis, she led me into her bedroom. "I want to show you my lovely little prie-dieu, dear," she said, making it sound as if we were embarking on a furniture tour. On the shelf of the prie-dieu lay an open spiral notebook with a list of names down each page in her wobbly handwriting. Not wishing to appear nosy, I hung back, but she insisted I kneel down on the prie-dieu and try it out for myself. "I really don't know how much longer I'll be able to kneel on it myself." After I had knelt down, she stood above me and pointed to the open notebook. "This is for when I do my intercessory prayers, dear. These are the people I pray for every day."

My name was at the bottom of the list. She had wanted me to see it.

I've grown so recklessly comfortable with this faithful quorum of winter early birds that I don't prepare for my musings in the aisle. I try not to have anything at all up my sleeve, trusting to their goodwill and inviting the spirit of the moment to send me some opportune thoughts. So far neither they nor the spirit has let me down.

This morning I describe how I almost collided with our monk-houseguest as he materialized out of the fog in front of the church and his seasonal admonition about watching for the master of the house. And that whole constellation of images in scripture about readiness and return, about the urgency of staying awake and being on the lookout for unscheduled landlords — or thieves; of keeping one's lamps trimmed and lit for the arrival of the bridegroom.

How do you prepare for the awaited, the hoped for? We all know how to do that. You clean the house, get rid of the rubbish, box up the excess and the superfluous, the things that aren't really you anymore, and take them to the dump and to the rummage sale. That's the repentance part of the preparation. Then you get out your best serving dishes and iron the tablecloth and napkins and put out new candles — as we're starting to do here today. Then (here I thought of Chase's flushings and splashings and my comment to Adrian) you clean yourself up and, if you've still got a bit of time left over, you sit down and compose yourself in joy and thanksgiving for the imminent embrace.

But how do we prepare for the unknown, the *un*announced, the thing we cannot even imagine yet? For the unknown is not always an occasion for joy when it arrives. Sometimes it takes things away from us, like the thief we're told to be on the alert for. Sometimes it walks right in our front door like a visitor and makes off with things we hold most dear, or turns our lives completely inside out. Do we, should we, then, prepare any differently for the advent of the *unwelcome* eventuality? In the literal world, yes. We buy insurance policies and install smoke and burglar alarms and, if we are wealthy and really jittery, we hire security guards, who can be trusted to announce over the intercom, "Your bridegroom, or your landlord, is at the gate. Want to buzz him in?"

But we're talking about inner life here,

about God's domain, as Jesus called it; and in inner-world terms, as people drawn to the light, we go about preparing for the hoped for and the unforeseen in exactly the same way. You clean your house and make yourself ready, you light your candles, you say "Come, Lord, come," and then you compose yourself and wait for the knock.

After the service, Marie Baird presents me with a paperback book covered in the beautiful peacock tapestry wrapping paper from her gift shop on Main Street, The Gilded Peacock. Her husband, who cuts my hair and what's left of Adrian's, has his styling shop above.

"This is for you, the only one of his you said you hadn't read. I got so excited when I found it. But the cover was so trashy I had to protect you from it."

I open it up and it's *The Greater Trumps* by Charles Williams. Other than Adrian and my father, Marie is the only other fan of Charles Williams novels I've ever met. "Oh, Marie, what a treasure. Thank you. Where did you find it?"

"Vincent and I were down in Mountain City this week, buying his hair supplies, and we passed this dingy little magic shop. Though Vincent said it has the reputation for selling other things besides magic. He didn't want me to go in, but there it was right in the window with its awful cover. I suppose they thought it was just a book about the tarot. I don't want to spoil your enjoyment of finding it for yourself, but halfway through the novel there's the most helpful description I ever read of how someone actually goes about praying for people. Well, I'm off to open up the shop. I'm setting up the crèche in the window today; that makes me feel less ambivalent about staying open on Sunday. But that's when busy people Christmas-shop in the literal world, isn't it? I loved what you said about house-cleaning. I'd never thought of repentance that way, but it makes perfect sense!"

I leave her in animated dialogue with Professor Mallory, who's telling about his Guggenheim Christmas spent in Florence and about the Italian tradition of building new caves for their crèche scenes each year with freshly gathered stones and moss.

Addie Rogers says she has something boring to discuss with me, but if I can come to tea on Wednesday, which is Estelle's day, Estelle will make us her special fruit cake. "Something boring" usually means Addie's son has been after her again to make her burial plans. She thanks me for keeping the church so warm, and this reminds me to put the thermostat back to 68 before I go home for breakfast.

I was alarmed to see Charles Tye's car

parked outside the rectory, but things soon clarified themselves. Jennifer's friend Sue had come down with flu, so Jennifer had spent last night in her new home with the bride and groom. Charles, delivering her early to church for her ten o'clock duties, had taken the opportunity to look in on Adrian. He was on his way downstairs again with his doctor's bag when I came in.

"His chest rattles like a box of Crackerjacks, so I took some slides. I'll drop them by the hospital lab, I'm headed down the mountain now to see Uncle Cratis. Your man is to stay home. With all the exotic new flu strains socializing with one another around town, he doesn't need a secondary bacterial infection. I told him the world could spare him for a week. It's been known to spare me for longer than that."

"What did he say?"

Charles laughed and pulled at his beard. "He said I was one to talk, out making house calls the morning after my wedding. Jennifer's in the kitchen with the rest of your gang. Young Chase seems pretty much recovered, that's the resiliency of youth for you. Get Jenn to tell you how she decorated our bridal chamber. Gus wants to have the whole wall laminated to preserve it."

I went up to check on Adrian, who was sitting up in bed talking over the phone to Jefferson, reading off a list of things to be done at the school. I tucked Marie's peacock-papered Charles Williams halfway under his pillow and signaled I would be back later.

Down in the kitchen, our quick-change monk had shed his habit and was demonstrating the technique of omelet-making to his young watchers. Charles was right, Chase did look better. His slabs of black hair were damp-combed, and his clean olive shirt had a stripe of plum running through it which exactly matched his hooded pullover. He looked like any slightly moody, well-cared-for young teenager slouched over the breakfast table at home. I must tell Adrian this, it would reassure him.

Tony tilted the pan so they could see the sizzling brown butter pooled inside. "Has to be hot enough so if you spit on it the butter spits back. I won't spit, but I've known many a fine chef who made a practice of it. Now after you pour your egg in, you have to keep shaking the pan. Not violently, just an oscillating, trembly motion." He demonstrated. "Just pretend you've got the shakes."

"That shouldn't be hard for an alcoholic," said Chase, with his bleak laugh.

"I can't believe you said that, Chase," Jennifer admonished him.

"Why? I didn't mean him. I was referring to myself."

"That's still rude."

"How so, Miss Manners?"

"Telling things like that about yourself makes people feel uncomfortable."

"Well, your dad did it at the party last night and it sure made a big hit."

"That was different," said Jennifer, offended.

"Oh, yes? How?"

You could see the machinery fiercely at work behind her furrowed brow. "Well, because. His story had a happy ending. Otherwise he wouldn't have told it."

"Why shouldn't mine have a happy ending, too?"

"You should wait until it does, and then you can get up in public and tell all the horror stories you like. Only it still won't be good manners. My dad only said he'd been miserable for a while, he didn't go into gruesome detail."

"For a twelve-year-old, you know, you are a very aggressive arguer."

"Who would like what on their omelet?" inquired Tony from the stove. "Margaret? You're the one who has to go to work."

"What about me?" said Jennifer. "I'm the server today. I'm also doing the preface for her sermon."

"See there?" said Chase. "She can't stop herself. She has to win every round." But enjoyment flashed across his acorn-brown face.

"I can offer ham and cheese. Or just cheese. Or cheese and ham." Tony cut his eyes at me to see if I appreciated his humor. He seemed to be in a cheerful mood. Was he lightened by the prospect of dumping some awful secret on me at two o'clock and then riding off into the sunset an absolved man?

"I'd love ham and cheese," I said.

"Jennifer?"

"Thank you, Tony, but please see to the others first," Jennifer primly replied. "I already had some cereal with my mother and dad earlier." Then she flushed self-consciously, probably from her use of the word mother, and drew herself up with dignity. "Gus said she wanted to get over to the nursing home early to put in the white heath while the ground was still damp, before coming to the ten o'clock. I told her she didn't have to come, but she said she wouldn't miss hearing me read my thing."

"Tell how you fixed up their room," said Chase. "I saw it before the newlyweds did," he boasted. "She took me upstairs and showed me during the reception. To get me away from the booze."

"There you go again," said Jennifer. "Why don't *you* tell them about it?"

"She had taped these hundreds and hundreds of photos on the wall, of them at —"

"Not *hundreds*."

"Who's telling this story, anyway? Okay, there were *numerous* photos of them. Taken when they were babies and little kids, and then their school pictures and graduation pictures, and him in his lab coat, and her in her truck loaded with lumber, and then the two of them together after they met, and some with Jennifer when she was little and then more recently. It was this whole history of two people, artistically pasted together. And then she'd put a big box at the top and written on the wall above it in red script with sparkles stuck all over it: 'Love Conquers All.' "

"May I make just one teeny correction?" said Jennifer. "Nothing was *pasted,* that would have been intrusive. And I didn't write directly on the wall. It was all done with masking tape, which won't leave any marks."

"From what Charles tells me," I said, "Gus wants to make it a permanent part of their room."

"Yes, she mentioned that at breakfast," said Jennifer with obvious satisfaction. "Of course, we'll have to take it all down and repaste it on a big board first before she laminates it. Otherwise it wouldn't be secure. I'm not bragging or anything, but it wasn't easy to get all those pictures. Especially hers. I had to resort to all kinds of tricks."

"It was a cool thing to do," Chase said. "I wish someone would do it for me."

"Perhaps I will sometime," Jennifer told him with a saucy toss of her head.

"It won't happen," he said sneeringly.

"It will if I say it will," she assured him a little less confidently, drawing back from his malign smile.

"You'll have to resort to more than tricks, then, Miss Marvel. How are you going to do it when nobody's saved any pictures of me?"

Adrian was leafing through *The Greater Trumps* when I brought him a second cup of tea sent by Tony.

"I can't remember if I've read this one or not. Sybil the fey sister seems familiar, but the others don't."

"Marie says there's a wonderful passage about how to pray for people."

"Ah, then I will read it and try it on Chase. I've tried everything else."

I related the kitchen scene between Chase and Jennifer. "Up until then, they were getting along so well. She was lightening him up, and bossing him like a nanny, and he was insulting her like a big brother, with occasional glances of awe. And at the reception last night she actually took him upstairs and showed him the wall of snapshots she'd done for her father and Gus."

"Ah, vintage Chase. He burrows his way into your sympathy and when your guard's down he lashes out — or deposits something nasty at your feet. I hope Jennifer held her own."

"She did, but you could see the hurt surprise. She's so adept at playing the mature woman that people tend to forget she's still basically a little girl. You don't think that's true, do you? That nobody saved any pictures of Chase?"

Adrian got a strange look on his face. "He's probably exaggerating. However, these things are possible. Nobody saved any of me that I know of."

I must have looked stricken, because he immediately added lightly, "Well, the good news is, Tony announced his afternoon departure when he brought up my hyssop tea. Said he'd already spoken to you about it."

"Mmm."

"That's a skeptical sound. You know something I don't?"

"Not yet, but . . ." I told Adrian about the two o'clock appointment in the sacristy.

He raised his eyebrows, intrigued. "For the sacrament of penance — or reconciliation, as we're supposed to call it now?"

"He's not sure yet. Something he wants to get off his chest, he said."

"Well, if it's under the seal, I'll just have to live under the same roof with you and my unrequited curiosity. I have a good idea what it is, though, don't you?"

"What?"

"That he's not what he says he is, and was simply imposing on our hospitality."

"But if he's leaving today anyway, why destroy his cover? He might need us for references at his next stop."

"Maybe we were so nice to him that his conscience is hurting him."

"Maybe, but I'm still undecided whether he's genuine or fake. His contradictions have a certain authenticity about them."

"Yes, he's an appealing old bird in his way. We'll probably miss him when he's gone."

"I'll hold off on the missing part until I see what he's left me with. Are you resigned to being under house arrest for a week?"

"I must be. I don't even feel like reading."

"That's the fever. Just drift and sleep — and think, if you feel like it."

"I'll think about my sins. The great season of spiritual hygiene, my wife the priest calls it. Jefferson's going to call the principal at the high school first thing Monday morning about admitting Chase. He should be able to start on Tuesday. Jefferson was very willing to take over as interim headmaster. He said something that makes me wonder if he hasn't been waiting for me to come to my senses and ask him."

"What was that?"

"He said, 'Despite my illustrious surname, Bonner, I'm really more of a Truman. And when the giants aren't available, Trumans have their uses.' "

"That was a compliment to you."

"I don't think he meant me. Sandlin was

the giant. I've just been trying to impersonate one until we can find another one. But I'm coming around to the realization that we aren't going to find a replacement for Hiram. There aren't that many warm, intuitive neurobiologists with leadership skills just waiting to be asked to be headmaster of a tiny experimental school in the mountains of North Carolina. That's why I was so taken with Jefferson's comment. He knows his limitations and is willing to serve with them. Not that Truman wasn't a giant in his own way."

"You know your limitations, too, and are willing to serve with them. I wouldn't go turning over the school to Jefferson on that account."

"What are Chase's plans?" He changed the subject.

"Chase has decided to go to church. I hope he doesn't make Jennifer nervous."

"And Tony?"

"I think he's hoping to bring you breakfast, if you want it, and then slip into a back pew."

"Who rings your bell?" Chase wanted to know, looking up at our square bell tower as he and Jennifer accompanied me across the lawn to church.

"Van usually does it."

"Could I ever do it?"

"Well — ask Van. I'm sure Van would be willing to let you ring it if he showed you how first. He has a fixed way of doing it."

"No longer than a minute. Twelve strokes, three at a time. Then finish out the minute with just plain ringing?"

"How do you know that?" asked Jennifer.

"Father Bonner let me do it at the school. I was training to be his sacristan before I fell from grace and ruined my chances."

Jennifer opened her mouth to say something, then gave a little shudder and clamped it shut.

In winter at All Saints High Balsam, thirty people at the ten o'clock is considered a crowd, and that's what we had this morning. I'd noticed in the past that if there'd been a big wedding or funeral the day before, a residual community spirit seemed to draw parishioners back to the place where they had shared it.

When Jennifer and I entered the chancel from the sacristy, I saw most of the parishioners who had been at Gus's wedding in their accustomed places, but it wasn't until after the Great Litany, when I was seated for Van's reading of the first lesson, that I looked out and saw Grace Munger in the act of shedding her red cape, assisted by the person next to her, who happened to be Chase. There was something positively *annunciatory* about her, as she settled into her aisle seat. She had the air of someone who had come for a purpose. And so she had.

We had two substitute organists, one too slow and one too fast, and this morning it was the fast one. Unprepared for her bouncy rendition of the somber "Let All Mortal Flesh Keep Silence," the congregation balked and stumbled, there were a few exasperated raised eyebrows, and some people literally obeyed the hymn and fell silent. Only a few voices kept up, Grace Munger's rather harsh soprano being the most assertive. I found myself feeling defensive about All Saints' lackluster musical prowess, which she would undoubtedly equate with spiritual lukewarmth.

During the Gospel, which I always read standing midway down the aisle, I was so close to her that I could hear her breathe. She could have reached out easily and laid her red nails right on top of the book that Jennifer held open for me.

Then Jennifer mounted to the pulpit. I had instructed her to count to twenty silently before she began to read, and I could feel her honoring every digit, despite her eagerness to start.

"The Genealogy of Jesus Christ, from the first chapter of Matthew. 'The story of the origin of Jesus Christ, son of David, son of Abraham:

" 'Abraham was the father of Isaac;
Isaac was the father of Jacob;

Jacob was the father of Judah and his brothers;

Judah was the father of Perez and Zerah by Tamar;

Perez was the father of Hezron;

Hezron was the father of Aram;

Aram was the father of Amminadab;

Amminadab was the father of Nahshon;

Nahshon was the father of Salmon;

Salmon was the father of Boaz by Rahab;

Boaz was the father of Obed by Ruth;

Obed was the father of Jesse;

Jesse was the father of David the king.

David was the father of Solomon by Uriah's wife;

Solomon was the father of Rehoboam;

Rehoboam was the father of Abijah . . .' "

The baffled looks could be seen kicking in before Jennifer got to Amminadab and had spread over most faces by the time she reached Rehoboam. If I had dared to do this part of the sermon, there would have been raised eyebrows before Perez and silent mutiny before Boaz. The novelty was this handsome girl in her alb, graciously doling out the unpronounceable and obscure names in her precise, ringing voice as if they had been one-of-a-kind charms handmade by herself for them to take home and hang on their Christmas trees. Added to the attraction was that everyone knew her; many had been present yesterday at her triumphal acquisition of a new mother.

The recitation of the genealogy took three minutes and ten seconds; Jennifer had clocked it beforehand with her stopwatch. By the time she had launched, with Jeconiah, into the final fourteen-generation home stretch to Jesus, most faces were alternating between polite resignation and piqued interest ("What is Pastor Margaret going to spring on us now?"). The exceptions were Chase Zorn, whose eyes were riveted on Jennifer, and his pew neighbor Grace Munger, whose haughty countenance maintained an emphatic attention throughout; periodically she gave small brisk nods, as though she wanted it clear that all of these names were perfectly familiar to her.

"Thus the total generations from Abraham to David were fourteen generations; and from David to the Babylonian Exile fourteen more generations; and finally from the Babylonian Exile to the Christ fourteen more generations."

Jennifer bowed and returned to her server's bench and I replaced her in the pulpit.

"Back when I was in seminary in New York, I once heard Raymond Brown, the Roman Catholic priest and scholar, give a talk on preparing for Advent. I was so struck with his insights that I forgot to take notes and could have kicked myself later. But last summer when I was away in New York, I came across a monograph of his, *A Coming of Christ in Advent* in my seminary's bookstore, and guess what? Inside was the 'lost lecture' in the form of an essay. There's no way I can do justice to all of it, but I do want to touch on the points that were so illuminating to me. If anyone's appetite is whetted for more, the monograph will be on the library shelves in the crypt.

"As you know, we have two stories of Jesus' conception and birth. Only two, Matthew's and Luke's, and they are very different from each other. When we reread them, it comes as a shock to some of us just *how* different. Did Mary and Joseph live in a house in Bethlehem where Jesus was born; or did they live in Nazareth and go to register for a Roman census in Bethlehem, where Jesus was born in a stable because the inn was full? Did they flee from their house in Bethlehem into Egypt to escape Herod's child-killing rampage after he'd been tipped off by the magi's arrival; or did they return peacefully home to Nazareth after the Bethlehem census-taking with nary a mention of Herod?

"Our Christmas pageants usually combine the two stories, but when biblical scholars attempt to reconcile the conflicting material, they can't. Raymond Brown suggests that we

411

might do better to recognize that the Holy Spirit was content to give us two different accounts and that the way to interpret them faithfully is to treat them separately. Not try to force a harmony out of some mistaken notion that if scripture is inspired it has to be historical as well."

(Here I allowed myself a wary glance in Grace's direction. She did not look as if she were about to rise up and correct me.)

"We must accept that there is no way of knowing precisely how historical the Infancy Narratives are, or where Matthew and Luke got them. Does this limitation of knowledge rob them of their value?

"Not at all. It frees us to concentrate on the inspired meaning of the narratives, what the two evangelists were trying to teach us in their different narrative voices, the religious message on which they agree.

"In his monograph Father Brown writes that he's been conducting a somewhat solitary campaign to urge pastors to preach the Matthean genealogy during Advent. And I'm finally getting around to doing it, now that I'm a pastor myself. He says that those three minutes and ten seconds worth of tongue-twisting names that Jennifer has just read aloud to us contain the essential theology of the Old and New Testaments for the whole Church, Orthodox, Roman Catholic, and Protestant alike.

"Now that's a pretty bold and sweeping ecumenical statement. But Brown tells us Zwingli was already preaching it back during the Reformation. Zwingli preached that Matthew's genealogy contained the essential theology of the Reformation: that of salvation by grace.

"The 'story of the origin of Jesus Christ' begins with Abraham begetting Isaac; no mention of that deserving elder son, poor unfairly banished Ishmael. Then Isaac begets Jacob; not a word about older brother Esau whose birthright Jacob stole. Jacob begets Judah 'and his brothers'; why is Judah chosen and not the good and extraordinary Joseph?

"What's going on here? According to Matthew, who is being faithful to Old Testament theology, God does not necessarily select the noblest or most deserving person to carry out Divine purposes.

"Now that's the interesting part. For reasons unknown to us, God may select the Judahs who sell their brothers into slavery, the Jacobs who cheat their way to first place, the Davids who steal wives and murder rivals — but also compose profound and beautiful psalms of praise.

"And what about the five women Matthew chooses to include? Not a mention of Sarah or Rebekah or Rachel, the upstanding patriarchal wives of Israel. Instead *Tamar,* a Canaanite, who disguised herself as a prostitute and seduced her father-in-law Judah to get a son out of him. And *Rahab,* another Canaanite and a real prostitute this time. And *Ruth* the Moabite, another outsider. And Bathsheba, mother of Solomon, is named only as the wife of Uriah, whom King David had killed so he could marry her himself. Every one of these women used as God's instrument had scandal or aspersion attached to her — as does the fifth and final woman named in the genealogy: Mary, the mother of Jesus, with her unconventional pregnancy.

"But this will fit right in with Jesus' coming ministry to tax collectors and sinners and prostitutes and lepers, to 'those who need a physician,' not those who are already righteous.

"Matthew's genealogy is showing us how the story of Jesus Christ contained — and would continue to contain — the flawed and the afflicted and insulted, the cunning and the weak-willed and the misunderstood.

"His is an equal opportunity ministry for crooks and saints.

"And what about that final fourteen generations of unknown, or unremarkable, names Jennifer read to us? Who was Azor, or Achim? Who was Eliud, who was Eleazar? Or even this Matthan, who was, according to Matthew, Jesus' great-grandfather? What did they do? What kind of men were they? We don't know. You won't find their names in the concordance, or in any biblical *Who's Who.*

"And this is, of course, where the message settles directly upon us. If so much powerful stuff can have been accomplished down through the millennia via the agency of wastrels, betrayers, and outcasts, and through people who were such complex mixtures of sinner and saint, and through so many obscure and undistinguished others, isn't that a pretty hopeful testament to the likelihood that God is using us, with our individual flaws and gifts, in all manner of peculiar and unexpected ways?

"Who of us can say we're not in the process of being used right now, this first Sunday in Advent, to fulfill some purpose whose grace and goodness would boggle our imagination if we could even begin to get our minds around it?

"Let me conclude my sermon with Father Brown, since he's been both the prod and mentor for it. He suggests that a thoughtful reflection on Matthew's genealogy encourages us during this liturgical season of Advent to continue the story of the sequence of Jesus Christ in this way:

" 'Jesus called Peter and Paul . . . Paul called Timothy . . . someone called you . . . and you must call someone else.' Amen."

I switched off the hanging lamp over the

pulpit desk and descended the steps, carrying with me an equivocal afterimage of Grace Munger bulked solid as a monolith in her aisle seat, her red-lipsticked mouth a hard line, her eyes tightly shut. Whether in prayer or in deep disgust over my homily, it was impossible to tell.

After the Nicene Creed came the Exchange of the Peace. As Jennifer and I were greeting each other, I thought of Helen Britt's husband slipping out to buy his newspaper to escape the Peace; I wondered how she was getting along without him. Undemonstrative All Saints High Balsam had reached its own *via media* in regard to the Peace: some people shook hands or clasped pairs of hands, some hailed one another cavalierly across the aisle, a few marrieds discreetly touched cheeks or lips, but nobody made a prolonged exhibition.

As rector, I varied my techniques: sometimes I greeted the servers and a few people in the front pews; sometimes I walked the entire length of the nave, shaking hands with everybody on the aisles and anyone else who reached out; if there were under fifteen, I did everybody.

Today, I chose the aisle method. I was moving along briskly until I reached Grace's pew, where I was obliged to wait until she had released a bug-eyed Chase from her embrace and finished saying something to him. No sooner had I reached out my hand to her than I was tugged sideways and likewise enveloped in a mammoth embrace.

"The Peace of the Lord, Margaret," she boomed victoriously over the top of my head.

"Peace to you, Grace," I mumbled into her bosom, my cheek mashed against the Byzantine cross. As I regained my balance and proceeded on down the aisle, several parishioners sent me looks of condolence. Gus, who had come in a bit late, but in time to hear Jennifer read, pressed her cheek against mine and then, with a cool smile, reached down and put my lopsided chasuble to rights.

After the Peace came announcement time. Before I arrived, the rector made all the announcements. If you wanted to announce something, you wrote it on a piece of paper and gave it to him before the service. But I had changed all that, in the interests of "the ministry of all," and thus it could be fairly murmured, as I'm sure it was afterward, that I was hoist by my own petard.

I began by reminding them that by popular request we were moving the ten-thirty Christmas Eve Mass to nine P.M. this year. "I guess we're all getting a little older." (Dutiful chuckles.) Then I asked for volunteers to decorate the church during the final week in Advent. "And everyone please do join us in the crypt for coffee immediately following

417

this service. Are there any other announcements?"

A single hand went up.

"Grace?"

Grace Munger rose.

"Thank you, Reverend Bonner. First let me compliment you on your stirring sermon. If I had any nervousness about standing up among you today, it was completely overcome by your closing words. Or that Catholic priest's closing words, whichever it was. It comes down to the same thing when we're dealing with God's plans. Jesus called Paul and Paul called Timothy, and someone called Reverend Bonner . . . and someone called me."

Smiling fiercely with the childlike little teeth, she looked around her and allowed a pregnant pause before continuing.

"And now here I am, calling you. My name is Grace Munger. Some of you may remember my father, the Reverend Joel Munger of Free Will Baptist. I moved away from High Balsam some time ago, but now I've been called back. Yes, that word *called*, again! I've been called back to organize a Millennium Birthday March for Jesus. I'm sure you've seen the announcements in the paper, but I came here today to extend a personal invitation to your congregation. I've already had several productive conversations with Reverend Bonner about it, and when we

418

breakfasted together at the Horseshoe Diner at dawn yesterday morning, she asked me to join you at worship. Many churches in the area are already committed to the march, including the other Episcopal congregation, St. Francis-in-the-Valley. Reverend Kevin Dowd informed me only this morning that he will be playing some favorite hymns on both his French horn and recorder in the parade. Though not on both at the same time, of course."

She left space for laughter here, but everyone was far too nonplussed to do anything but gape.

"The march will begin officially at ten o'clock A.M. on the Saturday before Christmas, December eighteenth, right here in High Balsam, because it is the highest point east of the Mississippi, and Our Lord deserves the highest, doesn't he? But at nine-thirty we'll gather at Great Thunder Falls, where the old Cherokees used to gather to invoke their ancestral spirits on important occasions. There will be a short prayer service, during which we'll ask the Lord to heal the deep social and economic rifts that have recently blighted this community. Then we'll march under police escort, praising aloud with whatever instruments the Lord has given us, down Main Street, and then circle around on Cusauga Street to the Community Park for our worship service and rally.

"Some churches are marching as a congregation, others are sending representatives, but do, please, let us make this a hundred percent, all-out effort of God's people to honor the two thousandth birthday of the Lord and Savior we all share. I will take Reverend Bonner up on her invitation to join you at coffee hour, where I hope you will introduce yourselves and let me know what instruments or talents you would be willing to bring to this joyous occasion, whether trumpet or timbrel or dance or stringed instruments, as the final psalm says, or just the voice or the body God gave you. Whatever it is, God wants it. 'Let every thing that hath breath praise the Lord.' Amen."

Grace Munger sat down.

"Are there any other announcements?" I asked.

There were not.

"Walk in Love, as Christ loved us and gave himself for us, an offering and sacrifice to God."

The organist struck up the offertory hymn, "Deck Thyself, My Soul, with Gladness," which was more compatible to her calliope style, and I turned with relief toward the altar where, at least for the next few moments, there were no people to face.

XIII

Confession

In any society certain offenses which seriously endanger or disrupt the community or bring scandal upon it result in separation from the community for the offender. After appropriate penalties, self-examination, testing, and reeducation, the person may be reincorporated into the community. So far as we can trace historically, all cultures have had various expiatory penalties for those who violate the communal codes and, where it was felt reasonable, have conducted rituals which might restore the penitent sinners to good favor in the group.

— Marion J. Hatchett,
"The Reconciliation of a Penitent,"
Commentary on the American Prayer Book

Coffee hour was late getting started because Lucinda Lord had forgotten to nip downstairs during the offertory hymn and turn on the machine. "It completely slipped my mind, Pastor Margaret. For the first time in twenty-six years, when it was my week to do the coffee, I forgot to turn on the pot." She seemed unduly upset.

"Listen," I said, "any one of us could have forgotten, after that announcement. Something as unpredictable as that has a way of throwing off the things we do by rote."

"Well — that's kind of you, but I honestly don't know what's happening to me — senility, I suppose. You didn't really tell her we were going to be in that march, did you?"

"I did not. But Grace has a way of coming to her own conclusions."

"How do you know her? She left town so many years ago."

"I met her Friday evening when she came by the rectory to drop off some materials about the march. And Saturday morning I was at the Horseshoe Diner after a hospital call and she joined me in my booth."

"She made it sound like you two were *in cahoots*."

"A little bit, yes."

"Do you know who her father was, and about the fire?"

"Yes, several people have filled me in."

"Did they tell you there were some people in town who thought Grace set the fire herself?"

"No," I said, "you're the first."

"Oh, dear, I probably shouldn't have mentioned it. It was just an old rumor anyway. And I know it's wrong to gossip at coffee hour just after receiving the sacrament. I'm surprised about St. Francis-in-the-Valley participating, I truly am."

"She did make it sound that way, but let's wait. Kevin Dowd's playing his instruments doesn't necessarily mean St. Francis's congregation is committed."

"True! He isn't even their rector, he's only a fill-in. Still — it makes us look bad. Whatever could have possessed him?"

"Grace, perhaps?"

Lucinda laughed sportingly and made her usual comment about our groaning coffee machine. "It sounds more and more like a wounded animal every Sunday."

I excused myself and went over to greet our visitor, who stood in a little knot of people at the entrance of the crypt. She was addressing Chase while the rest looked on: Buddy Freedgood wore the avid expression he got when he hoped something exciting would happen; Cass Morrissey appeared all set to pounce on Grace with her grocery list of personal questions; Van Wyck Sluder and Tim Stancil hovered together at the edge, their elder masculine presences on courtly alert to provide the voice of calm hospitality or middle-of-the-road reason if called upon.

". . . from around here?" Grace was quizzing Chase.

"No, ma'am," said Chase, lowering his head so the black wings of hair fell forward fetchingly. "I'm from South Carolina."

"Oh. I thought maybe you were one of the Cherokee nation," pursued Grace, studying him intently.

Cass Morrissey looked embarrassed: Grace's probing had gone too far even for her.

Chase shrugged. "You're not the first to think so. But as far as I've been able to figure it, I'm a mixture of Inca and Spanish. I was purchased by my father from an orphanage in Peru when I was a baby, but they forgot to send along my family tree with my papers."

The speech had the facile delivery of having been pulled out of Chase's pocket on many occasions before this. But in his adopted lowland drawl, in a tone cannily pitched between modesty and insolence, it produced its effect. Standing chest-high to Grace, the brown-faced boy shimmered according to your personal reading of the moment: exotic little victim or, as Adrian had proudly described him, a boy who could give as good as he got.

"I have always wanted to visit the ancient ruins of Machu Picchu." Judge Stancil came to the rescue with a kindly bow toward Chase.

"I wouldn't mind visiting them myself, sir," Chase said, switching to his prep school boy mode, respectfully humoring an authority figure.

"Are you, er — affiliated with the international March for Jesus group, Miss Munger?" Van inquired.

"No, I am not," said Grace. "This is something I've been called up here to do personally."

"By old friends from your father's church, I'll bet," Cass Morrissey put in. "I remember your father. I mean, I didn't have the pleasure of knowing him personally, but from his reputation. His revivals drew people from four states."

"More than four," Grace coldly corrected her. "I *was* appealed to by a few old acquaintances who cherish my father's memory, but that alone wouldn't have brought me up here with no resources other than my skills. I'm here because I had no choice. As I told the Reverend Bonner here . . ." Five gleaming red nails flashed out and firmly laid hold of my shoulder. ". . . the Lord himself asked me to do it. I'm not in the habit of turning the Lord down."

Stunned, polite silence. Eyes drifted to the crypt's Sheetrock ceiling or down to shoes; then, with nowhere else to go, swiveled expectantly toward the rector for corroboration or enlightenment.

"Did God actually speak to you?" Chase asked Grace.

A ripple of something — gratitude? relief? — emanated from the others and traveled affectionately toward the boy. I could have hugged him on the spot myself.

"Yes," said Grace, "He did. The Lord often speaks to people when He wants them for something. He calls them by name and tells them what He wants them to do. Read your Bible."

"Was it — in English?" Chase pressed on. If there was guile behind his interrogation, it was well-hidden.

"Of course in English," Grace snapped back. "That's my language. He speaks to people in the language they understand when He gives them their instructions. He isn't going to call me in *Russian,* just as He didn't call the Hebrew prophets in American English." She tapped the side of her marvelously structured coiffure and leered at him with the childlike teeth. "Use your head." Then, seeing she had impressed him, she proceeded to pounce. "You would be such an asset to our march on the eighteenth. Do you play an instrument?"

"No ma'am," said Chase, "but I can whistle just about anything. Is this a parade where you can dress up?"

"You *could,* I suppose . . ." She looked dubious. "Dress up as what?"

"I don't know. Maybe a prophet or something? With a long beard and a sign." He laughed. A mistake.

"This isn't an occasion to make fun of things," Grace told him, frowning. "This is a

426

time for everybody to come together and throw down their animosities and praise the one who's in charge of it all. Most people are marching just as themselves and carrying banners either with their church's name or a suitable scripture quote. Except for the Bikers for Christ: they won't be marching on foot, they'll be riding their motorcycles in formation."

"Who are the Bikers for Christ?" I asked.

"*You* know," she said chummily, "the group I had to rush off to speak to on Saturday — cutting short our breakfast talk."

"You mentioned a bikers' group, that's all."

"Yes, that's all it was *then*. They saw my ad in the *Clampitt Clarion* and asked me to come down and speak to them. Many of them have been laid off, and their spirits are low. They needed a little pep talk. I told them they should call themselves Bikers for Christ. Focusing your energies and giving yourself a name is the first step when you've been disenfranchised. Dedicate yourselves to him as Bikers for Christ and put your future in His hands, I said. And that's exactly what we did, right then and there."

"People are coming all the way up here from Clampitt for your march?" Buddy Freedgood asked.

"You think thirty miles is too far to go for Christ? When you've just put him in charge of your future?"

Buddy Freedgood was silenced.

"But, now, I would *hope*," Judge Tim Stancil said, speaking up in his cautious, deferential voice, "nobody gets the idea that your march is going to bring about — well, any sudden miracles, Miss Munger. As you must realize, we're in volatile times around here. People are hurting, and when people are hurting they're prone to act rashly. The shooting on Main Street last summer, with all the attendant publicity, and now the firebombing trial coming up first thing in the new year, and journalists already on the scent for some picturesque trouble that will win them a Pulitzer — surely, you must know —"

"Of course I know," Grace impatiently cut him off. "I'm in the publicity business myself. I have to keep up with the media, it's part of my job. If everything was milk and honey up here and people weren't hurting and confused, I'd still be sleeping in my comfortable apartment down in Mountain City, rather than paying seventy-five dollars a night to Mrs. Fletcher at the High Balsam Inn."

"Do I take it, then, that you're on a kind of *mission* in High Balsam?" the judge courteously persisted.

"The Lord called; I answered." She fixed that maddeningly implicating gaze on me again. "Just as in your pastor's excellent sermon today: when you are called as an instrument, you'd better go."

I'd had enough of her implications. "What is it you hope to be an instrument *of,* Grace?" I asked her. Not as courteously as Tim Stancil, either; Grace ran roughshod over courtesy.

"God's will," Grace said, as if I had asked an idiotic question. "If every able-bodied Christian person regardless of rank, income, or denomination comes out on December eighteenth with the intention of praising Christ and placing their futures completely in his hands, something will change here." She looked around at us, tawny eyes flashing with fervor. "Of this I have been assured."

"But have you been assured it will be a *constructive* change?" It was Gus, who had just come over with Jennifer to join the circle around our interesting visitor.

Grace failed to suppress a look of pure fury at Gus, who had caught her off guard with her level-headed sangfroid. But then, switching to the placating tactics she had used on me after returning from the toilet in the Horseshoe Diner, she replied quietly to Gus, "I wouldn't be here if I didn't think it was constructive, I can assure you of that," and, before anyone could accuse her of sailing past the heart of the question, hurried on to congratulate Gus on her marriage ("I saw the write-up in the *Mountain City Times* this morning" — with a look at Judge Stancil, you see I do keep up with the media) and on from

429

there to praise Jennifer's reading of scripture ("I always tripped over Amminadab, myself").

"Coffee's ready, at long last!" called Lucinda.

"And I can vouch for the drop dead brownies," said Buddy Freedgood. "My wife made them this morning, and I had three of them warm with my breakfast."

As everyone drifted toward the table, Buddy asked the judge hopefully, "Anything new from the pesky journalists on your answering machine?"

"Nothing new as of this morning," said Tim Stancil, sighing, "but there's always tomorrow." He seemed dispirited after his exchange with Grace.

"Pastor Margaret," said Lucinda, "can I have a word with you?"

We went over to a corner by ourselves.

"Food Pantry," announced Lucinda, with an odd little smile.

"What about it?" I asked.

"Don't you remember, we agreed to switch months with First Methodist, on account of their renovations?"

"Oh, right. We agreed to do December here in the crypt, didn't we?"

"We surely did, Pastor Margaret." She was beaming now. "Every Saturday morning in December — which *includes* the eighteenth. So we have a prior commitment!"

"We do, indeed. Not that we need one to say no, but it's nice to have a fence of prior commitment around us. I'm a little weary of being nakedly besieged."

"Isn't it the truth. I was ecstatic when I remembered. I had to stop myself from dancing a jig right in front of the coffee urn. I may be losing my marbles, but at least I remembered *one* important thing, didn't I?"

"You certainly did," I said.

"Go on," croaked Adrian, sitting up in bed. "This is better than Trollope."

"Maybe just because it's closer to home."

"I wonder how he would have done Grace."

"Grace is done enough as she is."

"So did you set her straight about the eighteenth?"

"Before she left, I told her about the Food Pantry, but I also made it clear that the issues were separate. That even if we didn't have the prior commitment to feed the poor, we still wouldn't feel it was part of our ministry as a parish to join this march."

"How did she take it?"

"Surprisingly mildly. Which worries me a little. Oh, by the way, Lucinda told me some people here believed Grace set the fire that burned up her parents."

Adrian fell back on the pillow with congested laughter. "Good old parish coffee hours. Where else can you collect so much exciting dirt in such a short time? I'm sorry I missed it; I want to experience this Grace Munger for myself."

"I could invite her over this afternoon."

"No thank you. I've already exceeded my sociability threshold with Tony. What a chatterbox he is. I finally had to send him on an errand."

"So he was with you. I wondered why he never showed up at church. What did you two talk about?"

"Oh, the abbey. And his great friend and supporter, the late Father Cecil. He seemed to want to impress me with how close they'd been. He grilled me quite a bit about my life, too. He was particularly impressed that I was a gunnery officer in the Navy, whereas my Zurich stint interested him much less. I think he would have really liked to hear more about the orphanage, but I wasn't in the mood to tell my Little Orphan Adrian stories. Then I had a coughing fit, and he said I needed a good humidifier, so I sent him to the drugstore to buy one. Where is Chase? I wish I could have been there when he asked was it in English. That boy goes straight for the jugular. I enjoy it, when the blood's not running down *my* neck."

"Gus and Jennifer borrowed him for the day. They're going to get pizza and then move the rest of Charles's stuff over to the house in Gus's truck. They'll bring him home this evening about nine."

"So after Tony leaves, we'll have the place to ourselves for a few hours. I'm looking forward to it, even though I feel lousy."

"I just hope Tony doesn't tell me anything too awful before he leaves."

"We've already discussed one likelihood. But if he's what he says he is, it will probably be something less dramatic: a tepid prayer life, animosity toward a brother monk. Or possibly that he's got a whole collection of clippings in his suitcase about nice church couples he plans to hit up for hospitality after he leaves us. Did you ever hear that old joke about the clergyman who went on a coast-to-coast vacation of the country?"

"No."

"Well, since he already had the names and addresses of all the families he was going to stay with, he decided to save himself time and bother by writing all his thank-you notes before he left home and sealing them in stamped envelopes, which he would then mail one by one as he made his way cross-country. The only trouble was, he left them all behind in the first house on his itinerary. He realized his mistake as soon as he unpacked in place number two, and phoned back to his last hostess, to ask her to put them all in a big envelope and send them to his next address. 'Oh, don't worry,' she said, 'we've already taken care of it for you, Father. My husband dropped the whole stack in the mailbox on his way to the office. You just go ahead and enjoy the rest of your trip!' "

We were laughing when Tony came upstairs bearing the assembled new humidifier. I stopped myself just short of asking Adrian to repeat the story. Tony might think we had been making comparisons between him and the clergyman.

While the three of us were deciding where to set up the machine before Tony filled it with tap water, the doorbell rang.

"Now who could that be?" I said.

"Grace Munger for lunch?" suggested Adrian.

"Had I better add a few more potatoes to my potato soup?" I heard Tony ask Adrian seriously as I went downstairs.

It was a gaunt-faced young woman in jeans and a cardigan that came to her knees but didn't look warm. Her chapped hands held up a Stove Top stuffing canister that had been partially papered over and scribbled on. "Hi, you the minister of the church here?"

"Yes I am, how can I help you?"

"We're collecting money for Christmas toys for poor kids. Any cash you can spare would be much appreciated."

"Which group are you with?"

Her eyes narrowed. "I don't get your meaning."

"I just wondered if you were from a church or —"

"No, it's just some of us out collecting on our own. These days there's a whole lot of people in this area can't even put food on the table for their kids. We're just trying to help out with some toys, that's all."

"In that case, I can help you. Do you know The Gilded Peacock, on Main Street?"

"The gift shop?"

"That's the one. The lady who runs it gives away toys every Christmas season to any charitable group or family who comes in and asks. They're nice toys, she chooses them herself from the catalogues. Just go in and ask for Marie Baird. She's open Sundays."

The young woman didn't look at all happy with this news, and I didn't feel any happier to have called her bluff. During this season, toys for kids was a choice ruse for panhandlers, the rest of the year the favorite request was an urgently needed bus ticket, to a place just far away enough to cover the price of the needed booze or narcotic.

"Marie Baird at The Gilded Peacock," she repeated, looking at me levelly for the first time. Her pinpointy-pupiled blue eyes were rock hard with pride. This one would carry her lie away with her without backing down. "Much obliged for your time."

"You're welcome. Good luck with the toys." I stood at the door and watched her go down the rectory walk. She turned left, in the direction of the shops, proceeding purposefully along in her stiff-backed, pigeon-toed gait. She looked cold. She probably knew I was watching. Maybe she would bluff it out right to the end, actually go into The Gilded Peacock and ask Marie for a few free toys. Perhaps the toys would even find their way under some needy child's tree. Nevertheless I felt less good about the day and my place in it as I shut the door on all her unvoiced needs. I remembered Tim Stancil's weary sigh at coffee hour. There were enough needs and hurts in this town already, without manifestos and Millennium marches hinting at easy rescues.

Adrian wanted to go downstairs for our last meal with Tony, prepared by Tony, but he felt woozy when he got out of bed. So we brought the potato soup and toasted cheese sandwiches up on trays and kept him company.

"Will you be spending any time in Mountain City," Adrian asked our departing guest, "or going straight on to your next destination?"

"What would you suggest?" Tony asked him respectfully, spooning his soup toward himself.

"Well, there's always the famous millionaire's castle in Mountain City, which brings visitors from all over the world. If you want to spend the better part of a day seeing in detail how one very rich man chose to spend some of his money at the turn of the last century. Napoleon's chess set is there, but Margaret's and my favorite part of the tour was the servants' quarters, which were opened to the public only a few years ago. The grounds of the estate are beautiful to walk in, even at this time of year. And, as you probably know, there are a number of our churches in Mountain City, ranging from smoky-high Anglo-Catholic to no-frills Protestant Episcopal."

"Your late prior Father Cecil did his prayer school at Our Lady's," I put in.

"Yes, that's the smokiest of the bunch," said Adrian. "Father Devereaux is rector there. Please give him our regards if you happen to see him."

"Father Devereaux," Tony repeated with a dutiful nod, as if storing away the information, but he looked a trifle forlorn.

Presently, I excused myself to do some homework for the Commission on Ministry meeting at the diocese next week. I expected Tony would follow me, but he said, "Leave those dishes, Margaret, I'll bring everything down when I come," and began telling Adrian what promised to be another extended anecdote about his late great prior, Father Cecil.

In a folder on my desk, as yet unopened,

were six five-page autobiographies from applicants aspiring to be priests that I and some other clergy, including the bishop, would be interviewing at the two-day meeting next week. Since I had almost an hour before my appointment with Tony, I thought I might as well get started on them.

Once, my autobiography had lain like this in folders with those of other aspirants, on desks of people who would be either well-disposed, lukewarm, or downright opposed to our wanting to be ordained. It was an awesome responsibility to discern, on the basis of some parish evaluation forms, a five-page autobiography, and two sets of meetings with someone, whether that person had a call to the ministry. It was even more difficult when the interviewers were split in their votes. The part of the process I liked least, on my present side of the fence, was having to phone the rector of the sponsoring parish whose candidate had been turned down for postulancy. But the most taxing part of all was writing the letter to the rejected applicant, explaining the decision of the commission and trying to enumerate the person's perceived strengths that she or he could bring to another field of service. I always imagined how I would have felt had I received such a letter, and wondered what other "field of service" I would be in now, and whether, if I had still married Adrian, I would feel resentful that he got to be a priest and I didn't, and how it would have affected our marriage. But I had learned to temper my sadness for the rejected applicants by keeping ready a mental list of the priests I had known who definitely should have been stopped long before ordination.

I opened the folder and leafed quickly through the papers. All were word-processed, though some formats were more eye-pleasing than others, with spiffy alternating fonts, "sight-bite" paragraphing, and catchy headings. The paper on top, by a twenty-six-year-old high school English teacher, with its skinny margins and infrequent paragraph breaks, had the least artfulness both in format and content, but I was immediately hooked by his candor.

My best friend in college described his acceptance of faith as having occurred in the company of 10,000 people at a revival held by a well-known Christian evangelist. He just walked down to the stage and was saved. For a long time I was bothered by the fact that my faith did not come like his, that is, did not come in one epiphanic moment of insight. No, I was faithless for quite a while, then ambivalent, then skeptical, and then when I finally decided, in college, to choose to believe, to acknowledge that I had a religious nature in spite of intellectual qualms, the study of philosophy helped me make the reconciliation, in particular the philosophy of pragmatism as presented by William James. According to James, truth = whatever works best in the way of helping individuals make sense of their existence. So, I felt free to have faith. But faith in what?

Here begins the second phase. I tried different things. I went to synagogue services, I went to a Wiccan service, and I attended Quaker meetings for about four months. But I could not concentrate in the Quaker meetings, Judaism was too big of a cultural change, and the Wiccan ceremony seemed to me a shadow of the Episcopal liturgy I had grown up with. So I returned to the church of my childhood (which I left at 12 because I could not be a hypocrite and recite creeds I did not believe). I could now return because pragmatism and Pascal's wager, and also Kierkegaard's image of the leap of faith, helped me bridge the gap between the seen and the unseen, between rationality and mystery. The beauty of pragmatism for me is that it allows one to find truth in many places. So science and Christianity, or Hinduism and Christianity, can be true simultaneously. I think God is at work in everything, but Christianity is the best way for me to understand that work. I am committed to it because it provides me with a sense of hope and relief: whatever I do, God is willing to forgive and start over as long as I am willing to start over and let myself be forgiven. Further, besides offering forgiveness and new life, Christianity is based on ethics which correspond to my notion of appropriate living and action. The simplest articulation of these ethics, to love God and to love one's neighbor as oneself, makes sense to me as a basic outline for conduct.

But I continued to worry that my faith lacked the necessary evangelical zeal. It then occurred to me that I needed to reconsider my criteria for evaluating my belief. Specifically, I should stop assuming that belief must come in certain forms to be genuine. In places ranging from George Herbert's poetry to Flannery O'Connor's stories to the Old Testament, I encountered emphasis on the mystery of God's methods and began to understand that accepting and appreciating this mystery is part of belief, that God's methods cannot be categorized. Faith, for instance, enters an individual's life however God wants it to, and I need not worry that my faith did not come in a flash, but evolved. I see that how I claimed faith has nothing to do with the strength of my faith.

By considering how and why I came to believe, I have reached a clearer idea of who I want to help, and what sort of help I want to offer. I see more clearly that my desire to help others involves the desire for them to be helped in the way I have been helped . . .

Here I closed the folder. I owed this applicant a full engagement with his so-far rigorously cleared trail up the mountain of vocation; I was already looking forward to meeting him, seeing how the person would match up with his documents. But the more imminent meeting with Tony was nibbling at my attention, so I went next door to the church with time to spare.

It was still moderately warm from the ten o'clock, but to play it safe I turned the thermostat back up to 68, in case Tony's hour went over.

In the sacristy, I arranged the chairs for a face-to-face encounter, and put a prayer book on the table beside Tony's chair. I also prepared the kneeling desk facing our makeshift confessional, in case he chose to go that route. I had planned to go into the chancel and lurk in the shadows for a while, readying myself for God knew what sort of disclosure, but the sacristy felt cozier, and I ended up sinking to my knees upon the lamb cushion, embroidered by Lucinda's mother, at the kneeling desk, staring straight ahead at the closed door with the confessional screen cut into it. Back in Romulus, my father had kept an old kneeling desk similar to this in his study. Once when I was little I had come upon him praying and asked him where exactly God was when he knelt there. "Where exactly?" he had repeated. He squinched his eyes shut, as though calculating the exact location. "Well, honey, I'd say about six inches inside that wall."

At ten minutes before two I heard the soft pebbly crunch of approaching footsteps on the walkway leading around the side of the church to the sacristy door. The footsteps came close, then retreated, then returned and made more scuffling sounds on the gravel. But no knock. Curious, I finally opened the door to see what was going on. Tony leaned with his back against the handrail of the walkway, pulling fiercely on a hand-rolled cigarette. In the thin sunlight the boyish reddish-brown fringe against his ghastly pale old forehead looked particularly bizarre.

"I was a little early," he apologized in his quavery voice.

"That's okay, I'm ready anytime you are."

"Perhaps I'll just finish up this little soldier, if that's all right," he said with attempted jauntiness. When he held up the glowing stub between his thumb and forefinger, his hand was shaking.

"That's fine. Just walk on in whenever you're ready." I closed the door. I realized I was nervous.

Almost at once there was a timid knock, and I opened it again. "That was quick," I said.

"I decided I'd had enough. Don't worry, I didn't stub it out on your grounds." He patted the deep pocket of his habit. "It's in here."

"Is that completely safe?"

"If you're an old veteran at conserving butt ends, it is."

We stood facing each other, both at a momentary loss for words.

Then I showed him where he could hang his duffel coat. "Have you decided how you'd like to go about this?" I asked.

"Oh yes." A quavery little cackle.

I waited.

"Would it be possible — do you think I could — could we just talk?"

"You mean outside the rite of reconciliation?" I asked.

"Outside, yes. You know, without the confidential seal."

"Sure, we could make it just a pastoral session, but I couldn't give you absolution then."

"Then maybe I'll forgo the absolution for now."

"But why would you want to forgo the seal? Most people are grateful for it."

"What I would like," he hurried on, "is to tell you a story kind of like the doctor did at the wedding reception yesterday. Maybe I shouldn't have confused the issue when I asked you earlier. I guess I hadn't thought it out as clearly as I should have."

"Well, let's be sure we're clear about it now. You don't want the sacrament, you just want to tell me a story?"

"That's right." He looked relieved. "Without the enforced confidentiality. That's the way I've decided I want to do it."

"But a pastoral session still isn't a public meeting, Tony. Just because it's not under the seal doesn't mean I'm going to go out and blab about it."

"But you could use — discretion, couldn't you?" Now he seemed to be pleading. "I would tell you the story, then say good-bye, and after I was gone — years from now, even — if there ever came a time when you thought there might be a benefit in telling it to anybody, well, you would have my blessing."

"I admit I'm perplexed by this, Tony."

"You won't be, Margaret, if you'll hear me out."

"Let's sit down, then."

He started for the chair I usually sat in,

445

then hesitated. "This all right?"

I started to say it was fine, they were both almost identical armchairs, but then I realized I very much desired the security of my habitual seat, with its view of the polished oak vestment cupboards and the folded stole on top that Adrian had given me for my ordination, which I had gotten out for Tony's confession, and, on the wall above, the Celtic cross I'd bought on Lindisfarne Island on my twenty-second birthday, after having scattered my father's hair cuttings from our last barbering session in the border of veronica, yarrow, sea campion, and gorse growing along an inside wall of the ruined priory.

"Why don't you take that one," I said, indicating the armchair beside the table with the prayer book on it.

We each sat down. He spent some time plucking at his skirts and rearranging the folds of his habit. I noticed he had cleaned his black Nikes since I last saw them. His face was going through some amazing changes: one second I saw a tough and cunning boy determined to show no emotion when he was dealt his well-deserved punishment; the next, I was gazing upon a sorrowful, weather-beaten old man with foolish orange hair.

"Here." I stuck out my hand. "Let's pray first." His hand in mine was ice-cold and trembly, yet he held on tight.

"O God, whose power working in us can

accomplish infinitely more than we ask or imagine, please be close to us now, in this hour, while Tony tells his story. And in all our hours still to come, help us to support one another in kindness and integrity of heart. Amen."

"Amen," said Tony.

Silence.

He cleared his throat. "What I thought was —" Here his smoker's cough kicked in, the one that sounded like a car engine trying to turn over.

I waited as he took a handkerchief out of the deep pocket where he kept his tobacco pouch, coughed into it, then wiped his lips daintily and stuffed it back in the pocket. I wondered if Adrian and I were still folded together in the other pocket.

"What I'd like to do," he began again, "is to tell this the way the doctor did. You know, like a story about some other man. When I was listening to him I got the idea. I think I could go through with it better this way, if that's all right with you."

"Of course it is," I assured him. "It's a time-honored form of storytelling."

"Oh well, that's good, then." He sat up straighter in the armchair and folded his hands neatly in his lap. Now he looked like an old monk with orange hair about to impart some spiritual advice.

"Once there was this scrappy young man

447

who thought he was different. Like many young men his age, he thought he had a special destiny. He went his own way as much as he could, he didn't like being told what to do, and though a few of his teachers told him he was smart and could go far in life if he'd get rid of his attitude, he went right on being the same. He was the kind of young man who'd pick a fight with a soft stick of butter and lie to you if you asked him which way to the corner. The more questions you asked him, the farther from the truth you got; he didn't even know why he did it most of the time. Later in life, someone told him it was like the way a wolf will lure you away from her den, going off in all kinds of false directions to protect her young. This was someone who kept trying to help him, after he'd messed up so bad the rest of the world had given up on him. This person's theory was that there was something in the young man — some little mustard seed of integrity, as he put it — that he felt he needed to protect. That's an odd notion, isn't it, protecting the little mustard seed of truth inside you by covering it with lies?

"He came from an assembly line family the way some people come from farming or brewing or seagoing families. His French-Canadian grandfather had emigrated to Motor City to work in the Ford plant, and his father and big brother worked there now, and he was expected to take his place on the assembly line as soon as he was done with school. Keep up the great family tradition of being a cog in a wheel that produced a car every fifty-five seconds to the glory of Henry Ford and his shareholders, and suffering from chronic hemorrhoids in the bargain. Well, he didn't think so, but if he'd kept his thoughts to himself he might have gone on living with his folks a while longer and finished high school.

"One Sunday when they were all sitting around the dinner table, the gorge rose up in him as it often did on the wrong occasions and he found himself laughing and telling them a story about an older friend of his who'd recently gone to work at the Ford plant. The friend got mad when the company doctor cut off his hemorrhoid, slapped a Kotex between his buns, and told him he could go back to work now. The friend decided that from then on he would make it a point of honor to neglect every fifth generator shaft that came past him. They came past at five to ten a minute, which meant five hundred an hour, and four thousand in an eight-hour shift. It gave him the satisfaction of knowing that every day he sent out eight hundred Ford generator shafts with his personal stamp of sabotage on them. Well, nobody else at the table found the story funny. The father and mother were scandalized and wanted to know who it was so they could get him fired, and his brother told him if he had half the brain of a normal human being he wouldn't find it funny, either. The next thing you know, Scrappy lights into the brother like a fighting cock, and big brother ends up in the hospital with two smashed ribs and a handful of broken fingers, unable to work on the assembly line for six weeks, and Scrappy quits school and leaves home to work on the river. The friend who made the eight hundred mistakes a day didn't exist. The story had just sprouted inside his head at the Sunday dinner table and grown bigger and bigger until it sprang him out of his home.

"He liked working on the river, he managed to stay out of fights — most of the time — and even let up on the lying some; maybe because people on the river didn't ask as many personal questions as they did in Dearborn. Also he came under the influence of a friend — a friend who really existed this time — as fine a fellow as he'd ever been privileged to call a friend. He and his friend planned to buy a tug and eventually start their own tugboat company. Then here came the war and the friend enlisted in the Army and got himself killed almost as soon as he set foot overseas. By this time Scrappy had joined up himself and was being inducted into the rigors of warfare at a reception center, learning how to make a bunk bed so tight that a dime bounces off it, and if it doesn't, a loathsome little corporal tears it up and makes him do it over. He takes the General Classification Test and surprises even himself by scoring high enough to volunteer for parachute training, which appeals to his sense of having a special destiny. But he never gets there, because in his third week of basic training he has an urgent phone call from his dead friend's girl. She's six months pregnant from the last time her soldier was home on leave, and she asks if he'll marry her so her lover's baby won't bear the stigma of illegitimacy.

"It was a pretty heavy-duty request, but our hero said yes. Let's call him that just this once, because it's the nearest he's ever going to get to being one in his life. Maybe this is a good place to explain something else. He admired this girl, he used to envy his friend for being loved by such a superior girl; in fact, he'd fantasized some about her, himself. Yet he also knew even as he was agreeing to marry her that she would never have married someone like him if she hadn't been in a fix.

"Well, he went to the commander of his training company and requested special leave to get married. He said it was his baby. The commander, a second lieutenant younger than he was, not only denied the request but made some snide remarks about the 'lady' waiting awfully long to inform him of the 'happy event,' and even suggested 'man-to-man' that the baby might not be his and that one day he would be thankful Military Law had prevented him from making a cuckold of himself. In peacetime, that prissy young lieutenant would have been collecting his teeth off the floor, but Scrappy still had some wits about him. He went AWOL instead, got married, started back the same afternoon, and in rage and frustration beat up the MP who tried to arrest him just when he thought he'd made it back to his unit with nobody the wiser.

"He spent the next two years at Fort Leavenworth. Then the Army transferred him to a new disciplinary barracks where they were experimenting with rehabilitating prisoners who hadn't done anything too bad and returning them to active duty so they could earn an honorable discharge if the war lasted that long.

"During all this time, he'd been writing to the woman who was his legal wife, though they never had consummated their marriage. The baby had been stillborn at eight months, and she had gone to work in a factory that made gas masks from old rubber tires. The whole situation was peculiar as hell to them both. They hardly knew each other, their reason to be married was gone, but they still had to keep up their story. She told people that he was in the administrative and guard unit at Leavenworth, and entertained the other women at the factory with stories about the prisoners, which she got out of his letters. He talked about her superiority and showed his wedding snapshots of him and his smiling pregnant bride to the other jailbirds. When his case came up for review, he told his commandant that he was determined to bring her back an honorable discharge even if it came home with him in a coffin, and it was probably this more than anything that got him his second chance.

"At the new disciplinary barracks, he was put to work stripping down old Army vehicles and rebuilding them with new parts. At least it wasn't the Ford assembly line; he got to use some ingenuity and see one job through to the end. The commanding officer of his guard unit liked him and said he was going to recommend him for infantry training to prepare him for active duty. But that commanding officer retired suddenly due to ill health and the son of a bitch who replaced him had it in for our boy on first sight. He had him transferred out of the motor shop to the equipage shop, where prisoners repaired Army clothing. And there he remained until the war ended and he was demobilized with no honorable discharge.

"It was a strange bus ride home. Here he was, looking like millions of GIs about to hit the streets in search of a job and a life, but he had three invisible strikes against him in his pocket. As for home, he was going to an address in a town he'd never lived in, to share a one-room efficiency he'd never seen, with the woman who was legally his wife until they could both figure out what to do with their future — together or apart.

"But things have a way of deciding themselves, when the fever of the times is all around you. There was a homecoming of sorts, because she had a place and they were alone in the world and everybody was singing that happy times were here again and the lights had gone on all over the world and you'd be so nice to come home to. Her mother was dead, she'd left her drunken father when she was sixteen and finished high school on her own, living with the guy she loved, the nice guy who worked on the river. And Scrappy's assembly line family had let him know what they thought of him after he wrote from Leavenworth. He never contacted them again. So here they were in their efficiency, a lonely young woman and a virile man going on twenty-eight who'd been without his freedom for four years, and they were legally married to each other. They had built up a kind of friendship in their letters, and I guess she must have found something appealing about him, too, because for a while it was sweet.

"Well, as our young friend Chase would

say, 'You don't have to have very much intelligence to figure out what happened next.' They both wanted the baby, but it was a bad time for her. She couldn't keep anything down, and then she developed a lung problem the doctor said had been caused by breathing fumes from the burning rubber in the factory. He also predicted she would probably miscarry and indicated it would be just as well for her health. Her first pregnancy had been calm and easy, before she ever set foot in any factory, and the poor little fellow still hadn't made it. So what chance did this ill-starred little creature have? Nevertheless, this baby was brought to term. This was before the days when the doctor could turn on a machine and show you whether you were getting a boy or a girl, so they had names ready for both. In either case, they both wanted to name the child after the guy who worked on the river; it was a nice-sounding name, it reflected the French-Canadian heritage of all three of them, and it was equally suited to boy or girl. If it turned out to be a girl, her middle name would be the first name of the mother, and if it was a boy his middle name would be the middle name of the father, who'd never liked his first name much.

"Well, it was a boy. Margaret, I've been looking at that little sign on the wall that says 'Thank you for not smoking,' but do you think I could just finish up that little butt end in my pocket?"

"Do," I said abruptly.

He was shaking like a leaf as he reached down into his pocket and fumbled around. "Now if I can only find my matches —"

"Here!" I leapt up and snatched the candlelighter from its wall hook. I switched on the flame too high and almost scorched his dyed fringe. "What did you name him?" I asked harshly.

Tony took a deep puff. The butt end seemed to glow red forever. At last the old man released his pungent plume of forbidden smoke into the sacristy, regretfully regarded the embers before crushing them between his thumb and forefinger, and looked up at me with tearful, beseeching eyes. "We named him Adrian Anthony Bonner."

"But my husband doesn't have a middle name," I said, when I felt I could speak in a normal tone of voice.

"He probably didn't remember," he said miserably. "And it's possible we neglected to give the fathers his middle name. It was a bad day for all of us. We really did intend to come back as soon as I could find work, but —"

Here he broke down. As he wept, he continued to massage the crushed butt end between his thumb and forefinger until I pulled some Puffs from the little box on the shelf beside the *Book of Occasional Services* and handed them over. "Listen," I said, "why

456

don't we go outside and continued this in the garth? That way, you can smoke all you want, and a little fresh air might do us both good." I very much needed an intermission to sort out my feelings and begin to deal with the impending consequences of what I had just heard.

We put on our coats and went out into the brisk afternoon, down the steps to the garth. He made himself another cigarette as we walked. I looked up at the second-floor bedroom window and thought of my Adrian, either dozing or coughing or worrying about the school, totally innocent of the fact that his wife was pacing around and around the hibernating English borders with her father-in-law. I could not remotely imagine what I was going to do.

"You couldn't find work, then," I prodded Tony, holding in reserve all the other things I desperately wished to know.

"There had been work, but that was part of the problem, see. He — or no, we're not doing it that way anymore, are we?" He looked wistfully over at me for guidance. I suspected a return to his "storytelling" form would be easier on him, but mightn't it also be an easier container for evasions and lies? Hadn't he already described himself as a born liar?

"You had work, but there was a problem with it?"

"We — this fellow and I — had a little partnership that traded in black-market auto parts. He procured the parts people needed, no questions asked, a little more money paid, and I installed them. My 'military training' came in handy, and my partner couldn't have cared less about the dishonorable discharge. We had a good thing going, as long as it lasted. I used to take the boy to work with me when she wasn't feeling well."

"That's where you two were playing when he chipped his tooth."

"That was the place. Oh, dear, when he brought up that tooth yesterday and I was looking right at it! I thought he might recognize me then. But I guess I've changed more than I'd like to think."

"Would you have recognized him if you hadn't known who he was?"

"Well, I don't know. The tooth, of course. But on the other hand, I'd seen his picture. If I hadn't seen the picture, I'd probably have been expecting more hair. At least I'm not responsible for that. Baldness comes from the mother's side."

"Is his mother still alive?"

"She died eight months after we left him with the fathers. Cancer. Thirty-one years old. We didn't even know she had it. We were always worrying about her lungs, you see. She had this other bleeding that went on for months, but we assumed it was the after-

458

effects of — you see, we had to leave town very suddenly when my partnership closed down, and she'd had a miscarriage in the car. That's when we hit bottom and decided he'd be better off with the fathers until we could get our lives back together. But, as you see, we never did."

Ah, God — if my heart constricts like this while I'm asking these things, what will it do to my husband's heart?

"But *you* could have come back for him. I would think you would have wanted him more than ever, after you lost her. Why didn't you come back for him? Or at least let him know where you were?"

"So help me, Margaret, I kept meaning to. Then I'd think, well, I'll wait a little longer, until I've got a steady job. Then it was, I'll wait until I've got a decent home to bring him to. Then a little later it became: he might not be so happy to see me come back alone. He might not be so glad to see me, period. He's in a safe, respectable place, getting his education from the Catholic fathers, and every day that passes I grow dimmer in his mind. After that, I went to prison for a while, and when I got out I thought: he's a young man now, with a sense of his own special destiny like I had once, and what's it going to do to his sense of special destiny if an ex-con failure shows up at his doorstep and says hi, let me introduce myself, I'm your dad? Of course by

459

then I didn't even know where his doorstep was, because he would have been almost twenty by then and not in the place where we left him. Then once again I got busy trying to put my life back together, working at this and that, wondering if I'd ever get on top of things, and the next thing I knew I was back in prison. Prison is easier to go back to than most people think.

"This time I was in for a longer spell. What had started off as a quietly planned theft that would have hurt nobody and given some wealthy people in the area a little excitement buying new jewelry their insurance would completely pay for — well, unfortunately things got out of hand and turned into an armed robbery. My partner who did the leg-work got the tip of his earlobe grazed by a cop, nobody else was hurt, but he ended up claiming I was the mastermind and told about the other times we'd done it — it involved a little jewelry store I was managing up in the Catskills. That lady who ran the Catskill resort where I taught dancing until my mishap with the samba: remember I was telling you about her? Well, she got me the job; I guess she wanted me to stay around for the winter. It was her young cousin who did the legwork and got his ear nicked; he was the one who double-crossed me to get himself a lighter sentence."

"So you were the man in the prison story

you told at the reception last night?"

"Yes, I was the man in that story, too, Margaret. Sometimes it seems like I've been the man in every story but my own. Father Cecil — he was the one who kept believing in me when everyone else had given up, liked to say I kept 'reinventing myself.' I'd say to him, 'What's the difference between reinventing yourself and starting over with a new lie?' That's the way we talked. He'd offer his elevating reasons why I was the way I was, and I'd shoot them down."

I looked over at the bizarre figure strolling along beside me in his old duffel coat and Benedictine skirts. He'd gone through another cigarette. We must have done the four sides of the garth dozens of times by now, but he seemed ready for dozens more, he actually seemed to be deriving momentum from the exercise. Quite likely he associated the pacing of small outdoor enclosures with his recreation time in prison. If anyone were looking down on us from the rectory, they might well think: what a sweet sight they make down there, the old monk and the serious young woman in her collar; what could they be talking about so intently, going around and around like that? God, no doubt. And feel vastly reassured by the picture we made.

"I take it, then," I said rather caustically, "that you met Father Cecil when he came on his visits to your prison in New York."

"No, it was more amazing than that!" He was suddenly elated. "Father Cecil and I had *already met* at Fort Harrison."

"Fort Harrison?" I resented his new buoyancy. He'd shed his load; now I was about to assume the burden of it.

"Fort Benjamin Harrison. That's the Disciplinary Barracks they sent me to from Leavenworth. They also had a school for chaplains there, see, and he was assigned to stay on as an Army chaplain at Harrison after he finished his training. He was six years younger than I was — it seems unfair that such a useful man is dead when I'm still knocking around — he wasn't in the order then. Back then he had plans to be a labor lawyer, but he found his true vocation at Fort Harrison. Later when we discovered each other again at the, er, facility in New York, he was kind enough to say that knowing people like me had made him realize that soul work was more interesting to him than industrial relations. The amazing thing to me was, he was as optimistic as ever that my little mustard seed of integrity could still be cultivated into something fine.

"And when the parole board finally said good-bye and good luck to me at sixty-one, the time when most men my age were looking forward to receiving their gold watches for retirement, Father Cecil took me on as cook and gardener and general man of all work at the Transfiguration. Thanks to him, I was gainfully employed at the abbey for nineteen years. I liked living with the monks, though there are always tensions between people, just like in any family. But monks are supposed to try harder, and generally they do. And after so many years inside, I found their routines came easy to me. Prison life and monastery life have many things in common. So, in a way, I have been a sort of honorary lay brother, though I admit I pushed things a bit far by wearing the habit on this trip."

"Whose habit is it, then?"

"It was his. Father Cecil's." He cut his eyes over at me, then added in an apparent attempt to disarm, "He looked a lot better in it than I do."

But I was in no mood for being disarmed. "Why did you come to us dressed as a monk — in a dead monk's clothes — implying you were a monk? What could possibly be gained by such a deception?"

"It was probably wrong of me, but —"

"There's no probably about it."

"I guess the reasoning behind it was you were much more likely to accept me as a nice old monk than an ex-con. I needed to gain myself a little time, so I could get to meet my boy, see how the land lay. Please try to see it from my side."

"I'm trying to see it from my *husband's* side, and that's where all my compassion is going at this moment —"

"He's a fine man, any fellow would be proud to have him for a son. I don't deserve him, but having met him, I can go away feeling my life hasn't been a total waste. And that's why I wanted to come clean before I got on the bus this afternoon, Margaret. One of these days, maybe you'll find it in your heart to tell him we had this little talk and —"

"Let's leave the bus out of this for a minute, Tony. And please let's postpone the scenario of your riding bravely off into the sunset and delegating the consequences of your charade to me. Don't you know how much this information is bound to affect Adrian? How did you happen to find him, anyway? *Was* it simply that you came across our picture in *Episcopal Life* —"

"No, our new prior, Father Ted, was actually the one who came across it." Now he sounded penitent, but maybe that was an act, too. "Father Ted brought it into the kitchen, folded back to the page, and said, 'This might be of interest to you, Tony.' Even before he became prior, while Father Cecil was still around to stick up for me, Father Ted was always inquiring whether I had any connections I could go and live with when it became 'inoperable' for me to stay on at the Transfiguration. Well, the instant I saw that name under the picture, he must have known from my face he'd hit pay dirt, because he said,

'It's a fairly old issue of the paper, but they're probably still there after three years. Would you like me to make some discreet inquiries on your behalf?' I said no, but I wouldn't mind going down there and having a discreet look myself. 'That can easily be arranged,' he said. He looked as cheerful as I've ever seen him. 'We'll take care of the travel part,' he said. 'You've earned a sabbatical, Tony.' I don't think Father Ted ever liked me very much, if you want to know the truth, Margaret."

"I very much want to know the truth, Tony."

Either he missed my tone or let it go by.

"You see," he went on, "it was general knowledge among the monks that I'd left a child with the Catholic fathers back in the early fifties. Father Cecil had put out a few feelers through Catholic channels, but all he could learn was that the place had closed down in the late fifties and all of the children had been placed elsewhere." He set about producing another hand-rolled smoke. "When Father Ted was driving me off to the bus station with my millennium ticket, he said, 'What a pity Father Cecil never thought to look up the name Bonner in our own Episcopal Clergy Directory. It was the orphanage being R.C. that put him off the trail. And here he's been right under our noses in the abbey library for the past fifteen years!' "

"What about the grandmother in Manistee?" I asked.

"The grandmother in . . . ?" He looked genuinely perplexed.

"In Adrian's file at the orphanage, there was a lady in Manistee, Michigan, listed as his maternal grandmother. But you said your wife's mother was dead."

"Oh, now, I'd forgotten all about that! You're right, Margaret, she was dead; I mean, Evette's mother was dead. But you see, we were afraid the fathers might not take him in at all if there was no person to contact in emergency, so I snatched at the first name that popped into my head, which was the name of Adrian's mother. I mean the first Adrian, the one I'd worked on the river with. He'd always spoken so well of his mother. She was dead, too, but she *had* lived in Manistee."

"And what was her name?"

"Well, let's see, his name was Rameau. So she was — oh, yes, I remember now: Ida Rameau. Mrs. Ida Rameau."

"And was your first name Joe?"

The man of many stories reached into the deep pocket of his dead friend's habit and withdrew a thin black wallet. He opened it and tweaked out a little document which he presented to me as proudly as if it had been a diploma from the Academy of Truthtelling itself: a New York State driver's license issued to Joseph Anthony Bonner. The mug shot was Tony all right, but his hair in the photo was the same color as his open-necked white shirt. Had he dyed it to make it easier for his boy to recognize him from the days of old?

O God, please tell me in American English, what do I do now?

Adrian was asleep when I returned. The room pulsed with his feverish choppy breathing against the steady background hum of the new humidifier. I took off my collar and sat down in the armchair by the window.

"Mmfh?" he inquired. The tumble of bed-clothes shifted. I waited for him to wake and start asking questions, but he turned over on his left side, uttered a deep, yielding groan, and went back to wherever he had been.

I was glad to have the remission, thankful to sit quietly with the side view of his face — the sharp-cut bridge of his nose where it joined his forehead, the wide, sloping, high forehead, with all the marvelous, troubled, complex thoughts churning behind it and only a few damp wisps of hair left at the center. ("At least I'm not responsible for that. Baldness comes from the mother's side.")

Did Tony's story change anything about my feelings for Adrian? Without a second's hesitation I could answer no. I had wanted the Adrian he had made of himself out of the materials of his difficult and uncertain history, and what I had wanted I had got: the man who now lay sleeping right in front of me, drawing deep, coarse-grained breaths. If I had gone beyond wanting him now, it was only because I had somehow slipped into a brand-new place, unknown as recently as forty-eight hours before: a place where the idea of "wanting" Adrian seemed as superfluous as "wanting" myself. We were both here, for better for worse — that had been *done*. The wanting had been replaced by an emotion closer to curiosity, a profound curiosity as to what God was going to do with us next, and the desire to be able to recognize it as it came to us, and to meet it with imagination and courage of heart.

But would Tony's confession change anything about Adrian's feelings about himself? That, I admit, filled me with some trepidation. He already labored under so many doubts about himself. What would it do to him to learn, at this point in his life, that this old ex-con who had sidled into our house posing as a monk was none other than his own progenitor, the flesh and blood father who had abandoned him to a childhood of mystery and dispossession? Would it turn him more against himself? Or would the sheer outrageousness of it provide something

like an electric shock strong enough to cata-
pult him into another place altogether?

He continued to sleep and I continued to
sit there. Sounds drifted up from below. The
guest who had been going to depart was settling in again. They were tentative sounds,
grateful and humble and a bit apologetic —
perhaps *meant* to sound that way? That the
newly revealed member of our family was a
con artist was not in question.

Daylight drained slowly out of the room.
At some point it became too dark to see outlines. I was floating, open-eyed, in a kind of
sensate gloaming when Adrian suddenly
raised himself up on the pillow and spoke to
me.

"How strange," he said.

"What?"

"I was dreaming about you sitting in that
chair, watching over me, and you're really
there."

"Yes, I'm really here. How do you feel?"

"Surreal. But it's pleasanter than coughing
and aching. When I was last in the bathroom,
I swigged some of that out-of-date codeine
syrup from my last bronchitis. It must still
have some kick. What time is it?"

I squinted across the room at the green
digitals. "Just turned five."

"Wasn't — Didn't you see him off on the
bus?"

"No, Tony is still here."

"He's staying *another* night?"

"A little longer than that. I invited him to stay for Christmas."

"What?" He attempted to sit up. "Wait, let me turn on the light."

"No," I said, "don't turn on the light. Let's talk in the dark for a while."

"Is it that bad?"

"Not bad, just — different than we expected."

"You went through with the confession, then."

"It was a confession, yes, but it wasn't under the seal."

"*Hmmf,*" he said. He cleared his congested throat. "Well, you must have had a good reason for asking him to stay."

"I didn't see what else I could do under the circumstances."

In the gray soup of the room, the new humidifier hummed on, dispersing its vapor. He waited for me to continue. My eyes were adjusted to the dark and I could see the pale disk of his face, the shadows of the eyes, but not the expression.

"He would like . . . not to have his story generally known until he's had a chance to prove himself — whatever that might mean." I was fishing my words, one by one, out of the gray soup.

"I take it I'm included in the general class."

"That's up to you."

"How so?" He seemed surprised.

"It was not under the seal. And my first loyalty is to you. That much I am sure of. Anything you want to ask me, I will answer."

"This is sounding rather strange, Margaret."

"It is strange. It's beyond where I can reason. All I have to guide me is a sort of moment-to-moment intuition and my love for you."

Another clearing of the throat. "If I've somehow managed to retain your love, I think I could put up with the devil until Christmas."

"Well, he's not the devil," I said. Not knowing what more to say.

"Strange," he said again. "Of course, *I'm* feeling spacey and strange. I suppose that adds to the strangeness. You do what you think best. I completely trust you. I was on the verge of saying something like that to you in the dream, it just came back to me. I was about to tell you in the dream that you're the first person I have ever let myself trust completely. Did you ever play that horrible game, 'Falling,' when you were a child?"

"Where you have to close your eyes and fall backward and trust the others to catch you? Yes, I played it, but I hated it. I hated it from the falling point of view, and almost as much from the catcher's point of view. I used to worry, what if my hand slips or something and I let the faller down?"

"I saw that happen more than once on the orphanage playground. It was considered a great joke. I refused to play at all. I just couldn't trust."

"That shows more intelligence," I said, "than a lack of trust."

What a blessing that you feel spacey and strange. Let it all mix together in the eventide of your sickroom: the dream woman in the chair and the real woman, the strange little man with the secret you need to know whenever you are ready to ask, children falling backward on a playground, being caught and not-caught. Play with it all in your fever-fantasies, entertain phantom possibilities; if they grow too threatening, send them back where they came from, refuse to play for a while. Let it mix together in the vaporous merciful gloom. Let spaciness be your air bag against the impact of too-sudden clarity.

Let it dawn on you slowly.

XIV

The Rector's Day Off

Adrian: X ray & blood culture
install new cartridge
order communion wafers
gutters!
stern letter to Internet Abusers Anon.
Lucinda
call T. Stancil: who is Paul Pike?
3 p.m. haircut (cancelled)
tea with Grace M.
　　　— M.B.'s appointment book,
　　　　first Monday in Advent, *1999*

Monday was officially my day off. Which meant I got to work on my overload of chores in any order I liked. Which also meant, as my father used to say about his day off, "your interruptions don't have to make appointments."

Last night Adrian's temperature had risen to 102, despite the antibiotic. We were having a small argument about whether to call Charles at home (I was for it) when Charles called us. He was still down at the hospital.

"Listen, Margaret, I want Adrian to get an

X ray and a blood culture. There's too much mean-spirited bacteria on the loose around here; I lost Uncle Cratis to strep pneumonia this afternoon."

"Oh Charles, I'm sorry."

"Damn thing just snuck up on us." Grief and anger at himself were thick in his voice. "I want to know exactly what's going on in Adrian's lungs. So bundle him up good and bring him over to the clinic tomorrow morning. If there's a morning fog, wait till it lifts; he doesn't need to be breathing in that stuff, either."

I had spent the night on the pull-out bed in my study, to leave Adrian the full range of his sickroom, and then, rising early, had slipped over to the church before anyone began to stir. I microwaved a cup of coffee and a frozen hot cross bun in the parish kitchen and took them up to my office. I read morning prayer. Outside it began to drizzle. I stood at the window and watched the brick walk in the garth below change from dull grayish-pink to a glossy tile-red in a matter of moments. For some reason the transformation made me feel better, as though I had accomplished something myself. If only it could be as simple as that.

As I was collecting my things to go downstairs the night before, Adrian had looked up at me with flushed cheeks and asked suddenly: "Did he really come from the Abbey of the Transfiguration?"

"Yes. He's been living there for the past nineteen years."

"Surprising," he murmured almost crossly. "Why?"

"I don't know, I found it easier to write him off as a complete phony. Coming out of another setting altogether."

"But we're all more or less products of mixed settings," I said. "I definitely wouldn't write him off," I cautiously added.

He looked pensive, then closed his eyes and slipped farther under the covers. He didn't ask anything more.

I took Adrian to the clinic for his X ray and blood culture. It was pneumonia. Charles switched him to a broad-spectrum antibiotic in case it turned out to be one of the bacterial strains, prescribed a new cough syrup, and ordered him back to bed. "Total rest until further notice, you hear?"

"But I'm feeling a little better now," Adrian said.

"That's word for word what Uncle Cratis said to me Friday night," Charles told him.

We stopped off at the drugstore; Adrian waited on the bench for the pharmacist to fill his prescriptions, and I went down the street in the drizzle to collect the mail from the post office, where I ran into Dick Miller, the Lutheran pastor.

"Hear you had a visitor at your ten o'clock," he said.

"Now who in the world told you that?"

"The visitor herself." He laughed. "She phoned me to tell me how warm and gracious you all were to her."

"Well, if that's all she told you, it's okay. Because that's all there is to report."

"And about Father Dowd's fife and drum — or whatever he's going to play in the parade. She said you had Food Pantry and couldn't commit yourself as a congregation. I told her we didn't have Food Pantry and weren't committing ourselves. But I'm glad I ran into you, Margaret. I've been thinking, it might be nice to do something ourselves to welcome in the millennium. Not to bring down the rapture, nothing spectacular, just a solemn evensong to celebrate the occasion and thank God we made it this far. Our two congregations, and whoever else wants to join in."

"What a wonderful idea. Let's do it."

"Your place or mine?" He winked. "I know I shouldn't say it, but yours is prettier."

"Come to us, then. But our organist is on leave."

"We'll bring ours. We'll provide the music and the refreshments, how's that?"

"Our hospitality committee would never take that lying down. We'll split the refreshments."

"And if Kevin wants to bring his folks and play his fife and drum, we can accommodate him, too." The Lutheran pastor threw back his curly head and laughed. Come to think of it, I had never seen Dick Miller in an unsociable mood. I wondered what his secret was. Adrian would probably say he was an extrovert feeling type, which I supposed went a long way.

When we returned home, Tony and Chase were playing blackjack for money at the kitchen table; something meaty and tomatoey was bubbling away in a big pot on the stove.

"Mr. Jefferson phoned," Chase reported to Adrian.

"Oh. I'll call him back right away."

"You don't need to. It was just about my school. He said to tell you he's set everything up with the principal. I report for duty tomorrow morning." He made a long face at Adrian. "My last chance to become a decent member of society."

"Something like that," agreed Adrian, smiling. "We must find someone to drive you."

"No problem," said Chase. "The school bus picks up some other kids in front of the hardware store at seven-thirty. It will be kind of cool. I haven't been inside a public school since I got kicked out of third grade."

"Otherwise I said I'd be glad to drive him,"

said Tony. "If I had the use of a vehicle."

"And I told him I could drive myself if I had the use of a vehicle," said Chase. He looked provocatively from one to the other of us. "And a license, of course."

"You've done a fair amount of driving without one, haven't you?" Adrian reminded him. But in passing, he ran his hand over Chase's head, very lightly so as not to disturb the hairstyling. Momentarily the boy shimmered, like a cat being stroked. An odd expression crossed Tony's face. Was he remembering a time when he had stroked a boy's hair?

"Well, I'm going to report back to bed," Adrian said. "Actually, I was feeling pretty good after I got dressed, but Dr. Charles informs me I have pneumonia."

Chase slammed down his cards, faceup. "You're kidding."

"Why should I be kidding?" Adrian asked, frowning. Then he saw Chase's distress. "Oh, I get it. You think this has something to do with your wishing it on me when we were having our swamp chase on Friday night."

Chase hung his head.

"As I recall, you wished yourself into oblivion as well. Well, Mr. Zorn, you won't get rid of either of us that easily."

"I don't want to get rid of you," murmured Chase.

"I know you don't," Adrian said. He

started to leave the kitchen, then turned back. "I don't want to get rid of you, either."

"Come on, Z-man, let's deal us both another round," Tony said, gathering up Chase's cards. "Won't do to play with an exposed hand." Cackling merrily, he shot me a glance loaded with conspiracy.

After Adrian was tucked away between clean sheets, having settled himself in to be a responsible invalid, the table on his side stocked with the updated medications, I went over to the church to "drop in" on Lucinda Lord in the sacristy. Monday was her morning to Brasso the brass, polish silver, dig old wax out of candleholders, and whatever other housekeeping she deemed due. Despite her lighthearted affability and her cultivated facade of being a bit of a flibbertigibbet, Lucinda was an intensely proud and private person who set great store on being in control and keeping her worries to herself. She was not one for confidences or "counseling" with the rector.

When I had casually initiated these drop-ins as a way of knowing her better, she had at first resisted me: "You don't want to spoil your hands with those nasty chemicals, Pastor Margaret. Priests are supposed to pamper their hands."

"I enjoy polishing things. I did it in my father's church after our chief altar guild person found she was allergic to metal polish.

Besides, it's good for a pastor's morale to wipe some stuff over a dark, dull surface and evoke instant shine."

"Well . . . at least put on these rubber gloves, then." She had capitulated.

Gradually over an accumulation of these Mondays, as we polished and scraped and discoursed on noninvasive topics, I was able to work up a faint shape, sort of like a poor brass rubbing, of Lucinda's unvoiced cares. The way she dealt socially with her husband's drinking and incivility was to turn your attention toward the positive aspects of his behavior. "Cal has never been a man of moderation in anything, but most especially when it comes to giving people gifts," she once cheerfully "confided" while buffing a silver paten until she could see her face in it. Or prying a stubborn clump of wax from a votive, she might suddenly muse as though thinking aloud, "Now Cal is one whom you can always count on to speak his mind, he doesn't suffer fools gladly, whereas I tend to pussyfoot and appease people, even when I don't much care for them."

I sensed something unusual about Lucinda that Monday as soon as I stepped into the sacristy and found her brooding at the sink. Though she must have heard me come in, she did not look up immediately, and when she did, she made no attempt to assemble her face into its usual perky welcome. She appeared puzzled and distraught.

"Lucinda?"

"I just don't know what to do."

"Here, let's both sit down." I took her hand and guided her to the chairs. She glanced wildly around her, as if contemplating escape, then sank into one.

I waited until she could compose herself enough to speak.

"Something awful is happening to me, Pastor Margaret."

"What is it, Lucinda?"

"Well, I think I'm losing my mind. I don't mean going crazy, I mean that other, awful kind — I don't even want to say it aloud, but you know: where you're erased . . . bit by bit . . . a little each day."

I felt a chill in my heart. But then I quickly went over our recent times together and couldn't recall observing a single hint of the dread malady, except for her forgetting to turn on the coffee urn during the offertory hymn yesterday, but after Grace's spectacular disruption, who wouldn't have?

"Why do you think so?" I asked Lucinda.

"Just now I had all those votive glasses lined up in the piscina. Then I looked down at them and suddenly I couldn't for the life of me think why I had put them there. It's come back to me now — I was going to run warm water into them and let them sit for a few minutes so I could dig out the wax easier, but

481

when you came in, my mind was a complete blank."

"Oh, Lucinda, that happens to me all the time. I'll go upstairs to get something and then I can't remember what it was."

"But that's just it, Pastor Margaret. Lately it's been happening *a lot more* than my usual 'all the time.' I'll suddenly come to myself and it's like waking up in a strange place. I'll be in the supermarket where we've shopped for years, and I can't think where the paper towels are. I just can't remember. And on Saturday, when I was driving us to Gus's after the wedding, I suddenly realized I didn't have the slightest idea how to get there. I had to ask Cal how to get to the Eubanks house! He said, 'Hell, Lucinda, who's the drunk in this car, you or me? A house we've only been to about a thousand times? You should have let me drive.' "

It was the first time in my presence that Lucinda had ever spoken of her husband's drinking.

"Listen," I said, "before you worry yourself sick over this, why not go and have yourself checked out. There are lots of other things that cause memory and concentration lapses: metabolic imbalances, certain medications, viral infections . . . even more serious things that can still be fixed if you catch them in time. To give you an example from my own life, my father was in the middle of a lecture once and he suddenly blanked completely. He couldn't even remember how to speak for a minute. We later learned that he had been having a TIA — a transient ischemic attack, which often precedes a stroke. If we'd known what it was at the time, he might be alive now. A checkup and a simple aspirin a day could have made all the difference. I'm not trying to alarm you, but why don't you put both our minds at rest by having a general medical workup?"

"You're very dear to say that about *both* our minds, Pastor Margaret, but I've been down in the den since six this morning looking up . . . that disease in all our medical books, and the only comfort I still have is that I haven't been diagnosed yet. I suppose that's what's called denial, but I don't think I'm a brave enough person to face it. I'd rather court dying from a stroke any day than being told that my circuits are going to come gradually unplugged until I'm like poor Fanny Mait-low."

Lucinda had been one of the parish's true models of faithfulness in her visits to the mother of our organist-on-leave during her slow and painful unplugging; now it pleas-antly occurred to me that maybe I was wit-nessing a simple case of sympathetic trans-ference. I say pleasantly, because I was starting to feel ominous twinges on Lucinda's behalf. People Lucinda's age and younger were diagnosed with Alzheimer's every day. Why should she or any of us be exempt?

"You've been very loyal about going to see Fanny Maitlow," I said. "Lots of parishioners went at the beginning, but you've stuck it out. I'm wondering if maybe your close connection to Fanny's illness has made you extra sensitive to the ravages of it?"

"That could be," she conceded with a brave laugh. "Wouldn't it be nice to think so!" Her bright, carefully mascaraed eyes filled with tears, but she preempted my reaching for the trusty box of Puffs by whipping out her own lacy pocket handkerchief and blotting away the wetness.

"Let's find out what's going on, Lucinda."

"Maybe it would be best. Only I hate to worry Cal. He gets so upset about the littlest thing. But I just don't know if I can face it alone."

"Will you let me face it with you? It can be our deep dark secret while we check it out. And afterward, too, if you want."

"But what if it turns out it *can't* be kept a secret?"

"Then we'll face that eventuality, too. But I promise you, Lucinda, you won't be alone."

"Well," she said presently, firming herself back into her Capable Lucinda mold, "that's good to know. You're very sweet to keep me company, Pastor Margaret. But now our sink water's gone cold and we'll have to soften that wax all over again before we can dig out those votives."

We duly cleaned all the little red and blue glass votive holders and put in fresh candles and Lucinda lined them up carefully on a tray and tripped into the nave to replace them in the votive stands. Then we got out the tall candlesticks for the high altar at Christmas, and the Elsa Van Wyck Memorial Ciborium with Van's grandmother's diamonds and garnets encrusted in the base, and the Georgian silver thurible that had once been Lucinda's great-aunt's best muffineer, and the wafter box and the silver wine ewer, and we polished all of them up, Lucinda afterward returning each shining item to its proper place inside the safe. Not once did she betray signs of any erasures or unpluggings, and I found myself petitioning, as we are wont to do for our friends and those we love, for a special exemption. Please let Lucinda, because she is our Lucinda, be spared this particular cup of human suffering.

Kevin Dowd was all but bursting with abject humility when I returned his call.

"Margaret, I wanted to tell you before anyone else did. I've given in about the Jesus parade."

"I know. Grace Munger announced it here in church yesterday."

"In All Saints? You mean she actually came

to All Saints High Balsam?"

"She did, and we didn't throw her to the high horses."

"Wait a minute. Does that mean *you've* also —"

"It means she was here, she took communion, she made her announcement at announcement time, and we treated her like a human being. As far as I know, that's all. Nobody came forward with any musical offerings, except one boy admitted he could whistle."

"Well, I'm no great musician myself, but I marched in my high school band, and I must say it's a relief to have her off my case. What was that old song about an irresistible force meeting an immovable object? Something had to give and I gave. When I told my temporary flock after church yesterday, you know a couple of them even thanked me, and the senior warden said he was *relieved!* He told me, 'Better you put on your dog collar, Father, and blow your horns with the fundamentalists, than have them come down here and do mischief to St. Francis's physical plant.' "

"He didn't really think they would go that far, did he?"

"Why not? Look at that barracks burning mess that's getting so much attention. I just saw on the news this morning where they're transferring the case to Judge Stancil's court because feeling is running so high in Jasper."

"But the security guards in Jasper were destroying something that they believed threatened their livelihood."

"Well, but remember a few years ago when all the black churches were getting torched? Now with this social and economic unrest, why shouldn't the worm turn the other way and disenfranchised people start burning down uppity white churches? That's what the senior warden was suggesting at coffee hour. Oh, and he was telling me about Grace Munger's own history. Do you know, Margaret, there's a rumor that she set the fire because her parents had disgraced themselves? Had you heard that?"

"Yes. We have our coffee hour, too, Kevin."

I was debating whether to write the stern letter to the Internet Abusers about dropping their cigarette butts and plastic cups and chewing gum wads in the churchyard before or after I changed the cartridge on the printer. The sooner I wrote it, the more thermal units of indignation I could draw on from the dialogue with that "immovable object," Kevin Dowd. But the print density would be more forceful with a fresh load of toner. While I was dithering thus, my office phone rang. As it was officially my day off, I let the machine answer. After the silence during which my recorded voice announced times of services and invited the caller to leave a message, a man began to speak briskly.

"My name is Paul Pike and I'm trying to reach the Reverend Margaret Bonner on a matter of some importance. I can be reached at —"

I picked up. "Hello, this is Margaret Bonner. How can I help you?"

"Ah." The voice conveyed satisfaction that I was not going to waste any more of his time by hiding behind my machine. "Paul Pike here. I'm a reporter from the *Mountain City Times*, but I also do features for Syndicated Press International. I'm working up an in-depth feature article about your area. Can we get together and talk sometime in the next few days?"

"What is the in-depth article on specifically?" I asked.

"What is it on specifically?" There was just the slightest touch of condescension as he repeated my choice of phrasing. He was not a southerner. "Its *focus* is on High Balsam, as I explained. Specifically what I want to do is to describe a small community in this state that might serve as a paradigm for American community concerns at the turn of the millennium. You know, all the issues and elements that are uppermost on our minds. A kind of target town where, if you do close-ups, you can see the seeds of the future already sprouting."

"That's quite an assignment you've given yourself." My turn to wield a touch of condescension.

"I thrive on challenges. Especially those I set for myself. As I see it, High Balsam is the ideal place for the kind of article I have in mind. It's small enough — but also it has to be *unusual* enough — to merit people's interest."

I wondered if the "unusualness" had anything to do with last summer's shooting and the recent change of venue to our county for the security guards trial. Was Mr. Pike one of Tim Stancil's journalists on the scent of picturesque troubles that could earn them a Pulitzer, or had he other fish to fry? Bad pun, Margaret! But something in the man's tone provoked my insolence.

"And which issue or element would our conversation address?"

"Your church, naturally. How you as its leader see its role in the community right now. I won't kid you that you're the only clergy person I want to interview, but you're one of my top priorities. So if we could set up —"

"Why is that? Why am I one of your top priorities?"

"Well, because I've heard you're an interesting person" (a little flattery to gain time) "and also you represent —" (ah, here it came) " — your parish represents the elite of this community. The movers and shakers. People of consequence." An insinuating chuckle: "All Saints High Horse?"

"I hardly think our parish has the monopoly on people of consequence," I said, not even bothering to respond to the other old chestnut, which I sometimes felt I wore on a chain around my neck along with my silver cross. "Look, Mr. Pike, why don't we do this? Why don't you send me a list of the questions you want to ask and give me a few days to look them over. If I think I can be of help, I'll get back to you in Mountain City and we can set up a phone interview."

"I'd want to talk with you in person, Reverend Bonner. A journalist isn't usually asked to submit his questions in advance, but I can fax you a list of probable topics, if you'd feel more comfortable. After all, I haven't written the series yet, have I?" He made it sound as if he were humoring someone difficult or slow-witted, or both. "Does All Saints have a facsimile machine?"

"You've got to be kidding." I laughed. "With all of us movers and shakers over here?"

He didn't laugh.

I gave him the fax number.

Who does he remind me of? I asked myself, after we hung up. That blinkered, bludgeoning *will* — without an ounce of humorous selfperspective. The answer came immediately, of course: who else but Grace?

I made a note to phone Tim Stancil. I wanted to find out if he knew anything about Paul Pike before I went and committed myself to an interview. We agreed to press interviews so easily, like schoolchildren eager to give the correct answers. But reporters, unlike most teachers, didn't always have our best interests at heart. Often they didn't even want to hear the correct answers; they wanted to finagle it so that their answers — the ones that would make the best stories — could be attributed to us. I remembered my father once taking Georgie Gaines, now Harriet's husband, to task for misquoting him in our local newspaper. This was in Georgie's journalist phase, slightly before his seminary phase, and he was writing an article about our corner cross and the legislator who was to help us get historic status so the town wouldn't chop off the corner. My father was explaining that the figure on the cross was called the corpus, when Georgie asked, "What is his name?"

Daddy, raising his eyebrows, had replied, "Well, I think we can take it for granted everybody knows his name . . . or perhaps we can't anymore."

"No, sir," Georgie had said, "I meant the name of the legislator."

491

But when the story appeared in the *Romulus Record*, Georgie had reshaped my father's comment into, "You can't even take for granted that everybody knows Christ's name anymore," making him come across as a cynical old fuddy-duddy.

"It presented our exchange in a false context," Daddy had lectured Georgie later. "Whether you end up as a minister or an ace reporter, you're going to have to be able to discern exactly where, in certain shady areas, a truth turns into a lie. The line can be almost invisible, but it's always there for the sharp-sighted few."

Whether Paul Pike was among the sharp-sighted few, I couldn't say. It was possible. But somehow I had my doubts.

Georgie had come to mind because I knew that a package from Harriet lay right there on my desk with the rest of the church mail. I had spotted it while talking with Dick Miller, guessed what was probably in it, then tossed the pile of mail in the backseat without mentioning it to Adrian on the way home.

I unstapled it now with a stoical resolve. I had known since hearing the teaser on the radio interview that I was going to have to confront it, and here it was on this drizzly Monday: the new "memoir" album I had intended to go out and buy and listen to in private, to see how bad the damage was. *An Evening Gone*. Lyrics and music by Ben

MacGruder. Vocals and instrumentals by Melody Station. On the cover was a cove in moonlight. In the shadows of the cove was a rowboat. In the rowboat was an airbrushed couple, naked on a blanket. At least she didn't remotely resemble me. But I could feel the scratch of that blanket now. An old Army blanket of Dr. MacGruder's, kept in their boathouse at the lake. This was the music video. What further pictures awaited me inside?

A memo-sized note from Harriet fell out:

Don't expect you to be thrilled about this, but Baby Brother made me promise I'd send it. You can always dispose of it at your next church rummage sale. H.

The curt missive, void of personal news, scribbled on a prescription blank, brought it home to me how far apart we had grown. My fault as much as hers. More mine, I'm sure she thought. She must have watched it already. Had she and Georgie watched it together and had a good laugh? ("Serves her right for trifling with my brother's affections.") Would Harriet actually say that, or was it my own inner voice of guilt putting words in her mouth?

I happened to glance through one of the glass sidebars of the office entrance and saw Chase in a hooded sweatshirt catapulting himself down the walk in his forward-pitched little trot. I got up to unlatch the door, which I kept locked from the inside so I could wander around the rest of the church as I pleased.

"This just came for you." He reached inside the shirt and handed over a white envelope he'd been protecting from the drizzle. The letterhead was from the High Balsam Inn and I had no trouble recognizing the handwriting. The envelope wasn't stamped.

"She brought it herself?"

"I said you were over at the church but she didn't want to disturb you." He shifted from one foot to the other.

"Come in for a minute, Chase. Can you by any chance change the toner on a printer?"

He tossed back his hood and stepped inside. With a coy dip of his head he made the shiny black swags of hair droop forward, and through their partial curtain he evaluated my workstation.

"It's the same dinosaur model my therapist had before he upgraded. I used to change his. You can't do it yourself?"

"I can, but I'll waste too much time concentrating on the directions. I'm trying to conserve my wrath for a scathing letter I need to write."

His interest picked up. "Who's the lucky recipient?"

I told him about the Internet Abusers

who'd been littering the churchyard after their weekly meetings.

"Hey, you know what you could write?"

"What?"

"You could say, 'Your computer is your sacred space. Well, this is my sacred space. How would you feel if you woke up one morning and found your screen all crapped up with gum, and butts stubbed out on your keyboard?'"

It was obvious why Adrian didn't want to give up on him. But of course, I quickly reminded myself, Chase hadn't gotten to know me well enough yet to figure out the most effective way to let me down.

While he was unpacking the cartridge, I read Grace's communication, much shorter than her last.

Dear Reverend Bonner,

I want to thank you for the reception you and your congregation gave me yesterday. It was not at all lukewarm. As I left the church, I picked up one of your newsletters and see on the calendar that Monday is your day off. I'm taking a day off myself. This weather makes a person a little discouraged of heart. Would you care to come over and have tea with me this afternoon? It would be a great honor to me if you would accept. Any time after three would be fine. Mrs. Fletcher will bring it to the room. My phone extension is room 2. Hoping to hear from you.

Grace Munger

"Now what?" I said. "Well, maybe — oh, but . . . Don't mind me, Chase, I'm just talking to myself."

"That's okay. I do it all the time. It helps you find out what you're really going to do." He shook the cartridge back and forth with a rapturous ferocity.

"How true. Well, I think I'm really going to postpone my haircut."

I called Vincent Baird and changed our appointment, then phoned the inn and pressed 2. When a husky, deflated voice answered, I thought I'd reached the wrong room. But the voice was Grace's. Perhaps she'd been napping. Or praying? However, my acceptance of her invitation to tea imparted an immediate surge of the old bossy assurance. "I'm so glad," she declared in the tone of someone who has finally bagged an apostate. After which she gave me directions to her room that would have sufficed for a three-year-old with a bad sense of direction.

"All done," Chase announced as I hung up.

"So fast?" I marveled.

"That's as long as it's supposed to take. Are we going to be good to the planet and mail this old one back in the postage paid box?"

"Absolutely." I penciled in my haircut for next Monday in the book. "Now, one more phone call to order the communion wafers, and then write the letter and then . . . oh dear, I still have to find someone to come and clean our gutters at the rectory. Adrian certainly can't do it with his pneumonia, and I didn't want him doing it anyway."

"Why won't he just go ahead and be the headmaster?" He was tenderly boxing up the worn-out cartridge as if putting an expired pet to rest.

"Well, I —" His direct question had caught me off guard. After reflecting a minute, I said, "Why don't you ask *him* that, Chase?"

"I already did."

"What did he say?"

"Probably the same thing he says to everybody. It's not his thing, he's better at the one-on-one stuff, nobody can ever replace Dr. Sandlin — who I never met 'cause he was dead before I came. But you know what *I* think?"

"What do you think?" I asked reluctantly. I was interested in hearing, but was decidedly uneasy about discussing my husband behind his back with Chase.

"I think he's afraid." He'd finished packing up the cartridge. "Do you have any tape for this?"

I rummaged about in a drawer, glad for the interruption. "Will this do?" I handed over a roll of Scotch tape.

"Clear packing tape would be better."

"Sorry, no packing tape."

He shrugged, then began sealing the box methodically, first securing the flaps with frugal little strips, then lengthwise with long strips, then crisscross with more strips. He appeared totally absorbed in his task.

I thought about turning on the computer and starting my letter to the Internet Abusers. But he had me in thrall; did he know it? I wanted to hear anything else he had to say about Adrian — if there was any more — though I was certainly not going to reintroduce the subject myself.

"When I was little," Chase said, adding more lengthwise strips of tape, "my dad would tie a length of fishing tackle to a hundred-dollar bill. Then he'd lay the bill down on the floor in the downstairs hallway. I'd come downstairs and run to pick up the bill, and at the last second he'd whisk it away and laugh. Father Bonner does worse than that. He comes out and shines on you and then goes back under his thundercloud." He added more tape: this was going to be one sealed package. "He withdraws and broods and doesn't delegate. I think he's afraid."

I took the bait. "Afraid of what, Chase?"

"Contact," said Chase. "He's afraid of too much close human contact." He added several more unnecessary strips of tape. "Just like my dad. I really pick 'em, don't I?" He scrutinized the package, obviously satisfied. His minesweeping glance ranged over the other contents on my desk. "Hey, cool! How come you have this?"

He picked up Ben's music video with the naked couple in the rowboat, full moon shining down on their flanks.

"His sister sent it to me."

"Wait a minute. Are you telling me you *know* Ben MacGruder?"

"His sister was my best friend. We grew up together in Virginia. Of course he was somewhat younger." Already distancing myself.

"Man, I don't believe this." He was doing a little dance, holding the album at arm's length in front of him like a partner. "Can we watch it?"

"Well —"

"Come on, it's your day off. We've got the VCR right here."

So we did. I'd had Van bring it up to the office so we could screen a Cistercian's video presentation on Centering Prayer for possible use in the Adult Study Group.

"He's your best friend's *brother*. Aren't you curious?"

If that's the word for it.

"Okay, let's watch," I said, waving him toward the machine. "You do the honors."

We sat down together on the saggy sofa, beneath my framed diploma from General.

Summer clouds bowled across the screen. Fast-forwarded clouds, technology hurrying nature along for artistic purposes. "O God, our help in a—ges past . . ." Ben's tenor seemed to rise out of their shapes, a pure-in-heart voice with nothing but praise on its mind, a voice I remembered from church in Romulus.

Chase jumped up and raised the volume. A little too loud for my comfort, but I let it go. He plopped back down and gave a little wriggle toward me. I could get to love this boy, I thought.

"What are those little kids doing?" he asked.

Was it possible he didn't know?

"They're having an Easter egg hunt," I said.

"Oh." He was silent.

"Easter shadows on a lawn
Children of an evening gone
We ran and plundered
Filled our baskets —
All but you: the preacher's daughter.

You turned and walked away
You — the only one I wanted
Ever since that evening gone . . ."

There she went, the little girl. Blond, thank God, in a silly pink frou-frou dress Ruth would never have bought for me.

*"You — walking away from me even then
Toward something only you could see.
Something absent and unseen."*

Off she marched, resolutely down a swanky greensward, away from the egg hunt, away from the other children. The major, now dead, would have been pleased to see her suburban lawn transformed into a luxury landscape out of *Brideshead Revisited*. I'm sure she always thought of it that way — at least in comparison to everybody else's.

The little boy actor — in a sailor suit, no less — ran after the little girl. He was not nearly as cute as Ben had been at three, but in the interests of romantic credulity, the producers (with Ben's approval?) had closed the three-year age gap between himself and his six-year-old beloved. These were both children of five or six.

Chase watched the screen hungrily. Was it possible he had never been to an Easter egg hunt? Quite possible, I decided, after thinking about it for a second or two.

Then back to the sky. Getting darker now. The fast-forwarded movement from afternoon into evening. Clouds swirling and purpling to reveal the round, rising disk of full moon — which then shape-shifted into Ben's face. A narrower, older face, crested with up-to-the-minute plumage in a paler shade of blond.

Then Ben's soft "confessional" voice-over, like those passages in country and western, where the teller elegizes in his speaking voice against an instrumental backdrop.

"This is my memoir of an evening gone. About love found . . . and love lost."

Zip from sky to rowboat. Couple in rowboat. Surely no full moon can give that much light. Even with Ben's tell-all face framed in its circle. There must be spotlights cleverly hidden in the trees. Oh, dear.

Chase said: "I don't know if I ought to let you watch this R-rated part or not, what do you think?"

I laughed, but I was embarrassed. How close up were we going to get and how far was this writhing young pair of actors allowed to go? I had watched very few of these music videos and had no idea what the current parameters were.

"You gave yourself to me
You took me as your own
But you don't like to be reminded —
Oh no, you don't like to be reminded
of that *evening gone.*

"They aren't really doing it," Chase reassured me. "It's all movement and light tricks. First of all, there's this Actors' Guild code.

They're probably even wearing body stockings, to prevent disease."

"Thank you," I said. "That's good to know." (Parson at All Saints High Balsam watches pornography in the church office with a minor.)

More quick-change scenery. Dark and darker. What now? Why did everything have to move so fast, your eyes got jittery.

> *"You always went looking for*
> *The absent and unseen*
> *But when you planned to wed a shadow*
> *I asked, 'What can this mean?' "*

"Look at *that* creep," said Chase.

A gloomy-looking older man in a black clerical robe, a dank Torquemada, had just etherealized out of a nasty-looking mist. He beckoned unsmilingly, then turned and disappeared into the mist again.

> *" 'It means,' you said, 'he's what I want,*
> *He's been my fate all along;*
> *If you have any more laments,*
> *Please save them for your song.' "*

Two black-winged angels are ceremoniously robing the girl in something limp and black, resembling an unwashed choir robe. She then walks purposefully off into the mist after the gloomy figure.

"I don't get it, did she die or what?" asked Chase. "Is the creep in black supposed to be death?"

"You'd have to ask the artist," I said.

More fast-forward clouds, lovers' flanks flashing and tumbling on color-scapes of clouds. Meant to represent time passing? A regurgitation of memories? One's eyes ached and swiveled to keep up. Children with baskets ran once more across the Brideshead lawn, then faded, leaving only a huge close-up of the lost girl's face.

"But you knew him. Did he ever have a girlfriend who died?"

"I don't think so. Maybe it's a symbol."

"A symbol for *what?*" Chase pursued.

"Well, *I* don't know," I said testily, "lost love or something."

> *"Can anyone explain*
> *Why everything about you*
> *Still calls out to me*
> *From that evening gone?"*

More clouds, then moving out fast, a thousand miles up, faster, farther, astronaut's view now, cribbed from NASA space shots, the voice doing a repeat on the refrain, soaring up higher the second time around — bursting through the tenor barrier in a final "gone."

Going, going, gone, I thought. And good

riddance. Or is there more to come?

"Not many pop singers can make a high D," said Chase, "but so far *Rap-Chapel*'s still my favorite. This album's sort of weird. At least so far."

We played the rest of it. The Nubian folk songs — some good dancers in Egyptian costume, except the action was too fast, you'd single out a figure in firelight only to have it snatched away from you. At last, the Mahasi wedding song where art reverses life and the guy gets his girl. The Egyptian priest figure joining them together was played by the same gloomy actor who represented Adrian, slinking off into the mist.

("So in a larger sense," Ben had said on the radio, "the album has a happy ending." "If you're willing to go back to ancient Egypt to get her," said the interviewer. "Well, what other choice did I have?" Ben had replied with a rueful laugh.)

Chase heaved himself up from the sofa. "I don't know," he said with a sad little sigh. He pushed the rewind button. "What did you think?"

"I liked the *last* ones especially. The instrumentals were unusual; the dancers had such vitality." I was studiously reading the liner notes on the back of the slipcase. "Let's see, they used a *darabukka*, that's a goblet-shaped drum, and then something called a *tambura*, which is a five-string lyre, it says.

The last song, the wedding song, is based on an ancient rhythm known as 'moon fever.' "

It could have been worse, I was thinking. If Ben will just spare the details in the interviews, I can handle this much.

"Yeah, but he already did that on *Mattokki Moon Fever*. He's repeating himself. I liked *Inner-City Rap-Chapel* better. When I took my wild ride to Florida in my dad's friend's car I played it the whole trip — until I smashed up, that is. I guess you want to write your scathing letter now."

"What?" For a minute I thought he meant to Ben.

"To those Internet litterers."

"Oh, right. I don't know, maybe I'll call around and find someone to clean the gutters first."

"Your wrath has worn off," he accused.

"A little." My emotions were admittedly in other places on the spectrum.

He comes out and shines on you, Chase had said of Adrian, *and then goes back under his thundercloud. He withdraws and broods and doesn't delegate . . . he's afraid of too much close human contact.*

But when you planned to wed a shadow
I asked, "What can this mean?"

That dreary actor in black, withdrawing into the mist.

I ached and I fumed. I wanted others to see Adrian as I knew he could be.

"Would it be okay if I looked around the church?" Chase was asking.

"Anything of special interest?"

"Could I maybe go up to the bell tower?"

"Well — I guess so. I'll have to show you where we hide the key. Oh, come on, I'll take you up myself."

"Avoiding your chores," he teased, looking almost happy — for Chase.

"I need a break. I haven't been up there myself since Van took me on the building tour. And even then I didn't go all the way up."

"Why not?"

"Well, for one thing, I was wearing a straight skirt, which would have been awkward on the ladders. And for another, Van didn't offer. He just tipped up the hatch so I could look into the chamber and see they had a nice bell up there."

"Why do you say they?" This boy missed *nothing*.

"I wasn't the rector yet. They were still interviewing people for the job."

"Oh. I think they were smart to pick you."

"Thank you. Just between us, I think they were, too."

"Why?"

"Because I understand what they love about the church and what's positive about it. My father was the pastor of a parish similar to this in a lot of ways, and I learned from him. He also understood when they needed stretching and that you had to go about it without rupturing them in the process. He didn't always succeed, of course. I'm sure I don't either."

We went down the north aisle of the nave. I switched on the lights to the choir loft. We climbed the wooden stairs.

"The organ," commented Chase, running his small brown hand across the pipes in the case. "It sounded bigger from downstairs."

"It's a relatively small one. In a slow tune without much ornamentation, you'll sometimes hear this funny little quaver. That's because back in the forties the rector's cat jumped into the pipes, and they could never restore one of the delicate ones to its original shape."

"Ha, that's funny."

"Is it?"

"No, I mean — this old lady that used to take care of me — she was blind, but when I was real little I didn't know it. She had this teeny little book, like an address book, that she read stories out of. Or I thought she was reading stories out of. There was one about a mouse that lived behind the organ pipes in the organ loft. Just like your rector's cat. Only the mouse never hurt anything. On Sundays, though, he had to come out because it was too loud for him."

"I expect it was."

I took down the stone replica of a Canterbury cross from the wall behind the bell rope and removed the key hanging on the nail behind.

"Neat hiding place."

I unlocked the door to the bell tower. Inside was a narrow winding metal stairway leading to the hatch at the top. "Be my guest," I said, waving him up the round stairs.

"You're wearing pants, you could come, too."

"I'll do the stairs, but not the ladders. I'm not too happy on ladders. I'll watch you from the open hatch. You can tell me how things look up there. Go ahead, you go first."

He clambered up the metal stairs. When you couldn't see the childish acorn-shaped face, he might have been any smallish man in jeans and work boots going up to inspect a tower. Except I could hear his excited boy-breaths as I followed behind, clinging tight to my railing.

When he opened the hatch, some minor debris dropped down on us.

"Sorry about that," he called back.

"No problem." Now I understood why Van had taken his handkerchief out and cautiously wiped around the hatch as he was slowly lifting it up.

Chase boosted himself, agile as a monkey,

through the open space and explored the confines of the tower. "Phew," he called back, "you could use a strong room spray up here. Can you open those shutter-things?"

"No, the louvers are there to keep birds and bats out."

He scrambled up the metal rungs of the first ladder. Then the second.

"Phew. Well, *some* little somebody's been in here because there's lots of you-know-what all over the top of your bell."

"Oh, dear. A whole lot?"

"A whole guano-factory of it." Swinging out from the ladder, he dangled a boot within an inch of the bell's flaring mouth. "If I pushed hard with my foot, do you think I could make this thing ring?"

"You could. I'd rather you wouldn't."

"Listen, can I ask you something?"

"Yes."

"Are you a rector or a preacher?"

"Both. I'm rector of All Saints, and I'm a preacher when I preach. People just call you different things at different times."

"What about your dad?"

"What about him?"

"Was he both, too?"

"Yes. Why?"

"Then were you the preacher's daughter?"

"Well, yes. Why?"

Now I saw where this was going.

"Then you're her, aren't you? You're the

510

girl in the song. Aren't you?"

"It's possible," I said.

"I *thought* so! Oh, man — oops —"

His boot tipped the bell. It rang. Not at its full voice, but loudly enough. A single ring.

"Sorry about that," he called down. "I really didn't mean to do it."

"Come down now. Before you do something else you didn't mean to."

"Man, I don't believe this. *You're* the girl that Ben MacGruder loved and lost! Hey, wait a minute, the creepy guy in black? Was that — *Father Bonner?*" His voice went up an octave.

"He certainly isn't the Father Bonner I know," I said, backing down the metal stairway. I added lamely, "Different things appear differently to different people. Listen, Chase, if that bell gives one more peep, I am going to be really cross with you."

XV

The Freelance Apostle

Adrian was sleeping, or so I thought, when I returned to change clothes. I stood in front of the open closet. What to wear?

"Going out?"

"Oh! I thought you were asleep."

"Just playing possum. In case it was Tony."

"Has he been disturbing you?"

"He's been *taking care* of me. Exhausting old extrovert. He brought me some delicious beef and tomato soup and stayed to watch me eat it. Talkety-talkety-talk. How does he manage when they go on silent retreat?"

"Maybe he talks to the birds, like St. Francis." I felt protective on behalf of them both. I didn't want to lead Adrian into saying anything about Tony that would cause him remorse later. "What did he talk about?"

"His usual variety act. The late great Father Cecil, the colorful inmates they ministered to, more of his potpourri past. He was married once, he told me. She died young. I suppose you've heard all this and more." A guarded note crept into his tone.

"Yes," I said. "I'm trying to decide whether

or not to wear a skirt."

"Where are you going?"

"Grace Munger hand-delivered an invitation to have tea with her. And I accepted. I cancelled my haircut to go and have tea with this woman who's been driving me up the wall. Can you explain it?"

"I would have done the same thing. An invitation from the shadow is hard to resist. 'Why do I love hating her so much? What can I find out about her that will enrage me even more?' It's energizing, in an upside-down way. Did I hear the church bell ring, Margaret, or was I dreaming it?"

"Chase pushed it with his foot. I took him on a tour to the tower. He said he didn't mean to. His foot slipped."

"Has he been bothering you?"

"Not at all, he's good company. He changed the toner on the office printer, and told me stories about his childhood. The father baiting him with a hundred-dollar bill and the old blind woman reading stories to him from a tiny address book."

"I've heard about the hundred-dollar bill. The address book, no. Well, I'm glad he wasn't in your way."

I was about to mention us watching the music video, then decided to leave it alone. Leave the dank Torquemada figure and the writhers in the rowboat until he was feeling more robust.

"Tony asked if he could borrow one of our cars," I said. "He wants to do some bulk shopping this afternoon. Also he says there are a few things Chase needs for school tomorrow. If you have any objection to him using yours, I'll take it and leave mine for him."

"Let him take mine, it's shabbier."

"Now, help me decide what to wear."

"Will she be expecting a collar?"

"She knows it's my day off. I'd like it to be just two women having tea together. Without my parson clothes, maybe we can venture onto other topics besides the Jesus March. I *am* rather curious about her, she's such a strange mixture of things. But I want to look nice. She always wears skirts and looks good."

"By all means wear a skirt, then. But you always look good whatever you wear. Or don't wear for that matter."

"Oh Adrian, I love you."

"I love you, too, though I'll never understand why —"

"Don't spoil it, okay?"

"Wait a minute. How do we know that old cenobite has a license to drive?"

"He does."

"You're sure?"

"Yes, I've seen it." I tugged down my paisley skirt and a burnt-orange tunic pullover. I prepared myself for the next question, if he should choose to ask it. I even foresaw the eventuality of having to cancel my date with Grace in order to answer him fully.

But he chose not to ask it. After a pause, he murmured, "My car keys are there on the dresser. I think I *will* sleep now."

If it hadn't been raining, I would have walked to the High Balsam Inn. I might have taken my umbrella and walked anyway and risked a few hairs out of place if I hadn't been going to see the fastidiously groomed Grace. Door-to-door was a brisk uphill constitutional of about seven minutes from one building on the National Register of Historic Places to another. Though sometimes it seemed to me that everything in High Balsam was on the National Register of Historic Places.

The inn, built as a private house in the Victorian style, was famous in the regional guidebooks for its ubiquitous wood fanciwork. The former owner, a clerk of court in the early years of the century, had allowed county prisoners to work off their sentences by improving his home. To judge by the evidence both outside and in, there must have been a lot of prisoners with wood-carving skills, or a lot of prisoners desperate enough for their liberty to develop some.

As I was picking my way across the antique-jammed lounge, Mrs. Fletcher's son-in-law, whose name had momentarily

515

slipped my mind, came through a swing door carrying a tray of folded napkins.

"Hey there, Reverend! Mom's made one of her great almond pound cakes and it's you we have to thank."

"How is that?"

"Soon as Gracie told us you wanted to pay her a call on your day off, Mom started right in breaking the eggs."

Just like Grace. *I* wanted to pay *her* a call. Oh, well, as Adrian had so astutely pointed out, it gave me one more reason to love to hate her. I had become aware of a lantern-jawed man in a Stetson hat and a string tie watching me from behind his newspaper in his club chair.

"What are you doing here?" I asked the son-in-law, whose name I wished I could recall. He drove a service truck for Century Fuel and had repaired our furnace twice last winter. "Is it your day off, too?"

"Since the first of November, every day has been my day off, Reverend Bonner. I was one of the casualties of Century's downsizing. I'm sure you read about it. End of the century, end of Century for me." He laughed wanly at his little joke. "I been with them eighteen years, ever since I got out of high school, and then bam, just like that. Handshake from the boss, slips me an envelope with my severance pay inside. 'Sorry about this, Pat, but the median income of our customer base has dipped and people are doing without the fancy service contracts. They're learning to fix their own furnaces.' So now I'm folding napkins and setting up for my mom-in-law. And telling my woes to Mr. Pike here, who's kind enough to listen."

Pat for Patrick, now I remembered. At the mention of *his* name, the lantern-faced man in the Stetson laid down his *Wall Street Journal* and rose from the club chair. He ambled over in his pressed jeans and Western boots. "Howdy-do, Reverend," he drawled, looking me over from head to toe. "You're in mufti, I see."

"I had no idea you were already on the scene," I said.

"Oh, I always do my research on the scene. That's the way I was taught."

But no one taught you to take off your hat indoors, did they? Or maybe he thought all us hillbillies wore hats indoors and went around drawling howdy-do.

"Mr. Pike's going to be with us to see the new millennium in," Pat informed me proudly. "He's doing a big international story about High Balsam as a — what was the word you used?"

"Paradigm, example," supplied Paul Pike. " 'A city set on a hill cannot be hid.' " He sent me a slantwise insider's smirk from under the Stetson brim. "That kind of approach. I've already been in touch with Reverend Bonner.

I'm much looking forward to having the benefits of her perspective."

"I'll wait to have your list of questions first," I reminded him. "Well, I'd better run along. When Grace invited me, she said three." I hoped Pat picked up on the *invited.* It was so hard to keep straight lines with some people: Kevin Dowd and Grace, and now Paul Pike.

Up the floral-carpeted central staircase. What was the story of the prisoner who had dug this acorn and leaf motif into the oak banister, carving his way toward early parole? Yesterday's session with Tony had forged a familial bond between me and the miscreants of the world; now I was more attentive to the specifics of what the late Father Cecil would have called their "misplaced creativity."

("Once you reach the top of the staircase, go *straight ahead* down the main hall. Don't take any of the corridors to the left or right.")

The old floors joggled and squeaked under the carpeting. Every wainscoting, door head, and molding bore some prisoner-whittled ornamentation, some better than others. I must bring Adrian over here, with his interest in woodwork. And the provenance of all this decoration would certainly beguile Tony. Bring them both, after the bomb shell had been detonated — with, one fervently hoped, no more damage than from a champagne bottle being safely uncorked — and watch them running their fingers side by side along fretworks and scrollworks in the corridors of the High Balsam Inn.

("Hey, look at this." Would Adrian say Father, or Dad, or just Tony? "Yep, some felon sure knew how to wield a scroll saw, didn't he?")

Baking smells wafted up from below. The almond pound cake?

("Keep going straight down the main hall until you can't go any further. Then you've got to turn *right* and go all the way to the end till you reach the door with number two on it. There's a carving of a face with some leaves and fruit above the door. That is my room.")

I knocked, perusing the carving. The crudely executed Bacchus with his headdress of grapes seemed an inappropriate escutcheon for Grace. She should have had an evangelistic beast with a profile as finely carved as hers. When I felt the vibration of her carpeted approach from the other side, an alluring nervousness stirred in me. I realized I had no idea what was going to transpire.

She greeted me in a floor-length garment of deep purple crushed velvet with bands of gold silk on the bell sleeves. Its A-line cut concealed her natural contours and imparted a liturgical, almost mythical aspect to her stately amplitude. She wore the gold Byzantine cross and her hair was done up to perfection. She might have been a priestess of some

519

esoteric sect, welcoming me to her inner sanctum, and here I had gone and left my symbolic togs at home!

"Reverend Bonner. Please come in. Let me take your coat."

"Oh, what a grand room."

"Yes, it's her best room," replied Grace equably. She shook drops of moisture from my raincoat before hanging it in the closet near the door. I crossed the expanse of floral carpeting between a large canopied bed and a writing table covered with paperwork. Outside the expanse of windows were High Balsam's panoramic stack of mountain ranges misted by a scrim of rain. The valley below us was dotted with fast-moving clumps of cloud, which caused landmarks to appear and then vanish capriciously.

"If it weren't so patchy today, I could point out my father's church better," said Grace, joining me at the windows. "See the tip of the white steeple over to the left? No, it's gone now."

"I saw it. Actually, I've been inside Free Will Baptist. We had an interdenominational open house a few years back. All of us went to visit one another's churches."

"Won't you sit down?" She indicated the two wing chairs facing each other above a low table in front of the windows. She gave no sign of having heard what I had just said. Previously I had attributed these tunings-out of hers to a simple steamrollering ahead toward the goal, but now I wasn't so sure. If I had learned anything from our few exchanges, it was that nothing about Grace was unmixedly simple.

I sat down and she arranged herself and the capacious vestmentlike robe in the other chair. She wore black flats and opaque black stockings. No bare skin was visible except her hands, wrists, and face. I allowed myself to be assessed in an oblique way, resisting the urge to dilute the tension with the kind of surface talk Lucinda and I excelled in for making our safe contacts with each other. If there was a larger-than-life encounter to be had with this larger-than-life presence, I wanted to be adventuresome enough to meet it unsafely.

"That is an attractive skirt and top," Grace at last pronounced with authority. "I like those rich colors on you."

"Well, thank you," I said, feeling pleased to have come up to the mark.

"Mrs. Fletcher will be bringing up our tea directly. You were very prompt."

"Not too prompt, I hope."

"Oh, no. I was ready for you."

By ready did she mean the end result of having stood before her mirror and coiling up her hair to perfection, or was she alluding to more latent Machiavellian preparations — interlaced with prayer?

Speaking of prayer, my chair faced the

empty fireplace from which God's voice had informed Grace as recently as Friday evening that I was her sister and that she was accountable for me and my flock. Would we get on the subject of prayer? A smile tugged at my heart when I recalled Chase asking her straight-out if God spoke to her in English.

"Normally, Mrs. Fletcher likes guests to take their tea in the lounge," Grace said. "But she's given me a dispensation."

"That was nice of her. This room is very agreeable."

"That's not the reason," said Grace. "There's a person staying here who's been making a nuisance of himself, a journalist from Mountain City. He lurks behind his newspaper in the lounge and waits for me to go in or out."

"You must mean Paul Pike."

"Yes." She didn't appear curious as to how I knew the name, but then that was Grace. "I've taken to driving to the diner for breakfast, even though breakfast is included in my room price. Tea is extra, and she doesn't do dinner in the winter. He asks too many questions. He has every right to do his feature article, but I, for one, don't wish to be misinterpreted in it."

"He called me, too, this morning, about the article," I said. "I assumed he was phoning from Mountain City. But I just ran into him downstairs. Like you said, he lies in

522

wait behind his paper."

"Oh, yes?" any other person would have jumped in, "what did he ask *you?*" But not Grace. "In my business, we work closely with the press," she went on, with not the merest nod to my contribution. "I have found it's always smart to make your presentation the way you want it and not get sidetracked into any careless talk. Otherwise you find your purpose woven into *their* package — or distorted out of shape."

"What do you think Paul Pike's package is?" I knew better than to ask what her purpose was.

"To draw attention to himself and feel superior by putting us down."

"Us?"

"High Balsam people. Believers. Folks who have fallen on hard times and are hurting — and are calling on the Lord to turn their lives around. And I'm one of them, Reverend Bonner, I know where they're coming from." She smiled coldly at me, then narrowed her eyes at the mountain peaks hidden in rain clouds.

"You are one of them," I repeated softly, hoping to elicit more.

"When I was a child, I thought it was a sign of God's favor that we lived on top of the world. What I hadn't been prepared for when I came back to organize this march was the apathy. When I was growing up, there was such enthusiasm and commitment in my father's church. He had only to say, 'We need to raise X amount of dollars to send a missionary family to El Salvador,' and the money would pour in. Or he'd say, 'It's time to get organized for the Big Meeting' — that's what we called our yearly revival — and it was like the Lord saying let there be light. Dad said the word and everything fell into place. Banjos and mandolins and portable organs dropped from the skies. Along with folks who knew how to play them. The tent got rented and raised and the food overflowed the tables and it never rained or even sprinkled and people came from near and far to hear the preaching and slept out under the stars. My father measured the success of the Big Meeting by the number of souls he converted or reavowed, and I got to write the numbers on the board." Her tawny eyes glittered with excitement. "It was like an auction — the prices going up and up!"

A timid knock at the door.

"Come in," called Grace.

The door swung open and in rolled a squeaky wooden trolley which appeared at first to be self-propelled. But presently a pin-curled scalp became discernible behind the approaching bounty. The innkeeper, whom I often saw at the post office, was so curved by bone loss that she couldn't hold her head up, but she never seemed aware of being under any disadvantage as she smiled at the ground below, or cocked her head up and around in order to aim a spate of chirpy patter in the direction of someone she knew.

"Let me give you a hand, Mrs. Fletcher." As Grace glided across the room to intercept the trolley, I suddenly remembered Madelyn Farley's little stage figures which she made by rolling up cones of bristol board shaped much like Grace's garment and taping the narrow ends around the necks of champagne corks. Then she would glide these bodiless little cones around her miniature set until she was satisfied with how the life-sized production was going to look from different angles of the theater.

As they began unloading tea-things onto the low table, Mrs. Fletcher darted friendly side peeks in my direction, keeping up a hospitable monologue. It was too bad about the rainy day, wasn't it, but better on a day like today when it didn't matter than on the Saturday of Grace's big parade. When Grace had informed her I would be joining her for tea this afternoon, she had right away begun to make the batter for her almond pound cake. Then, ducking her pin-curled head around to Grace's side, the bent little lady inquired of her star boarder whether we should allow "any *Pikes*" lurking in the vicinity to have a piece of almond pound cake and dissolved into eerie high-pitched giggles.

"Anyone would be pleased to have a piece of your pound cake," Grace replied coolly. "Thank you, Mrs. Fletcher, we can manage the rest."

"You don't want me to pour your tea for you?"

"No, thank you. Reverend Bonner and I have things to talk about."

"Of course you must, with the parade coming up and all. Should I leave you the trolley?"

"Yes, leave the trolley."

"You were telling about how your father got things done," I said as Grace poured the tea.

"I was pretty much finished with that," she said. "Do you take lemon or milk?"

"Milk, please."

"I'll let you put in your own sugar." She handed across my cup. "No, I surely was *not* prepared for the apathy I've had to deal with." She poured her own tea, daintily laid a lemon slice on the side of the saucer, and frowningly rejected my offer of the bowl of sugar cubes. "I will have been here two weeks tomorrow, and only thirty churches are firmly committed to the Birthday March. By that I mean they're in rehearsal, making their banners and costumes, procuring their sound equipment, and keeping in touch with the organizer."

"Thirty sounds like a gracious lot to me," I

said. "In my experience, everybody considers it a success when eight or ten churches agree to do *anything* together at the same time."

"In the western part of this county alone, Reverend Bonner, there are a total of 172 Christian congregations. You can get out the phone books and look them up yourself. And it's not every day we have a new millennium with its hope of new beginnings."

"That's true," I conceded, readying myself for the hard sell.

"Please take a sandwich. The pink fillings are ham salad; Mrs. Fletcher makes an excellent ham salad. The other one is her special combination of cheese and piccalilli. You ought to try them both. I'm not talking just about your mainline American Protestant churches, but all those cranky, independent little chapels hidden away in the coves."

"Have you been visiting those, too?" I took both kinds of sandwich, happy to do her bidding in this small thing.

"The ones I could find, or that my car could reach. The ones who answered their phones." She laid two of the crustless triangles in the center of her plate, long sides facing. "I encountered a different kind of resistance from these people. I was prepared for it, because I remember Dad saying they kept to their own ways and were suspicious of outsiders. But I couldn't shortchange the Lord by not making the effort. However, a person can only do so much." She chose a triangle, nipped off the tiniest corner with her child-like teeth, and chewed it in her fastidious movie star manner.

"Well, I think most of us would be quite pleased with ourselves," I reiterated, "if we had managed to line up thirty churches to do something as a group."

"We answer to the Lord according to our talents, Reverend Bonner. I don't know you well enough to judge what your talents are, though from what I observed yesterday one of them is putting together an effective worship service."

"Thank you."

She nodded curtly. "My main talent is getting difficult things done. That's what I was known for at Brent and Bolling, and that's what I'm known for in my mission work."

"I'd like to hear more about your mission work," I said.

"The Lord calls, I answer. It's that simple."

"Are you affiliated with a particular church?"

"That's what *your* people kept asking me. No, I'm not affiliated with any church, Reverend Bonner, though I'm happy to say I'm welcomed in most of them, including yours. It's just between the Lord and me. He summons, I go. I'm a freelance apostle. As I wrote you in the letter, friends of my father, remembering his great evangelical gifts, naturally

528

thought of me to bring the Spirit to this broken community. But they wouldn't have got me up here by themselves. The Lord had to persuade me. It's strictly between the Lord and me."

"The wrestling match," I said.

She scowled, affronted either by my familiarity or the lightness of my response — or both. My punishment came swiftly.

"At least now that Father Dowd is joining us and the Evangelical Lutherans from Clampitt are coming, *all* the mainline Protestant denominations in the area will be represented," she said, as if continuing the conversation we had not been having.

"That must please you," I commented warily.

She nodded, taking a prim sip of tea. "But this morning I had an unexpected setback. The person from Clampitt who's coaching the girls in liturgical dancing phones me at seven o'clock and announces she won't be coming anymore unless she's paid. I couldn't believe my ears. *Nobody* is getting paid, I told her. We are doing this for the Lord. She says, yes but there's lots of us don't have a big advertising agency behind our work for the Lord. I am on a *leave of absence,* I told her. Leave of absence means you don't get paid. And for all I know, I may not have a job when I get back, but that's a chance I was willing to take for the Lord. And furthermore, even

529

when I was an active account executive at Brent and Bolling, they were certainly not 'behind' my work in the field in any way! I had to keep my mission work completely separate from my job. I booked my own lodgings and never identified myself as representing anybody other than myself. I paid my own travel and per diems out of my own pocket. Yes, she says, but you had something *in* your pocket to pay out of, didn't you?" Grace raised up her palms in a gesture of exasperation and let them fall into the lap of her purple robe.

"So what did you do?" I asked. According to Smathers, she had no job to go back to. I could so clearly picture her checking her haughty, well-groomed self into a Days Inn in some hot little lowland town at the outset of one of her missions: signing the register simply Grace Munger in the bold, school-girlish handwriting, scrupulously leaving the "firm represented" space blank, and paying with cash or her personal credit card, before going out to case the local abortion clinic for her next day's matinee.

"What did I do? I did what she expected me to do. I offered to pay her to finish teaching the girls their flag dance. It's the centerpiece of this parade and she knows it. I'll pay you out of my own pocket, I told her."

What could I say? This march is really important to you, isn't it? But I did not think she would appreciate such a sentiment coming from my mouth.

"I'll tell you one thing," she said. "If I did have access to all the resources I was used to having at my fingertips at Brent and Bolling, I could put on a Millennium March that this place would never forget. However, it's in His hands now. Just before you arrived, I finished turning the whole thing over to the Lord."

"That's probably a good idea," I said.

We sipped our tea and looked away from each other to the blurred mountainscape outside. I squashed an unwise urge to offer support and encouragement.

"After I got off the phone with the liturgical dance person," Grace said, "I looked out and saw the rain starting."

"I saw the rain starting, too. I was in my office over at the church."

In her customary way she went on as if I were not part of the dialogue. "I thought to myself, well, and what if I wake up on Saturday the eighteenth to this kind of weather or worse? What do I do then? Dad always had good weather, but that doesn't mean I will. God took a different approach with my father. He gave him the good things first, then removed them one by one. Only, unlike Job, my father didn't wait around to get them back. That's when I became discouraged of heart, and remembered it was your day off. I decided to take a day off myself. That's when I wrote my note to you."

"I'm glad you did. This is precisely the time of year when we need to take days off and sip tea and contemplate the awesome mystery that's getting ready to happen again. Yet everything around us conspires to distract us."

She favored me with a brusque nod of agreement before forging right on. "I said, Lord, I've done my best to make this march a success, and will continue to do so, right down to the last detail on Saturday the eighteenth, whatever weather you choose to send. If I have to empty my pockets and overdraw on my resources, I will do so gladly, because I gave you my promise. And you in turn gave me yours."

"Which was?"

"As I told your people on Sunday," she said, a trifle impatiently, "something will change."

That's when Gus had inquired with her level-headed sangfroid whether Grace had been assured it would be a *constructive* change. As Grace had wriggled out of it in the crypt, I asked again.

She drew herself up; I waited for the rebuff. But no, the freelance apostle was simply mustering the Lord's message as it had been conveyed to her. "I had it from Him again this morning. Something important will change," she pronounced slowly, her voice stout with conviction. "It will change because we are doing this for Him. Whether it is merely something that will change in this community or something of more cosmic significance, that is not for me to say. All He has given me to know is that by doing this for Him I will help bring important change in some way."

I found myself gazing at the empty grate, in which a blazing log fire would have added the consummate touch to this interesting tea party, if Grace had not had her particular history. Had "what the Lord had given her to know" on this latest occasion also issued from the grate? Ruminations, sparked by Lucinda's post-Communion rumor, reeled through my head. If young Grace had started the fire, had there been a voice instructing her, and whence had *it* issued? In the tradition of biblical narrative, I could imagine it so clearly: the scripture-soaked preacher's daughter in her white nightgown, hearing God's voice summoning her, as He'd summoned others before, to do his difficult biddings: "Grace, you must get up now." "Behold, here I am, Lord." "In the kitchen, you will find some rags and a small can of lighter fluid. Offer unto me the burnt offering of your father and mother and then run like hell."

"If we put Christ in charge of our future,"

Grace was saying, "something will change, make no mistake about it. I know that old judge of yours thinks I'm a simpleminded fundamentalist who will bring a lot of trouble to the area by promising miracles to the disenfranchised, but that's not what it's all about."

"What *is* it all about, Grace?"

"It's about turning your life over to Christ, Reverend Bonner. Don't you understand? *That's* the miracle. Don't you believe that? Don't you subscribe to that — you, a minister of God yourself — even if you *do* refuse to join our march for reasons I'm still not clear about?"

Without giving me a chance to answer, she plunged on.

"Look at Jonah. The Lord sent him to Nineveh and they turned themselves completely around. The Lord was so impressed He decided to spare them. Don't you believe that if all of us come out in honor of His Son's birthday, rain or shine, in the last days of this millennium, that the force of it, the sheer force of us lifting our voices in praise and offering our lives to Him, can bring change?"

I waited for a second, to see if she was really asking for a reply, or merely catching her breath.

"I believe everything that happens brings change, Grace. As for marches, for whatever purpose, history certainly has shown that they can bring change, sometimes for the improvement of people's lot, sometimes to whip people up for the worst sort of carnage or evil. You said a minute ago that you're still not clear about why I refuse to join your march. Well, I'd like you to be clear. I believe we need change, but not apocalyptic change. We need the change that comes out of foundation, not fireworks. We need the change that comes out of present healing. And there are people all around us committed to that — doctors, builders, worshipers, ministers, seekers and searchers, people of goodwill. We need less display and more unassuming deeds behind the scenes. I don't believe the changes we need can come out of *any* kind of sheer force, even if it's just the sheer force of lifting our voices in a body during a parade. Nothing is going to change significantly in this community, or any other, until each of us makes room for God's kingdom inside ourselves and lets it change us from within. That's what I think Jesus' ministry was all about: giving hospitality to God's kingdom inside yourself and letting it change you. He went around teaching people what the kingdom was and what it wasn't and how to prepare for it and to recognize it. Since it was a spiritual kingdom and you couldn't see it, he taught in parables and metaphors, so people could have pictures of what it was like. He went on foot, with a few followers, and did a great deal of his teaching one-on-one. A woman at a well. A man in darkness. The nearest thing to a manifesto he ever expressed was love the Lord your God with all your heart, soul, and mind, and love your neighbor as yourself. Nowhere did he advocate 'traditional morals and family values.' Nowhere did he urge people to take charge of their lives. On the contrary, he went around telling them to abandon their families and lose their lives. And nowhere in the Gospels do we ever hear mention of Jesus organizing a parade to get God's attention."

Had I gone too far with that last?

Her haughty face had tipped up a notch or two, but the tawny eyes regarded me steadily. She seemed to be reflecting intensely on something. Was it possible that I had made contact with the freelance apostle at last?

"Is the old monk still staying with you?" she asked after a minute.

"Well, yes," I said, thrown off balance. "We've asked him to stay through Christmas."

"How nice," she said, smiling at me with the childlike teeth as if I had just handed over a gift. "I have been so hoping he would still be here to join us for the march."

XVI

Transfiguration Stew

Dynamics in a household shift with the presence of any guest. Throw in a resident teenager and season with the peculiar specifics of our situation, and what you've got is a drastically changed life.

During the last year I had become accustomed to what really amounted to a semi-monastic existence at home, broken up with smatterings of domesticity. I had a busy husband who was less there than not there, and in his not-there portions, I had returned to my solitary ways. While Adrian was out at Fair Haven in his dual capacity of acting headmaster and chaplain, I ate alone, slept alone, and talked to myself and God. These interludes were by no means forlorn. As an only child with a busy father and no mother, I had grown to rely on my inner resources and really did enjoy keeping company with myself and having plenty of time to absorb my experiences before having new ones. Those times when Adrian was out at the school would have been occasions for romantic replenishment as well, if we hadn't been in our celibate period following the death of Hiram Sandlin and Adrian's subsequent grief and depression. Meditating on an absent lover is an excellent way of banking the flame when you're expecting him home again.

Our celibate period had at last ended on the Friday before Advent when so much had shown up on our doorstep at once, including the pneumonia that had reinstated the celibacy; but now, because of all those arrivals, there was no opportunity to meditate on anything at all. At first this lack of focusing-time felt like the missing luxury it was, then the distraction began to gnaw at my spirit.

Whatever I was doing, at home or in the parish, I was already where I had to be next, or stuck in where I had been, and guessing what the new people in our lives were up to in my absence and how it was going to affect everything else in our lives. While choosing Christmas music with the organist, which was one of my favorite tasks of the season, I was worrying whether Tony was upstairs bothering Adrian and whether the recognition scene when it came would be acrimonious or joyful — or something unimaginable — and whether we should go all out and get a ten-foot Christmas tree for Chase.

While taking tea with Addie Rogers in her magnificent old dining room and listening to her animated story of how her husband had once stocked his private lake with bass so when the governor came to spend the weekend with them he would be sure to catch something, I was so busy speculating on when she was going to get around to discussing her burial plans that I did not realize right away that she'd finished her story and was waiting for me to laugh. Fortunately I had retained the sound of the final words and resorted to the wool gatherer's ploy of repeating them back to her.

"They jumped in the boat?"

"Yes, my dear, those poor fish were so fresh from the hatchery they hadn't even had time to orient themselves, and before the governor even got his line in the water, they were throwing themselves all over him!"

While talking on the phone to Dick Miller about our combined Millennial Evensong Service, I was feeling remorseful about my inattentiveness to Addie Rogers. While I was dashing off a thank-you note to Addie Rogers (and enclosing a burial form to follow up on our discussion, which in due time had taken place) I was remembering the wild elation in Grace's voice and the way her eyes had glittered when she said, "It was like an auction — the prices going up and up!"

Then I had to copy over my note, because instead of signing "Margaret" I had signed "Grace."

Now that Adrian's pneumonia had been diagnosed as streptococcal, his main assignment in life was to swallow his broad-spectrum antibiotics and his aspirins, drink lots of fluids, assuage his cough with the new cough medicine, and get plenty of rest, leaving the cares to others. "Up to two weeks" of this had been prescribed by Dr. Charles, who checked frequently by phone to see how Adrian was progressing. He apologized for making himself scarce, but the flu had reached epidemic proportions in town, and fifteen of the twenty-four acute care beds down at Bruton Memorial were occupied by pneumonia or pleurisy cases who needed their antibiotics intravenously.

"We caught Adrian's early, Margaret, before it got dire, but we've got to keep those liquids flowing through him. Tell him if he isn't getting up to pee at least once an hour, he's not drinking enough liquids."

Those days when I was carrying up trays or sitting with Adrian and filling him in on life downstairs were as near as I got to quiet time. They also came as a grateful reminder that we were a marriage of true minds. There was nobody in the world I would rather talk to than my husband. And now that our bodies had gotten back together, there seemed no limit to what we might make of each other — once Adrian got over his illness and decided what to do about the school and discovered and came to terms with the identity of the stranger in our midst, and — was I leaving anything out?

During this crammed Advent, I did occasionally have a wishful fantasy of myself felled by a less-than-dire case of something that would send me to bed and let others take over. Oddly, these fantasies were enough to fortify my energies and restore perspective. Adrian was in bed and the school was getting along without him, just as it had continued to function after the death of its matchless founder. Tim Stancil was home with a bad case of laryngitis and another judge was holding court for him. Cass Morrissey and Judy Freedgood, our Food Pantry representatives, were down with flu, so Tony and I were filling in for them on Saturday mornings.

If I were to come down with something, I would be ordered to bed and the chores I had been writing in and rescheduling and checking off in my Daily Reminder book with little self-important sighs would get done by others. A gung-ho Kevin Dowd would be flushed out of some other employment; or a retired priest, sufficiently rested and bored enough somewhere in western Carolina, would snap on his old collar and return with relief to the Christmas fray. The world could do without any one of us as long as the work kept getting done. In one of the happier TV news items, we watched a nursing mother cat suckling two orphaned baby squirrels who had fallen out of their nest. Even Jesus had known better than to set out to work all by himself.

Meanwhile, I was alive and well — just a little distracted was all.

On the first Tuesday in Advent, Chase left the rectory in his forward-tilting run-walk to catch the bus to public high school. He was wearing his green anorak from Fair Haven, but the school crest had been covered over with a cutout of a Chinese Foo dog he and Tony had found in some fabric shop and which Tony had expertly stitched on the night before.

"That's his emblem now," Tony said. "He chose it himself. Everybody starting over needs a new emblem." I was touched and impressed that Tony had foreseen something Adrian and I had totally overlooked: namely, that Chase would have had less of a brand-new start if he'd showed up wearing the Fair Haven crest. Whereas under the badge of the Foo dog (a strikingly congenial image for Chase) he could present his history at his own pace. Just as Tony, under the effrontery of his monk's robe, could be said to be protecting his own history from premature exposure?

By the end of his first week at High Balsam High, Chase was transferred into advance sections of tenth-grade algebra and English. Every day he brought home a new triumph, always reported with a downcast expression that would have served equally well for an admission of misconduct or failure. Then he would add some undercutting demurral before any of us had the chance to praise him. The promotions into honors algebra and English were explained away by a shrugging reminder that "everyone knew" public schools were a year or two behind the private ones. A girl in his class had told him he should try out for the male lead in the spring play, *Look Homeward Angel*, but: "I'm new and she's just trying to be nice. Besides, whoever heard of a *short* leading man?"

"You've already got a leading man's head of hair," Tony said. "By next spring you may have shot up some. When I was sixteen, I grew three inches in six months."

"Yes, but you're still short," Chase reminded him.

I would run upstairs to fill Adrian in on life below, and especially to report praiseworthy things about Tony: his many kindnesses to Chase; his bon mots; his helpful ideas about household management ("It's nothing, Margaret. Don't forget, I've lived a great portion of my life in community, so to speak"); his tact and shrewdness with certain of the Food Pantry recipients, both the ones who were too shy or embarrassed to take their full allotment, and the ones who liked to fudge a little and get more. ("Here, Don, take a can of this pink salmon. Well, I know you don't *need* it, but the FDA sent us six cases, and I can give

543

you a fail-safe recipe for salmon croquettes. Oh, Polly, let's see now, your card here says your two oldest children are in school, so they get their lunches there, don't they? So maybe four cans of Spaghetti-O's would be enough for yours and the little one's lunch? Here, let me put those others back for you.")

After Adrian's blood cultures showed he had strep pneumonia, we moved Chase downstairs to my study. The arrangement suited everyone better. I could sleep in Adrian's study and be close by if he needed anything in the night, and the bathroom belonged to just the two of us again.

"And if Chase wakes up in the middle of the night and wants to win more money off me in blackjack," said Tony, "he has only to tap on my door and call softly 'Praise be to God,' and I'll hit the ground running. That's been my wake-up call, you know, for nineteen years. After I'm gone, of course, he'll move into my sun porch room. I offered to switch with him now, so he could start settling in, but he wouldn't hear of it."

"Far be it from me to push an old holy man out of his room," said Chase. "Where are you going after Christmas? Back to your abbey?"

"Not *right* away." Tony picked up a pack of cards and treated them to an embellishing riffle. "I'd like to have a good look around first."

"At *what?*"

"Oh, new developments in the world."

"Like what?"

"Well, anything at all. I like to watch things starting out. Like you, for example."

"*I'm* starting out?" Chase squealed incredulously. "Most people would say I'm already finished."

"Now, that's more my kind of line," Tony said, shuffling twice and expertly dealing the cards. "And besides, if there's one thing I've learned in my eighty years, it's that no man is ever finished."

Chase looked unconvinced. You could see his mouth puckering for his next rebuttal.

But Tony, shoulders already shaking up and down with silent laughter, cut him off at the pass. "Nope, my friend, no man is ever finished. If all else fails, he can always serve as a bad example to others."

When I reported this exchange to Adrian, he cracked up at the punch line. This was followed by a round of coughing and the drinking of water. Then his mood abruptly changed. It was the first day he had wanted to get out of bed, and he was sitting in a chair by the window, a sweater over his pajamas, a blanket over his knees, his books and liquids arranged on a table beside him. Now I watched his face go dark.

"Oh yes," he mused sarcastically, "it's always fun to watch things *starting out*. Staying around and seeing them through is what separates the men from the boys."

"What are you referring to, Adrian?"

He gave me a sharp look and started to say something, then apparently changed his mind.

"I'm just feeling contrary," he said. "But maybe that's a good sign. Maybe it means I'm getting better."

Right after that, I left for the Commission on Ministry Conference in Mountain City, which turned out to be a welcome retreat from the accelerating Advent pace. The bishop, who'd no doubt planned it that way, preached the first evening on "Conversion of Life." He'd just come back from Florence, where he had seen the Fra Angelico frescoes in the Monastery of San Marco, and his illustration came from the Annunciation fresco located at the top of the stairs of the monks' dormitory. The placement was significant, he said. Every time a monk went upstairs to his cell he had to look at Mary saying yes again, which reminded him that he had vowed to do no less. Then he went on to talk about "ongoing conversion," how our repeated dyings and risings continued to produce fruit. While he was speaking, I saw myself running up to Adrian's sickroom bearing fresh supplies of liquids and stories from downstairs. Even without a fresco to remind me, every time I climbed the stairs I was saying yes again to the life I had chosen. I still wanted the man, sick and well, mellow and dark, and I still wanted the work, in all its uncertainty, serenity, and frazzlement. Now that the courtship period was over in both cases, I really did hope — as I sat in the rustic diocese chapel, lapsing back into my long-term thought patterns that first evening away from home — that the marriages would be long, because I wanted to see what they would make of me.

As the bishop, a peripatetic preacher, strolled back and forth across the transept, discoursing on spiritual second winds, and I was both listening to him and thinking these things, the knowledge suddenly caught me sidewise, but as manifestly as though Adrian himself had slipped into the seat next to me: *Adrian knows. He knows who Tony is.*

I had offered to tell him what I knew about Tony, because it hadn't been under the seal. But he hadn't asked. Why hadn't he asked? Had some part of him both known and not wanted to know?

And how and when had he known, and why was he keeping it bottled up inside himself?

There were six aspirants to the priesthood. Four clergy interviewers met with each aspirant. The twenty-six-year-old high school English teacher who had written so candidly about his unepiphanic hike up the mountain of faith until he stumbled into the mysterious chapel of acceptance turned out to be as solid as his paper and even more likable in person. He was one of the two candidates who received a unanimous yes from the commission.

Another aspirant, the dean of a business school who had written an impressive but cold paper on why she felt she was being called to offer her administrative skills to God in the second half of life, ran her interview like a meeting she was chairing. She told us that her favorite passage in scripture was the Wise and Foolish Virgins because she had always identified with people who made it a point to keep their lamps filled. "My theology of pastoral care is based on personal accountability," she concluded crisply. She was unanimously turned down.

I left the conference feeling renewed and invigorated, even though I was the one who had to call the sponsoring rector of the wise virgin and to write the letter to the rejected aspirant, explaining our decision and trying to steer her toward perceived strengths that didn't have to do with ordination.

It was a dissemblingly mild day for December; the digital thermometer above my rearview mirror had registered 62 when I left Mountain City, and had dropped only to 59 when I started the final ascent to High Balsam. If the trees had not been bare it could have passed for early May. Maybe Grace would be phenomenally lucky in her weather. I hadn't seen her again since our tea, but Tony had received one of her hand-delivered notes the day after saying how glad she was to hear he was staying over Christmas and therefore could be in the march. She offered to make him a banner.

Tony had consulted me. "Margaret, I'm betwixt and between. I more or less said I would, you remember, that first evening. If I'm still here, I said. I didn't expect to be, that was before your kind invitation, but here I am. What do *you* think I ought to do?"

"Whatever you want to. You're our guest, you're not my parishioner. And I wouldn't try to stop any parishioner who wanted to march, either."

"She's a very insistent lady."

"Yes, she is. But I can't subscribe to some of her causes."

"I see your point." He hesitated uncertainly. "If I *did* go, I'd tell her I'd prefer to make my own banner. But I wouldn't want to offend you or Adrian."

"You won't offend me, but why don't you discuss it with Adrian?"

"Good idea."

He had reported back rather crestfallen. "I don't know, Margaret."

"What did Adrian say?"

"He asked me if I planned to wear my

habit. I said I thought that was the main reason she wanted me. He said if that was all she wanted, why didn't she get herself a bunch of habits and dress people up in them since there were all kinds of people going around dressed up as things they weren't, anyway. I told him about her offering to make me a banner and how I would rather make my own — that is, if I did march — and he said, 'Well, if I were you, I wouldn't put anything on it that represents more than yourself.' "

"What did he mean by that?"

"I asked him. He said he wouldn't put anything on it connected to the Benedictine order or my monastery. I told him I hadn't intended to. I had more in mind a colorful angel, blowing a trumpet, maybe. Something fairly simple that I could cut out of felt and stitch on."

"That sounds good. There are some angel books in my study. You might find ideas in them."

"But I'm wondering, Margaret, whether I haven't overstayed my welcome."

"What makes you say that?"

"Oh, you've given up your study to Chase because I'm in the room he's supposed to have, and —"

"That's not a problem. I have Adrian's study upstairs, where I can be right there if he needs me, and I have my office at the church." (Where we were having this conversation.)

"And also, he seemed to like me better at first. That first morning, when he came down and found me in the kitchen and I made him the hyssop tea and brought out all my remedies, he was downright charmed, if I say so myself. I could see it and feel it, even though he was sick. I thought, now, this is a better beginning than I had the right to hope for. I even went so far as to think maybe he'd recognize me. Something about me would catch at his memory and — But he's definitely less charmed now. It might have been better for me to have just gone on and boarded that bus. Later when the mood was right, you could have told him. And he would either want to get in touch or he wouldn't."

"Look, Tony, you were the one who wanted to give him the chance to know you better. And he *is* still sick. Dr. Charles says he'll probably be feeling low for quite a while. As for recognizing you, well, you were absent from his life for a very long time."

"I know," he said, with a penitent droop of his shoulders. "I deserve whatever I get. But what if he decides he dislikes me before he recognizes me? That wouldn't be too good, now would it?"

"It wouldn't be ideal, no, but it's a chance you'll have to take. We've all got chances to take about this. It's not exactly your everyday occurrence, is it? We all need to feel our way. And we've taken on Chase as well. There are all manner of new quantum unknowns knocking against each other in this household."

"You've got a point there. I guess I'll just see it through till Christmas. Keep trying to make myself useful."

"You certainly are being that. And you're so wonderful with Chase. You've certainly won him over."

"Win a few, lose a few," he said gloomily.

A statement worthy of Adrian. Well, he was his son's father.

"Please don't jump-start the ending, Tony. Give things a chance to evolve, with a little help from God."

"You're right," he had quickly agreed. "Give God a chance to get His two cents in, as Father Cecil used to say."

When I turned into our street, I saw Adrian in his khakis and a sweater standing on the lawn midway between the church and the rectory. His back was to me and he seemed to be gazing up at the sky. At first I took him to be engaging in a little nature worship after having been inside for so long. I pulled over to the curb, switched off the ignition, and jumped out. I didn't want to wait any longer to be with him.

When he saw it was me, his pale, drawn

face brightened. "You're early," he said. "How nice."

"I left right after breakfast and drove fast."

"Is this December, or am I still running a fever?"

"It's Friday, the second week in Advent, and it was sixty-two degrees when I left Mountain City."

"Down there in the flats, too, where it's a mere 2,500 feet above sea level."

"How are you feeling?"

"Much, much better. It's good to be among the living again."

"My Lord," I said. "What is Tony doing on our roof?"

"He and Chase are cleaning the gutters. They wanted to surprise you."

Tony, whose head and shoulders had just appeared above the steepest part of the rectory roof, shot up a hand in greeting. "Welcome home, Margaret," he shouted in his crackly old voice.

"But where is Chase?"

"He's behind the house holding the ladder and emptying the leaves. They've rigged up a very efficient bucket and rope system."

"But why isn't Chase on the roof and Tony holding the ladder?"

"He volunteered, but Tony vetoed it. Wanted to show off, I think. It's not every eighty-year-old who can prance around on pitched roofs."

"My Lord," I repeated. Tony had disappeared again.

"Yes," said Adrian, his arm going around my shoulders. "Our amazing little miracle man. Come, let's bring in your stuff."

"Oh, it can wait."

"No, it can't. I want all of you back in the house."

Adrian sat in the chair and watched me while I unpacked. The bed was made, the medicines had been removed, and the windows were open to the unseasonable balmy air. I took a quick survey of the books on his table: a new biography of Aelred of Rievaulx from Cambridge University Press, Caroline Walker Bynum's *Jesus as Mother: Studies in the Sprituality of the High Middle Ages*, and a textbook called *Ministering to Young Alcoholics*. So he had returned to his full-strength reading regime.

"How did it go?" he asked.

"Good, on the whole. We rejected one, accepted five. Two unanimously: if they're any indication, the Church has a future."

"And if I know you, you volunteered to write the letter to the rejectee."

"I'm not looking forward to it, but I'd rather be the one to write it. I always pretend it's me who got rejected, and then I write the kind of letter I could bear."

"And who are you this time?" He was

looking at me with such unconcealed pleasure that I felt self-conscious as I made my trips between closet and suitcase and dresser drawers.

"I'm a competent, disciplined woman who's worked very hard to get where I am and now need to develop my neglected feeling qualities. I identify with the wise virgins, but I need to learn to share my oil."

"Ah." He was smiling. "And how is our bishop?"

"In fine form. He sent his best wishes for your recovery, but said you seemed to him the kind of person who'd know how to make good use of an enforced Advent retreat."

"I've been doing my best not to waste it."

I was unpacked. I hefted my empty suitcase to its overhead closet shelf and went over and perched on the arm of the chair. He pulled me over into his lap and we rested with our heads together, the sunshine pouring through the window onto our backs.

"You look wonderful," he said. "Now, ordinarily the next thing you'd expect me to say is, 'It must be because you've been away from me,' but I'm not going to say it, except in quotes. The bishop was right; I've got a few things to show for my enforced Advent retreat. You'll have to settle for 'I'm so glad you're back.' "

"I'll happily settle for that." There was something I wanted to tell him, was now the right time, or not?

Then from outside our window came the scrape of the ladder being moved nearer. Someone was climbing up. There followed the clatter of a bucket being hauled up and the clump of footsteps patrolling over our heads.

"Genetically, at least, it's not the end of the world," said Adrian, stroking my hair. "If he's up there on the roof at eighty, that should up my percentage for being around for our golden anniversary."

"How long have you known?"

"I first *admitted* to myself that I knew on the afternoon you went to see Grace Munger. But I think it had been bubbling up ever since you asked him to stay. You were being so delicate and careful that I was pretty sure it had something to do with me. You know how when you're sick your mind is freer to jump around and make these intuitive connections. That day you went to see Grace Munger, he'd brought me some soup and was sitting in this chair talking a blue streak, and something about the situation felt lived through before: like a childhood memory of lying in a bed, being captive to a garrulous grown-up who wanted to hang around when all I wanted to do was sleep. But nobody sat up with me at the orphanage, and they certainly didn't at the Schmidts. The only time Gerhard ever came close to my bed was to drag me out of it. But I pushed it down, the memory, I wasn't ready to know yet. But when you told me you'd seen his driver's license, it all added up."

"So you've known since that afternoon." I closed my eyes in relief, my head still resting against his. "I'm glad. I felt so torn. I hated keeping it from you."

"You didn't keep it from me. You said your first loyalty was to me and you would answer anything I asked. But you also said he wanted a chance to prove himself before his story became generally known. You said the whole thing was beyond where you could reason; that all you had to go on was your intuition and your love for me."

"I pulled those words out of the dark. One by one."

"And I trusted every one of them. I think I told you, you're the only person I've ever let myself trust completely."

"You did."

"Now I have a confession to make. After you left to have tea with Grace, I waited until Tony and Chase went off on their shopping expedition and then I picked up the phone and got the number of the Abbey of the Transfiguration. I was expecting to reach some underling. I was simply planning to ask if they had someone called Tony there and see how far that got me. But when the prior himself answered, I didn't feel I wanted to go on with this cloak and dagger approach any longer. As soon as I identified myself, he said he'd been expecting my call. We had a fairly long conversation, though he's a retentive sort. I gather, as much from what he didn't say, that Tony was the pet prodigal of the late prior, but not a favorite with him. Then he came across my name in that church paper. It must have seemed like a sign straight from heaven. He showed it to Tony, the order made up a purse for Tony, three thousand dollars, no less, for his services and out of respect for the late prior, and they bought him a millennium bus pass, and I'm assuming you can fill in from there. They're not expecting him back. I found myself protecting him a little. I mean, I didn't tell the prior he'd showed up wearing a Benedictine habit. Whose was it, by the way, the old prior's?"

"You guessed it. Does Tony know about any of this?"

"No. I wanted to get some command over myself first. I have some very conflicting feelings, as you might imagine. After I'd spoken to the prior, what I wanted more than anything was to go to sleep and wake up and have it all be a dream. It has the classic aspects of one, doesn't it? The man who has carefully fathered himself through intellectual effort, and through theories of God and the psyche, is visited in a dream by a comic crook posing as a monk, who is then revealed as his real father. Only it's not a dream."

"Oh, Adrian." He had spoken so bitterly.

"Not to tell you about the phone call was cowardly of me. I wasn't ready to hear your feelings about being presented with such a father-in-law. Especially when your father was such a thoroughly decent man. Will you accept my apology?"

"For the father-in-law?"

"That, too." At least I'd made him laugh. "And for keeping the phone call from you. When you've been so scrupulously above-board with me the whole way."

"No apology is necessary in either case. At least we don't have to play cloak and dagger with each other anymore. Tony specifically didn't want the sacrament of confession, because he *wanted* me to tell you when I thought the time was right. He said he'd like to tell me his story, then leave on the five o'clock bus, and if I ever felt there might be a benefit in relaying it to 'anybody,' I would have his blessing. I was puzzled, but I agreed."

"Do you think he ever meant to get on the five o'clock bus?"

"I've had some doubts," I admitted.

He shifted his legs. "I suppose, now that you're home, it's only a matter of time until we have the coming out party. I just wish I felt more open-armed toward the deserting old schemer."

"Don't rush things, then. Maybe you should hear more of his story first."

He sighed. "I wonder how much of it is true. He shows up disguised as a monk, how many other costumes are there under that one? Do I look like him? Tell me honestly, Margaret."

"There's a resemblance in the sharpness of your noses and chins," I ventured cautiously. "But both of you have *strong* noses and chins. It's hard to get a true focus on him with that hair. On the driver's license it was white, by the way."

"I suppose I should be grateful for small favors," he commented dryly.

We heard the bucket come thump-thumping down the side of the ladder, then Chase calling, "Yuk, these ones are all rotten and soupy!" Then the light-footed descent of the old man calling back in his cracked voice, "Wait, don't empty them . . . I might be able to use them in my Transfiguration stew." And the boy's high-pitched shriek of laughter.

"He might have made a good father," said Adrian. "Just think of that. He might have had all those years emptying gutters with *me*."

"Well, thank God that's over," I said, relapsing against his chest.

"What's over, my love?"

"Us keeping what we knew from each other. I hated that part of it."

"Listen, Margaret, I have something else to confess."

"What?"

"My leg has gone to sleep."

"Oh dear, I'm sorry!" I jumped up.

"No wait, I was just going to suggest we move over to the bed. I like talking when we're all wrapped up in each other. After all, that's how we began our life together." He rose unsteadily, stamped on the leg, then limped over to the door and locked it. "Why don't you close those blinds, so people going up and down ladders won't see in."

We began by lying on top of the covers and pulling a blanket over us. "I suppose the wife he said died young was my mother," he tentatively began.

"Yes."

"If *that's* the truth," he said caustically.

"If that's the truth, yes. But let's assume it is."

"What was she like? I mean, as far as you could tell, was she — assuming she *was* my mother — someone I'd care to hear more about?"

"Yes," I could tell him.

He sighed. A shudder went through his body. I guessed he was thinking of Father Mountjoy's warning story about discovering his own degraded mother.

If that story had been true.

We lay there, lightly wrapped together, and I dispensed, piecemeal, the information he asked for, in the order he asked it, no less and no more. He could only take so much at a

561

time, who could blame him? After a while we undressed and got under the covers, exhausted in the presence of all our complicated murals, true and untrue, embroidered, fabulated, or dissembled, or however they had seemed to us at the time. We loved each other gently and slept through the rest of the afternoon.

"This is like no stew I've eaten before," said Adrian.

"That can mean anything," Tony said.

"No, I like it," Adrian assured him. "It's subtle. I identify chicken, carrots, onions —"

"Wrong," said Tony. "No onions. Onions aren't subtle."

"Then what are these oniony-looking bits?"

"Do they *taste* like onions?"

"Well, I assumed they did . . ."

"Never assume anything. Use your tasters."

Obediently Adrian separated out a transparent sliver with his fork and raised it to his mouth.

"It's celery, anyone would know that," Chase blurted out.

"Thank you, sir, for letting me discover it for myself," said Adrian. "A real Socratic education one can get, with you living in the house."

"But there's something else in there that you'll never guess," said Chase. "Which gives it its special flavor. I was only helping you save your wits for the really important mystery."

"I'm afraid I already know what it is," I said.

"You probably do," agreed Tony humbly. "You're a subtle cook yourself."

"What is it?" demanded Chase.

"It's an essence," I said, "of something quite plentiful and ordinary."

"Oh, pox and putrefaction, she's got it," said Chase.

"Putrefaction, yes," I went on, "but first they must fade and shrivel and drop and crumble and soak up moisture and dirt and then rot for a while into a soupy mess in the gutter until someone says, 'Wait, don't empty those, I can use them in my Transfiguration stew!'" I felt as light-headed as though we'd been drinking wine, which we hadn't been, now that Chase was living with us. "The real mystery is how the chef got all the yukky brown out."

"She hasn't guessed!" cried Chase. "But somebody sure was eavesdropping on us."

"When it's right outside your window, it's not eavesdropping," Adrian told him.

"Anyone else want to hazard a guess?" asked Tony happily. "Or does everybody give up?"

"We give up," Adrian said. "We are no match for your secrets."

"Peanuts," said Tony, laying his hands palms up on the table, the abdicating magician. "Someone gave the abbey a bushel basket, and Father Cecil brought them to me and said, 'See what you can do with these, Tony, and if you can't dream up anything, toss 'em to the squirrels.' I felt my pride was at stake. Then I had this idea of shucking them and grinding them up in the Cuisinart with some chicken broth and a little sherry, and to make a long story short, it became the basis for what came to be known as my Transfiguration stew. A particular favorite during Lent, when less is more."

"Wait a minute," Chase said. "Aren't monks supposed to give up alcohol during Lent?"

Tony, growing surer of himself each day he found himself still among us, was hardly fazed. "Right you are, my boy. Nothing slips past *you,* does it? What I did, you see, was substitute a little ginger ale. During Lent."

Adrian sent me a glance: well, there he is, the nimble quick-change artist I bring you as a father-in-law. If one version doesn't wash, just brazenly whip out another.

But was there the faintest wry acceptance in the glance?

The phone rang.

"Now who wants what from whom?" Adrian said. But he reached over expectantly and grabbed the receiver.

It was Jefferson. Despite recent campus restrictions, the flu epidemic in town had infiltrated the school. Six infirmary beds filled this afternoon. Should he send the rest of the kids home early for Christmas vacation?

"Let's wait on that, Baxter. Some of them aren't expected home at all, you know, and some are going home with friends. But nobody's going to be happy if they bring the bug home with them. My inclination would be to call that nursing supply service and get more infirmary help. Prepare for a siege. Prepare for Christmas at Fair Haven with a bunch of sick kids. No, I'm not being pessimistic at all. Just the opposite. It could be very comforting for them to know they can just fall apart and be sick and we'll still provide Christmas for them."

He leaned back in his chair and let Baxter have his say; he nodded once or twice and rolled his eyes a couple of times. "I've been thinking about that, too. No, I mean on the premises, on the staff. Of course we can afford it. Someone fairly young, just out of a medical residency . . . now wait a minute, let me finish, Baxter. It's my feeling that if we stopped fretting about not having Sandlin's medical and scientific know-how to rely on anymore, we could get back to utilizing the talents God gave us. Yes, of course, I'm willing to discuss it. I was coming out to the school tomorrow anyway. Oh, I'm a new man. Almost. Not as fit as I'd like to be yet, but the wheels are cranking upstairs again. Yes, that sounds good, Baxter. See you then."

"You're going back to work," announced Chase as soon as Adrian hung up.

"Any objection?" Adrian asked him.

"No, sir. Just don't forget about us poor orphans at home here."

"I'm hardly the person to forget about orphans," replied Adrian caustically.

Then blushed to the roots of all the hair he had left.

Making little humming noises in his throat, Tony sprang up and busily cleared plates.

"You know what I think?" Chase went on, tapping a nervous beat with his fingernail on the table. "I think you should just go ahead and be the real headmaster."

"Oh, you do, do you?" Adrian scowled. "Would you care to tell us why?"

"Because you're the obvious person. Mr. Jefferson's nice and tries hard, but he doesn't fit the image of a headmaster. And some person from outside would just have to start from square one and might not understand what the whole point of the school is."

"I see. And what is the point?"

"Well, you explained it to me *yourself*. *You're* the one who wrote it into the handbook. To provide a *fair haven*, in the full sense of what both words can mean, for messes like me, until we can find our own structures and learn how to think and feel."

"That's pretty good for a renegade like you, only I don't recall writing the word 'mess' anywhere in our handbook."

"And some person from outside," Chase continued, watching Adrian closely, "wouldn't have known the *founder*. They wouldn't have any direct connection to the spirit of Dr. Sandlin."

"I see. No apostolic succession." Adrian's scowl was dissolving at the edges.

"If they *do* all come down with the flu," said Tony, with his back to us at the sink, "I could go out there and be Father Christmas for you. A few pillows in the right places, a white wig and beard, and a sack full of presents, and I'll look like the real thing."

"Oh, I'm sure you'd have no trouble looking like the real thing" was Adrian's calm reply.

"Hey, I know what," said Chase excitedly, corraling us with his quick dark eyes. "Let's get a movie and watch it together right here in the kitchen. We'll get something that everybody likes. Tony and I watched *The Shawshank Redemption* the other night, he'd never seen it before, but we could get something more high-minded for the reverends: *Hamlet*, or something."

"I hate to tell you, but the place closed ten minutes ago," said Tony. "We got a later start on supper than usual because — well, we just did."

"Because the reverends slept late!" Chase impertinently finished for him. During the latter part of the meal, he had become more and more keyed up. Now he seemed almost frantic to keep us all here. "Hey, I know," he said. "We could watch the new Ben Mac-Gruder album."

"Oh, is there a new Ben MacGruder album?" said Adrian. "That shows how out of touch I am. It's time I did get back out to the school."

"It's just barely out," said Chase. "*She* has it over at the church. He sent it to her!"

"No," I corrected him, "his *sister* sent it." To Adrian I said, "It came when you were sick. Chase and I watched it over at the office."

"Ben MacGruder is a favorite with some of our younger monks at the Transfiguration," Tony commented, returning to wipe the table with a sponge.

"Ben's older sister Harriet was Margaret's best friend," Adrian explained to Tony. "The MacGruders were members of her father's church."

"And she was the preacher's daughter and Ben MacGruder was in love with her!" Chase uttered his high-pitched squeal of a laugh. "That's what the album's all about."

"Is it really?" Adrian asked me.

568

"It's not all about anything," I said crossly. "The first song is some kind of . . . mishmash of a 'memoir' about his youth, and the rest is just Egyptian folk music. It's jittery and disorganized. Neither Chase nor I gave it a very high mark."

"But still," said Adrian, "that first part. Let's watch it. I'm curious."

"Don't anyone leave the room," ordered an ecstatic Chase. "I'll be right back. Oh, wait a minute, I'll need the key, won't I?"

I handed over the key.

Our kitchen TV was larger than the modest hand-me-down set at the church. All the more room for roiling clouds and writhing spotlit bodies when the time came.

" 'O God, our help in ages past,' " Adrian hummed along with Ben in his adequate baritone as the camera panned across the svelte Brideshead lawn, zooming in on particular children's faces.

"It's an Easter egg hunt," Chase explained.

"*The* Easter egg hunt?" Adrian asked me.

"A Hollywood version of it, maybe."

"That's you in the pink dress?"

"A dress Ruth would never have bought me and I wouldn't have worn if she had." Even as I was saying it I realized that it wasn't true. I would have worn any dress Ruth bought me if she had liked it. Long before she left us, I must have sensed she was tenuous property; I

569

went to great pains not to disappoint her.

"And where are you off to, looking so sad and determined?"

"Toward something that isn't there," I said curtly. "Listen to the words."

"You — walking away from me even then
Toward something only you could see
Something absent and unseen."

"Hmm," mused Adrian, interest picking up. "Metaphysical?"

"He has such a pure voice," said Tony. "Did he have lessons as a child, Margaret?"

"I believe so."

Time for the roiling clouds of evening and the rising moon shape-shifting into Ben's face, and his confiding spoken plaint:

"This is my memoir of an evening gone.
About love found . . . and love lost."

"Here it comes." Chase giggled. "Persons in need of supervision shut your peepers."

The rowboat rocked, the acrobatic couple heaved and quivered in light too bright for any moon — which was also Ben's face.

"You gave yourself to me
You took me as your own
But you don't like to be reminded —
Oh no, you don't like to be reminded."

570

"Hmm," said Adrian, "I can see why you're displeased."

"They're not really doing what it looks like," said Chase. "There's this actor's code. They're probably even wearing body stockings."

"A little more left to the imagination might have been better," Tony tentatively contributed.

Dark and darker on the screen. To match my mood.

"You always went looking for
The absent and unseen
But when you planned to wed a shadow
I asked, 'What can this mean?' "

"Here he comes," announced Chase, cutting a glance at me, then Adrian. "The rival!"

The dank Torquemada in the clerical robe unsmilingly beckoned the woman.

"Is that supposed to be me?" asked Adrian.

"That's exactly what *I* asked!" cried Chase.

Adrian laughed. "Well, at least he's given me some hair."

I liked Adrian for that.

The woman, in her dank black choir robe/wedding garment, disappeared into the fog after Torquemada.

"Even our monks who like Ben Mac-Gruder may take offense at his religious stereotyping," said Tony.

We watched the Nubian stuff.

"Your eyes don't know where to focus," said Tony. "But that may be the trend now. I haven't watched much of this sort of thing."

When it was over, Adrian was quiet. He leaned forward propped on his elbows and studied the empty screen while Chase rewound the tape.

"Anyone want to watch it again?" Chase asked.

"Once was too much for me," I said gloomily. For me, at least, the euphoria of homecoming was over.

"I think I get it," Adrian suddenly said.

"What?" I asked, not sure I wanted to hear.

"His album is struggling with a theme. In the title song, the lover loses his girl to dismal Father Shadow. But on a mythical level, he's dealing with the Bride of Death motif . . . the descent into the underworld. And in the set of Nubian songs he lets Orpheus retrieve his beloved a bit more each time by taking the same three people, reversing the winners, and rewriting the script. He didn't quite pull it off, but he has a more interesting mind than I gave him credit for."

My husband, the exegete. I thanked God for his classical and Jungian leanings; and above all, on this occasion, for his abstract mind.

"I think you may be giving Ben credit for

572

your own interesting mind," I nevertheless felt bound to say.

"But he would have done better to order his vestments from Almy's," Adrian said.

Tony rolled himself a smoke. The daily spectacle had lost none of its fascination for any of us. Chase watched, entranced, his frantic energies for the moment quiescent. And I was reminded — probably Adrian was, too — of where this meticulous little ritual of Tony's had been brought to perfection.

When Tony stepped outside to light up, in deference to Adrian's mending lungs, Chase's hypernervous antennae ranged over the room once more and lit on me. He cocked his head and asked: "Didn't you love him back at least a *little* bit?"

"Who?" I asked, knowing who.

"I think he means Ben MacGruder," said Adrian.

"No," I said, "I liked Ben. In some ways he was more fun to be with than his sister. But I can't say I ever loved him."

"Well, but, did you ever . . ." The boy's voice rose to a whinnying squeal. "But maybe I'd better not ask any more."

"Right you are, sir. That is more than enough."

Adrian cut him off with such devastating sharpness that if I hadn't been ready to kill Chase, I might have found it in my heart to be sorry for him.

★ ★ ★

As we undressed for bed, Adrian regressed into his old mode.

"What have I brought on you, Margaret? This boy, this *father*. You'd be perfectly in your rights to go live somewhere else."

"It'll work out," I said, more confidently than I felt. I was really tired. The idea of a hermitage seemed not at all unappealing: maybe I could be a part-time Julian of Norwich.

"He's too intelligent for his own good," Adrian went on. He was sitting in the chair, untying his first shoe.

"You're talking about Chase now."

"Of course I'm talking about Chase," he said curtly, untying the second shoe. "Who else would I be talking about?"

"Well, Tony is intelligent, too," I said. "This house is just bursting at the seams with intelligent people," I added caustically.

"It gets out of hand," Adrian went on, ignoring my remark. "Whenever he's not sufficiently occupied, or if he feels the slightest threat of abandonment, he starts looking for something to destroy."

He removed both shoes, held them in one hand and regarded them as a pair, then placed them side by side on the floor. The first time I ever saw him do this, on our wedding night, I was deeply moved. I had never seen anyone take off their shoes in this measured and considered fashion, untying one and then the other, followed by the loving examination and orderly placement. It must have something to do with his orphanhood, I had thought.

"He didn't destroy anything that I know of," I said, kicking my own shoes rather neatly into their designated corner of the closet.

"He was rude and insinuating."

"Yes, he was, but you handled it. You were the perfect image of the headmaster who knows when to wield the rod of iron."

"That was presumptuous of him, too. Nobody asked his opinion of my credentials to be headmaster."

I took a fresh nightgown out of the drawer. Then I was uncertain what to do with it. We were going to spend the night in the same room for the first time since his pneumonia. Though we had spent the latter part of this afternoon naked, and though he had come to bed naked in the dark on that Friday evening before Advent, we had never, in our marriage, undressed for bed in the same room with the lights on. If this sounds unbearably quaint, I can assure you from the confidences I have been privileged to hear as a pastor, as well as from my own limited experience, that more rampant modesty takes place behind closed doors than the average modern-day sophisticate would ever dream of.

"I think he was right about you, though," I said, still holding the folded gown. "You do fit the image of a headmaster, and you do have all the credentials, as well as the right of apostolic succession to Hiram, as you yourself put it."

Adrian sat quietly in the chair in his socks, appearing to ponder my words. Then he looked up. "Was he right about you, too?" he countered.

"What do you mean?"

"Oh, come on, Margaret, you know what I mean. Didn't you love Ben MacGruder back just a little? And all the rest that went with it."

It was the sudden roughness in his voice more than the questions that made me go cold.

"No, I never was in love with Ben," I said evenly. "As for what you call 'all the rest,' that was over long before I met you or even knew of your existence. I regretted it then, and I regret it now, for the precise reason that I *didn't* love him. If I had loved him, I wouldn't have felt bad about it afterward. And he might not have stayed so . . . obsessed about me and written that silly song."

Adrian pulled himself up straighter in the chair. He rested his hands on the arms. His expression became aloof and abstracted.

"What are you thinking?" I asked.

"Too many things at once," he said. "I need some time to sort it out."

"Well, if it has anything to do with me, I'd rather you let me help you sort it out."

He looked at me sharply. "I'm not sure that's a good idea. At least, not tonight."

"Why not?" I sat down on the foot of the bed, facing him. I hugged the gown to my chest.

"It's like . . ." He searched for words. ". . . like uncovering a whole new side to a period in history you'd believed yourself to be thoroughly familiar with. In scholarship I always found it exciting to have the foundations shaken. But it's — when it's my own foundations, I need to take some time."

"Adrian, please speak to me directly. Why are your foundations shaken?"

"I had misconceptions. But that song . . . and then Chase asking his rude questions, were instrumental to my belated awakening."

"Your belated awakening to what, Adrian?"

"Well, to my own arrogant naivete."

"About *what?*"

My voice had risen. Adrian looked pained as he continued his torturous search for words. "I guess I thought . . . I had no right to think . . . but I assumed, I suppose from the kind of life you led with your father . . . and from something about you . . . something in your demeanor . . . that you had never . . . this is difficult for me."

"You thought I was a virgin." My mouth went dry.

"If you insist on going on with this, please understand me." He passed a hand over his eyes. "I'm not blaming anyone but myself for being so . . . well, obtuse. There's no reason in the world you should have been. A young woman, attractive and full of life . . ." He turned his hands palms up on the chair arms. "It was perfectly normal for you to have all the lovers you liked."

"As long as we're into this, Ben was my only . . . I won't call him lover because I didn't love him —"

"From the evidence of that song, he surely loved you. Doesn't that count as a lover?"

"Please let me finish. Please let's not quibble about words. When I was twenty, before I met you, I had the bad judgment to take Ben MacGruder as a . . . physical partner. It was bad judgment because I didn't love him and he did love me, and after a few months I felt so uncomfortable with the situation that I broke it off. I have never been in love with anyone but you, Adrian."

"Yes, as I recall, you did say — and write that — after we got engaged. But I assumed that to mean —"

"Are you saying that if you had known about Ben, your feelings would have been different?"

"I'm not saying anything, Margaret. Please don't put words into my mouth."

"You assumed it to mean *what*, then?"

"I don't know."

"Would it have made a difference if you had known?"

"I honestly can't say. I don't know what I would have done."

I was stunned.

"What I mean to say is," he stumbled on, "I don't know if I would have risked asking you to marry me."

"Why not?"

"Because," he said in a choked voice, "I only had experience with one woman before you."

"So? I don't understand. Did you love her?"

"We liked each other, but, no, we weren't in love. She was my best friend in Zurich. We were training together at the institute; she was Swedish and recently divorced. We had apartments in the same house. She was kind enough to break in a thirty-five-year-old virgin who had just given up flagellating himself."

"Well, that makes us even, then."

He didn't reply.

"Doesn't it? One each, before we ever met each other. By today's standards, I would say we were both still pretty virginal."

"You don't understand," he said, shaking his head as if to clear it.

"What don't I understand?"

"Look," he said, "I didn't want to go into this tonight. I told you I needed time to take it in. For me there's been a lot to take in lately. This boy Chase, who may be too much for us all. Then my deserting old parent sneaks back into my life posing as a man who's taken a lifelong vow of stability. And we still haven't had *that* little recognition scene yet. And now this new thing."

"But you *knew* Ben, Adrian. He was always hanging around our house. He was there the afternoon we met. I saw you watch him flinging himself around our garden. I'd broken off with him by then, but I assumed you thought of him as a pesky boyfriend —"

"Any ignoramus could have seen he adored you, but you were aloof from him, you seemed annoyed by him —"

"Well, I was! I wanted him to be in outer space. I wanted to concentrate on you. I already knew you were important to me."

"Later your father confided to me that Ben had a crush on you. He laughed about it in a kind way. He said, 'She brushes him off like a puppy, but she doesn't have it in her to be mean.' And I made some comment about Ben being such a virile, attractive young man, and Walter said, 'Yes, but if I know Margaret, the person she chooses will be a very different caliber of man.' It was because of your father that I first dared to think you might some day look at me."

"You and he discussed it?"

"No, no, nothing like that. But he told me things about you that made me feel we'd be very compatible, despite the big difference in our ages. Shortly before he died, he told me he thought you admired me. Something about the way he said it indicated that he wasn't displeased. Your father didn't know about you and Ben, I take it."

"He knew I liked Ben as a friend and that I wished Ben didn't love me. Which is the thing that matters, I think. However, if he had known, I don't believe *he* would have repudiated me."

"I hope you're not implying that I repudiate you, Margaret. I just said there's been a lot for me to take in lately and I need time to assimilate —"

"Well, *you* implied that if you had known about Ben you might not have married me."

"I did not. By God, I did not say that. I said I didn't know if I would have risked asking you to marry me."

"You didn't ask me right out. We sort of tacitly worked up to it."

"I know. And even then I wasn't sure —"

"You weren't *sure?*"

"Please don't finish my sentences for me, Margaret. It's hard enough to formulate them. I told you I needed time to sort it all out. I haven't had time to formulate things properly."

"Sorry I jumped the gun. I should go away and wait it out until you formulate properly how to tell me I have shaken your foundations and undermined our whole history together."

"Margaret, let's both stop right now before one of us says something that can't be unsaid."

I was too far gone to stop. "You've already made one such unforgettable contribution. You said you didn't know what you would have done if you had known."

"All right. Since you're determined to carve my clumsy remark in stone, will you at least allow me some elaboration on it?"

"Go ahead."

"When I said I didn't know what I would have done, what I meant was — now, please let me think this out . . ." He was trembling. "What I meant was, if I had known you'd had experience with a young man with everything in the world to recommend him, a vital, good-looking young man, at the peak of his virility, I might have been more reluctant to . . . well, to risk your making unkind comparisons between us —"

"Good *God*, Adrian —"

"No, please, let me finish. As it was, I never would have dreamed of foisting myself on you as a husband if Ulla hadn't proved to me I was a functioning male."

"How insulting! Me with my secret little

scorecard, adding up the points! I loved you, Adrian, *you!* When you love someone, you want the way that person expresses himself through his body. You aren't keeping track of *performance.*"

He got shakily to his feet. "Well, I'm sure mine left a lot to be desired," he said.

He got a clean pair of pajamas out of his drawer and stood holding them in front of him. If I hadn't been so furious and hurt, I would have found it funny: the two of us hugging our nightclothes to our fully-dressed bodies like shields. I admit I found it slightly ludicrous anyway.

"But, you see," he concluded with a thin smile, "all this time I've congratulated myself that you wouldn't know the difference because I was all you'd ever known."

"Well, I wish you *had* been! But what am I supposed to do about it now? Take the veil? Brand my nether parts with a hot iron? Go off to the desert and slather myself with camel dung?"

"How about something a little less dramatic?" But a smile of appreciation flickered across his strained countenance. Adrian always admired a bit of drama and flamboyance in other people. "How about just being patient with me until I absorb all of this — new history?"

That's enough, don't say any more, a sensible voice inside me warned. But his last plea had set me off again.

"Too bad you threw your little medieval whip into the Zurich lake," I said. "I might have taken up flagellation myself. You could have shown me the drill and then stood by and watched me scourge myself into a penitential frenzy over my besmirched history. Who knows? It might have turned you on."

"I don't think so," he said quietly, after a minute. He took his pajamas and went into the bathroom to undress.

What would happen next? After such an exchange, anything I did would be overweighted with significance: if I took off one more item of clothing, if I turned down the bed in which we had spent a loving afternoon, if I picked up my Daily Office book, if I opened the blinds which I had closed earlier and stood looking out at the night . . .

It seemed most neutral to sit down in the chair he had vacated, put the folded nightgown on my lap, clasp my hands on top of it and wait.

It took a long time, but he came back in his pajamas. He hung up whatever hadn't been left behind in the bathroom hamper. I observed him out of the side of my eye; he appeared to be relying on his peripheral vision as well. Now he was coming over to the chair. He kissed me very lightly on top of my head and reached across me to get a book from the table.

"I'm going to read for a while in the next room," he said.

There were all sorts of things fighting to get out of my mouth: Good night, damn you. Good night, my father's old bed is made up and there aren't any books on it anymore to keep you from sleeping there. Good night, I still love you but I'm mad as a spitfire.

There was still something else I had wanted to tell him, but now was hardly the time.

"Fine," I said, not moving.

The door clicked softly behind him.

I sat on for a while, not raising my eyes. Then I deigned to look at the remaining books on the table. *Ministering to Young Alcoholics* was still there. So was Caroline Walker Bynum's *Jesus as Mother*. The new biography of Aelred, Abbot of Rievaulx was gone.

Back to the monastery.

XVII
Countdown to Armageddon

The term Armageddon was introduced
when the sixth plague bowl was emptied
of its contents (Rev. 16:12–16). This is
the only occurrence of the name in scripture. It means in Hebrew "mountain
[Ar] of Megiddo." Zechariah in a parallel context shows God victorious over
all opposition at the site of Bigath-
meggedon, plain of Megiddo (Zech.
12:10). Megiddo, whether as mountain
or plain, served the prophetic imagination as a place to muster and concentrate
our faith, lest we be indolent in the crisis.
> — Eugene H. Peterson,
> *Reversed Thunder:*
> *The Revelation of John and*
> *the Praying Imagination*

The weather had been so inconstant since my
return from the conference in Mountain City
that it was a main topic of conversation with
everyone — that and the flu epidemic. A week
of freakish warm days had culminated in a
major snowstorm prediction that turned out to
be a fluke: a mere inch fell in High Balsam and

was already melted by morning, disappointing Tony's shoveling plans and Chase's hopes for a school closing. Then came a cold snap, followed by another warming trend, but this time accompanied by high winds that brought down trees and strewed fallen limbs and caused power outages. The Power and Light Company had to take on extra part-time help, giving Mrs. Fletcher's out-of-work son-in-law some extra Christmas income.

The regional newscasters, trying to beat new life into the tired theme of Millennium, quipped about "End-time upheavals" or took the opposite approach, topping the current weather anomalies with old ones from their files. ("On April nineteenth, 1900, folks, a blizzard struck the Smokies *in twenty minutes flat*. Everything was frozen in motion. Seventeen cattle climbed on one another for warmth and froze to death in a solid block.")

Returning home in the wee hours from a hospital emergency, I switched on the radio and caught Whispering Dan dipping into Revelation, accompanied by suitably menacing tremolos on his electric organ, and cobbling together a promise of "cataclysmic happenings right here in our midst . . . good buddies . . . which will wipe out central strongholds of the Unredeemed . . . before the New Year."

On the night of the third Sunday in Advent, Kevin Dowd was taken by ambulance to Bruton Memorial. He asked the triage nurse to phone me from the E.R.: if it wasn't too much trouble, could I bring the sacrament to him? I was already in bed when the call came, but took a strange pleasure in the inconvenience. I had been reading Charles Williams's *The Greater Trumps*, obstinately willing myself to stay awake to see how long Adrian would prolong *his* reading marathon in the next room. This was three days after the kitchen-viewing of *An Evening Gone* and our subsequent . . . what? Quarrel? Misunderstanding? Falling out? Schism?

> She emptied her mind of all thoughts and pictures; she held it empty till the sudden change in it gave her the consciousness of the spreading out of the stronger will within; then she allowed that now unimportant daily mind to bear the image and memory of Nancy into its presence. She did not, in the ordinary sense, "pray for" Nancy; she did not presume to suggest to Omniscience that it would be a thoroughly good thing if It did. She merely held her own thought of Nancy stable in the midst of Omniscience.

I had just finished reading this passage in which Sybil the mystic prays for her bewitched niece, then realized it must be the intercessory prayer passage Marie Baird had praised. Ordinarily my impulse would have been to go and knock on Adrian's door and share it with him. But under the circumstances, my visit might be interpreted as "making up," and I didn't want to make up, not until I had, to appropriate my husband's provoking phrases, "sorted my feelings out" and "formulated things properly."

Then the triage nurse had phoned. I considered going next door to inform Adrian. Then I decided to wait until I was dressed. While I was dressing I recalled the last time I had been called out into the night, the night of our reunion, and how Adrian had poured coins into my pocket and said, as if pronouncing another wedding vow, "Take all my quarters."

What a difference between that night and this. And all because of that stupid song.

It was far deeper than that, of course. As Adrian had said, the song had been only the instrument of his belated awakening. I'd had all the opportunities in the world to tell him about Ben, in all those letters before we married, if I had chosen. And, I had chosen *not*. I had known very well that I was putting an unthreatening self forward and leaving out the equivocal parts. The maddening thing was that I now realized my instinct had been right. If Adrian had been that uncertain about his "performance," he might never have risked offering himself if he had known about seventeen-year-old Ben. My instinct had known what I hadn't. In that sense, I *had* remained virginal. Because, before I was married, it had never crossed my conscious mind that men worried about such things as performance.

Yet my instinct had led me to keep back this ambiguous part of my past for later — perhaps gambling that later would never materialize. If I could just *have* Adrian. But "later" had now arrived, and with what bad timing! Our home was already crowded to bursting with threatening arrivals demanding to be assimilated. Would this one be the one that brought the house down? It seemed so unfair. So out of proportion. I hadn't committed murder; I hadn't even, like certain people, been to jail. This was not Old Testament times, when wives could be put away for adultery. Wait a minute, I hadn't committed adultery! It was so hard to keep my lines clear, even in my thoughts. On the other hand, maybe something *had* been murdered: Adrian's illusion of me as Father Melancholy's perfect maiden-daughter. And how did I feel about that? Didn't I mourn her a little? Had I enjoyed wearing her image, if it brought me Adrian's esteem? Well, if that was all he esteemed about me, too bad. Death to his illusions. Maybe we should have a funeral ceremony and bury her. Erect a nice gravestone. I could chisel it myself until my hands wept blood. MARGARET GOWER BONNER, VIRGIN WIFE OF ADRIAN. REST IN PEACE AND IGNORANCE.

Oh, there was "sorting" and "formulating" to be done on both sides, but in the meantime I intended to cherish my hot coal of umbrage, holding it close to my chest, guarding its heat, even if it was slowly searing a hole in my heart.

At the last minute I took *The Greater Trumps* along with me to Adrian's room. I knocked and he didn't answer for a moment. Then there was a muffled "Come in."

He was lying on my father's bed, propped on pillows and covered with a blanket. His reading glasses were folded on the table beside him, on top of Aelred of Rievaulx. He had clearly been asleep.

"I'm off down the mountain to the hospital. Kevin Dowd's in Emergency."

"What?" He shot up. "Has he been in an accident?"

"No, but the nurse said he's been vomiting black stuff and can't urinate. They brought him in by ambulance."

Adrian held up his wrist and squinted at his watch. "Couldn't it wait until morning?"

"He asked for the sacrament."

"Oh. Well . . ." He was already on his feet. His hair, where it still grew abundantly on the sides, was sticking straight up, a sight I would normally have found irresistible.

To prevent myself from any demonstration of endearment, I shoved *The Greater Trumps* at him. "Where I've turned the page down is that passage about intercessory prayer," I said.

He gazed down, perplexed, at the thing in his hands, as though he'd never laid eyes on a book before.

"That Marie Baird said was in there. The one you were looking for when you were sick, but couldn't find. See you in the morning."

I was down the stairs and out of the house, without looking back.

When I pulled aside his curtain in the E.R., Kevin Dowd began to cry. A tube ascended out of his nose into a plastic container hanging above. The container was about a third full of sludge-colored gunk. From under his hospital gown, pale yellow fluid inched slowly along through a catheter into a clear plastic bag below his bed.

"They're draining me from both ends, Margaret. I'm pretty sure I'm dying, and now I can't even swallow the sacrament . . . as you can see."

"Well, we'll work out something for you, Kevin. And let's hope you're wrong about the dying. What happened?"

"I don't know. I kept wanting to pee all day, and nothing much would come out. I haven't been able to eat, no appetite. Then, about nine o'clock, this evil stuff started spewing out of my mouth . . . just like in *The Exorcist*." He pointed to the plastic container hanging above his head. "They've already taken away three full buckets of it. You should have come earlier. It was just pouring out of this tube in my nose like a geyser. Now it's tapered off some." He seemed disappointed that I'd missed the high point.

A thin white-haired doctor came in, assessed the level of the sludge, nodded respectfully to me and then discreetly dropped the sheet over the exposed urine bag after checking its level.

"Any idea what it is yet, Doctor?" Kevin asked woefully.

"We won't have the blood analysis until morning, but I'm admitting you because of the internal bleeding."

"Will I be going upstairs, then?"

"We're going to make you comfortable right where you are."

"Am I that bad?"

"No, but they've got a full house upstairs tonight. All seventy beds taken."

"But what about — is the ICU full, too?"

The doctor's face lit with a slight surprised smile. "You're hardly *that* bad off," he assured him. "My guess is an ulcer, though it could be that new medication you're taking. The one for your toenail fungus. I've seen violent reactions to it before." On the way out he tweaked Kevin's exposed big toe, which did have a crumbly yellow nail. "However, internal bleeding means we've got to keep you till we're sure."

Driving back up the mountain at two in the morning, I tuned into Whispering Dan to keep myself awake. I had touched a tincted host to Kevin's lips and then swallowed it myself, anointed him with oil, and then kept him company for a while to assuage his hurt pride for not being thought mortally ill. He asked me to read some psalms from the prayer book, which I did, and found solace in doing, while occasional spurts of coffee-colored sludge continued to percolate sluggishly up through his esophagus and out through the tube in his nostril and into the plastic bucket.

Many things had passed through my mind as I read, including the night when I had summoned Adrian to the Intensive Care Unit in Romulus, where my father lay unconscious, never to regain consciousness again. Adrian had come with his Oil Stock and stole, sooner than I thought it humanly possible to get there, and we had agreed Daddy would have wanted the Ancient Western form of Extreme Unction, had he been able to ask for it: the ritual in which all seats of the senses are anointed: the eyes, the ears, the nostrils, the lips, the hands (palms of the hands for lay persons, backs of hands for priests), the feet.

And the following night Adrian had come to the rectory and I handed over a suitcase full of my father's things: a brand-new set of Fruit of the Loom underwear, knee-length black socks, his Johnston & Murphy black wing-tipped shoes, the black trousers from his best suit, a clerical shirt I had ironed myself, and a collar: the old starched kind, not the plastic.

I'd had a moral dilemma about the gold collar stud. Should it be buried with Daddy, or could I keep it?

Then Adrian and I had gone over to the sacristy to select the vestments my father would be buried in, and I had told him about my dilemma.

"This stud was given to him by Father Traherne, the person Daddy considered his spiritual father," I began.

"Yes, I know," Adrian said. "He talked about Father Traherne very often to me."

"But, on the other hand . . ." and then I got rather emotional, telling Adrian how I had taken the stud out of Daddy's collar just after he had fallen. "It was still warm from his neck."

And Adrian had offered his own collar stud. "Your father was my Father Traherne," he said. "I don't have a gold stud, but I'll take the one I'm wearing and when I'm vesting his body at the mortuary, I promise I'll take it from my own warm neck and —"

Then Adrian had broken down. He put his squarish hands over his face and, standing quite straight, sobbed like a child. I stood equally as straight, not two feet away from him, letting my hands hang down at my sides, though I wanted to put them on him.

I had told him I was sure my father had loved him. And could not prevent myself from adding, "And for what it's worth, I want you to know I also love you. For his sake, and also because of what you are."

He held out his hands to me. They were wet.

"Oh, Margaret, what are we going to do without him?" he said.

"I don't know," I said.

Then he put his arms around me and held me, for a quarter of a minute or so, before going over to the mortuary to vest my father. Morticians dress the dead every day, but they prefer to have another priest vest a dead priest. To make sure everything goes on in the right order.

By the middle of Advent, Adrian, though still not up to full strength, had reassumed command out at Fair Haven. The infirmary was full, and four sick girls had been installed in a "flu cottage." Tony, in his element as healthy, indestructible eighty-year-old of sundry skills, traveled back and forth to the school with Adrian. He played blackjack with the kids on the mend in the infirmary and told colorful cautionary tales derived from his and Father Cecil's "prison ministry"; he took apart the pipe under the bathroom sink in the flu cottage to rescue a diamond earring a girl had dropped down the drain; he made flu powder pancakes in the infirmary kitchen. He had repaired the band wheel on Della Jefferson's late mother's old sewing machine, and was running up a Father Christmas outfit for himself, as well as a costume for Chase to wear in Grace's march. "Chase thought up the idea himself," Tony reported to Adrian. "He has quite a sense of humor, that boy. But it's nothing offensive, and doesn't represent anything other than himself." Some girls in Chase's class were going to be part of the liturgical dancing group in the march.

I learned of Tony's doings at the school through Adrian's beguiled reportage, always armored with skepticism. Was Adrian protecting himself from too much enthusiasm? Determined to be a slow forgiver? Nourishing his own little hot coal of umbrage against the orange-haired deserter? Yet, in the days following our "Ben night," as I had come to think of it, our talks about Tony and Chase had become our safest mode of companionship. Adrian would tell about Tony's doings at the school; I would tell about the arrival of Chase's Christmas box from his father and Chase's subsequent little skit for Jennifer, who had dropped by, in which Radford Zorn, flying off to purchase rails from Siberia, scribbles his secretary a check for a thousand dollars and tells her to "go buy whatever you think guys of his age get . . . you know all his hang-ups and his sizes . . . he's been quiet lately, so you can sign it 'Love, Dad.' "

"How did Jennifer react?" Adrian wanted to know.

"The way I expected. She immediately told Chase *she* already had her Christmas present for him, and nobody had copied *her* signature."

"She's very fond of him," said Adrian. He frowned, started to say something else, then censored it. Probably something to do with ways Chase might find to let her down. Then he said, "Sometimes I believe he knows I know. I'm speaking about Tony now."

"What makes you think so?"

"He has this way of sidling his eyes at me when we're together in the car. As if he's waiting for me to speak. Or he'll say things."

"Like what?"

"Well, this morning when we were driving out to the school, he brought up the subject of my being headmaster. He said, 'You have it in you to be a better leader and father than anyone else those kids are likely to meet. Just because your own father was a bad example, you shouldn't sell your own capacities short.' "

I refrained from saying I agreed with Tony. I hadn't forgotten that, on the "Ben night," it had been my saying that Chase was right, that Adrian did fit the image of headmaster, that had caused Adrian to counterattack with, "Was he right about you, too?" Since that night until Adrian himself brought it up now, we had avoided any discussion of his capacity to fill the permanent role of headmaster. I also refrained from taking what, in different circumstances, would have been a perfect opportunity to say more on the subject of fatherhood.

"What did you answer?" was all I asked.

"Well, I was on the brink of ending the suspense then and there. It was on the tip of my tongue to say something that would convey to him in no uncertain terms that I knew who he was. But something stronger held me back. I don't know what it was. Maybe just that I wanted to punish him some more. Here he's waited forty-seven years — now it's my turn to wait. Something that simple, perhaps. So I merely replied that being a bad example had its uses, too, I supposed."

" 'No man is finished as long as he can serve as a bad example to others,' " I quoted Tony, feeling a little sad on his behalf and on behalf of the rest of us. All these things we were withholding from each other to protect ourselves.

"Exactly," Adrian responded with a dry laugh.

After two more parish-related postponements following the one to make space for the tea with Grace, I was finally seated in Vincent Baird's high barber chair, having my hair cut. Vincent let you choose: you could go into a curtained cubicle, or you could sit up front in one of the communal chairs facing the long mirror, tipped to reflect the activity on Main Street below. Ladies (and a few gentlemen, too, Vincent confided) sitting out coloring jobs and permanents tended to prefer the privacy of the cubicle. I had been known to opt for my cut behind the curtain on days when I felt I could not absorb one more human contact, but this afternoon my mood was both sociable and spectatorly. Perhaps it was the influence of the Christmas season.

"This capricious weather," murmured Vincent, combing back my wet hair, then waiting for its archings and curves to decide where they wanted to form. "Marie says it upsets shoppers. A lady came storming into the Peacock this morning and said, 'How can I buy paper napkins with snowmen on them when we're still cooking outside on the grill?' Marie suggested she buy one packet of snowmen and made her a present of a leftover summer

600

packet with ladybugs on them. 'Now you'll be safe either way,' Marie told her. 'Ladybugs can show up any time of year.' " With the tail of the comb he delicately straightened the roadbed of my natural parting and, somewhat in the same manner as a man beginning a trek through the woods, paused to study the terrain that lay below him. "It's been a while," he commented, picking up the scissors.

"I know. This haircut was originally scheduled for two weeks ago. Am I too far gone?"

"Never. Just gives me a little extra to work with. You've got nice thick hair. Ever worn it longer?"

"Not since I took up my present occupation."

"That figures." He picked up a damp swatch and snipped at an angle.

("All this nice hair," Adrian had said, standing behind me in my seminary room. I had never worn it long since that haircut.)

I gazed past myself in the mirror and there was Grace in her trademark red cape down below on Main Street, walking beside a man in a Stetson hat. Paul Pike. "Hah," I said aloud, wondering what it signified. Had she given in, or was he pursuing her? They looked like congenial strollers.

"Chief of police was in this morning," said Vincent, seeing what I was seeing. "He says she's been pestering him ragged about alternate routes to cover all the weather possibilities. If it's snowing even lightly, she wants the trucks carrying the sound equipment to be allowed to detour through Laurel Ridge Estates so they won't get stuck on that steep grade from Great Thunder Falls into the village. And if it's raining, she wants permission for them to have their rally inside the armory, which they can't because there's that antique car show booked. He told me he was praying for decent weather and no animosities. He's had it up to here, he said, with anonymous phone threats since Judge Tim agreed to have the barracks burning trial after the New Year."

How refreshing to hear it called simply "the New Year," after all the hoo-ha surrounding Millennium.

"It's asking for trouble to schedule anything outdoors for this time of year," I said.

The interesting duo had strolled outside the mirror's range. Only then did it occur to me that Paul Pike, who had called me on the day this haircut was first postponed, had never followed up on his interview. The promised faxed questions had never arrived. And that was two weeks ago.

"She's probably wishing Jesus celebrated His birthday in the summer," commented Vincent, taking another strategic snip. "Does anybody know for sure when He *was* born?"

"No," I said, knowing he could handle it.

"There must have been *some* reason for December twenty-fifth, though."

"There was. The Church of Rome had to come up with something to keep all the Christians from running off to the pagan feast of the sun god on December twenty-fifth."

"Now that makes sense." His snipping took on a confident, intuitive rhythm. "Now isn't that interesting. Of course, none of it makes a hoot of difference to the real stuff, does it?"

"No," I said.

After Vincent's, I went along to the Balsam Bookworm. There was a browsing cove in back, hidden by a high shelf from the rest of the store, where chairs had been placed on either side of a reading table. From the Religion section, whose space had tripled during the six years we had lived here (Meaning what? End-time nerves had reached High Balsam? The fulfillment of André Malraux's prophecy that the twenty-first century would be a religious century or it wouldn't be at all?), I took down a handsome volume I had been appraising earlier, a collection of essays about holy women, with high-quality color plates lavished throughout the text, and squirreled it off to the browsing cove. The author, the prioress of a double monastery in Oxfordshire, had scrupulously documented her material, which her modest, workmanlike style honored — though, as I turned the pages, I found myself wishing for the sort of emotional details the stories of these women — except for St. Teresa, who had provided her own — always left out. In the chapter on St. Hilda of Whitby, I read, "No one knows why, at thirty-three, Hilda renounced her home and all she possessed and began monastic training, under Aidan's guidance, in Northumbria. Since Bede never referred to Hilda as a virgin, as he did Etheldreda and Aelffled, some historians have suggested she may have been married, or widowed."

These straightforward and unremarkable sentences ignited old creative aspirations in me. My research on Hilda, gathered during a medieval honors project in college, had been seized on by Madelyn, who saw in the scant evidence of the seventh-century abbess's life a heroine worthy of her "hot wand," as she liked to call her art. But she died before she could finish transforming it into an evening-length theater piece. Her notes and stage directions for "Abbess of Motherwit" were in my possession still. Myself and Madelyn as collaborators: that would be a strange match. Yet it had a turn-about symmetry. She had taken my unwitting father's lessons in liturgy and "collaged" them into iconoclastic theater pieces debunking the religion behind this liturgy. Why shouldn't I add my own inspiration to her unfinished portrait of this tough, wise Anglo-Saxon woman and combine all our efforts into a spirited piece of liturgical theater for use in our church?

I was already at work, fleshing Hilda's intriguing unknowns into possibilities for a dramatic rendering — had Hilda, that other "nonvirgin," ever been pregnant? Had she ever brought a child to term? What had happened to her husband, if she had one, and what had he been like? How had her passion for God evolved? — when a redness suddenly bulked large at the edge of my creative fugue.

I looked up and there was Grace in her cape.

"You were reading." Pronounced much in the same way she had accused me of praying the morning she stood over me at the Horseshoe Diner.

"Hello, Grace."

"Mind if I sit down for a minute?"

No longer pretending to be friendlier than I felt — it washed right off Grace — I simply dipped my head toward the other chair. What tack would she take today? And what had she done with her Stetson-hatted companion?

"I heard Father Dowd is in the hospital," she began.

"Yes," I said.

"Do you know what's wrong with him?"

"When I talked to him last, he said they think it was a reaction to a medication."

"Do you know when he'll be out?"

"No, but you could call him at the hospital. He has a phone in his room."

"Oh, then he's well enough to talk?"

"Apparently so. I spoke to him this morning. He's still weak, he says. He lost a lot of blood and had to have transfusions."

"I suppose that means he won't be out in time for the Birthday March."

"I really don't know, Grace. Why don't you call him yourself? It's early in the week. He may be feeling fine by Saturday."

"I doubt that," she said, with a look that clearly implicated me in his defection. There went her Episcopalian contingent.

"I saw you with Paul Pike." I decided to counterattack. "Will he be joining the march?"

"I expect he'll want to cover it," said Grace. No reference to last time, when she had called him a nuisance.

"I know you said something about not wanting to be misinterpreted by journalists," I reminded her.

"Oh, I'm not worried about that so much anymore," she replied airily. "Mr. Pike isn't like some I've met. He listens intelligently and doesn't put words into your mouth. We could use the coverage. Reverend Bonner, will you not reconsider? What would it cost you and a few of your congregation to join us on Saturday and be a part of this community and raise your voice along with the rest of us and allow the Spirit to come over you? I know you have that Food Pantry commitment, but you and I both know you could manage it if you wanted."

"We already *are* a part of this community, Grace. As for raised voices, I'm not sure we wouldn't do better with fewer of them. The Spirit we need isn't going to get whipped into existence by a rally, but it may just make itself heard if we stay very quiet and direct our hearing toward it. I've explained to you at least twice already how I feel about your manifesto and about your march. The age of conquering through the sheer force of evangelism, through the amassing of *quotas,* is over."

"That is a matter of opinion," bristled Grace.

"Well, fine. I'm conveying my opinion, then. I'm not against marches or parades or ceremonies, but I don't believe this march, however many or few come out on Saturday, is going to heal or change anything, or serve any need. I'm beginning to wonder whether it hasn't got more to do with your own needs."

Grace blushed violently. I saw conflicting emotions battling for voice on her haughty countenance. What would come out? A retaliatory tirade like the one in the Horseshoe Diner against "lukewarm elites" like myself? Or was there still a remaining stratagem at the bottom of her bag to rope me into the march?

"Well," she said at last, squaring her broad shoulders and rising, "I'll leave you to your book." Her voice, surprisingly low and gentle, was anticlimactic to what had gone before. Looming above me once more in the red cape, she inquired, as if in polite afterthought, "What are you reading?"

I closed the book and pushed it across to her.

"*Holy Passion*," she read aloud, "*The Feminine Journey to God.*"

When pronounced with such obdurate flatness, the title sounded quixotic. She bestowed one hand lightly on the book's cover but seemed only to be contemplating her pale skin and flawlessly enameled nails against its dark background. Then, without further comment, she gave me a pitying look and left me to myself in the browsing cove.

But her oppressive spirit remained behind, and after a minute I picked up the book and left. As I stood chatting with the young woman at the register while we waited for my card to clear, I saw Grace Munger walking away from the store with Paul Pike.

I had a funeral mass scheduled for two that afternoon. I stopped by the church to check out Lucinda's preparations, which I would have been loath to do if she hadn't confided in me about her memory lapses. She had taken my advice and made appointments for medical tests in Mountain City for the week after Christmas. We planned to drive down together, and afterward shop for fabric for a new Easter altar frontal.

At home, I found Adrian in my study, writing something on a pad.

"Oh, I was just leaving you a note."

He seemed so flustered by my appearance that I jokingly asked if he'd rather I stepped outside till he finished.

"No, no, of course not. I was just — Tony and I were heading out to the school, and I wanted to let you know where we were."

"Please remember what Charles said. Just because your two weeks are up doesn't mean you can't have a relapse."

"Point taken. But it's nice to be back in the swing of things, in moderation. I see you've been to the bookstore."

"I bought a present for myself." I took *Holy Passion* out of the bag and handed it over.

He hefted it admiringly. "I'd like to read this myself. Who's going to assist you at the funeral?"

"Van was going to, but he says he's coughing too much to be of use. He's still coming, though, because he knew her."

"So you'll be alone?"

"Oh, I can manage fine. It's not going to be much of a crowd. She was very old, all her contemporaries are gone, except for Addie

Rogers. And so many people are down with colds or flu."

"Well. Tony's out in the car waiting. See you at supper. I've made chili."

"You *are* feeling better, aren't you?"

"Yes, I — things are falling into place." He started to say something else, then kissed me lightly on the forehead and left.

I looked down at the notepad on my desk.

"Wednesday, 1:10 P.M.," he had written. "My dearest Margaret, I —"

Not his customary salutation for a note scribbled to apprise me of his movements. What else had he been about to write?

I went over to the church early, to allow myself some quiet time in the chancel before the hearse arrived and I went out to meet the body.

Dorcas Yates had been born in 1901, arrived here from Pennsylvania as a young teacher, never married. Her only surviving contemporary in the parish was Addie Rogers. Van had been in her eighth-grade class. In her late sixties she had retired and moved to Florida for her health.

Lucinda had replaced the rose-colored Gaudete Sunday frontal with the violet one we would be using until Christmas. Everything was precisely as it should be. The vessels for the Eucharist were in their proper places, my vestments pressed and laid out for me to put on.

I had never known anyone named Dorcas. Had it been a popular name for girls at the turn of the century, or had her parents specifically intended to name their child after the woman of good works in Jaffa whom the apostle Peter is supposed to have raised from the dead? She had prepaid all her funeral and burial expenses and left detailed instructions with a Daytona Beach undertaker. Send the embalmed body to High Balsam, which she considered home. Simple, straightforward Burial Rite One with Eucharist. No eulogies or hymns. Interment in the local cemetery, flat stone with name and birth and death years only. DORCAS YATES 1901–1999; plot long ago purchased. The only touch of personal vanity, if it could be called that, was her stipulation that each mourner be given a sprig of rosemary for remembrance, an old Anglican custom dating back to the seventeenth century. Van said she'd read Grail stories to them in the eighth grade and brought them homemade fudge ("a little too soft, but nobody minded"). She had taught them the rudiments of some mysterious game with letters instead of numbers, and then one day she said, "Boys and girls, it may interest you to know that you have been doing algebra for quite some time now."

She had worshiped in All Saints High Balsam before it had pews. The church she had looked back on as her home parish, all those retired years down in Florida, would have been the shorter building, before Gus's grandfather extended the sanctuary in the mid-sixties and made the crypt into a downstairs parish hall. But she would have known these same plaster walls and leaded windows, the prided timber-trussed ceiling of the nave, the sanctuary paneling from local chestnut trees, and, after the chestnut ran out, the wormy chestnut they (" 'made do with,' ha ha") in the narthex under the bell tower. (Van's cough would not stop him from tolling the bell today.) A schoolteacher who read Grail stories to her class would have loved and taken pride in her church's English-derived features and treasures: the Crucifixion rood screen, the carved lectern with its student-of-William-Morris's grapevine and pelican motif. Even if her fudge was too soft, she would have done her bit for her parish family at potluck suppers and coffee hours.

Though I had never laid eyes on the lady, I found I could hold her presence in my mind. Perhaps the fact that I had not known her made it easier. There weren't all those loose ends and rough edges and projections a personal acquaintance carries with it. It was her essence I held, the completed destiny of a woman named Dorcas Yates who had made her journey through the century that held her, and who had left behind some memories of her usefulness and dedication.

A side-gift of my contemplation of Dorcas Yates was that it brought the essences of others into clarity. I could receive them, as they presented themselves, in the same tranquil spirit I was able to receive hers. Though I did know them, did, in fact, live with three of them, I could observe them from a distance, yet not feel distant from them. It was just that they weren't acting on me now. They were simply present with me in this moment of consideration, holding themselves up for perusal: Grace marching inexorably toward her march; Chase safely contained, for a couple more hours, at the public high school; Tony and Adrian driving out to Fair Haven, each waiting for the other to break the big silence; Margaret collecting herself in the chancel before a funeral. Yes, I could peruse myself as one of them, too.

And, with the ones closest to me, I was able to feel what propelled them. I could close my eyes and, as it were, run my fingers along the essential contours of their being.

The volatile boy, seething with intelligence and mistrust, testing to the limit anyone who dared to love him.

The wily old scapegrace with energy and charm to burn, looking for a place to alight in old age where he might share his sagas of pluck and misadventure, show off the skills acquired through his checkered career, and garner all the love and respect he'd be the first to tell you he hadn't earned.

And his abandoned son the self-doubter, dogged pursuer of the trustworthy and true, seeker of "purple fish" profundities, self-taught orphan and unsure husband — galvanized out of his coping trance by an overload of revelations.

And the woman who went after that essential seeking soul in him and married herself to him and all his difficulties: the ones glimpsed and the ones to be revealed later.

Lord, grant us passage through these and all our other transitions, teach us to befriend our own strange and unsightly edges so that we may better befriend others, and keep us alive in imagination and courage of heart, "that we may so pass through things temporal that we lose not the things eternal."

And now let us welcome home your servant, Dorcas, and give thanks for all the ways, remembered and forgotten, she made her century a better place.

When I returned to the sacristy to vest, the outside door suddenly opened and there was Adrian.

"Oh," I said, "I thought you'd already left." Yet there was a fitting inevitability about his suddenly being here, when I had just been so close to him in contemplation.

"No, we're still here," he said. "I've come to assist the priest with the funeral mass." He was carrying his alb over his arm.

614

"Well, thank you," I said. "Even though she could have managed alone."

"Don't I know that. But she's not alone."

After the funeral, the eccentric weather performed another pirouette. As our modest little convoy of hearse and cars — and Gus's truck, in which I was riding — departed for the cemetery, a dusting of snow began to drift down through mixed sunshine and cloud. In the uncommon sunlight, the flakes took on the substantial look of tiny pieces of bread being flung down randomly from the sky, and I told Gus about Grace's retort to Sandi, when the waitress had asked what she would do if it rained or snowed on the day of the march. If the Lord could drop down manna on His disobedient people, why should it be a problem for Him to provide appropriate weather for a birthday march in His son's honor?

"But how can she be so sure what God's idea of 'appropriate' is for this occasion?" was Gus's arch reply.

It was good to be with Gus again, we hadn't had any time together since our dramatic walk through her woods on the morning of her wedding. "I was surprised when you showed up today," I said. "Did you know Dorcas Yates well?"

"Well enough to feel guilty as sin. She was a dear old thing, but completely out of touch.

615

Or at least, when we were heartless twelve-year-olds, we thought she was. She had retired from teaching and for two awful months she substituted for our Girl Scout leader, who'd had a baby. Poor Miss Yates. We were such little beasts, and I'm afraid I was the ringleader." Here her laughter bubbled up and splashed all over her contriteness.

"All right, you might as well tell me."

"She had some antiquated concept of what a Girl Scout meeting should be like. The first week, we made bookmarks while she read us a story about King Arthur and his Round Table. Then we had brownies and milk. The next week we learned to tie knots out of the Scout handbook; she tied them with us, and messed up hers. Then we had brownies and milk. One week she brought a lot of old magazines and we were supposed to cut out pictures and assemble 'paste-ups' of our aspirations. That was by far her most successful venture, actually. Followed by brownies and milk, of course. Our troop met down in the church crypt, which Grandpop had by then remodeled, and our regular leader always put us through a rigorous warm-up of miming and jumping exercises, designed, I now realize, to burn off some of our ferocious afterschool energies so she could deal with us.

"Well, about this time, my cousin Smathers, who's just got his driver's license, comes to visit from Mountain City, and I'm

616

telling him about our deadly Scout meetings, and we devise a plan to liven things up. The next meeting, I say, 'Miss Yates, please will you teach us to make delicious brownies like yours?' Poor thing was so pleased, and grateful, too, because she was probably running out of ideas of what to do with us. So the next meeting we brought all the supplies, including a little package of hashish shavings, which Smathers and I had run through the carrot grater at my house, and we made the brownies in the crypt kitchen. We found some way to distract her so we could mix the shavings in with the batter, and then she read us a King Arthur story while we waited for them to bake. And then, well, we all ate them, and a few girls got spacey or downright silly, but Miss Yates sort of went crazy. First she got really giggly, then she broke down and started crying, and then she got angry and snarled at us like a witch and called us little fiends and made us put on our coats and go outside. Then she locked us out of the crypt. By the time our mothers came to get us, we were all milling around in the cold, feeling sorry for ourselves. One girl's mother knocked and knocked at the crypt door, but Miss Yates wouldn't open for her. We all were made to write her notes of apology, but that was the end of her Girl Scouting. She sent us each an identical note of apology back, saying her capacities weren't what they once were, and she would always remember our earlier, happier meetings and hoped we would all fulfill our aspiration paste-ups. Oh God, Margaret, I laugh, but I still feel guilty about it."

"Do you remember what your aspiration paste-up was like?"

"Oh, some houses and buildings — I was already going around boasting that I was going to be an architect like Grandpop — and then I'd also cut out this couple in a romantic illustration and pasted them in the bottom corner as an afterthought. Architecture first, love afterward, I guess was what I had in mind. So, Miss Yates, I *have* fulfilled my aspiration paste-up. Too bad I can't tell you."

"Why don't you tell her, anyway. When I'm sprinkling the sod on her coffin."

"I'll do just that. I've missed you, Margaret."

"Same here. These weeks have been something else, with Advent and our expanded household."

"Speaking of that, Jenn tells me old Tony is like a member of the family. Is that right?"

"That's right."

"Have breakfast with me tomorrow morning at the Horseshoe."

"I'd be delighted. What time?"

"Is seven too early?"

"Seven's fine."

Gus was already waiting in her truck when

I pulled into the diner parking lot next morning. The sun was just rising through the mist, and the freakish warm days had at last conceded to the seasonable winter bite; the lady who'd bought the snowman napkins from Marie was one day nearer to using them.

"Hey, I've had a more adventurous idea. Can you spare an extra hour, Margaret?"

"It just so happens I'm free all morning."

"Then let's get take-out breakfasts and you follow me in your car to my site and I'll show you the house we're building before the workmen get there. We can picnic in the living room, which doesn't have an outside wall yet, and then I'll take you to a very special waterfall I know."

We did just that. Sat on the edge of a living room perched in the tops of trees that still had clouds in them and dangled our legs over the side into empty space. We sipped steaming coffee from Gus's thermos and ate ham and biscuit sandwiches — I had a well-done fried egg inside mine as well.

"A room always looks so much better before the outside wall goes up," Gus mused sadly. "Not to mention the furniture people deface it with."

"What kind of furniture will these people deface it up with, do you think?"

"Oh, whatever *Architectural Digest* is pushing in the next few months. He's made gobs of money in Mountain City real estate and recently purchased himself a flighty young wife. God knows what she'll find to do up here. You can only make decorating your country house last so long. Smathers conned me into this job. They're acquaintances of his."

"How did he con you into it?"

"I said, 'The last thing this mountain needs is another 'millionaire's hideaway' glinting down from its bald space of slaughtered trees.' 'True,' he says, 'but they've purchased the acreage that abuts on Great Silence Falls.' 'Then you should be asking me to shoot them instead of building their monstrous house,' I said. 'You know how I feel about Great Silence Falls.' 'If you build it, it won't be monstrous and you can save lots of trees,' he says. 'And you can have free rein with your taste, because they want to be seen as people of taste and they have none.' That more or less did it."

"I never heard of Great Silence Falls. What an evocative name. Like someone announcing a solemn moment: 'Great silence falls.' "

"It was Grandpop's name. To contrast with Great Thunder Falls. You'll see why when we go up there. Its map name is Saligugi Falls. The locals call it Cooter Falls. Saligugi is Cherokee for water turtle. Cooter is hillbilly for turtle."

I stopped swinging my feet because I suddenly felt dizzy. I edged backward away from the overhang until I could bury my head between my knees.

"What is it?" came Gus's concerned voice through my unhappy turbulence.

"I think I have to throw up." I tried to get to my feet.

"No, no, just do it here. Hang your head over the side. I'll hold you."

"I hate to —"

"Don't worry, I've got you." She grabbed me firmly around the waist from behind. I leaned forward and spewed my breakfast down into the cloud-festooned treetops.

Afterward, she quietly waited for me to put myself to rights with the leftover paper napkins.

"How are you feeling now?"

"Totally fine. I shouldn't have ordered that fried egg. I should have been sensible like you and just had the ham."

"Do you still feel like going to the falls? It's only about a quarter mile, but it's rocky and straight-up steep. Should we leave it for another day?"

"No, I'm perfectly fine now. I really and truly am, Gus."

Any other woman friend would have been unable to resist a voiced innuendo, or at the very least a significant glance, but Gus was gallant, unintrusive Gus, and her warm sidelong squeeze of my shoulders, followed by her characteristic reticence, was communication enough.

She was right. The ascent was sufficiently rough and vertical to make both of us huff and puff and stop frequently to hear our hearts thudding. We held hands to balance each other, and kept our focus in the service of our feet, cautiously picking their way around rocks and mud puddles.

"You can't even get up here in the wet months," Gus said. "The only ones who use this path then *are* the water turtles."

We heard the water before we saw it. Less of a roar than the sound of someone running a bath at full force. Presently the volume increased and we came in sight of the falls, modest by the standards of the "stars," like Elk or Looking Glass or Whitewater. Gus led us around a recessed ledge behind the falling waters, and, lo and behold, behind that was a shallow cave where you could sit in dryness and hear an altogether different sound.

"It's like listening to the way the waterfall hears itself," I said. "The way we hear the sound of our voices from inside our skulls."

"I knew you'd appreciate it. Don't you know the Cherokees found something wonderful to do in here? Of course, only two or three of them could comfortably fit in at one time, but Grandpop said he liked to think of couples courting, or pledging their love, or old people climbing in here to crouch and meditate about death. Only thing is, it's cold. The sun doesn't come in till much later, this time of year. You tell me when you've had enough."

"Not yet."

"Watching you and Adrian bowing to each other up at the altar during communion yesterday was so strange."

"In what way?"

"Well, it was very moving. It was like some graceful little ceremony of mutual regard."

"We were trained by the same Eucharistic teacher at General Seminary. He told us we should always comport ourselves at the altar like creatures showing good manners before their creator."

"No, but the way you bowed to *each other*. Every time he handed you something, or you handed something back to him. I know that was part of the Church ritual, too, but I was lying awake last night thinking about it in a different way. I was thinking, maybe couples ought to have little rituals like that, where they bow to each other. Maybe once at the beginning of the day and once at the end. Maybe at other times, too. As a way of acknowledging to each other — oh, I don't know, that there really is a sacred aspect of what they're trying to do with each other."

I'll take that home to Adrian, I thought:

he'll like it as much as I do. I thought: perhaps we've both exhausted our stockpiles of umbrage over that wretched music video and can bend from the waist and get on with what we are trying to do with each other.

Will today be the day I find the right time and the right words to tell him what partly belongs to him anyway?

But no, the rest of that day had a different agenda in mind for us.

Adrian was waiting for me when I got home.

"I thought you two were leaving for school right after breakfast," I said.

"I sent Tony on ahead to pay his cheer-up calls. Maybe if I could ask you to run me out later in your car."

"Is anything wrong?"

He had a combative look, but it was not directed at me. "You were wondering yesterday why Paul Pike never followed up on his questions to you. Well, your answer is in today's edition of the *Mountain City Times*. He had all the ammunition he needed and didn't want to have to water it down with mitigating truths."

"Oh, dear."

"Tony and I *had* started out to the school. Then we stopped to pick up the paper and I made him bring me back. Your phone has been ringing nonstop."

"Where's the paper?"

"In the kitchen."

"Good. I need something to eat."

"I thought you were having breakfast with Gus."

"I did, but — well, I need a little something else. We went on a hike to a waterfall."

He followed me into the kitchen. The phone in my study, which was also the church line, rang three times, then someone — it sounded like Van's laconic style — left a brief message and hung up.

The Mountain City paper, which High Balsam people referred to simply as "the *Times*," lay folded on the table, showing the bottom half of the front page, which, along with a large square of red that turned out to be an unflattering photo of Grace with her arms outspread, shot from below, which gave her a double chin, was completely taken up with part one of Paul Pike's series, "Countdown to Armageddon in a Paradigm Town."

Today's offering bore the headline "Polarized Heights: Raised Voices versus 'Movers and Shakers' in High Balsam's Worship Community." Below Grace's picture, which made her look like a haranguing hysteric, the caption read: *Prophetess of the Peaks, Grace Munger. "If we all come out and raise our voices on Saturday, the Lord has promised me something will change."*

"Perfidious creep," Adrian said, pacing up

and down while I skimmed the piece.

After the predictable opening ("This is the Southern Highlands town famous for its hospitality where a poor man killed a rich man last summer over a condescending tone of voice . . .") came the (also predictable) gory replay of the Main Street shooting, followed by the reminder that the poor man, now convicted and in prison, had worked for the security company that guarded the rich man's estate. Then came a restatement of the theme: the plummeting of fortunes for the have-nots (Mrs. Fletcher's napkin-folding son-in-law's "End of the century, end of Century Oil for me" was quoted) contrasted with the fortified silences of those lucky enough to have achieved safe living in troubled times, and what would be the outcome of this widening chasm in a "city on a hill that cannot be hid"? This led to Grace's impending march in High Balsam, and how God had promised her "change" in return for her mobilization of the worshiping community. This was followed by an overview of Saturday's march highlights and a list of participating groups. " 'I am still praying that every congregation on this mountain will join us in raising our voices in praise,' says Miss Munger, 'though there are a few holdouts, such as the rector of All Saints High Balsam, who assures me the days of evangelism and public demonstrations are past and we'd do better to stay quietly at home and be changed from within.' "

"Damn it, Grace, I did *not* say quietly at home. I said *quiet*. Or maybe he changed it."

"A nice scurrile collaboration, it looks to me," muttered Adrian, still pacing.

Up until now I had been standing, still intent on getting something in my stomach before I confronted this thing in earnest, but here I sat down.

In person, the Reverend Margaret Bonner, a slight, unimposing thirty-something woman who goes about town in jeans or schoolgirlish skirt-and-sweater combos, seems an odd choice for the rector of the elite Old Guard congregation of All Saints High Balsam Episcopal Church (nicknamed "All Saints High Horse" by many locals). "I guess you'd have to say we do have our share of people of consequence," admitted a shop owner, himself a member of All Saints, who asked to remain unidentified. One such prominent parishioner in the news lately is Judge Timothy Stancil, who replies in cryptic monosyllables, or retreats behind his prep school Latin, when queried about the upcoming Jasper firebombing trial of the security guards, which has been transferred from Judge Henry Molton's court to Judge Stancil's.

(An old UNC buddy of Stancil's, Judge Molton took the heat off Stancil last September by hosting the shooting trial of the High Balsam Security guard in *his* court.)

Approached by phone for an interview to talk about the nexus of social, economic, and religious issues coming to a head in her community, the Reverend Margaret Bonner responded with similar Olympian chill, though without resorting to dead languages, merely to slang. This reporter was required to submit his questions pending a "possible" interview. When asked whether All Saints had a facsimile machine, the Reverend Bonner's reply was, "Are you kidding? With all us movers and shakers over here?"

I slammed the paper down. "I'm going to fortify myself with coffee and toast before I read the rest of this malicious garbage."

"You would never have said anything like that," said Adrian.

"Oh, but that's exactly what I did say. The problem is, Mr. Pike left out what he said first."

"I'd like to flatten *him* through a fax machine," said Adrian.

"And there I was, feeling I'd made a fashion statement with my paisley skirt and chenille tunic when I went over to the inn to have tea." I surprised myself by bursting into genuine laughter.

"You're pretty amazing to be able to laugh about it."

"No, I'm just a little light-headed, is all. Wait until I eat something, and then I'll be good and offended."

Which I was. After I did read through the whole of "Polarized Heights: Raised Voices versus 'Movers and Shakers,' " I figured out what Grace must have been doing when she tracked me down in the browsing cove yesterday. She had been giving me one last chance to relent before she threw me to Pike.

The piece went on to quote Grace's account of her father's evangelistic triumphs in High Balsam before his untimely end. Dad saying the word, banjos, organs, tents, and food raining from the skies — but no rain, ever; hundreds of souls converging from far and near to fall on their knees and be converted and reavowed ... and Dad's daughter getting to write the numbers on the board. And Grace coming through her trial by fire, in which her parents perished, Grace marked as God's own, and sent back by Him to the scene of her childhood to organize this Endtime March. "Despite what my friend the Reverend Bonner believes, Our Lord Himself said faith can move mountains. . . ."

Then the projective sops: how, in these last

two weeks of the old millennium, or (Pike playing it safe) in the weeks just *after* the year 2000, when the trial of the security guards got under way, would the nexus of social, economic, and religious issues come to a head in our paradigm town? Would there be riots, class war, burnings, and lootings? Would Grace Munger's God honor His debt to her and bring change? And if so, what *kind* of change? "As Tacitus would say: '*Deos fortioribus adesse.*' Which, for the benefit of those without prep school Latin, translates: 'The Gods are on the side of the stronger.'

"But who, in this community under surveillance, will turn out to be the stronger?"

Part Two of Paul Pike's "Countdown to Armageddon" was promised for next week.

I drove Adrian out to the school.

"What are your plans for the rest of the day?" he asked.

"Well, instead of writing some Christmas cards, I guess I'll answer my phone messages and write a letter to the *Times*. And call the bishop before he calls me — if he hasn't left a message already. Oh, and this afternoon, I have a meeting with Dick Miller about our joint End-time Evensong service. Liturgical life goes on — fortunately — despite the slings and arrows of the day-to-day."

"What will you say in your letter?"

"I'll clear up the context of the 'movers and

shakers' quote, and say I am still waiting for Mr. Pike's promised list of questions if he hasn't already decided on his own what the answers are. It'll be brief. I expect there'll be other mail postmarked High Balsam from our epistolary 'people of consequence.' Poor Buddy Freedgood, what an asinine quote to have to live down. I also, surprisingly, feel sorry for Grace. What a horrible picture."

"She comes across as a bit of a madwoman."

"The sad thing is, she predicted it herself, before she succumbed. She said he'd make us all look small so he could look down on the whole thing and feel superior. I wonder if my recalcitrance had anything to do with driving her into the Pike's maw. But you have to admit she makes good copy, I don't blame him for wooing her first. Much more colorful than the slight, unimposing reverend with her Olympian chill."

Adrian's arm suddenly went around me.

"But it will certainly focus attention on Saturday's march," I said. "Maybe that's enough compensation for her. She can offer it up to the Lord."

XVIII

Armageddon

On Thursday they were predicting light snow beginning on Friday. But clearing up by Saturday morning.

But Friday, the day before Grace's march, was cold, blue-skied, and sunny. The light snow forecast had been moved forward to midday Saturday.

Then it was changed to "sometime Saturday morning" and upped to four to six inches.

Driving around Paul Pike's "city set on a hill," attending to parish business, I would catch myself listening to the radio's shifting weather reports as if I were Grace. She must be going crazy, I would think. Then I'd think: no, maybe not; maybe God is assuring her right this moment that He has every intention of providing appropriate weather for her march. But then, as Gus would say, how could she be so sure she and God had the same definition of what the appropriate weather would be?

I know this sounds strange, but I felt close to Grace in these countdown hours before the march. I don't mean I liked her any better, but that I kept thinking about her. I wondered what her reaction to part one of "Countdown to Armageddon" had been. Had she felt betrayed or misrepresented, or was she pleased to have the publicity? Did she have anyone she could discuss it with? Had she recoiled at the first sight of her haranguing image? Did she feel any shame about her remarks concerning me, or was she able to say with St. Paul, and finally stick to it this time, "From such withdraw thyself."

Despite the trouble she had caused me, I felt — I don't know: that she was a riddle sent to me to solve?

Heading out to see Professor Mallory in his rented farmhouse after he had broken his leg during one of his Guyot-tracking mountain expeditions — he would have frozen to death if the ranger had not forced him to carry a modular phone — I passed Grace in her dark gray sedan, headed in the opposite direction. She appeared extremely intent on something; perhaps she, too, was listening to the weather report? Her jaw seemed uptilted a few more degrees than usual. A reaction to the picture with the double chin? Just as I had reacted to Paul Pike's unflattering fashion assessment by wearing my clericals more than usual after the article appeared?

Parishioners and friends had, of course, left their cards of outrage and condolence on my answering machine. I called everyone back. The bishop had *not* called, but when I dutifully called him to qualify my wretched "movers and shakers" retort, he good-naturedly responded with a story of how a casual irony of his own, made to a friend at a diocesan convention years ago, had been overheard by an unctuous delegate, reported to others as his literal statement, and caused him several months of discomfort. Nevertheless I noticed that he did not discourage me from writing the editor of the *Mountain City Times* and setting the record straight in print.

Judge Tim Stancil was writing his own letter, to set the record straight about his "retreating behind Latin quotes," which had nothing at all to do with prep school, but were ("at least, I had assumed they were") familiar to any newspaperman conversant with the law of the land. He was going to suggest Mr. Pike invest in a *Black's Law Dictionary*. He also would remind those who might have been confused by Mr. Pike's article that judges did not decide among themselves in some buddy-buddy back room to "host" one another's trials: attorneys for the defense and the prosecution had to *request* a change of venue. The judge of the court could then say yes or no.

"I had it in my Daily Reminder book to call you and ask who this person was before I granted him an interview," I told Tim. "Then Advent got busier, and I thought, 'Oh well,

I'll wait till the faxed questions come, and then I'll call Tim.' Big mistake."

"I wouldn't fret too much over it, Margaret. All I'd have been able to tell you was he rubbed me the wrong way in our single conversation and I didn't tell him a damn thing more than I would have told the devil. He is a small-time devil, in his way, a provocateur straining to make something happen that will coincide with the Big Two-oh-oh-oh. Then if by chance something sensational *does* transpire in the next few weeks, he can pull out his little fly-spotted set of clippings and say: 'Looky here, everybody, I saw it coming.' Meanwhile, you and I have to get on with quotidian business, if you'll pardon the Latin derivative."

On Friday evening's six o'clock weather report, a full-blown snowstorm was predicted for the next day. Our household of four was gathered for supper in the kitchen. Stew, bread, and a salad that Chase had taken such pains to build on a platter that everyone was a little shy about disassembling it.

"Well, that's that," said Adrian, punching the Off button on the TV with an air of satisfaction. "Now everybody can stay quietly at home tomorrow and be changed from within." He sent me a comradely look as he quoted my sentiments as reported by Grace to Paul Pike. He laid a hand gingerly on my forearm, then quickly removed it, as though I might snatch away my arm if he didn't.

Since the morning of the article, he had alternated between watching me as one keeps an eye on someone who's been dealt a blow to the head, and making short, awkward courting overtures. The courting part was a little unsettling. It was the way he might have acted when we first met, if he had known he wanted me, and hadn't had much experience with women. Which he hadn't. But of course, he hadn't known he wanted me then, and so he could conduct himself unselfconsciously in my presence and stay in his attractive bubble of remoteness.

And now, here we were, six years married, the incomplete man making his first clumsy, adolescent attempts to woo the nonmaiden. It was certainly food for thought.

"But she said probably not until midmorning," protested Chase.

"She, who?" Adrian asked.

"The *weather* girl. Cindy Lou Fowler. On the TV you just turned off."

"Oh, the weather. I thought we'd finished with that."

"Besides. What happened to the last 'major snowstorm' they were predicting? One measly inch."

"True," said Tony, "I didn't even get to use the new shovel."

"And even if it *is* going to be one, she said

not until mid-morning," Chase reiterated. "We'll be almost finished by then."

"We who?" Adrian asked, frowning.

"Well, *you* know." Chase's voice rose. "The people on the march."

Adrian put down his spoon. "Wait a minute, let me be clear about this. After all the ill-feeling that article has stirred up, you were still intending to go out there tomorrow morning and be part of that thing?"

"Well, *I* didn't have anything to do with the article."

"But the person who's organizing the march did, didn't she? Let's not be disingenuous, Chase."

"I'm not sure I know what disingenuous means, sir."

"Lacking in straightforwardness, playing a double game."

"Would anyone like more beef stew?" asked Tony. "Adrian?"

"Not right now." Adrian transferred his scrutiny to the chef. "*You* certainly weren't planning to take part in that thing after the article, were you?"

"Well, now, I — if you think it would be a bad idea —"

"If *I* think? Can't you think for yourself?"

Tony looked miserably down at his plate.

"If *I* think," Adrian repeated, shaking his head. "Neither of you is exactly unknown around town. And everyone who knows *us* knows whose roof you've been sleeping under. What does it say to them if you take part in an event that Margaret has been publicized as wanting no part of? Surely you both must have thought of *that*."

"But *she* never said anything after the article came out," protested Chase. "And Tony said you didn't care if we marched as long as we didn't represent anything except ourselves."

"I said that before the article. And after the article, I had assumed we were all in agreement. As for Margaret, she's right here, she can speak for herself."

What was I going to say? The article, which I was sick of hearing about, had come out on Wednesday. The four of us had discussed it at supper Wednesday night. Nobody had brought up the subject of the march then, and I supposed if I had thought about it I would have assumed, as Adrian had, that nobody in this house would still feel like going. The truth was, I *hadn't* given it any thought, there had been more urgent things waiting to be thought about when I had a few precious spare moments in which to think them. Now, I admit, I was a little vexed with Chase, as much for going on about it as still wanting to be in it. I was vexed, as well, by Tony's cowardly hedging, and with Adrian for putting me on the spot. Adrian was so combative lately. Yet I knew he was trying to defend me, that all kinds of new things were waking up in him and fighting to come out and he would have to learn to modulate their expression over time.

"As far as I'm concerned," I said, "this Advent could have done very well without Grace's Birthday March for Jesus, and Paul Pike's article, and the flu epidemic, and a few other things." Such as Ben MacGruder's music video. "Nevertheless, they're part of the package, as will be the weather tomorrow and whatever else God chooses to send. I'm not going to cross anyone off my Christmas list if he marches in Grace's parade, but if I'm stating my preference, I'd say we'd present a more united family front if none of us showed up. This is all probably rhetorical, anyway. Cindy Lou Fowler has already spoken with her little weather wand."

"But Tony's already made my costume!" Chase wailed.

"Your *costume?*" Adrian shouted. "Great God Almighty, haven't we had enough of costumes in this house?"

"Why do you have to get so emotional about everything lately?" Chase shouted back.

"Now now, you two —" said Tony placatingly.

Adrian shot the peacemaker an incredulous, withering look, slammed down his napkin and went upstairs.

Tony, subdued, began clearing dishes.

"No, don't take mine away," I said. Breakfast has been touch and go lately; I intended to finish my supper.

"You guys hardly made a dent in my beautiful salad," said Chase.

"Here," I pushed my plate over. "Give me a sampling of everything again, but go easy on the vinaigrette."

"He's just so *moody*," Chase whined. "Either he's running from you or he's yelling at you."

"He's just recovering from pneumonia, and he's got a lot of things on his mind," I said. "All the flu cases at the school. Whoa, that's enough vinaigrette."

"You always wet down your salad."

"I prefer it a little drier at the moment."

"We have plenty of flu cases at our school, too."

"And all of us crowding him in his own house," said Tony sorrowfully from the sink. "That's got to be a strain on him."

"Well, I didn't invite myself here," said Chase. "He talked my dad into it. If it had been left to my dad, I'd be in my jail cell now. At least it would be my own private jail cell."

"Not anymore it wouldn't," said Tony. "They're doubling and tripling them up nowadays. Too many people wanting to get in."

"This is my house, too," I said. "In fact, it's

officially my rectory. It may be a little crowded until we sort things out, but everyone under the roof at this moment is both wanted and loved. By Adrian and by me. I can assure you both of that."

"You're very kind," murmured Tony. But he sounded dubious.

"I don't *believe* this," said Chase. "All that work on my costume for nothing."

"Well, I don't know what it is," I said, "but maybe you'll be able to use it for something else."

"No, it was *perfect* for this occasion," said Chase bitterly.

Tony dried his hands on a towel, sighed sadly, and left the kitchen.

Chase sat on, watching me eat. "So *moody*," he repeated, hoping to draw me into a discussion about Adrian.

"Do you have homework to do?" I asked.

"It's Friday. I have all weekend to do it. Especially now that nothing interesting is going to happen."

"Why not go ahead and do it anyway? Then if something interesting does happen, you'll be glad you're free."

He slumped forward on his elbows without replying. He grabbed his front swags of hair in his two fists and pulled his head slowly from side to side.

"As a matter of fact," I said, "I'm going to take my own advice." I carried my plate and utensils to the sink, rinsed them, and put them in the dishwasher. "If anyone wants me, I'll be over at the church working on my sermon."

"Then if anything interesting does happen, you'll be glad you're free," he singsonged back, just barely short of a taunt.

"Mmm-hmm," I replied, not rising to it.

I was planning to do a sermon reflecting on the closing prayer for the Fourth Sunday in Advent, which asks God to "make us grow in faith and love" in order to celebrate the imminent feast. How glibly and thoughtlessly that phrase "make us grow" slides off our tongues. As if growth were always a happy, shapely matter: leaves unfurling, blossoms opening, hearts and minds joyously stretching toward more light. Whereas the fact of the matter was, when we asked for growth we were asking for a mess. Exploding tempers, privately nursed little petri dishes of resentments, insecure stumblings into dangerous new places. (Witness the transformation stew going on at our house.)

My office phone rang. It was Gus. "Sorry to interrupt your sermon-writing, dear."

"How did you know that's what I'm doing?"

"Chase has been on the phone with Jennifer. She's invited him to come over and play with us and stay overnight in the maid's

642

room. If you can spare him, I'll be glad to come get him."

"I think we just might be able to spare him. He's in a rotten mood."

"So Jenn said. That woman and her blasted *march*. I don't know if it'll do much good, but I said he could bring his costume over here and model it for us."

"So there goes *your* evening."

"Oh, Jenn and I were just rattling around over here. We were going to rearrange the linen closet. Her idea of fun. The doctor is out on a call, what else is new? Chase will provide us with a change of tempo."

"Chase certainly can be counted on to do that."

"If there's a snowstorm tomorrow morning, we'll keep him here. If not, he can go out to the woods with Jennifer and me to cut greenery for the church. How's that?"

"What can I ever, possibly, do for you in return?"

"Just write another one of your good sermons."

It would have been a good sermon, too, because it was one I myself urgently needed to hear and draw strength from. But it was a sermon destined neither to be finished nor preached that Sunday.

I worked on it for a time, until I heard Gus's truck arrive and depart. It was calming to be alone in my office, quietly matching ideas about human struggle with apt phrases, without real people's ragged edges catching against mine. The lights were off in Tony's room, formerly the Seducer's Sun Porch. Unless Chase wanted to play cards or watch a movie, Tony retired to his quarters. He turned his light out early: a habit ingrained in him from the abbey — and the institutions prior to it? Passing his door, I often heard old-time pop songs or jazz playing low on the little clock radio by his bed, where I could picture him lying in the dark under our hospitality icon of the three angel-visitors, toting up his welcome quotient for the day and plotting how to make himself even more indispensable on the morrow. I suspected he did not always step outside to smoke.

Adrian's study window wasn't visible from my office, but I felt I could locate him accurately enough within the realms of probability after the go-round in our kitchen; lying on my father's bed and escaping to twelfth-century monastic life in Rievaulx.

All quiet on the rectory front tonight, thanks to Gus.

I had just finished making a list of ways we grow in faith and was about to start in on ways we grow in love, when so many incoming thoughts pushed in at once that I needed a break. Since I didn't smoke, I stepped outside to pray.

644

The darkness was a thick, palpable dark. The clouds for Saturday must already be massed up there. It felt like stepping out into tomorrow's weather and tasting the wetness of snowfall before it fell.

"What are you, anyway?" I said. "And yet how close you are."

I stood outside for a while longer, then decided to lock up and go home. I wanted to speak to Adrian.

Who was not on my father's bed reading when I knocked, but standing by the window, looking out into the same dark I'd just come in from.

"Am I disturbing you?"

"Never. Done with your sermon already?"

"How did you know about that?"

"Oh, word gets around." He turned and held out his hands to me. "Chase came up to ask if it was all right with me if he went off with Gus. He said she was calling you at the church."

I went over to the window and leaned against him. "I thought you'd be off at the monastery in Rievaulx with Aelred."

"I wouldn't mind having Rievaulx's spacious layout to put some of this volatility into. Including my own. Have we taken on too many people at once, Margaret?"

"I don't *think* so." And here I had been about to alert him to the probability of another.

645

"Sorry I blew up. No, I'm not sorry. I'm not my old self. I don't know what I am anymore. It's time I leveled with him, though."

I knew who he meant.

"I keep waiting for the right moment, but it never seems to arrive."

"Yes, I know that predicament," I said.

"I have so many conflicting feelings about him. One minute, I'm admiring him and envying him a little, he's such a tough old bird. Then the next, I'm looking at that rust-canker dyed hair of his and thinking about his past and wondering how we're going to present him to the community. 'Baxter, Coach, members of the student body, I'd like you to meet my father, who dropped me off at the orphanage forty-seven years ago and just recently dropped back into my life.' . . . 'Van, Lucinda, members of All Saints High Balsam, meet Adrian's long-lost father . . . well, no actually he *isn't* a monk, he just stole that habit . . . but he's been everything else. You name it, he's been it. If you prefer not to name it, he's probably been that, too. Anyway, I know you'll all want to welcome him into your lives.' "

"The hair will grow out," I said. "And I'm sure you've noticed he hasn't been wearing the habit lately. And people already like him. They just take it for granted he's here."

"Too bad scripture doesn't provide us with

646

any suggestions for homecoming parties for prodigal fathers. Though he'd undoubtedly want to do all the cooking himself — with his little spices and herbs."

"I've fantasized a little on what I would feel if our situation were reversed," I said. "I mean, what if my mother had gone away and *not* been killed? Say she'd just disappeared, and then forty-seven years later this old nun — rather, an old woman posing as one — shows up at our door? I probably wouldn't have recognized her, even with all those photos my father and I pored over. And then the old nun confides to you who she is, and you say, look, you'd better stay on with us till Margaret has a chance to get used to this and gets to know you better and then we can figure out what to do. I would have slowly seen the light, perhaps nudged with a few hints from you, and I would have gone through the same conflicts you're going through: shock, fascination, resentment, embarrassment —"

"Yes, I am fascinated and repelled and deeply moved by this old man, and I'm angry as hell, and some other emotions I don't have names for yet. But, Margaret, even when we finally do come out and acknowledge each other, he can't go on living here. There's just not room. Chase needs that sun porch, and you need your study back, and, for the long-term, Chase himself may need to be somewhere else. That's what I've been up here trying to do: work out logistics for everybody. The ironic thing is, running Fair Haven seems like nothing compared to the problems in this house. I got nowhere and decided to admit defeat. That's what I was doing when you knocked, looking out at the dark and dumping it all into God's lap."

"It's a good dark for praying in," I said. "I took a break from my sermon to go outdoors and do the same thing. I was having too many ideas at once to find places for — not so different from having too many people and not enough rooms —"

He was starting to reply when we heard footsteps slowly climbing the stairs. We waited in silence. Presently Tony, carrying his folded habit, appeared in the doorway.

"Oh, dear," he said, hesitating.

"Come in," said Adrian.

Tony looked uncertainly from one to the other of us and almost stumbled over the threshold with his bundle. "I thought Margaret was over at the church, or I wouldn't have —"

"I'll be glad to leave," I told him, "if you wanted to see Adrian."

"Oh, no — no need for that." He was flustered. "I only wanted to — well —" His eyes diffidently met Adrian's. "After what you said at supper, I thought it was time I turned in my costume, is all."

The two men stood looking at each other.

Then Tony held out the habit to Adrian. There was a little velvet box, like a jeweler's ring box, resting on top.

After a measured pause, Adrian reached out his arms and accepted the bundle. His gesture was that of someone solemnly accepting a folded flag.

"What's in the box?" he asked in an unsteady voice.

"Something belonging to you," said Tony.

Adrian laid the habit on the bed and plucked up the little box. He seemed to move in slow motion. After taking a deep breath, he opened the box.

"I don't understand," he said, scowling down at the interior. "There's nothing in here but a —" He picked out something very small and held it up between his thumb and forefinger. "It looks like a piece of dirt."

"It's your tooth, Jou jou."

"*What?*"

"The piece of your tooth that fell off when I was chasing you around the shop —"

"No," Adrian said harshly, "what did you call me?"

"Jou jou. Don't you remember?"

Adrian replaced the shard and snapped the box shut. He stood quite still, looking at no one.

Tentatively, Tony reached out to touch him.

"Don't," Adrian pushed his arm away. "Don't you dare —"

"I'm sorry," murmured Tony, stepping back.

"Oh, you're sorry, all right," said Adrian. "You run away and then sneak back forty-seven years later in that damned disguise and then one evening you decide to 'turn in your costume' and call me some old nickname and expect me to run weeping into your arms."

"I don't expect it," Tony said miserably. "I only thought you might remember about the name. Your mother said I played with you too rough, like a toy — a *jou jou*. You started calling yourself that when you wanted to play. You'd say, 'Come and play with your Jou jou.' I never could resist it —"

"You did a pretty good job of resisting, until the monks kicked you out and you had to find yourself another retirement community. What good luck that your prior found old Jou jou for you in that church paper. Old Jou jou, complete with a generous wife with supernormal powers of empathy who could be counted on to harbor the old runaway parent with loving discretion until Jou jou could find it in his heart to forgive —"

"You *do* remember, then."

"Yes I remember, but I wish I didn't. I wish I had truly been able to tell you, 'Sorry, old man, that thing in the box may have once been a part of my tooth, but I have no memory of ever being anybody's Jou jou.' "

"I'm glad you remembered," said Tony softly. "I was afraid you wouldn't. That box, by the way, was your mother's. There was a diamond engagement ring in it, from someone else. A far better man than me, but he had the bad luck to get killed. You were my boy, but we named you after him. I sold the ring after she died, but I kept the box. I wanted it for that little piece of your tooth. It was all I had left of you."

"Well, that's your own damn fault, isn't it? You could have had the rest of me. You knew where I was."

"Yes, well . . . for a while I did. Then, maybe Margaret's told you, I went to prison for a while. I can tell you one thing: I have a lot more reason to be proud of you than you ever will of me. But at least I'm not in disguise anymore. I've given you back the costume."

"Oh yes," Adrian said bitterly, "the costume. But what about all the rest? You can't give that back, can you?"

"No, my boy, I can't. But —"

"All those years —" Adrian's voice broke. He turned away to the window and, standing very straight, with his back to us, began to sob.

On Saturday morning's *Smoky Mountain Roundup*, there was a little plug for Grace's march.

The snowstorm was now expected to begin mid-morning. The two anchors bantered in their down-home voices: "Well, Bud, still waitin' for the bottom to drop out." "Yeah, Ernie, the skies are so white and impacted out there it felt like I was walking through milk from the parking lot, but nary a flake yet." "Meanwhile, folks, seven more shopping days until Christmas, and only *fourteen* more days till the Big Rollover. By the way, Bud, if you were counting on a last-minute reservation for New Year's Eve dancing at the Rainbow Room at Rockefeller Center, forget it, it's been booked since 1975." "I don't know about you, Ernie, but I'm seeing out the old millennium right in my own aluminum-sided castle. Gonna get some take-out barbecue from Three Little Pigs, build a roaring fire, and cuddle up with the old lady." "Can't beat that, 'specially the take-out barbecue from Three Little Pigs. Closer to home, folks, up here at four thousand feet above the cares of the world, the Millennial Birthday March for Jesus is still slated for ten o'clock this morning. Marchers will congregate at nine-thirty at Great Thunder Falls for a short prayer session, then up to Main Street, and on to the Community Park for a worship rally. I repeat, the Millennium Birthday March for Jesus *is* still scheduled for ten o'clock this morning. The organizer, Grace Munger, was just on the phone to us and she says they're expecting about five hundred. 'We're ready, and we're leaving the weather to the Lord,' she says. Good Luck, Gracie, you got spunk!"

At eight-thirty Adrian and I headed over to the crypt. He was going to help me with Food Pantry since the other volunteers were sick. He slit open the cartons and we unpacked them. We worked together in peaceable, organized silence. He stomped on the empty cartons and stacked them flat; I arranged boxes of cornflakes, pyramid-style, on the shelves. The events of the previous evening had left us drained of emotional resonance. Before we had finally called it a night, Tony offered to pack up and leave on the morning bus, Adrian yelled at him, "That's right, run out on me again," then both of them had clasped hands and embraced, then Adrian said a few more nasty things and made Tony cry, and soon after that we all agreed it was time to go to bed and get some sleep. Logistically, nothing had been settled. This morning Tony had showed up first in the kitchen, as usual, and made oatmeal the hard way. We all three sat hunched over our bowls, watching Bud and Ernie banter back and forth on *Smoky Mountain Roundup*. Tony had assumed he'd be helping us with Food Pantry, but I asked him if he'd mind going out instead and buying food and supplies and delivering them to Professor Mallory before the snowstorm got going. I think he was as relieved as we were to have the respite.

Adrian slit open another box. "I remember *this* old friend from graduate school, when I didn't have a refrigerator."

We stacked the cans of condensed milk next to the cornflakes.

After all the food was unpacked, I showed him how to do the cards. "They give you their names, you pull up their cards, and write in today's date. If they haven't been for a while, ask if there's still the same number of people in their household. If this is their first time, make a card. Name and address, if they'll give you one, on the left-hand side. Household members in the upper right-hand corner. And be sure and put down the children's ages. We need that for reordering infant food, also to know who's in school and gets lunch there. And you put a check mark on that pad for every person served. You make marks for everybody in the household, not just the person who comes in."

"Got it," Adrian said, sitting down at the desk. He stuck a pencil behind his ear and gazed up at me with such sheep-eyed devotion that I found myself self-consciously looking away. Last night, I had fallen asleep with his arms around me and his tears wet on my back. If I hadn't been so wiped out by the emotional extravaganza of the previous hours, I would have turned around. As it was,

I settled for a drowsy elation that, despite the Ben video, my husband's manhood still seemed to be intact.

By nine the firstcomers were already crowding the hallway in the crypt, waiting for their turn. The procedure was to let in two persons, or families, at a time. Adrian filled in their cards while I accompanied them around the shelves, pointing out new items, urging the proud ones to take enough, and rationing the overacquisitive. Our first customer was one of the rapacious regulars, who had mastered a comic routine to divert you from what he was squirreling away in his knapsack.

"I see you all got chicken soup today, Pastor. Ever hear the one about the little chicken who felt sick, so his mama let him stay home from school?"

"No, Ray, I haven't."

"Well," his fingers worked the shelves rapidly, "come lunchtime, she brings him in this nice steaming bowl and he looks at it and he sniffs it and then he says, shocked, 'But Ma! You know what this is? This is *chicken* soup!' And she says, 'No one has to know, son.' "

"Whoops, three's the limit, Ray. Leave some for the sick little chickens."

Adrian and I worked together nonstop. The majority always came early, to get in on the good items. At ten there was a lull.

"I guess Grace's march is setting off from Great Thunder Falls about now," I said.

"Mmm," said Adrian, toting up the marks on his list.

"How many have we served?"

"Let's see . . . forty-seven. That's counting all the members of the households."

"I wonder if she really will have five hundred."

"Sounds a bit optimistic to me."

A few more customers dribbled in, including one of our longer-term faithfuls, Delmer, whose attrition rate seemed to be high in every area of his life but one. "Just call us the Amazing Stretching Family," he said, laughing, while Adrian was adding the new baby's name to the household list, which already numbered six. Today, Delmer brought along his two-year-old girl, and while he and I read the ingredients on different brands of baby formulas, Adrian entranced her by stomping on an empty box and asking her if she could carry it over and lay it on the stack with the others.

"But I've saved the best news for last, Reverend," said Delmer as he was leaving. He put down his two full bags of groceries and dug into his pocket and stuffed three crumpled bills into my hands. "I've got a part-time job. So you take this and put it toward something you need for your church."

Another lull. I flattened out Delmer's three bills, a five and two ones, and tucked them in my pocket. A dollar for each person, counting the new baby?

Adrian, at the desk, had been working intently on a card. He handed it to me. "Would you mind looking this over?" he asked quietly.

On the left-hand side he had printed: Adrian Anthony Bonner. Address: All Saint's Rectory, High Balsam. In the upper right-hand corner, under household members, he had listed: Margaret Gower Bonner, Joseph Anthony Bonner, Chase Zorn, aged 16. In the space below was today's date, December 18, 1999, and, below that, in his handwriting: Without you I am poor indeed. Love, Adrian.

"Have I got everything right?" he asked.

"Yes and no," I said, when I could speak.

I put the card down in front of him on the desk and picked up the pencil. Bending over him, I printed beneath Chase's name:

_____ Bonner, due (by the grace of God) Aug-Sept, 2000.

Jennifer Tye burst into the crypt with snowflakes on the shoulders of her black coat. "It's just started! And I hope Chase gets good and soaked, I could kill him — oh, goodness, Pastor Margaret, Father — excuse me, I thought it was Food Pantry down here —"

"It is," I said. "We were just taking a short affection break between customers."

"What has Chase done now?" Adrian asked.

"He tricked us! Oh, I am really mad. We were driving into town with the greens in back of the truck when he suddenly says, 'Listen, see you guys later, I've got somewhere to go.' And he jumps out of the truck and runs! Gus is *furious,* but what could we do? We couldn't bodily force him to come back. He'd planned the whole thing! Before we left our house, he said, 'Hey, you know what? Maybe I'll wear my costume to decorate the church with you all. That way, it won't be completely wasted.' And we encouraged him! We waited for him to go change! When he had it up his sleeve to join up with that old march the whole time. Can you believe such underhandedness?"

"I can believe it," Adrian said flatly. During Jennifer's report, I had watched the light from our brief joyful moment ebb from his face.

Gus came in, also covered in snowflakes. "I guess you've heard about our truant. If he'd been a little younger and slower, I would have parked that truck and run after him and beat his bottom raw when I caught up with him."

"What was the costume?" I thought I might as well ask.

"Oh, it was a full-length hair shirt Tony made out of some fake fur. Then there was a — what do you call that flat piece that hangs

658

down over the the habit?"

"Scapular."

"Yes, well, it was made out of a white sheet, and on the front it had 'Amazing Grace' painted on it in orange, and on the back it had 'To Save a Wretch Like Me.' He modeled it for us last night and whistled 'Amazing Grace.' It cracked us up, but of course it would have been wrong for him to join the march, after that piece in the paper. He said so himself, last night."

"You know what I think?" cried Jennifer. "I think when he called me up last night, he already had his plan made. He was just using us. I hope he gets soaked."

"There's a pretty good chance of that," said Gus with her customary equanimity. "It's coming down out there."

I looked at my watch. Ten-thirty. "Well," I said, "at least Grace got in most of her parade. But I, for one, will be glad when all this is over."

Adrian, pale and grim, said nothing.

"Come, Jenn, let's go upstairs and get started with the greens," said Gus.

"I hope his costume gets ruined," said Jennifer, following Gus out of the crypt. "I hope all the letters wash off his sheet."

"That would be symbolically appropriate," said Adrian after they'd gone, "but my question is, what do we do with the boy underneath *now?*"

A hooded person came in, stomping snow off his Wellingtons. He looked too prosperous and inconvenienced for someone showing up to collect free food. He knocked the hood back, saw Adrian, and brusquely laughed. "So you've been shanghaied out into this mess, too, Bonner." It was Cal Lord.

"You must have brought Lucinda," I said.

"Yep, she's upstairs doing her char number. She's all ass-backward this morning. She started out, got halfway to town, then had to come back, she'd forgotten the fair linen. I thought I'd do best to drive her the second time 'round so she wouldn't get stuck in the snow. Then we got held up on the way into town while that miserable Jesus parade straggled by with its damn police escort. Then we had to stop and buy the communion wine, and when we came out the skies had finally opened. She's got the credence table to set up and a couple of your vestments to iron, then we're out of here. You don't happen to have any hot coffee made, do you, Margaret?"

"We haven't had time to make any, but there's a kettle and a flame and a jar of freeze-dried in the cupboard, if you'd like to make some."

He winced. "I'll pass, thank you; can't stand the stuff. Well, Bonner, first time I've seen *you* out and about since the wedding. Saw that boy of yours in the parade, wearing some kind of drag, tagging alongside our

660

Prophetess of the Peaks. I'm surprised you'd let him participate after that hostile write-up about Margaret in the *Times*."

"He participated without our blessing," Adrian replied tersely.

"I seem to be one of the lucky few to escape this flu," said Cal, adroitly dropping the topic. "Lucinda says it's my contrariness. I myself ascribe it to regular visits from old Doc Jack Daniel's. Well, here's our monk, Father Tony — or is it *Brother* Tony, I never can remember."

"Please, just Tony," came the usual reply as the old man stepped into the crypt, brushing snow from his duffel coat. Flakes frosted his hair, rewarding us with a momentary preview of how he would look when the dye grew out: a senior citizen who could pass as a grizzled veteran of the Merchant Marine — or a wiry old teamster, respectfully retired on union dues.

Adrian said: "Actually, it's Tony Bonner. Tony is my father, Cal."

Cal's eyebrows went up. Was he being made the butt of a joke?

"But I've spent the last nineteen years cooking for the monks at the Transfiguration," Tony eased right in. "I guess maybe some of their habits may have rubbed off on me." Then, wincing, he cut his eyes shyly toward Adrian: "If you'll forgive the bad pun."

"Forgiven," said Adrian.

The two of them might have rehearsed it for months, it went off so smoothly.

"Well, I'm blowed," said Cal Lord.

"How is Professor Mallory?" I asked Tony.

"Very grateful for the home delivery. Fascinating fellow. I hope you'll send me out there again. He was telling me Cherokee snake myths while I heated his clam chowder. Would anyone here besides me drink a cup of coffee if I make it?"

"Are we talking perked?" asked Cal hopefully.

"You can have it perked, fried, or over light," Tony told him, cackling softly as he set to work.

"I have to check out the snow for myself," I said, getting my coat. "Back in a minute."

The first snowfall still sent a childish leap of ecstasy through my heart, even though the highway department would have removed tons of it from the streets of High Balsam before it melted into April's showers, and I would be gnashing my chewing gum as I skidded up and down the mountain curves between now and then.

It was really coming down. As I left the shelter of the eaves to climb the outside stone stairs, hefty flakes caromed at me, plopping with sizzles into my hair and eyelashes. The churchyard was already white, the walks covered; someone would be doing some heavy-duty shoveling before the eight o'clock service tomorrow.

I stood out in unprotected space, feeling possessive affection for our handsome square-towered church. Seen through its snowy curtain, it resembled a subtly tinted old engraving that might have been titled "Traditional Parish Church in Winter."

I breathed in the crisp white air and let the deluxe-sized flakes clatter down on me as they did on everything else. Surely, I thought, everything would work itself out. Hadn't we made progress already? Even since last evening, after I had stood outside tasting in advance the wetness of this very snowfall, hadn't we made notable progress?

Prudence did at last overcome childlike ecstasy, and I moved over into the shelter of the west porch entrance, with its *Venite adoremus* carved into the stone archway. Branches of juniper, pine, and balsam, cut from Gus's woods this morning for decorating the church, lay in a pile on the side of the porch, snow still on them. Well, *three* of us had made progress; but meanwhile the Amazing Grace boy had fallen from grace, disappointing Adrian (again), as well as me, and Jennifer, and Gus. As Adrian had just asked, what were we to do with him now?

From high in a fir tree a crow sent a raucous query into the white stillness; as if in answer came the distant sonic scrape of a jet cutting through the turbulence toward strato-spheric sunshine. Another silence, then the starting-up on Main Street of a merchant's snow blower.

Then, somewhere on the other side of the snow blower, I thought I heard "Onward Christian Soldiers." But it faded in and out of earshot, as if somebody were erratically turning the volume up and down. I was standing there trying to figure out where the tune was coming from when Jennifer nipped out from the church to gather up an armload of greens.

"Pastor Margaret, what are you doing out here?"

"Do you hear singing, Jennifer?"

She scrunched up her beautiful forehead and listened. "All I hear is a snow blower — no, wait a minute — it's 'Onward Christian Soldiers.' " She ran out to the sidewalk and stood on tiptoe in her boots, snow catching like spangles in her fly-ey hair. "Hey, it's the marchers. They're coming down Main Street. There's some sort of float — no, it's a flatbed truck with a loudspeaker. The sing-ing's coming out of the loudspeaker, but it keeps cutting off. Oh *God*, Pastor Margaret, I hate to tell you —"

"What?"

"They're turning into *our street.*"

"But it's not on the parade route." I went out to the sidewalk to have a look. "No, I don't think so," I said, "the flatbed truck isn't turning in." It was hard to see through the screen of careening flakes.

The erratic loudspeaker hymn suddenly switched off.

"The *truck* may have pulled over," reported Jennifer in an ominous little singsong, "but the *people* are still coming."

All too soon I saw she was right. The Millennial Birthday March for Jesus — or what looked to be the stalwart leavings of it — was headed up our street, led by the Freelance Apostle in sodden red cape and hood.

"Oh, shit." I knew exactly where this bedraggled remnant was being led; I only wondered whether Grace hadn't planned it this way long before the first flake fell.

"*What* did you say, Pastor Margaret?"

"I said, 'Visitors Welcome.' "

"Sure you did, *I* heard you. Oh, look, those poor people, their banners are all wet and runny. But, ha ha *ha* — there's Mr. Abominable Wretch and his costume is ruined and *his* letters are running all over the place. Serves him right. I'm going to get my mother." She darted for the church, calling back excitedly, "I want her to see this for herself."

"Christ, the royal Master . . ."

In the absence of the amplified backup,

someone in the group had started up the singing again. Other voices trickled in.

> *"leads against the foe;*
> *forward into ba-at-tle . . ."*

As I went forth to meet them, I recalled the words I used to think were the right ones when I sang this hymn as a child, marching around the Sunday school in my father's church:

> *"Christ, the royal master*
> *leans against the phone*
> *for word into battle . . ."*

Well, Daddy, what are the right words to say to this obstinate prophetess in her wet cape, dragging her parade to my church?

I've been watching you, honey. You'll find them.

Grace staggered forward. She had actually done the march in her high-heeled boots, which were soaked. "Reverend Bonner," she challenged hoarsely, "the Lord led us here — will you allow us to come in?"

"Of course," I told her. "We've been sitting quietly at home, waiting for company. Passing out a few groceries in the meantime."

Here came the police chief, in yellow rain hat and slicker, put-putting his motorcycle alongside the ragged line of marchers. "Pastor, I count sixty-five here who stuck it out. We've got the younger kids squared away in a school bus. Miss Munger said it would be okay with you if these people waited inside your church till we organize more transportation to get them back to their vehicles at Great Thunder Falls. *Is* it okay with you?"

"I've already invited them in," I said.

"Praise the Lord," Grace said, rather dully.

"Praise the Lord," echoed the police chief in a not very religious tone. Rolling his eyes in exasperation, he took a moment to brush the snow off his mustache, then proceeded to bark orders into his walkie-talkie.

"Bring your marchers down to the crypt," I said to Grace, "and let's see what we can do about getting everybody dried off."

The Repentant Sinner in his soggy hair shirt and washed away letters had slipped out of the line and was suddenly beside me. "I guess I've messed up good, haven't I?"

"You look pretty much of a mess. Go to the rectory and change your clothes and shoes. Then, if you'll take the advice of someone who cares about you, come back and apologize to Gus and Jennifer, and we'll take it from there."

"Is *he* over at the rectory? He'll probably kill me."

"Adrian's in the crypt, helping out with Food Pantry. He's hurt and disappointed, but you know he doesn't go around killing people. When are you going to stop testing people's limits, Chase?"

"I'm sorry," he whimpered, "and it wasn't even worth it. It started snowing almost as soon as we started and the girls' ribbons got too wet to do their liturgical dance, and there were hardly any spectators outside to watch us."

"Chase, please march up that sidewalk and change your clothes, apologize to Gus and Jennifer, then come back to the crypt as soon as you can and make yourself useful to your wet friends and comarchers."

I caught up with Grace and led the battered troops down to the crypt, cautioning them against the slippery stairs. "Please everybody hold onto the rail."

"Everybody hold onto the rail . . . hold onto the rail . . ." voices called out to those behind them, spirits somewhat revived by the prospect of shelter and completion.

"We've got visitors," I announced to Adrian and Cal and Tony. "Grace has brought her march here. Help me welcome sixty-five wet people."

"Holy Hannah, what next," said Cal Lord, making a sour face.

"Is Chase among them?" Adrian wanted to know.

"He's over at the rectory, changing clothes. He's coming right back to help."

★ ★ ★

When the hangers ran out, coats were spread on the tile floor. Drowned banners, dark colors bleeding into light letters and vice versa, were laid out to rest: MARANATHA! WONDERFUL COUNSELOR. BREAD OF LIFE. I WANT TO BE ONE OF THE 144,000! "BEHOLD, I COME QUICKLY." MORNING STAR MOTHERS GROUP. WE ARE READY WHEN YOU ARE, JESUS. 21ST CENTURY: DOOMSDAY OR PARADISE FOR OUR KIDS? — OUR CHOICE.

The liturgical dancing girls from Chase's school stood in a shivering knot, helping one another remove the wet ribbons tied to their fingers.

Tony had both our big urns on the boil, and a parade lady wearing a pink jersey with PROMISE KEEPER'S MOM stenciled on it was ripping open envelopes of Swiss Miss at his direction and shaking the contents into large aluminum serving pitchers. Lucinda Lord, who had dashed down the inside backstairs from the sacristy to lend a hand with the crowd, was setting out paper cups and Christmas napkins on the counter when she suddenly put her hands to her head and looked flustered.

"What have you forgotten *now?*" said Cal, trailing her with his cup of fresh coffee.

"Toilet paper . . . all these people . . ." She grabbed a six-pack from a cupboard, slit it expertly with a fingernail and shoved two rolls at him, almost spilling his coffee. "Be a sweetheart and put these in the men's room while I do the ladies'."

"Are you done with your char work upstairs?"

"Pretty much . . . I have to do one more little bit of ironing and put away the wine —"

"Lucinda, I am *out of* here in the next two minutes. If you wish to join me for the ride home, I'll be waiting in the car."

"All right, Cal, but do the men's room first. Then go wait in the car, and I'll be out in five minutes at the most."

Adrian came over to where I was helping the liturgical dancers untie the wet ribbons from their cold and reddened fingers. "I thought Chase was coming right back."

"He should be back by now. Unless he's still apologizing to Jennifer and Gus upstairs. That was on his agenda first."

"Jennifer and Gus are down here. They just came in."

"Oh, so they are."

"I'm going over to the rectory to look for him."

"Go easy on him. Or at least semi-easy."

Hardly had Adrian left the crypt than Chase made his jaunty entrance down the backstairs from the sacristy. He sauntered over to our group, but kept his distance from

670

me. "Here, Wendy," he said to the prettiest of the liturgical dancers, who towered over him, "let me help you with those silk ribbons. If you roll them up while they're wet, they'll dry flat." He was wearing a spiffy peacock-blue ski outfit with racer's stripes down the legs that I had never seen before.

"Where did *that* come from?" I asked.

"I raided my dad's Christmas box."

"It's not Christmas yet."

"Yeah, I know, but I wanted to look my best for my friends." His cheeks were pink and his whole countenance flushed with bravado.

"Adrian just went to look for you."

"Well, I'm here now. I made my apologies to Jennifer and her mom, and then I helped Mrs. Lord set up that lousy old ironing board, and now I'm here, making myself useful to my comarchers, like you said." There was just the edge of taunting in his reply, but when I tried to catch his eye, he ducked his head and concentrated his whole attention on wrapping Wendy's ribbon around his finger.

"I thought your parade costume was wonderful," another girl piped up. "Did you make it for him, Reverend Bonner?"

"No, someone else did."

"The old monk who lives with us," Chase told her. "Tony can do just about anything."

"It must be fascinating living with a monk,"

the girl went on, encouraged. "By the way, I'm Amy. We're in honors English together, but I sit about a mile behind you."

"The view of me is probably much better from there," said Chase, eliciting a round of admiring titters.

He handed back the rolled ribbon to pretty Wendy and was about to embark on another when Jennifer called angrily from the kitchen area, "*Well,* Chase, are you going to help out over here, or aren't you?"

"Excuse me, ladies, my babysitter is calling me." He bowed, leaving them behind in giggles. As he swaggered across the room, he stuck his hands in his pockets and began whistling "Amazing Grace" in his keen little mistral whistle. Whereupon the Promise Keeper's Mom plunked herself down at our upright piano and picked up the melody. Voices lifted eagerly in song, then flagged and faltered, until an old-timer who knew the words by heart began feeding the lines in the old tent-meeting style. By now the Swiss Miss was being served and Tony had broken open a couple of jumbo-sized bags of ginger snaps, which Jennifer and another parade lady were passing around.

Grace emerged from the ladies'. Obviously she had been setting herself to rights, but under the fluorescent lights she looked wiped out. Several marchers gathered around to speak to her and embrace her. Swaying a little, she seemed momentarily uplifted by the affection and the exuberant singing; but when she saw me heading toward her, the tired shoulders lifted and her face froze into its haughty mask.

"Well, Grace," I said, "everyone seems to be drying off. Would you like something hot to drink?"

"No thank you, I need to say a few words to my people, after this hymn is over, if that's all right with you."

I didn't quite follow the logic, but let it pass. "Where is your friend Mr. Pike?" I asked. "I thought surely he'd be covering the march after that provocative article in Wednesday's paper."

"Mr. Pike is not my friend, Reverend Bonner. I was planning to write you a long letter, but since you've chosen to bring it up now, when we are all sheltering in the basement of your church, you have a right to an answer. He used me and he used you, to play us off against each other for his purpose. I did not expect this. What I said to him about you was said off the record. He promised me not to use it. I was merely thinking aloud, speculating why it was you were being so rigid about not joining us —"

"Oh, come on, Grace. Since when does a seasoned media-maven like yourself play around with 'off the record'? You said yourself you were wary of him distorting *your*

673

purpose. What led you to talk to him at all?"

"I thought it might help the march. He promised to cover it, and I took a chance. But the day before the article appeared, he checked out of the inn. And when I read it, I knew why: he was afraid to face me. He broke two promises."

"Well, you had the march, anyway," I said. But it sounded like such cold comfort that I added, somewhat against my better judgment, "You've kept your promise to the Lord, anyway."

"We had about two hundred and fifty," she went on, without appearing to have heard my consolation prize. "What with the flu epidemic and those scary weather forecasts, that's not a bad turnout. The Bikers for Christ cancelled because they were afraid they wouldn't get home, and the liturgical dancing coach phoned me from Clampitt at six this morning saying it was already snowing down there, which I happen to know was a lie —"

The whole time she was talking to me, she must have been keeping track of "Amazing Grace," because when the feeder called out the opening lines of the last verse,

> "When we've been there
> Ten thousand years . . ."

she excused herself in mid-sentence and

stepped over to speak to the lady at the piano.

The next cluster of things happened quickly in succession. Though "in succession" isn't accurate. But "all at once" isn't right, either. A field theory style of narrative, rather than linear, would be useful here, whatever that might be like. What I mean to say is, things that had been stealthily ripening in a few separate souls now came to a head and "for better for worse" found outward expression, more or less at the same time, that Saturday morning inside All Saints High Balsam Church. The reason I can differentiate these ripenings, and put them in any sort of order now, is because I was required so many times during the weeks and months following that Saturday to give an account of what happened, and to report, as best I could remember, what had led to what, and, "if possible, in what order."

Even as the last echoes of "Amazing Grace" were reverberating around the crypt, the Promise Keeper's Mom struck up a fanfare of announcement chords on the piano and Grace waved her manicured hands aloft, indicating that she wished to speak.

"Brothers and Sisters in Christ," she cried into the elicited hush, "thank you for coming out today and lifting up your voices and banners in honor of Our Lord and Savior's birthday, and welcoming Him into His new millennium. Thank you for rededicating your lives to His purposes. In doing so, my friends, you have *taken charge of your lives* —"

"Praise the Lord!" shouted the old-timer who had been line-feeding the hymn.

"— taken charge of your lives," Grace insisted on completing her sentence, "in *His* name."

"Praise Him!" a woman's voice cried.

"Even though He sent us challenging weather, we know the Lord works in strange and mysterious ways, and this may have been part of His winnowing test —"

Here the outside door was flung open and the police chief stepped over the threshold, bringing a gust of flying snow and Adrian in his wake.

"We got buses here for y'all folks!" he was proudly announcing when, to his visible embarrassment, he was promptly shushed.

"Just give me one moment more, Chief," Grace called placatingly.

"His winnowing test to sort the lukewarm from the trustworthy and true —"

"Praise Him!"

The crypt door opened again. "Lucinda, where the *hell* are you — do you want us to spend the night overturned in a snowbank —" Cal Lord only looked more furious when shushed.

"Chase is here," I whispered to Adrian.

"He'd better be," he replied.

"The Lord has measured us today, and He has measured our city on a hill," Grace adamantly persisted, her voice rising, "and you can go home today knowing you are His people and you have made a difference. Because of you, something in this place will change!"

"More people will get sick," Cal snarled. To me he said, "Lucinda's locked me out of the sacristy. Where is she *now?* Did she forget to come out of the bathroom down here or what?"

"Maybe not today or tomorrow, but soon!" cried Grace. "As my friend Reverend Bonner said to me only moments ago, 'You have had your march, Grace; you have kept your promise to the Lord.' "

When was I going to learn to listen to my better judgment?

"And, my sisters and brothers in Christ, the Lord will keep His promise to us: 'Behold, I am coming soon. I will give recompense to each according to his deeds' —"

"Praise the Lord!"

"Bless you, Grace!"

"Bless you, Reverend Bonner," called the Promise Keeper's Mom.

"Blessed are they who wash their robes clean!" cried someone else.

"Blessed are those who are washed in the blood of the lamb!" shouted the old-timer.

"Blessed be all of you!" shouted the police

chief, who had recovered his authority. "Now every blessed one of you, put on your blessed coats and go out and get on the blessed buses, and let's get you all home safely!"

Lucinda, wearing her coat, came flying down the inside stairs from the sacristy.

Cal accosted her. "Lucinda, what do you mean locking me out of the sacristy?"

"I locked the *outside* door, Cal, because something's missing up there —"

"Well, I'm not surprised, with all this mob —"

"Shut *up,* Cal. Pastor Margaret —"

"What's up?"

"There's a jug of wine missing. I've checked every place I might have left it, and it's simply gone. This isn't my forgetfulness this time. Cal and I bought two gallon jugs of New York State port to last us through the Christmas communions. I opened one to set up for tomorrow, and when I went to put it back in the safe, the other one was gone. I may have left the safe open when I came down here to help out, but —"

"Someone obviously walked out with it while you were down here dispensing toilet paper to the masses," said Cal. "If that's all, we can buy *another* jug next week. I thought someone had taken at least the jeweled chalice, from the way you were going on."

"Well, it's my responsibility, and —"

"May we *please* get out of here now, before

this mob starts lining up for the buses?"

"Let me go back upstairs and check the sacristy one more time, maybe I did put it in some unlikely place —"

"Go on with Cal, if you want," I said. "I'll have a look around later, after everyone's gone."

"Obey your rector, Lucinda."

Adrian suddenly left my side and plunged through the marchers pressing around me to say good-bye. I was hugged by some, blessed by many, and invited to all sorts of worship services. I invited right back. I saw Chase go out with the liturgical dancers, and come back with snow on him. I briefly glimpsed Adrian bearing down on him and tapping him from behind on the shoulder.

"Reverend Bonner." Like the captain of a ship, Grace, looming in her red cape, had waited until last to leave.

"Well, Grace." I forestalled the threatened embrace by aggressively sticking out my hand.

Which she shook — and held onto. I was not to escape a last little peroration, it seemed.

"We may differ on some things, Reverend Bonner, but don't you feel, as I do, that it was God's purpose to gather us here for this rally at the end of the march?"

"I don't flatter myself that I can identify God's purposes as quickly and easily as you do," I said. "But I'll go as far as to say I feel it was Grace Munger's purpose to gather us here. And she has managed that."

I had been about to say, simply, "Grace's purpose," but that would have left her an opening for quoting me as having meant the other kind of grace. Which she was still perfectly capable of doing. *Almost* against my better judgment, I gave her hand a perfunctory parting squeeze before removing mine from her grasp. Quite likely, she would be capable of making something out of that, too.

"Well, whatever our differences," she said, "I will continue to regard you as my sister in Christ." The multicolored eyes flashed at me, I couldn't say for sure whether in threat or sisterly zeal, as she pulled up her hood. As she headed out into the swirling snow, she called back, "I still plan to write you that letter."

"Go with God," I shouted after her, as much to have the last word as to speed her on her way.

"We're going with God, too," said Gus, her arm around Jennifer, "while we can still see the road. You'll find the church upstairs all decorated. Your young man apologized, by the way. Was that your doing?"

"Let's call it a 'suggestion.'"

Gus laughed and gave me a hug.

"He may have apologized," said Jennifer, also hugging me, "but you might want to know, Pastor Margaret, he's acting *very* strange."

"Well," I said, shutting the heavy door against the last cries and blessings of the marchers boarding the buses, "Food Pantry is over and the birthday march is over. Great Silence Falls." I was getting to love that phrase.

We set about closing shop. The ever-efficient Tony hustled about the crypt, dropping cardboard cups and paper napkins into a plastic sack.

"Guess what, Margaret? I met the man whose father did the masonry on the church extension here, back in 'sixty-six. Nice fellow. The son, not the father, I mean." He cut his eyes at Adrian and cackled meaningfully, but Adrian, packing away Food Pantry surplus, either didn't hear or didn't respond.

"He was carrying a sound system on his truck, but he said they had an awful time. The volume kept cutting off. Probably a loose wire, I told him."

"You're not having Food Pantry next Saturday are you?" Adrian asked.

"Why not? Oh, no, of course not, next Saturday is Christmas, and the Lutherans are distributing the turkeys and hams this year. And the Saturday after that will be New Year's Day. So we're done with Food Pantry until May. You can go ahead and box things up."

"Hard to believe I'm going to see the Third Millennium," said Tony, twist-tying the plastic garbage sack. "What else is there to do down here, Margaret?"

"Just box up the rest of those cans and cereals with Adrian, and I'll go upstairs and take a final look for poor Lucinda's lost wine, and then we can go home. Where's Chase?"

"Chase is at the rectory, under house arrest," said Adrian grimly. He closed up a box and shoved it out of the way with his foot. "And there's no need to look for the wine. That little mystery, unfortunately, has been solved."

"Ah, no," I said.

"What's left of that port had better be on the kitchen table. With the top screwed on tight. If it had been a *corked* bottle, he wouldn't have had such an easy time."

"Now that's too bad," murmured Tony, shaking his head. He cleared the last shelf of cans and packed them away.

"What's too bad?" demanded Adrian curtly.

"That the boy backslid. It's partly my fault."

"How so? Don't tell me you've been tippling with him."

"Oh, dear me, no. Surprisingly, that's never been among my downfalls. I meant about the costume. I encouraged him by sewing it for him. And then he was disappointed when . . ." Having gone so far out on his limb, the old man could not retreat. ". . . well, when it was no longer appropriate for the two of us to be in that parade."

"In that case, I would share the blame, wouldn't I? For disappointing him. But people get disappointed every day, don't they? Are you suggesting we ought to try to exempt someone from disappointment because he happens to be an alcoholic?"

"No, certainly I wasn't suggesting that —"

"Besides, aren't we forgetting something here? He *was* in the parade. With his custom-made costume."

Adrian's voice was thickening by the second with aggressive sarcasm, and Tony was sounding tearful. Were we headed straight back to the father-son impasse of last evening? Was all the progress we'd made since then to be cancelled out because Chase had disappointed us once again?

"Can we go home now?" I said to Adrian. "The march is over, praise the Lord, and the missing jug of port has been redeemed, and the penitent wretch is safe at the rectory, and you have made your first introduction of your father to Cal Lord. Why don't we all go home and count our blessings and let the snow cover the rest of this day's sins? I, for one, could use a nice long nap."

Because my words had been uttered with a fair degree of vexation, I was surprised by their immediate peaceable effect. Adrian's sourness vanished dramatically. He looked around him as if he had just awakened and heard good news.

Which he had, from me, only an hour ago. But so much had happened in the meantime that even I myself had forgotten it.

"Yes, you must certainly have that nap," he said tenderly, his arm going around me. "I might even go so far as to join you."

"Well . . ." said Tony, busying himself with some last-minute shifting and straightening of the boxed-up supplies. "Now, let's see. I think comfort food is in order for supper. I've got some frozen cuts of round beef. Swiss steak and mashed potatoes might hit the spot."

We locked up and headed home. Tony pulled the hood on his duffel coat and trudged ahead through the slushy footsteps left by the marchers. He studied the sidewalk and planned his snow-shoveling strategies for the morrow. The funny thing was that from behind, with the black hood, he did look like a monk.

Adrian held onto me as though I were a frail old lady. "Have you been to the doctor yet?"

"It's hardly three weeks. I wanted to be sure before I got my hopes up — or anybody else's. But I'm fairly sure now. The signs are the same from the other time."

"Three weeks. That would make it —"

"That night you came home from chasing Chase. The Friday before Advent began."

"That was also the night Tony arrived. And you had to drive down the mountain to the hospital."

"Yes, a lot happened that night," I said.

"It's really too much," said Adrian with a small laugh.

"What is?"

"Him!" Indicating the black-hooded figure ahead, he lowered his voice. "I mean, he stays gone all these years and then slides into home base just in time to be a grandfather."

The missing jug of port was not on the kitchen table, and Chase was nowhere to be found in the house.

"Now let's think," Tony said, when Adrian returned out of breath from checking the upstairs. "No point in going off half-cocked here. First thing we do is check the garage."

Both cars were in the garage.

"Could he have gone with Gus and Jennifer?" Tony suggested.

"No, Gus would have let one of us know," I said.

"I told him to go and fetch that port, wherever it was, and come straight back here and put it on that table . . ." Adrian tapped a fingernail hard on the table as if ordering the jug to show itself. ". . . and wait for further instructions from me."

"Could he maybe — still be fetching the port?" Tony cautiously offered.

"That's a thought," I said. "Let's sit down and give him a few minutes." Adrian was breathing awfully fast from his up and down sprint.

"Good idea," said Tony. "How about some herb tea?"

"What herb have you got handy for fury?" bristled Adrian.

"Well, now, that would be chamomile," said Tony, making a beeline for the kettle. "Or Saint-John's-wort; we went through tons of that at the abbey — for antianxiety, you know. Valerian's effective, too; only thing is, it loosens up the bowels —"

The phone rang. "I'll bet that's the wretch," said Adrian. "What next?" He snatched it up. "Oh, Cal. Yes, she's right here." He handed over the receiver.

"Are you two home already?" I asked Cal.

"No, I'm in a pay phone outside the Country Hi-way Deli and Lucinda's in the car. She thinks she may have left the iron on. Chase set up her board in a different place and so she doesn't remember for sure whether she put it away or not. I told her you said you were going upstairs to look around, but she wouldn't let it wait ten more minutes till we got home. The church might burn down in the meantime. *Is* the church burning down?"

"Not that I know of, Cal, but I certainly will go over and check on the iron so she won't worry. She probably put it away and then forgot — because of it being in an unaccustomed place."

"What's going on with my wife? She's been so frantic and discombobulated lately. Do you know something I don't?"

"Listen, Cal, tell Lucinda I'm headed over there right now. And I'll call you at home as soon as I get back. The phone will probably be ringing when you two come in the door."

"I'll go with you," said Adrian as soon as I hung up.

"No need. I'll be right back for my tea."

The phone rang; I answered this time.

"I'm trying to reach Reverend Margaret Bonner."

"Speaking."

"This is Nancy at Commercial Alarms. The main sensor on your fire system just activated. Do you know about this?"

"No, I didn't. I'm not at the church. Did you say the main sensor? That's the one above the altar."

"Yes, ma'am."

"That means the fire's already inside the church."

"The smoke is, at any rate. You want me to call in the alarm?"

"Yes, please do."

"Will someone be over at the church?"

"I'm leaving now. It's right next door."

"I'm going, too," said Adrian.

"We'll all go," said Tony, switching off the kettle.

We pulled on boots and got back into wet coats. We hadn't reached the sidewalk before the siren on the roof of High Balsam Fire Company Number One (the only one) set up its revolving wail, summoning its volunteers from their workplaces and warm houses. The dispatcher would be calling them in, they would be throwing down tools, switching off TVs, bolting last bites of lunch, dashing for their vehicles, most equipped with revolving blue lights denoting their right to drive recklessly in an emergency, and, tires skidding in the fresh snow, hearts racing with the thrill of escape from the humdrum, heading for the station. But, once there, they still had to get into their firefighting clothes, organize themselves, get aboard the trucks . . .

"I don't see any smoke from this side," said Adrian. "But with the snow, it's hard to —"

"Let's hope the whole thing is a false alarm," said Tony, scuttling ahead of us. "In — well, a place where I was staying once, the whole building had to be evacuated at midnight because a false alarm went off. A fly had made her nest inside one of the main sensors, and when the babies hatched, all hell broke loose."

Then, in that brief pause in which the siren

catches its breath for a fresh ululation, came a single, not-very-forceful ring of our bell.

We stopped dead in our tracks. Nobody spoke. I saw the others realizing what it was we had just heard and the implications of it. If the bell rang, someone was in the church. I saw Adrian close his eyes; he was picturing something I had described to him not long ago: a boy in the bell tower, pushing the mouth of the bell with his foot. ("Oops — sorry about that. I really didn't mean to do it." "Come down now. Before you do something else you didn't mean to do.")

"Chase —" we both said at the same time.

"You mean the boy's in there?" cried Tony.

"I'm pretty sure he's up in the bell tower," I said.

We cut across the lawn. As we ran and stumbled erratically through the snow, I was struck by the absurd contrast between now and just a few minutes ago, when Adrian was guiding me up the sidewalk like a frail old lady.

Suddenly there was a pop-pop-pop: then an explosion of shattering glass. We rounded the west porch in time to see black smoke pouring out of the sacristy's single leaded window. Fire appeared suddenly, snaking across the sacristy roof like a shimmying dragon of flame materializing along its entire length.

"Chase!" I yelled, aiming my cry at the lou-vered windows of the tower. "Chase, come down! The church is on fire!"

"Could that be why he was ringing the bell?" panted Adrian. "Could he be trapped in the tower?"

"Maybe it hasn't reached the church yet —" I was fumbling for my keys, to open the door to the west porch.

"Wait," said Adrian, "feel the door first. They taught us that in shipboard fire drill. If it's hot, don't open it."

"But what *do* we do then?" I cried hope-lessly.

"Everybody wet down your handkerchiefs," Tony instructed. "Put them over your faces before you go in."

The door was not hot. We opened it a crack, then a crack more, just enough to look in. No fire or smoke at this end, but at the other end sparks were igniting westward across the central beam of the truss-timbered ceiling. Waist-high to ceiling in front of the altar hung a veil of impenetrable smoke, as if some malevolent thurifer had been madly censing up there with evil-smelling incense.

"Close it," said Adrian. "More air will feed the fire."

The two men knelt, rolling their handker-chiefs in snow. "I only have a Kleenex," I said. "Does anyone have a spare handker-chief?"

690

"You're not going in there and breathing that stuff," said Adrian. "Don't even think of it. You stand out here and keep calling to Chase. You have two lives to protect."

"That's right," agreed Tony, oblivious to Adrian's meaning. "You stay here and wait for the trucks."

"Wait, take this —" I detached a key from my key ring and gave it to Adrian. "The door to the tower might have locked behind him, or he may have locked it."

"And keep calling to Chase," said Adrian.

Before I could reply, they were inside. "Let's haul ass, and stay down low," I heard Tony say to Adrian as the door swung shut.

"Chase!" I called. "The — church — is — on — fire." I spaced my words, giving each a chance to float up in its separate little balloon of coherence. "Come — down — now. We — love — you."

But how much, if any, of this could be heard from three floors above, inside a louvered tower, with the siren bouncing off the impacted air of the snow-trapped skies, and your own head fuzzy with Communion port and scenarios of all the reproaches waiting for you when you came down?

God, please wrap them all in your wet handkerchief and bring them out safely.

The first to arrive was Mrs. Fletcher's son-in-law, Pat, tumbling out of his pickup in his boots and firefighter pants and helmet, his bulky waterproof coat swung over one arm. "Got here as quick as I could, Reverend. Luckily, this was my napkin-folding day, not my Power and Light day, so I was right across the street from the station. The volunteers are coming in slower than usual on account of this weather. Chief sent me on ahead to scope things out. Lord have mercy. This looks fully involved. The alarm we got just said the main sensor had activated."

At that moment the entire sacristy roof imploded on itself.

"What's in that wing, Reverend?"

"It's our sacristy. Where we keep the supplies and vestments and candles. Someone may have left an iron on. Also, there's smoke at the altar end of the main building and we saw sparks in the open trusses of the ceiling."

"Was there a door open between the main building and the — um — sa-cer-sty?"

"There could have been."

"There's no one in the church now, is there?"

"Yes. My husband and — his father just went in. We think there's a boy up in the bell tower. They've gone up to get him out."

"Shoot-fire, that changes everything. We got to do a rescue first, *then* suppression." Even as he was speaking to the fire chief on his portable radio, he was shrugging into his firefighter's coat with his free arm.

"Okay, Reverend, both our pumpers are on

their way. Lemme run and get my Survivair and then I'll need you to give me directions to that bell tower."

Which I did while he knelt down and strapped on his air pack.

"How long would you say they've been in the building?" he asked.

"Five minutes . . . no, maybe a little more."

"Now listen here, Reverend." He was breathing excitedly. "Seeing as we don't have no aerial ladder truck, I got to go up and help those folks down, and the sooner I get there, the better. Now, I want you to stand here and when the chief comes tell him to lay a line through this west door and back me up with a fog pattern. He'll know what I mean. Got that?"

"Lay a line through this door. Fog pattern."

"You got it."

His wide-eyed, excited face vanished behind a blue rubber and Plexiglas mask. He plonked on his helmet again, flipped a switch at his waist, and then cracked open the west door cautiously, drew a deep breath, and pushed his large, ungainly, fireproofed self into the church.

Now there were four inside, three without protective clothing and oxygen masks.

A line from an old memorization assignment chose this moment to jog egregiously through my head: "They also serve who only stand and wait." Whose line it was, or who was serving what purpose, or waiting for what, I couldn't have told you.

At last came the approaching sirens. Red light flashing through the downfall of flakes, firefighters riding its sides, the first engine careened into our street, shimmying a little on the slick turn — then the second one close behind.

Already a cluster of people was gathering; others ran toward the church from town. Fires are thrilling spectacles as long as you're only a spectator.

The chief jumped down from the first engine. I met him halfway and told him what I could: iron left on in what was now the collapsing sacristy; smoke seen — how long? ten minutes ago? — at altar end of main building; sparks igniting westward across open-trussed ceiling.

Four people inside, somewhere between the ground and the bell tower.

I gave him directions to the bell tower and conveyed Pat's request.

He relayed orders to the others. "Get a hand line up the choir staircase to the left, and another into the main body of the church. Try to keep the fire down at the east end.

"We get the folks out first," he said. "Then we fight the fire."

"Yes, please," I said, choking up for the first time.

Men were unreeling the flattened hoses from the pumpers, running with them across the snow-covered lawn. A policeman had arrived and was roping off the immediate area with orange tape.

Black smoke was now rising from the main roof.

"Who all's in there besides Patrick?" the chief asked me.

"A sixteen-year-old boy, an eighty-year-old man, and my husband."

The chief, who in his spare time ran a frame shop on Main Street and painted miniature landscapes of the area, which sold like hotcakes during the tourist season, spoke numbers and color codes into his portable radio. "And better give us an ambulance. Two if you got 'em."

"Just in case," he added to me.

. . . who only stand *and wait.*

Firefighters, slipping and sliding in their tall rubber boots. A flat hose, stretching from the pumper in through the open west porch door, from which smoke now gusted freely, suddenly becoming tumescent. More pickups with revolving blue lights arriving, people running, one man in shirtsleeves, reporting to the chief. Everyone wanting to help. To be in on the action.

Somebody asking, "Why don't they ventilate the roof first?"

Somebody else: "They's folks still inside."

A small man in a hooded anorak talking to a policeman, then ducking under the orange tape and crossing toward me.

Vincent Baird had been in the middle of his final Saturday appointment when the station siren sounded across the way and his customer, a volunteer fireman, leapt half barbered out of the chair.

"What can I do, Margaret?"

"Stand here and wait with me, Vincent, and pray for them to come out."

"Wait, I think someone's coming out now."

A masked firefighter — not Pat: too short, too small — with a boy, gasping and choking, slung over his shoulder. "We got us a broken leg here, looks like," he calls to the chief.

Moments pass. Then a dazed old man staggers out, looks confused by all the flashing and whirling red and blue lights, sits down suddenly in the snow and puts his hands over his face. The man in shirtsleeves comes running with an oxygen cylinder.

"Isn't that that old monk?" asks someone.

"Is that all of them?" Vincent asks me.

"Adrian's still in there. And the first volunteer, who went in."

Vincent's arm goes protectively around me. "Don't you worry, Margaret, they'll be out any second."

A second passes. Then another, and another.

A window blew out, or was knocked out, somewhere.

"How many gallons do them pumpers hold?" cried a querulous voice on the edge of the crowd. If spectators had failed to come out in the snow for Gracie's parade, they were making up for it now.

"They's folks still inside."

"Here, Margaret," said Vincent. "See? Here they come."

"Brick outside . . . slate roof . . . an oven . . ." The chief's voice. "Okay, soon as they're out, move in for a full response. Go easy on the water damage, if at all possible."

Pat's bulky shape, crouched low, emerged through the west door. Smoke escorted him on either side, and licking flames were now visible behind him in the sanctuary. He was dragging Adrian's limp form between his legs. Once clear of the door, he flung up his mask. "Get me oxygen over here," he yelled, "and call an ambulance."

"EMT vehicle's just arrived," someone called.

"Then we need to get him bagged fast!" cried Pat.

"It's the preacher's husband," someone said.

"Is he dead?"

697

"Maybe just passed out from smoke inhalation."

"Hey, that can kill you, too. Sometimes quicker'n fire."

XIX
Fourth Sunday in Advent

"Some of my best prayers have been arguments with God," a rabbi who attended my father's funeral confided in me. Later I always wished I had asked him what he meant by "best."

I know he didn't mean "best" in the sense of his most eloquent prayers. He wasn't a posing kind of man. Neither did I think his "best" meant that they got him what he was praying for. He seemed much too wise for that.

Had he meant his most honest prayers? The ones that didn't fool around with pretty language and diplomacy? Telling the harsh, nervy, barefaced truth to his creator about how he felt, being treated like this, and demanding help?

For the second time in my life, I found myself riding in the passenger seat of an ambulance, while, directly behind me, in hearing distance, a paramedic did emergency things to the body of the person I loved most in the world.

My father had been felled by a stroke outside his church on Good Friday during a reconsecration service for the vandalized crucifix that stood at our corner. Adrian had helped Daddy plan that service and choose the readings. Adrian himself had carried the aspersorium in the procession, and had stood in the ivy next to my father and read from Psalm 118 in a hoarse voice. ("I called to the Lord in my distress; the Lord answered by setting me free.") He had been coming down with acute bronchitis at the time.

In the ambulance then — as now — the driver communicated acronyms, vital signs, and medical history by radio to the emergency room. Twelve years ago I didn't know what all the acronyms stood for; it was a sunny spring day in Romulus and the nearest hospital was fifteen minutes away. Today I did know what the acronyms stood for, and that the ETA from High Balsam to the nearest hospital would be whatever time it took to drive fifteen miles down a spiraling, slippery road in a snowstorm.

The EMTs had radioed ahead for a paramedic to join us; we stopped at the Horseshoe Diner to pick him up. Minutes after he came aboard the serious stuff began: the things EMTs aren't licensed to do: put in the IV and start the heart monitor. Then the choking sound I remembered from the other time when I rode with Daddy. And even the same words, from the paramedic to the EMT assisting him: "Gag reflex normal." They were intubating him.

That blessed word "normal." But, as I already knew, you can have a normal gag reflex and still die.

The driver was a large rosy woman named Emily Jane. She wore her hair in a thick gray braid. The man who rode in back with the paramedic was her husband, Steve. Until two years ago they'd managed an Agway store out on the highway. They fantasized and fantasized about the free and wonderful life they could lead if only they could take early retirement. So they saved and saved and took it. Went on a couple of trips, went to visit the grandkids, then came back to High Balsam and almost died of boredom until they trained as EMTs.

As we were leaving the Horseshoe Diner with our paramedic aboard, Emily Jane glanced over at me and said firmly, "Buckle up, hon." And I remembered Helen Britt's strange derisive little snort when I had asked *her* to buckle up, as we drove away from the hospital with her husband's personal effects in the red plastic bag.

Tony, in considerable shock and respiratory distress — but not as bad as Adrian — and Chase, with a smashed ankle, and in some respiratory but more emotional distress, were following in a second ambulance.

Later, we would piece it together: Chase had rung the bell with his foot. Had not known there was a fire in the church, or even smoke on the other side of the door below his hatch. There was the bell, there was his foot; the two must meet again. Only he was fall-down drunk (as Charles Tye might put it) — and did fall down. He lost his grip on the ladder as he swung out to kick the bell, and fell to the cement floor of the tower. If he had fallen a little more to the left, he could have crashed through the hatch and been hurt a great deal more. Paradoxically, had he been less drunk, he might have been in much worse shape than he was.

Adrian had been first up the circular metal stairwell to the tower. When he climbed up through the hatch, he called back to Tony that Chase had fainted. Neither of them knew about the smashed ankle until he and Tony had started to maneuver the boy be-tween them down the circular stairwell. Adrian had the boy under the shoulders, and Tony had just taken hold of the feet, when Chase came to and began screaming bloody murder. By this time Pat, in his firefighting gear and mask, had gotten as far as the choir loft and heard Chase screaming. Finding the door to the tower locked from his side, and the church fast filling with smoke and flame, he was starting to kick it in when Tony opened it. All efforts then centered on getting Chase out, since he was the one who couldn't walk. Pat hoisted Chase over his shoulder. By then the smoke was thick in the choir loft. He instructed the two men to crawl down the choir steps backward, keeping their faces low to the ground to preserve oxygen. Pat went ahead with the boy. Tony followed on his hands and knees, with Adrian right behind him. Down they went backward, low to the ground as instructed. Then Tony no longer saw Adrian's feet on the stairs above. He started back up, feeling ahead of him for Adrian.

The first firefighters from the engines had entered the church by then. Pat handed Chase over to another man, and headed back to the choir loft. He found Tony, confused and coughing, trying to drag an unconscious Adrian down the choir stairs. Pat sent Tony out ahead, and followed with Adrian, dragging him between his legs. Keep him low, low. He was clammy and his lips were blue.

"Get me oxygen over here, and call an ambulance!"

"EMT vehicle's just arrived."

"Then we need to get him bagged fast!"

As the ambulance pulled away from All Saints High Balsam, men were on the roof with axes. The handsome square-towered building still stood, but it looked as if a child had taken black and orange crayons and scribbled across the "Traditional Parish Church in Winter" etching I had framed in my mind — how long ago? An hour, less?

Sparks were shooting twenty feet into the air, singeing the fir trees. Suddenly a crow side-swiped the column of sparks and spiraled drunkenly upward out of the smoke.

Emily Jane was radioing a new set of Adrian's vital signs to the E.R. Tachypnea. Tachycardia. B/P 100/70. Patient intubated. IV started. The E.R. was advised that patient was recuperating after pneumonia.

"He's in shipshape," I thought I heard coming out of the radio. But after Emily Jane snapped back angrily into her transmitter, "We have patient's wife riding with us," I realized I had misheard shit as ship.

A respiratory therapist was on duty and would be standing by. It would be helpful to know what toxic substances patient inhaled. Insulation? Asbestos? Polyester? Foam rubber? Chemicals for cleaning and polishing?

> *I called to the Lord in my distress;*
>   *the Lord answered by setting me free.*
> *The Lord is at my side, therefore I will not*
>   *fear;*
>   *what can anyone do to me?*

Don't *you* do it to me, God.

Most vestments have some polyester content. Sacristy armchairs filled with flammable stuff. Foam rubber kneelers. Silver and brass cleaners. Stain removers and furniture polishes.

Not this. Not now.

Please. Don't do it.

Later, during the winter months when we were holding our Sunday services in Mrs. Fletcher's summer dining room at the inn, the fire chief would come and speak to our congregation. People needed to be able to picture how something they loved was lost.

Depending on the number of volatiles, even a substantial edifice like All Saints High Balsam can be devastated in no time at all. Something is set going, not necessarily even a spark; heat can be enough for combustion to occur. And after that, given a continuing supply of oxygen and more heat, it's just a matter of how much food there is in the vicinity to feed the fire's appetite.

At the heat-into-spark stage, an appetizer is necessary. A vestment, say a blend of tropical wool and polyester, on which a hot iron has been set down and forgotten — or parked on its handle and fallen down on the garment: an iron from the vintage before those smart new ones that switch off if left unattended for more than one minute.

The wool scorches under the iron, the heat rises, then the polyester bursts into flame. The flame eats into the towel that has been pinned around the asbestos ironing-board cover. The towel burns through and splits. One flaming corner of the towel drops onto the legs of the old wooden ironing board, which ignites and topples against the arm of the fiberfill-upholstered chair. The appetizer course is now over.

Now that the fire has a substantial meal to consume, the temperature rises incredibly fast. It shoots up until the telephone on the sacristy wall melts; the lead in the window above the vestment press, in flames by now, also begins to melt.

If the room is closed off tightly, the fire will finish off everything in the room first, until a door collapses, or the ceiling is breached so that the fire can move into the rafters of the whole structure.

But if a door has been left open, or ajar, say by someone distracted for whatever reason, or confused by too many demands at once, the fire will leap on into the next space and begin to consume, in an upward, outward, V-shaped embrace, any volatiles in its path. If the space is big enough, and open enough, and continues to be generous in fuel — altar cushions, kneelers, cloth frontals, wooden pews, wooden floors, delicately wrought wooden crucifixion rood screens, carved lecterns with grapevine and pelican motifs, sanctuary paneling from the seasoned old wood of extinct chestnut trees, timber-trussed ceilings with their airy spaces — the whole substantial edifice can be beyond saving within a half hour of that first ignited fiber-filled chair.

But: this was a church of solid handmade Charleston bricks, built on the exact model of a seventeenth-century English stone parish church, when churches were built to last.

A brick church can be built on the exact model of an English parish church, but bricks are not masonry. English parish churches customarily have stone floors. Brick walls are not as thick as masonry. And in the older brick buildings, between the bricks and plaster is the lath. In an inside blaze, plaster falls off first, then the thin strips of lath are mere kindling wood.

And even masonry can be weakened beyond repair.

God, do not hand me that red plastic bag with Adrian's watch and belt and wedding ring inside. Not now, just when we were at last getting the mess out of the way and starting to make more of each other. Marriage is a call to development. Let us go on developing, then. You've got plenty of tread left in both of us. We're worth it! We can do more together than I can alone with my heart broken. Especially now, we are hitting our stride. Why would you want to redeem Adrian's father and bring him back from the dead and start this child inside of me and lay so many ghosts to rest and then say, ha ha, pulled the rug out from under you, didn't I, now if you will just take this red plastic bag, and go home and tend to your burnt church and rebuild your life —

I couldn't take it. I refuse to believe that you expect this of me. You've got to help me help Adrian. He can't pray for himself right now, so listen to me praying for him. You help him back there. Destroyed churches can be rebuilt by people; destroyed husbands can't. You come down here yourself, right now, and help him breathe.

A doctor tried an experiment with prayer. He took two groups of sick people. One group got prayed for, the other group did not. More people in the prayed-for group got better.

However, the people in the prayed-for group knew that they were being prayed for.

So? What does all that prove?

Nothing, except that empirical methodology, in that instance, suggested that prayer worked on those people.

But why?

Why not?

My father never regained consciousness.

Your father did.

But you've heard the rest of the story many times: and there was so much more to come.

The nurses in the E.R. had sterile sheets waiting, in case of hidden burns. The respiratory therapist was there. The doctor was there. They checked Adrian's lungs, ordered the respirator, the cardiac monitor, the antibiotics and sedation through the IV, the X rays, the EKG, the tests for blood gases. Before the sedation took effect, I looked into Adrian's eyes and knew he saw me and knew he knew he was seeing me. I needed that.

While the nurse was inserting the Foley catheter, I stepped outside in the hall. They were just bringing in Chase and Tony from the other ambulance. Tony still had on his oxygen mask, but he was conscious. When I bent over his gurney, his eyes darkened with expectations of hearing the worst.

"Adrian is conscious," I told him.

"But he's going to die, isn't he?" wailed Chase from the other gurney. "And it's my fault."

I stayed until the doctor saw to them. Chase was sedated and sent for X rays. Then I went back to Adrian.

They transferred him to the ICU and I stayed with him the rest of that day and evening. He seemed to be improving; his color was better. All that hundred-percent oxygen pouring through his lungs and tissues. He squeezed my hand and held onto it for a while, but it seemed too much effort for him to keep his eyes open. I got hopeful enough to leave him long enough to go to the toilet. Hopeful enough to make a few necessary phone calls, and to go and check on Tony and Chase, on their separate floors. Both were sleeping. They would set Chase's leg in the morning.

Charles Tye came. He talked to the doctors, spent quite some time watching Adrian while he slept, being breathed for by his respirator. Around midnight Charles drove me back to High Balsam in his GMC truck, on the road his grandfather had helped blast out of the rock. The snow had stopped; the road had been plowed, but there was nobody on it but us. Charles said, "I won't lie to you, Margaret, Adrian had a close call." Full recovery of the lungs was going to take a while, he said, and the next twenty-four hours would give us some idea *how* long. He would have to be monitored closely, to keep all those small airways at the base of the lungs open. Gus and Jennifer had a bed ready for me at their house. The rectory was off-limits for sleeping, in case any "hot spots" next door flared up again, but Jenn and Gus had been by and picked up a few of my things. Also, the fire chief reported some damage on the sun-porch side: water got in an open window while they were wetting down the trees. The sacristy and my office and the main body of the church were gone, but the firefighters had managed to save the crypt

710

and the tower structure.

Jennifer had prepared her room, formerly the master bedroom of Gus's parents, for me. My overnight bag had been unpacked and the items put away in the drawers. The fresh sheets were turned down, my prayer book and office book on the bedside table, my flannel nightgown arranged on top of the blanket like a graceful ghostly effigy, its arms crossed over the bodice. In the master bathroom my toiletries (including the squirt bottle of Stroup's Altar Fix) had been laid out on a folded face towel, just like in the best hotels. In the closet hung my new Roman-style cassock, with the buttons all the way down the front, and a pair of black shoes. Of course. Tomorrow was Sunday. Or rather, today was.

There was a wrapped candy on the pillow and a note.

Don't you worry, Pastor Margaret, my father says Father Bonner's going to be all right. He phoned from the hospital before you guys started home and told us that. And my dad wouldn't have told *us* that privately unless he was really sure. And my mother's going to rebuild the church as beautiful as before, and everything's going to be great. I *know* it.

LOVE CONQUERS ALL.
Now get some rest!
Love, Jennifer Tye

At ten A.M. the winter faithfuls who regularly attended either the early or the mid-morning mass gathered for a combined Morning Prayer service in front of the ruins that had been All Saints High Balsam this time yesterday. I had set this up from the hospital yesterday evening when I was making my other calls. If Adrian had gotten worse, Van was prepared to take over for me. Also present at the outdoor service were thirty or forty townspeople, several of whom had brought along their video cameras.

The sunshine played its indiscriminate sparkle over the debris of many recognizable things that we had neglected to imagine in any other shape than their whole, upright, admired-and-cared-for ones. Our perverse "End-time" weather had returned and the temperature was already in the forties and rising, making yesterday's snowstorm seem a fluke; but, at least until it melted, the snow contributed a partial shroud for the blackened pews, the sodden clumps of kneeler entrails (bad stuff that shouldn't be in anybody's lungs), the poor charred body of our carved pelican from the lectern, torturously twisted pieces of rood screen, giant charcoaled hulks of broken beams, the blob of organ with its garish grimace of melted keys.

The parishioners formed a semicircle facing the ruins, which had been all but embroidered with orange tape to keep people out.

I stood facing the congregation, next to our outdoor bulletin board. Except for some dents and scratches in its automotive paint, it had survived the fire wholly intact. Sermon material here, but I doubted I would use it any time soon.

"Lord, open our lips," I began.

"And our mouth shall proclaim your praise," came the response.

Mouth, singular: though composed this morning of the mouths of Van, Marie, Vincent, Addie Rogers and Adele, Gus, Jennifer (Charles had gone back to the hospital to check on Adrian and the others), Buddy Freedgood, (Judy Freedgood, Tim Stancil, and Cass Morrissey were at home with the flu), and Cal and Lucinda Lord.

Someone in the crowd must have rushed his film down to Mountain City after the service, because parishioners saw themselves on MCTV's "Sunday Evening Roundup" at six P.M. I didn't see it then because I was at the hospital with Adrian, but Van later acquired a copy of the whole tape and it became part of our archives.

"This is the Fourth Sunday in Advent," I said, after we had prayed the short form of Morning Prayer, "and it seems fitting that the image in today's Collect is that of a mansion: in this Collect we ask God to purify our conscience so that when His son comes He will find in us a 'mansion prepared for himself.'

"In the weeks and months to come, we will be giving much thought and prayer to mansions and dwelling places in their many aspects, both temporal and eternal, but this isn't going to be sermon time. Everybody's dressed warmly, but some of us standing here feel the cold more keenly than others and nobody else needs the flu. So this will be just a short farewell and thanksgiving for All Saints High Balsam in the form we knew it until yesterday. Each of us standing here cherishes some personal memory of something we will especially miss, a beautiful object that conveyed meaning, a particular place where we felt directly in the line of God's sight. I urge you to write these memories down while they are still vivid, and we will make a book of them.

"We loved our building, yet we know that the church is us. The church is what we make when we come together in the sacramental mystery of God incarnate. It's what we allow God to do through us in this corporate body.

"We're stripped down to essentials this morning, but look at us: *we're here*. Like the ancient Israelites, we carry our invisible God with us, even when we're without so much as a tent. And as people of God, what we need to be asking ourselves this morning is, what has God been doing here? What has God set in motion — through these circumstances —

that we can carry forward and make more of?

"Lucinda, our sacristan, will lead us in the first fourteen verses of Psalm 102. Please look over the shoulders of anyone who brought a prayer book. After that, Mrs. Fletcher, whose son-in-law, Patrick Murray, was the first volunteer fireman to arrive yesterday and who got Adrian and Tony and Chase out safely, has invited us all over to the inn for a breakfast buffet."

Lucinda stepped forward in her smart Chesterfield coat, mouton hat, and high-heeled boots. She looked as if she had lost a member of her immediate family and was bravely reading the lesson at the funeral service.

When you were little, you came running to me after church once and hid your face in my cassock.

"What's wrong?" I asked you.

"That old lady who keeps asking my name over and over again," you said, trembling against my legs.

"That's Mrs. Lord, she's lost parts of her memory, but she's a good person. She won't hurt you, darling."

"But she just said she burned down the church."

"Well, there was more to it than that. She left an iron on in the old church, but there was a lot of confusion that day. We had lots of visitors and people were running around and she just forgot."

"But what if she does it again? What if she burns down *our* church?"

"She won't," I assured you.

"How do you know she won't?"

"Because, first of all, she doesn't iron here anymore," I said, "and second of all, we've got a better iron that turns itself off if someone forgets about it."

You were always picky about your answers, but that one seemed to satisfy you. At least for the time being.

" 'Lord, hear my prayer, and let my cry come before you,' " Lucinda began.

" 'Hide not your face from me in the day of my trouble,' " came the scattered response as people craned toward the few available prayer books. Only Addie Rogers, in her ancient ranch mink and a pink mohair shawl covering her head, stubbornly closed her eyes and jutted her chin out and intoned the words from memory.

When we were reading, " 'I have become like a vulture in the wilderness, like an owl among the ruins,' " I looked up and met the beady eye of a crow — the same one who had spiraled drunkenly through yesterday's smoke? — gazing down on our proceedings from the singed limb of a fir tree.

I caught Gus in a cool moment of assessing

just how much needed to be done to the taped-off site before we could begin again.

Lucinda got all the way to verse fourteen like the trouper she was before she broke down.

" 'For your servants love — ' " She faltered and had to stop.

" 'For your servants love her very rubble, and are moved to pity even for her dust,' " we all finished for her.

Then we dispersed, in cars and on foot, for Mrs. Fletcher's breakfast at the inn, where we ate well in the time-honored country-style, exchanged information in warm and comfortable surroundings about what had befallen us, and began to plan the next chapter in our parish's story. It turned out to be a celebration breakfast for her son-in-law as well. Patrick Murray had become a local hero overnight. Everybody wanted, and needed, to hear the Fire Narrative. He didn't put himself unduly forward. It's just that he did get there first and get three people out who might not have gotten out otherwise, and people wanted to hear details. He never went begging for a job again. Century Oil's director came with his hat in hand to offer him his old job back, Power and Light wanted him full-time with benefits, and Gus was the lucky employer who snared him: he helped build the new All Saints High Balsam, and, as you know, is Gus and Jennifer's general manager of Eubanks and Tye Construction today.

When I arrived at the inn, Mrs. Fletcher, handing over an envelope with my name on it, told me that Grace, who had planned to leave High Balsam this morning, was feeling "real poorly" and had decided to stay over another day or two. She was running a fever, Mrs. Fletcher said. Inside the envelope, in a wilder version of Grace's usual handwriting, was a short, relatively incoherent missive, the sort of thing you would expect from someone running a fever. Later, as I watched beside Adrian in the ICU, I would reread it and ponder it. Grace seemed to be taking complete responsibility for the fire — hand in hand with the Lord, of course, and his mysterious ways — yet also apologizing to me for the suffering I must be going through because of it. It was signed "Your Sister in Christ. Grace Munger."

I joined the others for breakfast but took an early leave. I was anxious to get back to the hospital and first had to go by the rectory and pack some things for Adrian and Tony and Chase. Poor Chase's new peacock-blue ski outfit had been cut off him by the medics.

A black Range Rover, its engine running, was parked in front of the church — or rather, where the church had been. On the sidewalk with his back to me, surveying the ruin, stood a stocky, rumpled, red-haired man in outdoor gear. I pulled in behind the Rover. Its slush-splattered South Carolina license plate read ZORNUSA.

He turned around and watched me pick my way along the slippery sidewalk toward him. There had been nobody to shovel. Of course he knew who I was from my cassock and black coat. I had phoned him yesterday from the hospital, but had not expected to see him here.

He had a day's growth of red and gray stubble and aggressive little green eyes that squinted out sharply from sun-crinkled skin. "Radford Zorn," he said, squinching my Ninth Avenue wrist in his blunt handshake. "Got here as soon as the snowplows would let me. We got dumped on down in South Carolina, too. I've already been to the hospital and seen Chase."

"I'm headed back there now myself," I said.

He gave me a long assessing once-over. "Yeah, I reckon you are. Your husband's on a respirator, Chase tells me." He waved his hand at the mess in front of us and shook his head. "When my son goes on a destruction binge, there's never much left standing." But wasn't there just the faintest note of pride behind his grim sarcasm?

"He didn't set fire to the church," I said. "Someone else did that, inadvertently. And there's already someone else pushing forward

719

her divine claim to responsibility."

"He says if he hadn't stolen the church wine and hidden in the tower, the firemen would have had time to save the church."

"Maybe they would have, but the church — or rather, the building — is beside the point now, Mr. Zorn. What are we going to do to save Chase?"

He cocked his head sidewise, as if he had not heard me right. "Did you say 'we'?"

"I did."

"Now that my son has rewarded your efforts by putting your husband in intensive care, wouldn't you be wiser to turn over the saving to somebody else? That's why I drove up here on this god-awful road. To pick up his things and clear him out of your life. He can be discharged this afternoon, the hospital says."

"Discharged to what?"

"To my care, that's what," he snapped belligerently.

"But — excuse me, *do* you care?"

"*What?*"

"I said, do you care?"

"You are really *beyond* me, Mrs. Bonner!"

"Well, you are equally beyond me," I said. "My husband and my husband's eighty-year-old father went into that burning church to save Chase. Why should they risk their lives to have him 'cleared out of their lives' before they're even home from the hospital?"

"Hey, you're the one who phoned me —"

"It was my duty to phone you. He's your son, he'd been in an accident."

"Caused by himself. He's a self-loving little drunk."

"He's a self-hating alcoholic, and that needs some work. For God's sake, Mr. Zorn, think a minute. How can that boy possibly *know how* to love himself when he's had so little experience of feeling loved?"

"Well, who the hell has?" he exploded. "Excuse me, but I won't even begin to tell you what a fucked-up childhood I had, being moved around from one crappy mill town to another with an alcoholic mother *and* father. But I don't go around drinking and whining and destroying everything I touch. I made something of myself."

"That's great. You found yourself an outlet. You build Hometown theme parks without any crappy mills or alcoholic parents. Give him a chance to find himself an outlet. Maybe he'll end up building Loving Home theme parks, where people can leave off their kids for a week or two of virtual care."

He reared away from me and stood fingering his beard stubble. He seemed to be uncertain what manner of creature he was up against.

"So," he said grudgingly after a moment, "what do you suggest we do? Chase himself says he's hopeless. He told me so this morning."

"No man is hopeless," I said, "as long as he can serve as a bad example to others."

He gave me a wary look: was I referring to him?

"That's just one of my father-in-law's jokes," I said. "He spent eighteen years in a monastery and heard that one from his prior."

"Your father-in-law was in a monastery?"

"Among other things. My father-in-law's led an adventurous life. He's very fond of Chase, too, I might add."

"Look, Mrs. Bonner — or what am I supposed to call you? What are you suggesting we do here?"

"Mrs. Bonner is fine, I so seldom get called that. Margaret is fine, too. I'm not sure what to suggest, Mr. Zorn. I'll need to talk it over with my husband — when he's able to talk again. There are too many of us at present in the rectory, and now there's water damage in one of the bedrooms, as well. But if you can build complete hometowns, and we want to keep Chase in our lives, which we do, we ought to be able to come up with something workable for everybody concerned, don't you think?"

"What I think is, he's damn lucky already," said Radford Zorn, with a self-pitying twang surprisingly similar to Chase's, in *his* low moments.

EPILOGUE

Feast of the Epiphany, 2020.

So Adrian spent the last Christmas of the old century in the hospital and was released in the second week of the new millennium. You've heard him joke about his "Cistercian Retreat of '99," when he was denied speech. In our hours together in the ICU, as his lungs began their slow recuperation and he was slowly weaned off the respirator, he held up his end of the conversation on legal pads.

We took the pads home with us, twenty-three of them, and, as you often have caught me doing these past four years, I have drained every dram of solace and recall that I could, out of their compressed utterances. A single scribbled word like "feet" evokes so much: not only that Adrian had cold feet in the ICU that night of the Fourth Sunday in Advent and wanted a blanket over them, but also the cold feet he brought home from "chasing Chase" through the swamps out at the school, and that I wrapped between my warmer ones on that Friday night before Advent of '99 began — and you also had your beginnings.

"Father?" scribbled so often those first few days, evokes his concern for Tony before the old man was able to leave his bed and come upstairs to the ICU and sit with Adrian and entertain him with stories of their first six years together. Not all of them may have been a hundred percent true, but your father never grew tired of listening to them.

But that word "Father?" in Adrian's handwriting connects me with so much else that is important to his story. "Father," in its fullest sense, is, I believe, the goal Adrian was called to all along, from the time he lost his own father and was forced out into a wider meaning of the search: leading him through the grim scourge of Father Mountjoy's tutelage, the hellish indenture to Devil-father Schmidt, a brief escape to father-monks and then to Father Navy, into (and out of) theology, then across the waters to partake of the spirit of the Wise Old Man of Zurich, and throw away his whip. What a story, when you think of it! And so much further to go: ordination to priestly fatherhood — still not enough — more apprenticeships to spiritual fathers, including my own dear father, and into the more demanding territory that had been pulling him relentlessly on: his assumption of his own fatherhood to a flesh-and-blood daughter, and his acceptance of spiritual fatherhood to the sons and daughters of Fair Haven until his death at age sixty-nine.

724

That's quite a journey.

Still — I wish it could have been a longer one. I had hoped, until his lungs gave out on him a final time, that we could have our old age together, the sort I had envisioned on our wedding trip when we met that crusty sheep farmer — the one who kept a braying retirement home for old rams because he was still in love with his wife.

"So?" Madelyn Farley would say. "Next time through this vale of tears, choose a husband nearer your own age. Twenty years difference was exceeding even your mother's penchant for gamy old father-figures."

We keep hearing their voices. I wonder what my voice sounds like in your mind. I hope, overall, it's a sound you like. I also hope that my living voice will be around for you a lot longer. I would so much have loved to hear my mother's voice when she was my age. A Ruth of fifty-three, what would she have been like?

I also hope my obsessing over my lost mother and what I would have liked to know from her has not caused me to err in the other direction and tell you more than you wanted to know! But that is a risk I took — wanted to take. How proud she would have been of you today (God, she would be seventy-five now). Not only do you have her wicked sense of humor and her capacity for seeing through people — and yes, her short temper and im-

patience with anything less than perfection —
but you are lovely to behold in the same style
she was, with those neat ankles that look like
they were cut out carefully with paper scissors, and the rich hair trapping the colors of
the sunshine in it, and her physical sureness
of movement. You are altogether surer of
yourself than she was — or I was, certainly —
and you are, in addition to all *that,* sublimely
blessed with a rare tenderness toward the
specificities of the creatures and objects that
surround you. This tenderness already shows
itself in your precise art, where even the most
mundane things are rendered with a holy affection. Praise be to God, you got the art, too,
the gift she desired so much and died still
seeking. Those ink-board etchings you recently sent me from art school, "Scenes from
Rectory Life," as you entitled them, have
given me many hours of pleasure, though I'm
going to tear myself away from them long
enough to have the fire chief frame them, all
of them, before I take leave of High Balsam
for my next assignment: teaching two courses
a week at General Seminary, and writing the
rest of the time. I was due for a change, you
rightly said so yourself on your last visit.
Well, let's hope New York is big enough to
contain both of us for a while. Of course, I'll
be coming back to Great Silence Falls in the
summers, and I look forward to having your
company whenever I can get it. Isn't it some-

thing that I should have bought the house that those rich people abandoned before it was even finished because it was too isolated? How happy Gus was to get it back from them: she whittled it down in proportion and cut out more windows and kept it for her own, first as a guest house, then for Jennifer and her family until they outgrew it. When Gus offered to sell it to me this past winter and I said, "I can't take Great Silence Falls from you, Gus," she replied, "I've been saving it for you, so I could keep you. I just realized that."

If I behave with tact and discernment, I imagine the parishioners at All Saints will still be glad to see their former rector at Sunday services, even though it's the tradition for the preceding priest, however beloved in her day, to make herself scarce so her successor can shape his own leadership. Oh, well, I can always drive down the mountain to hear Kevin Dowd preach at St. Simon's Chapel in Clampitt. At fifty-two, he finally got called to lead a parish.

Here's another offering from your father's ICU pads, a verbose one this time, when Adrian was regaining strength and growing more impatient for speech. It was like having back our old epistolary days again, when I would present him with a narrative from my life in New York and he would explicate it from Romulus. Only it was better, because I could look at him and know I had married him, after all, and know he was improving every day and that God was letting us make more of each other for a while longer.

What elicited this interesting spate in the legal pad was that I had just come from seeing Grace, who was recovering from flu at the inn.

As soon as I finished telling Adrian about the visit, he snatched up his pad and began writing . . . and writing . . . and writing.

GM: Consider. She has just lost her job. Ever since the father's disgrace and the fire that killed the parents and scarred her and evicted her from her child's paradise, she has been between worlds, socially, economically, religiously. Coming back to High Balsam to organize the march was her attempt to reunite with her father's magic powers, an attempt that failed. She *is* a bit like Jonah. She expected a different outcome from the Lord. Decent weather. Voices raised in exultation, bringing a downpouring of healing energy from the skies. Solidarity, with herself leading the community out of Babylon and back to Zion. Paul Pike covering the parade. Herself as heroine and prophet. Instead, he caricatures her and decamps, it snows, and your church burns down and an All Saints parishioner takes all the credit *for that* away from the Lord. So glad to have seen her with my own eyes. What do you think she'll do now?

"She wouldn't give me a clue," I told him after reading the pad. "I asked her what her plans were, but either she looked through me, in that way of hers, or she circled right back to her awful revelation about the psychologist at that Episcopal boarding school who seduced her, and the abortion he and her adoptive parents talked her into and how that led to her *real* conversion. Or she rambled some more about God still wanting her to be my sister in Christ. Which she already is, of course. But when I pointed that out to her, she got impatient and rather angry. As though I was trying to steal her thunder. When I was leaving, I said, 'Let's keep in touch, Grace,' and I meant it. I really am curious to know what she'll do next."

So far, that curiosity has been left unsatisfied. I never heard from Grace after she left High Balsam, and she seems to have vanished from Mountain City as well — or at least the Mountain City Smathers Eubanks could be counted on to know about. Once, a few years ago, when I was on my way to lead a retreat in South Carolina, I passed a peculiar-looking little roadside church that had been made from a mobile home. The sign outside said

"Congregation of the Risen Grace," and gave times of Sunday services, and, at the bottom, in big bold Roman letters, just like the ones on our sign: VISITORS WELCOME. I suddenly became possessed with the certainty that this was Grace's church — some weird denomination she might have founded, who ever heard of "Risen Grace" otherwise? — and I was convinced that the Visitors Welcome was a message, and a challenge, for me to stop. Well, I've never admitted this to anyone, but I phoned ahead to the retreat house in Charleston and said I had been delayed — I'd been expected Saturday evening, but as my official preaching didn't begin until Sunday evening, I could do this. Yes, I stayed over in a crummy motel that had sand in the sheets in order to go to that ten o'clock service at the Congregation of the Risen Grace. A very enthusiastic Pentecostal service it was, and, as it turned out, the preacher was a woman. I was the only white member of the congregation, and they went overboard to make me feel at home at coffee hour. Somehow, I think I am still destined to meet Grace again, one way or another. Meanwhile I ponder her significance and her challenge to me.

"Chase and Tony?" reads another scribble on the ICU pad. That was when we were having our discussions about "logistics," who was going to live where, how we were going to keep Chase close and get him through high school, and where Adrian's father was going to live. Tony, our tough old bird, recovered *his* lungs and lived to the age of the average High Balsam geezer, ninety-six. He never did give up his hand-rolled cigarettes. He maintained his full faculties until Adrian abandoned *him,* after which he never came out of his grief; his spirit took leave of him before his heart stopped, but, as you know, we buried your grandfather less than half a year after your father. You read the lesson.

When someone has enough money, logistics can be worked out in no time. Radford Zorn bought and furnished a house in town, and Tony and Chase lived in it together rather splendidly until Chase (almost) finished high school and quit in his final semester when Radford Zorn was felled by a stroke. He never did go back to school. Well, as you've often remarked, he didn't need to, did he? Chase moved in with his father and did everything for him, and took over the business. He eventually added some creative touches of his own: his Orphanage and Prison theme park hotels for kids, possibly inspired by all the tales he'd heard from Adrian and Tony. He became the most devoted of sons until his father died. I think he surprised himself, but Adrian always said he wasn't surprised. As you well recall, Chase lavished embarrassingly expensive gifts on you when you were a child. I still remember how angry you were with me that time I intercepted that list you were preparing for him. He had asked you to write down what you wanted him to bring you the next time he came to see us, and I'm afraid you had let your imagination run wild. I hope Chase will eventually find someone he loves. You were too young to remember him courting Jennifer, but Jennifer, as Gus laughingly put it, was determined to hold out for a *really* needy man so she could be more useful.

So there we are. I've written you my Advent tale. It's my gift to you in return for your rectory drawings. Please accept with all my love this inner and outer chronicle of those last weeks of our old century and our old millennium — and the first weeks of your own beginnings — when so many things were on their way to us, things we neither anticipated nor, in some cases, ever could have imagined. This is the story of how we met them and were changed by them. May we continue to meet what is coming to us with courage of heart. "Until, Dear Lord," as my father used to pray, "you gather us into your household and assign us to our rightful rooms." Until then, he would always continue, "keep us generous and faithful and teach us to fear nothing but the loss of you."

How good it has been, throughout the

months of writing this, to bring Adrian close again in all his particulars. Just as you have brought back in such close focus so many dear things in your "Scenes from Rectory Life." There's our staircase, there's our stove, there's your bookcase in your sunporch bedroom, there's the view of the church — the new church, as I still think of it — as seen through your bedroom window.

All your drawings throb with things seen: you have looked and you have seen! What a rare and lucky person you are. And you have seen even what you never looked upon. Lucinda's ironing board. A Benedictine habit airing on its hanger on the dogwood tree.

You have been our gift since the very beginning. Now the gift of your art goads and inspires me to risk further narrative adventures of my own, as I journey toward my Last Interlocutor, the Final Narrative Goal.

ACKNOWLEDGMENTS

I thank the following for their generous help:

Father Gale D. Webbe, for driving me around the mountains of western North Carolina in search of the right place to set down the fictional town of High Balsam, and for his tales and homilies about the art of pastoring and headmastering during the course of these pleasant drives.

The Reverend David L. Bronson, for guidance on Anglican Church architecture and ceremonial, and for the three-year loan of Percy Dearmer's *The Parson's Handbook*.

The Reverend James C. Fenhagen, former dean and president of General Theological Seminary, for his warm and perceptive theological and ecclesiastical responses to the finished manuscript of *Evensong*.

The Reverend Janet Vincent-Scaringe, for invaluable information about running a parish and for her Advent notes written especially for me.

For their anecdotes, suggestions, sermons, and the examples of their ministries: the Right Reverend Robert H. Johnson, Bishop of Western North Carolina; the Reverend

Edward Gettys Meeks and the Reverend
Richard Price, of St. Mary's Parish,
Asheville, N.C.; the Very Reverend Neil
Zabriskie, dean emeritus of All Souls Ca-
thedral, Asheville; the Reverend Haywood
Spangler; the Reverend Robert J. Magliula
of Christ the King Parish, Stone Ridge,
N.Y.; and the Reverend Thomas P. Miller
of St. Gregory's Parish, Woodstock, N.Y.

Father Russ Ingersoll, Headmaster, and the
English classes of 1996 at Christ School,
Arden, N.C., for their imaginative assistance in figuring out the boy who would become Chase Zorn.

Dr. Peter S. Hawkins, Professor at Yale Divinity School, for his insight about the relationship of narrative to prayer.

The late Mari Basil, for our inspiring talks,
during the final months of her life, about
the Book of Revelation, Charles Williams,
and other intricacies and mysteries of faith.

Frances Halsband, AIA, for her notes and
sketches of bell towers.

Marie Duane and Kingston Hospital E.R.
Nurse Kathy Van Buran for medical details.

Lucy Beers for suggestions as to how a small
private school like Fair Haven might be
run.

Dr. C.T.B. Harris, Jungian analyst, for our
fruitful conversations about Margaret and
Adrian, and for his fine book, *Emasculation*

of the Unicorn: The Loss and Rebuilding of Masculinity in America, 1994.

Chief Michael Densen of the Woodstock Fire Company and Inspector Christopher Rea of the Kingston, N.Y., Fire Department, for their expert advice on fires and firefighting.

Jo Ann and Ken Traub of The Jewelry Store, Woodstock, N.Y., for their burglary stories.

My researcher Dan Starer, for his unusually adventuresome research, which helped shape the plot.

My publisher and editor Linda Grey, who focused her keen eyes on the horizon and helped me see the fully realized book coming into sight.

My stalwart and candid agent and dear friend of thirty years, John Hawkins.